Gaelen Foley holds a B.A. in English literature and it was while studying the Romantic poets, such as Wordsworth, Byron, and Shelley, that she first fell in love with the Regency period in which her novels are set. After college, she moonlighted as a waitress for five years to keep her daylight hours free for writing and honing her craft. Her dedication paid off in 1998 when her first novel was published. She went on to win the *Romantic Times Reviewers Choice Award* for Best First Historical Romance. Seven years and many awards later, this *USA Today* bestselling author is now published in ten languages. Foley lives in Pittsburgh, USA, with her husband, Eric, and a spoiled bichon frise. She is hard at work on her next book in the Knight family series.

D0654930

THE
DUKE

Gaelen Foley

PIATKUS

PIATKUS

First published in the US in 2000 by The Random House Publishing Group
First published in Great Britain in 2005 by Piatkus Books
This paperback edition published in 2005
Copyright © 2000 Gaelen Foley

A CIP catalogue record for this book is available from
the British Library

ISBN 978-0-7499-3651-8

Typeset in Great Britain by Phoenix Photsetting, Chatham, Kent
Printed and bound in Great Britain by
CPI Mackays, Chatham, ME5 8TD

Papers used by Piatkus are natural, renewable and recyclable
products sourced from well-managed forests and certified
in accordance with the rules of the Forest Stewardship Council.

Mixed Sources
Product group from well-managed
forests and other controlled sources
www.fsc.org Cert no. SGS-COC-004081
© 1996 Forest Stewardship Council

FSC

Piatkus
An imprint of
Little, Brown Book Group
100 Victoria Embankment
London EC4Y 0DY

An Hachette UK Company
www.hachette.co.uk

www.piatkus.co.uk

For Eric, and he knows why

For who so firm that cannot be seduced?

—SHAKESPEARE

ACKNOWLEDGMENTS

I would like to thank the following people for their extraordinary generosity to me in their respective fields of expertise: Mary Jo Putney, for her matchless tact in steering me out of a dead end in the planning stages; Richard Tames, eminent London historian, Blue Badge and British Museum tour guide, author of *American Walks in London* along with 130 other books, and all-around genius (read him, if you love London!); Sheila Tames, London and the Lakes guide and author, for also helping and bearing with me; Andrea Caweltia of the Rosenthal Archives of the Chicago Symphony Orchestra, for supplying me with the information I needed about period music and instruments; Dr. Jean Mason, professor of history at Duquesne University and enlightened reviewer for *The Romance Reader* online, for scouring the manuscript for historical and logic errors; David Tucker, director of The Original London Walks Company, for his courtesy and helpfulness; the always-ready-to-help members of the Beau Monde online group, who all deserve vouchers to Almack's in my opinion; Marina Richards, writing buddy, for reminding me to have the courage not to pull my punches with a story I needed to tell; and last but never least, heartfelt thanks to my editor, Shauna Summers, for being behind me every step of the way and allowing me the creative freedom to write books that break the rules.

Any mistakes, blunders, or misinformations are the author's own.

Georgiana's Brood: the Knight Miscellany

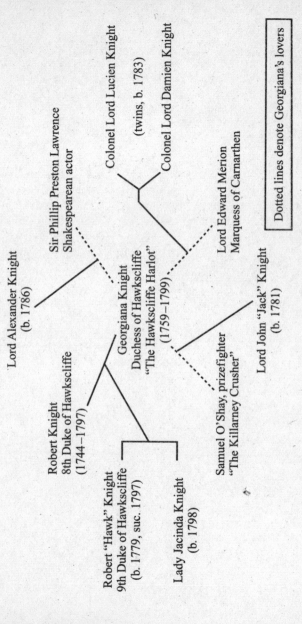

Dotted lines denote Georgiana's lovers

Robert Knight
8th Duke of Hawkscliffe
(1744–1797)

Georgiana Knight
Duchess of Hawkscliffe
"The Hawkscliffe Harlot"
(1759–1799)

Lord Alexander Knight
(b. 1786)

Sir Phillip Preston Lawrence
Shakespearean actor

Colonel Lord Lucien Knight

(twins, b. 1783)

Colonel Lord Damien Knight

Lord Edward Merion
Marquess of Carnarthen

Samuel O'Shay, prizefighter
"The Killarney Crusher"

Lord John "Jack" Knight
(b. 1781)

Robert "Hawk" Knight
9th Duke of Hawkscliffe
(b. 1779, suc. 1797)

Lady Jacinda Knight
(b. 1798)

⊰ CHAPTER ⊱
ONE

London, 1814

Many years ago, as a curly-headed youth on grand tour, he had fallen madly in love with beauty and so had stopped in Florence to take drafting lessons from a bonafide Italian master. Starry-eyed and romantical, he had followed the light-winged muses south to the Bay of Sorrento, where he had first heard the ancient Italian proverb "Revenge is a dish best served cold." He was an old man now, without illusions, cold and canny as a scheming pope. Beauty had betrayed him, but decades later, oddly enough, here on this gray English day, the Sicilian proverb held true.

A neat, slight-framed man, James Breckinridge, the earl of Coldfell, gripped the ivory head of his walking stick in gnarled fingers that ached with the needling April rain. He permitted his footman to assist him down from his luxurious black town coach while another held an umbrella over him.

The slumbrous quiet in this place was like a church, but for the pattering of the rain. He turned slowly, looked past the servants' blanked faces, past the jagged wrought-iron fence, into St. George's Burying Ground on the Uxbridge Road, just north of Hyde Park. Three weeks ago, he had buried his young bride here. Under a chilly gray drizzle, where the hill curved green, her marble monument rose

1

like an angry needle to the smoke-colored sky. Beneath it, just where Coldfell had expected to find him, stood the tall, powerful, brooding silhouette of a man; wind-blown and lost, the wide shoulders slumped as the gusty rain blew his black greatcoat around him.

Hawkscliffe.

Coldfell's mouth flattened into a thin line. He took the umbrella from the footman. "I shan't be long."

"Yes, my lord."

Leaning on his walking stick, he began the slow ascent up the graveled path.

The thirty-five-year-old Robert Knight, ninth duke of Hawkscliffe, appeared unaware of his approach, stony and immobile as the monument. He stood in bleak granite still-ness, the rain plastering his wavy black hair to his forehead, running in chilly rivulets down the stark planes of his cheeks, and dripping off his rugged profile as he stared down at the yellow daffodils that had been planted on her grave.

Coldfell winced at the ungentlemanly intrusion he was about to make on the other man's grief. Hawkscliffe was, after all, the only one of the younger generation he re-spected. Some of the old-school pigtail Tories found the young magnate's views alarmingly Whiggish, but none could deny that Hawkscliffe was twice the man his weak-willed father had been.

Why, Coldfell reflected as he hobbled up the path, he had seen Robert become a duke at the age of seventeen, managing three vast estates and raising four wild younger brothers and a little sister practically single-handedly. More recently, he had heard him deliver speeches in the Lords with a cool force and eloquence that had brought the whole house to its feet. Hawkscliffe's integrity was un-questioned; his honor rang true as a bell of finest sterling. Many of the younger set, like Coldfell's own idiot nephew and heir, Sir Dolph Breckinridge, considered the so-called paragon duke a rigid high stickler, but to wiser heads, Hawkscliffe was, in a word, impeccable.

It was pitiful to see what Lucy's death had done to him.

Ah, well. Men would see in a woman what they wanted to see.

Coldfell cleared his throat. Startled, Hawkscliffe jerked at the noise and spun around. Tumultuous emotion blazed in his dark eyes. Seeing Coldfell, his dazed expression of pain took on a stab of guilt. With his honorable nature, it had no doubt tormented the duke to have wanted an old friend's wife. Himself, he had never been that chivalrous. James nodded to him. "Hawkscliffe."

"Beg your pardon, my lord, I was just leaving," he mumbled, lowering his head.

"Stay, Your Grace, by all means," Coldfell answered, waving off the awkwardness. "Keep an old man company on this dreary day."

"As you wish, sir." Narrowing his eyes against the rain, Hawkscliffe looked away uncomfortably, surveying the jagged horizon of tombstones.

Coldfell hobbled to the brim of the grave, cursing his aching joints. When the weather was fine, he could hunt all day without tiring. But he had not been energetic enough for Lucy, had he?

Well, she had had her fashionable London burial, just as she would have liked. Having died at his house just outside London, she had a spot in the most exclusive cemetery in the city, complete with a Flaxman funerary monument, the height of good taste, sparing no expense. And well he should have to pay for this most expensive mistake—an old man's folly, he thought bitterly. Beauty indeed was his weakness. With nothing to recommend her but a magnificent mane of flame-colored hair and the most luscious thighs in Christendom, the twenty-six-year-old Lucy O'Malley had been an artist's model in Sheffield before she had bewitched him into making her his second countess. He had sworn her to keep quiet about her background, devising a false one for her. At least she had given *that* pledge sincerely, eager as she had been to join the ton.

Coldfell was merely glad he had not been forced to bury Lucy next to Margaret, his first wife, who was reverently enshrined at Seven Oaks, the ancestral pile in Leicestershire. Ah, wise Margaret, his heart's mate, whose only fault had been her failure to give him a son.

"I am—very sorry for your loss, my lord," Hawkscliffe said stiffly, avoiding his gaze.

Coldfell slid a furtive glance at the duke, then sighed, nodding. "It's hard to believe she's really gone. So young. So full of life."

"What will you do now?"

"I leave for Leicestershire tomorrow. A few weeks in the country will help, I warrant." A visit to Seven Oaks would also take him out of the way of suspicion when this man carried out the deed for him.

"I'm sure you will find it soothing," Hawkscliffe said— polite, automatic.

They were both silent for a long moment, Hawkscliffe brooding, Coldfell reflecting on the uneasiness of living anymore in his elegant villa in South Kensington with its four pretty acres of sculpted gardens—the site of Lucy's death.

" 'Lay her in the earth. And from her fair and unpolluted flesh may violets spring,' " Hawkscliffe quoted barely audibly.

Coldfell looked at him in pity. "Laertes' speech on Ophelia's grave."

The duke said nothing, merely stared at the carven letters on the monument: Lucy's name, her date of birth and death.

"I never touched her," he choked out abruptly, turning

to Coldfell in impetuous anguish. "You have my word as a gentleman. She never betrayed you."

Evenly, Coldfell held his gaze, then nodded as though satisfied, but of course he had already known.

"Ah, Robert," he said heavily after a long moment, "it is so strange, the way they found her. She went out to our pond every day to sketch the swans. How could she have slipped? Perhaps my brain is muddled with grief, but it makes no sense to me."

"She could never slip," he said vehemently. "She was graceful . . . so graceful."

Coldfell was taken aback by his ferocity. This was going to be easier than he'd hoped.

"Did your servants report anything strange that day, my lord, if I may presume to ask?" pursued the duke.

"Nothing."

"Did anyone see anything? Hear anything? She was in earshot of the house. Could they not hear her cries for help?"

"Perhaps she had no time to cry out before she fell beneath the water."

Hawkscliffe turned away again, his firm mouth grimly pursed. "My lord, I have the blackest suspicions."

Coldfell paused, watching him. "I wish that I could put your mind at ease, but I'm afraid that I, too, am haunted by severe doubts."

Hawkscliffe turned and stared penetratingly at him. His dark eyes glowed like hellfire. "Go on."

"It doesn't add up. There was no blood on the rock where they said she . . . struck her head. What am I to do? I am an old man. These sore limbs are weak. I haven't the strength," he said slowly, emphatically, "to do what a husband should."

"I do," vowed Hawkscliffe.

The earl felt his dry soul thrill to the resolve in the fiery young man's eyes.

"Whom do you suspect?" Hawkscliffe asked in tautly leashed savagery.

Coldfell had never seen the man look so wild and fierce. He had to hide his glee. All he need do was utter the name, provide a target for all that churning wrath, then Hawkscliffe would duel and the viper who had turned on him would be struck down. He was not above playing Lucy's devotees against each other to save himself and his sweet, flawed daughter, Juliet. What else could he do? He was nearly seventy, a little weaker every day. Dolph was in his prime, a brutally skilled hunter who had been blooded at the tender age of nine with his first stag.

The tremor that moved through his limbs was real. "May God forgive me," Coldfell said under his breath with a look of distress.

"Whom, Coldfell? Do you know something? I know this was no accident, even if the coroner said it was. You and I are not fools," he said hotly. "She was in that pond for four days before they found her. There is no telling what else might have been done to her before she was killed."

"I see our fears run a similar course, Robert. To think that she might have been . . . violated. Oh, God." He leaned on Hawkscliffe, who steadied him. "It's almost worse than her death itself."

Hawkscliffe's chiseled jaw tautened. "My lord, I beg of you. Tell me what you know."

"I don't *know*, Robert. I only suspect. Lucy said to me once—"

"Yes?"

Coldfell paused. So hungry for someone to punish, someone to blame, he thought, passing a shrewd glance over Robert's face, assessing his features like an artist preparing to sketch his portrait. It was the hard, noble face of a warrior. His raven hair flowed back richly from his broad forehead; beneath his wide, flared, charcoal black eyebrows, his piercing eyes burned with iron will; his hooked nose was aquiline, hawklike, his mouth, firm and clamped, yet there was a sensitivity about his lips that captivated women.

"She said there was a man who . . . frightened her."

"Who was he?" Hawkscliffe demanded.

Coldfell drew a breath and looked away, knowing he was handing down a death sentence.

He was glad of it.

"My nephew, Your Grace," he said, cool as a consummate Italian. "My heir, Dolph Breckinridge."

"Oranges here! Penny apiece, sir, thank you and good day! Who's next?"

In the hustle and bustle of a gray day in the City, she was as out of place as the bright, sweet oranges she sold on the hectic corner of Fleet Street and Chancery Lane, handing them out like small suns to the dark-clad working gentlemen who gusted by between the worlds of government and finance—Westminster and the City, respectively. Bank clerks and barristers, city scrubs, journalists, hacks, tailors, respectable shopkeepers—even a passing deacon who was hurrying toward St. Paul's stopped in his tracks at the sight of her, then, like the rest, was irresistibly lured.

If Miss Belinda Hamilton at all divined that it was some indescribable quality in herself that brought male foot traffic to a halt, she showed no sign of it, all businesslike efficiency, counting out change with her cold-reddened fingers poking through ragged gloves, determined, in all, to take her coming down in the world with a true lady's uncomplaining grace.

A few months ago, she had been preparing giggling debutantes for their entrance into Society at Mrs. Hall's

Academy for Young Ladies; now, here she was, tenaciously clinging to the outermost rim of respectability by pride alone.

A wheat blond tendril of her hair blew against her rosy cheek as she looked up at her next customer and gave him his change with a fresh smile, weary but cheerful.

"Oranges, here! Who's next, please?"

One of her regulars stepped to the fore, a portly barrister from one of the nearby Inns of Court. His black robes billowed and he sent her a chagrined smile as he clamped his legal wig atop his beefy head to keep the thing from blowing away. His gaze skipped down the length of her.

Bel looked away, picking out a large bright orange for him. She gave it a polish with the end of her apron, then leashed her large pride by sheer dint of will and put out her hand expectantly. "A copper, sir," she sighed.

The barrister hesitated, then placed in her hand, not a coin, but a paper bank note that almost blew away. Bel knit her brow and looked at it more closely. *Twenty pounds!* She suppressed an appalled gasp and pressed the note back into his sweaty palm, revolted, though it represented a sum equal to almost three months' worth of this work. "No, sir. *No.*"

"No?" he asked, with a glow in his small eyes. "Do but consider it, my dear."

"Sir, you insult me," she said, dealing him a frosty setdown like a baroness in a drawing room instead of a desperate and nigh-penniless girl alone on the streets of the great city.

"I'll double it," he whispered, leaning closer.

She lifted her chin. "I am not for sale."

At her grand, withering stare, his heavy-jowled face turned beet red. He fled in embarrassment, his wig slipping askew. Bel shuddered slightly, scratched her forehead to gather her ruffled composure, then turned to deal hurriedly with the rest of her customers. It hadn't taken long to realize that not all of them wished to buy oranges, a fact she politely allowed herself to ignore.

After her last customer had gone, she bent down over her large oval basket and began straightening up her oranges in tidy rows.

"Hey, ye wee bit o' muslin!" yelled one of the rough-faced costermongers across the street. "We ain't gonna tolerate you on our corner much longer, girly. We got mouths ta feed. You're runnin' us outta shop!"

"Aye, why don't you go make yer money on yer back?" yelled his companion. "Why hawk oranges when you can get more sellin' your pretty *peaches*?"

They roared like drunken Huns at their own hilarity.

"Shut up, you cretins!" she belted back in a rough-and-tumble tone that would have shocked her girls at Mrs. Hall's. But really, rudeness was all that got through to such low, vulgar creatures. They interpreted good manners as weakness or cowardice—and it was imperative in her circumstances not to show fear.

"You don't belong out here, Miss Prissy. Just a matter o' time till you're some rich man's ladybird."

"I am a gentleman's daughter!"

"Aye, you look like it in those rags."

They guffawed and she glanced around in belated, lady-like embarrassment just in time to see little Tommy, the street sweep, nearly get run over by a hackney coach. His brother, Andrew, yanked him back by the scruff of the neck in the nick of time. Gasping at the close call, Bel stifled her exasperation.

"Andy! Tommy!" she called.

"Hallo, Miss Bel!" The roguish, underfed pair waved.

She beckoned them over. They nearly plunged out under the wheels of a dray cart, and when they reached her side of the street safely she scolded them to be more careful, then gave them each a few pennies and an orange. With a troubled countenance, she watched the two ragged young-sters scramble back to their post, Tommy peeling his orange while Andrew plied all his merry charm trying to persuade a passing gentleman in a top hat to let him sweep the cross-ing before him.

She had thought her lot was bad until she discovered these children. They were an inspiration to her, with their high hearts and happy-go-lucky spirits in spite of the hellish conditions they endured. The streets were crawling with them—homeless, shoeless, half-naked, and starved. She had only become aware of the true, horrifying scale of the problem one frigid night in January, when snow had covered London in the greatest blizzard in memory. While the rich had held a winter festival on the frozen Thames, she had gone looking for Andrew and Tommy with the in-tent of bringing them into her single-room lodgings in a ramshackle City tenement, at least to give them a roof over their heads. Searching everywhere, she had been at last di-rected by a surly girl to a dark building that looked like a deserted warehouse. Upon stepping inside, she had raised her lantern and beheld a mass of shivering children huddled together. There must have been seventy of them.

This was a flash house, Andrew had explained when she found him there. The youngster hadn't needed to tell her what her adult reason instantly grasped—here, the boys were apprenticed as thieves, the girls as prostitutes. It had been the most shocking and horrible moment of her twenty-three years. Never in all her days as a refined country gentlewoman of Oxfordshire had she ever imag-ined such a nightmare.

The worst part of it was how little she could do to help. She didn't have the arrogance to tell them not to steal when they were starving. The greater crime was the heartless penal code that would hang any child over seven for a theft of five paltry shillings. All she could do besides lend a hand at the relief societies was to give the little wretches affection, mind them as best she could, and nag them to go to church.

She saw Tommy drop a piece of his orange on the ground and quickly pick it up, brush it off with his grubby fingers, and pop it into his mouth. She heaved a sigh and turned away just as a flashy, all-too-familiar phaeton turned the corner and began rolling toward her.

Her face paled. Her empty stomach clenched and made a knot. She quickly bent down and heaved her basket up into her arms as the thunder of the horses' hooves grew louder.

God, please don't let him see me.

As she strained with the basket and began hurrying away, the sleek phaeton slowed to a halt alongside her, traces jingling. She clamped her jaw, realizing it would gratify her tormentor too much if she fled. Better to stand and hold her ground, unpleasant as their long war was. Turning slowly, she braced herself for battle as the flamboyantly dressed Sir Dolph Breckinridge leaped down from his equipage, his requisite cheroot dangling from the side of his mouth.

Abandoning his phaeton to his groom—who had a black eye—he swaggered toward her. He was tall, tanned, and sinewy, with short-cropped sandy hair. Grinning, the glowing-tipped cheroot clamped between his wolfish white teeth, he was the very picture of what she had taught her girls at Mrs. Hall's to fear as A Nasty Man.

"Don't come near me with that thing," she warned.

"Yes, ma'am," he answered—today it amused him to obey her.

He tossed the cheroot carelessly onto the pavement and crushed it under one of his expensive champagne-polished boots, then stalked her slowly—just as he had for the past eight months. Since the early autumn of last year, Sir Dolph had been utterly, destructively obsessed with her. She had no idea why. Perhaps it was merely his nature to fix upon one object until he had captured or destroyed it. She only knew one thing for certain: Everything that had befallen her was his fault.

With a cold expression she turned away and walked on, carrying her basket of oranges. She could smell him coming after her. He always wore too much cologne.

"Going somewhere, my heart?"

Bel merely sent him a withering glare and turned to the passersby. "Oranges, here!"

His dashing smile widened, revealing his chipped tooth, the result of one of his countless brawls, as was his off-center nose.

Dolph was proud of his battle scars. Possessed of no sense of decorum whatsoever, he was wont to start pulling off his clothes at the slightest provocation in order to give anyone he met the chance to stand in awe of his illustrious scars. He was especially proud of the one that slanted across his muscled chest where a bear had once swiped him during a hunting trip in the Alps. Bel had seen the scar, God knew. He had shown it to her the first night they'd met, to her astonished humiliation, considering that they had been at a Hunt Ball. She only wished the bear had been more determined.

Dolph rubbed his hands together and feigned a shiver. "Chilly out here today. Bet you're hungry."

"Oranges! Sweet oranges, here, fresh from sunny Italy!"

"It's your last chance to change your mind about going to Brighton with me. I leave tomorrow. There will be other ladies present, if that's your concern." He waited, but she continued to ignore him. "The Regent's mistress is giving a rout at the farmhouse by the shore. Me and my friends are invited—"

"Oranges, a penny apiece!"

He growled in exasperation. "Of all the women in the world that I could have, doesn't it mean anything to you that you're the one I pick?"

"If you're going to come and bother me every day, you could at least buy an orange."

"A penny, right? Sorry, I don't carry such small change," he said with a short laugh. "Oranges give me hives and besides, why should I help you? You are a naughty thing, always running away from me. How much longer do you plan to put me off?"

"Until it works," she muttered, carrying her basket down the street.

Following her, Dolph laughed with gusto. His groom led the phaeton's team after them, following them down the street at a respectful distance.

Bel looked away in desperation, longing to catch a glimpse in the crowd of a scarlet uniform and then to see her darling, wayward Mick Braden marching toward her, come home from the war. Why, he was *Captain* Mick Braden now since his gallantry on the fields of France, she thought with a rush of pride in the cocksure young officer from her tiny home village of Kelmscot—the man she had more or less planned on marrying since she was sixteen.

"Bel, sweet, you're a noble quarry, but it's time to give up the game. You've proved yourself as resourceful as you're stubborn, as clever as you are fair. Every move I've made, you've countered with admirable spirit. I applaud you. Now, for God's sake, stop this nonsense and come home with me. You're disgracing yourself."

"It is honest work," she replied through gritted teeth. "Oranges, here!"

"Do you doubt my affection?"

"Affection?" She turned to him and set down her basket so harshly the oranges rolled about. "Look what you've done to me and my father. When you care for someone, you don't ruin their life!"

"I took that life away from you so I could give you a better one! I'm going to make you a countess, you thankless chit."

"I don't want to be a countess, Dolph. I only want you to leave me alone."

"Oh, I'm so sick of you and your airs," he sneered, grasping her arm. "You *are* mine. It's just a matter of time."

"Let go of me this instant."

His grip tightened with raw power. "Nothing is going to stop me from winning you in time, Bel. Can't you see? My actions *prove* my love."

"Your actions prove you are selfish beyond imagining."

His eyes narrowed to angry slashes. "Be fair—"

"Fair?" she cried as he released her arm. She jerked back. "You had my poor father thrown in the Fleet. You got me fired from the finishing school. We lost our house!"

"And you can have it all back—just like that!" He snapped his leather-gloved fingers, staring lecherously at her. "Just surrender. Say you'll be my wife. You can't win this one, Bel. It's not as though my offer is improper—anymore," he added with a slight sulk.

"You are supposed to marry Lord Coldfell's daughter."

"What would I do with a feebleminded deaf-mute for a wife? I daresay I deserve better than that."

"Dolph, that is unkind. You know I am engaged to Captain Braden," she said, stretching the truth just a bit, because their long understanding wasn't an actual, formal betrothal.

"Braden! Don't say that name to me. He is nothing! He's probably dead."

"He's alive. I saw the list in the *Times* after Toulouse."

"Then where is he, Bel? Where is your hero? In Paris?

Celebrating King Louie's return with the French whores? Because I don't see him here, if he loves you so much."

"He's coming," she said with far more conviction than she felt.

"Good, because I can't wait to meet the chap and thrash him. You're not marrying him."

"Well, I'm not marrying you. I know too well what you are." With her basket tucked under her arm, she lifted her chin and walked on.

"Oh, you are a proud wench," he said with a quick, dangerous sneer, but he schooled it to a taut, angry smile. "Very well. You still refuse to submit to me. Not today. Not yet. But soon."

"Never. You are wasting your time."

"Sweet, foolish, beautiful Miss Hamilton." His gaze moved possessively over her body. "You claim to know my nature. Don't you see that the more you run away, the more lusty I grow for the chase?"

She took a backward step, gripping an orange, half prepared to hurl it at him to drive him off.

With a gleam in his eyes and a smirk on his lips, Dolph took out another cheroot. "Until next time, sweet. I'll be in Brighton for several weeks, but rest assured, I will be back." He lit the cheroot, blew the smoke at her, then turned and climbed back up into his phaeton. With a roar, he whipped his cowering horses into an instantaneous gallop.

Flinching at the crack of leather, she stood at bay until his fancy phaeton had rolled away. The two costermongers across the way shouted mocking names at her that she was learning to dread with a whole new understanding. She ignored them, swallowed hard, and glanced down the street, praying to catch a glimpse of a smart red uniform, but there was still no sign of her rescuer yet.

After she had sold the rest of her oranges, it was time for her daily visit to Papa at the Fleet, where he had been incarcerated since Christmas for a debt of a little over three thousand pounds. The walk to the hulking, redbrick prison on Faringdon Street was long and chilly, and with every step, Bel fretted over the holes in her kid half boots. She dreamed as she walked of the snug, cozy, rose-covered cottage where she had lived in Kelmscot, a quaint village on the Thames a few miles outside Oxford.

Her father was a gentleman scholar and admittedly a bit of an eccentric. Alfred Hamilton liked nothing better than to while away his days poring over the ancient illuminated manuscripts that were his passion, or haunting nearby Oxford University's awe-inspiring Bodleian Library. Papa and she had lived a quiet, placid life that moved at the stately pace of the river, but then Dolph had come along and bullied their creditors into prosecuting her father for his unpaid debts. Papa had always been absentminded about such things. Bel tried to mind financial matters in their household, but, like a guilty child, her father had concealed from her just how seriously he had compromised the family finances with his uncontrollable fervor for snatching up any illuminated manuscripts that crossed his path. Ergo, he soon landed in the Fleet.

Moving hastily to London to be near him, Bel had found work at Mrs. Hall's posh finishing school in the hopes of mitigating their troubles, but then Dolph had contrived to have her dismissed. He had wanted her helpless and bereft of resources so she would have no choice but to turn to him for help. She shook her head to herself as she walked. *That* she would never do.

As the Fleet's huge, arched entrance came into sight between the towering walls of the prison yard, she grew nervous and began mentally rehearsing her plea to the warden to extend her just a fortnight's credit, at which time she could pay her father's chamber fees in full.

Doubt gnawed her as she trudged toward the huge front

doors. Realistically, she knew the chances were slim that any plea of hers would move the lumbering, scar-faced man. The Lord Himself writhing on the cross probably could not have moved the warden of the Fleet, who had been hardened, she'd heard, by years of overseeing prisons in the convict colony of New South Wales. He had even managed women's prisons, it was said, so she expected no chivalrous treatment based on her status as a Lady of Quality.

The various jailers and guards knew her from her daily visits. One of them conducted her through the long, rectangular lobby. As they neared the warden's office, she heard his deep, rough voice through the open door as he matter-of-factly abused one of his subordinates, citing codes and regulations like a true petty tyrant. She trembled at the thought of having to throw herself on the mercy of such a man.

As the guard led her past the office, the warden's colorless eyes, devoid of emotion, flicked to her. He was standing behind his desk, a big, square, brawny man with skin as weathered and tanned as a saddle. He had a whitish-pink scar that scored his brow and cheek and ran all the way down to his jaw. A ponderous ring of keys hung by the pistol and bludgeon at his belt. He nodded to her as she passed, then she could feel his gaze following her.

She shuddered as the guard led her up to her father's cell, though she knew the way herself by now. Arriving before the solid wood door, she wearily gave the guard the necessary coin. He pocketed it with a greasy smile, then turned the key and admitted her.

When she walked in, she found her father, Alfred Hamilton—dreamer, violin player, medieval scholar—in a state of absorption, poring over one of the rare and precious manuscripts that had landed him in debtor's prison. His round spectacles were perched on his nose. His snow white hair, wild and woolly, stuck out in all directions from under his beloved velvet fez.

"Hello?" she called in amusement.

At her greeting, he looked up in surprise, startled back into the present century. Then his lined, rosy-cheeked face broke out in a wreath of smiles, as though he had not just seen her yesterday and the day before that.

"What light through yonder window breaks? Why, it's Linda-bel!"

"Oh, Papa." She strode in and hugged him. He had called her Linda-bel since she was knee high and it was typical of him, since he seemed to do everything backwards. He sat down on his stool again. She stood beside him and affectionately patted his shoulder. "How are they treating you today? Have you had your dinner?"

"Yes, a mutton stew. I fear I shall turn Irish with all the mutton I eat," he exclaimed, clapping his thigh as he chuckled. "How I should love a good English steak. Ah, beef stew and a clutch of dinner rolls like you used to make—heaven!"

"Well, if turning Irish is the extent of your woes, I'm glad. You seem in good spirits."

"Always, my dear, always, though not everyone around here can say the same. Why, just this afternoon, I went down into the courtyard and saw so many long faces that I took my violin and entertained the whole block with airs from the North country. Soon some even took to cutting a reel. I don't mind telling you I received a rousing ovation!"

"Well done!" she said, laughing. She knew old Alfred had charmed most of the guards and all the other prisoners with his buoyant, gentle nature, his violin playing, and his tales of ancient chivalry, of dragons and knights and maidens fair, all of which helped to while away the hours of endless ennui for those imprisoned here.

For now, he had the stronger prisoners and some of the

kinder guards looking out for him, but the Fleet was no gentleman's club, and her gentlemanly father had never been exposed to such a place before. With such thoughts weighing almost constantly on her mind, her laughter ebbed away.

He lowered his spectacles on his nose and peered at her. "Now, now, I know that look. You mustn't worry over me, little damsel. The clouds will part. They always do. You just look after yourself and your young charges. Teaching is the noblest profession in the civilized world. Mind you, after your silly debutantes have finished their proper posture and walking lessons, tell them it never killed any young lady to remove the book from off the top of her head and open it for a change. Just like I taught you."

"Yes, Papa." She looked away.

Her father was a hopeless optimist, but surely he would not be so cheerful if she had not kept the truth from him. Determined not to worry him, she had been keeping up appearances, putting on a brave face. She had not told him of her unjust dismissal from Mrs. Hall's.

"Don't forget your Milton," he added. " 'The mind is its own place, and in itself can make a heav'n of hell, a hell of heav'n.' You look at these four walls and see a jail cell, but I see—an enchanter's study," he declared with a sudden grin.

"Oh, Papa. It's just—I don't know how I'm ever going to get you out of here. It's such a lot of money. You are my father and I would never reproach you, but sometimes I just wish . . . that you had *sold* the manuscripts instead of donating them to the Bodleian Library."

A rare, stern look of disapproval knit his bushy white eyebrows. "Sell them? Daughter, for shame! Think on your words. These are priceless works of art that I salvaged from the hands of unscrupulous dealers. Can you sell beauty? Can you sell truth? These books belong to all humanity."

"But to buy them, you spent the money that was earmarked for our rent and our carriage and our food, Papa."

"And I am the one who shall suffer for my principles, am I not? I consider myself in fine company in that regard—Saint Paul, Galileo. Well, you have everything you need, don't you? The school gives you room and board and other girls to talk to."

"Well, yes, but—"

"Then fret not over my welfare. In this life, we make our choices and we pay the price. I'm not afraid of whatever my fate holds."

"Yes, Papa," she murmured, lowering her head. She stewed at his deluded lecture but didn't dream of telling him that he was comfortable in his enchanter's study only because of her constant toil and sacrifices. Instead she brought their visit to a close. He no doubt was eager to get back to his work on the moldering text. She kissed him dutifully on the cheek and promised to return tomorrow. He patted her on the head fondly, then the jailer let her out.

She steeled herself as she followed the guard back down the stairwell. It was time to face the warden of the Fleet. The door at the back of the long lobby was open. She saw the prisoners shuffling inside from the courtyard, returning to their cells. It had begun to rain again. Bel heaved a disgusted sigh to think of her holey boots and the long walk home.

She tapped the guard on the shoulder. "May I speak to the warden privately for a moment, please?"

"Oh, sure, missy. He'll be 'appy to meet you—privately," the guard said with a knowing leer.

Bel scowled at him, but a moment later, she was shown into the office. The big, hulking warden rose at her entrance but did not smile. The guard closed the door as he left.

"Thank you for seeing me," she said nervously. "I am Miss Hamilton. My father, Mr. Alfred Hamilton, is in cell one-twelve-B. Do you mind if I sit?"

He sliced her a military nod. She eased warily into the chair across from his desk. She glanced around the small, cramped, gloomy office. There were racks of rifles fixed to the wall, a locked ammunition box, and a coiled bullwhip on a nail.

"What seems to be the problem?" he asked, brusque and impatient, his rough voice tinged with an Australian twang. Lord, but he made her nervous.

"Well, sir, you see, ah, the thing is—this month I'm afraid I have somehow come up short in regards to my father's chamber fees. I—I'm very sorry and I promise it will never happen again, but if you could just see clear to give me an extra fortnight just this once, then I could pay in full. . . ."

She faltered as his leathery face hardened. His skeptical stare seemed as though he half suspected she had spent the money on gin or something equally disreputable.

"This ain't no moneylender's, miss."

"I realize that, but . . . surely something can be done." She attempted to smile winningly at him. "I already work several jobs, but some young friends of mine needed shoes for the winter. . . ." Her voice trailed off. His expression told her clearly he didn't want to hear her excuses. "I'm in quite desperate straits, sir. That is all."

"Haven't ye menfolk to help ye? No brothers? Uncles? No husband?"

"No, sir, there's only me."

His gaze slid downward. "Well, let's 'ave a look." His keys jangled as he sat down at his desk and flipped through his ledger, then fingered a column. "Appears we've never 'ad delays on your account before."

"I have certainly done my best," she agreed, feeling a faint spark of hope.

"Mm-hmm." He sent her a glance with a gleam in his cold, glassy eyes that made her shrink back from him slightly. "Well, now." He stroked his scar. "Under the circumstances, I'm sure we can arrive at some satisfact'ry arrangement. Let me think on it. Jones!" he bellowed abruptly, summoning his assistant. "Call me carriage around for the young lass."

"Sir?" she asked, wide-eyed.

He looked at her after his assistant had disappeared. "You arrive here every day on foot, Miss Hamilton, so I've noticed. It's pourin' rain. My man will drive you home."

"Thank you, sir, that's very kind, but it's not necessary—"

"Yes, it is. G'day." Having summarily dismissed her, the warden of the Fleet went back to work.

"Good day," she replied uncertainly, rising. With a frown of gnawing uneasiness, she went back out to the front of the prison. She did not want to accept a ride from the man. It was far from proper. On the other hand, she didn't want to offend him, either, since he held Papa's fate in his hands. She bit her lip in indecision as she stood under the arched entrance while the rain fell, cold and dismal. She was essentially a practical woman. What if she got sick from walking home in this weather? She couldn't afford to miss a day's work. It wasn't as though the man would be in the carriage with her.

A battered ex-hackney coach pulled up, drawn by a sway-backed nag. A driver in a soggy top hat beckoned her over. Hesitating only a moment longer, Bel dashed over the pavement and let herself up into the cab.

All innocence, she told the warden's driver where she lived.

* * *

The duke of Hawkscliffe, when in Town, lived in a sumptuous urban palace with a view of Green Park. Behind a brick wall topped with wrought-iron spikes, Knight House stood in all its Palladian grandeur, aloof and impregnable, gleaming, cold and pearly in the black wet April night.

Long shadows from the lampposts sculpted the stark, elegant symmetry of its flawless facade, while great Newfoundland dogs and thick-bodied mastiffs padded the neatly groomed grounds, alert for intruders, but all around the vast mansion was silent. Through the front door, into the chandeliered opulence of the grand entrance and down the marbled corridors, a hollow stillness pervaded everywhere. The servants, brisk and hushed, cleared the dining room where the master had dined, as usual, alone.

Now he sat inert at the magnificent pianoforte in a corner of the dim library. He owned several of the instruments, being a bit of a collector and a musical connoisseur. He had a Clementi in the ballroom, a Broadwood grand in the drawing room, a Walter along with the dear old harpsichord in the music room—but this, his beloved Graf, the king of pianos, was his pride and joy. It was typical of his obstinate, highly private nature to keep his finest instrument locked away in a room where no one was ever invited. Anyone else who had paid such a sum for a pianoforte would have surely placed it on display in one of the state salons, but music was a very personal affair to Hawkscliffe and besides, there was no one to hear the Graf's mighty voice anyway.

He touched the keys mournfully with one hand, finding he could take no solace from it now. His music and his noble causes were forgotten. There was a session in the Lords tonight but he couldn't even bring himself to go.

Slouching on the bench, he stared down at the keys, black and white. The dim illumination from the low fire in the hearth flickered over his face, but it did not rout the chill in his heart that had descended three weeks ago, when Lucy had gone missing.

With the silver locket containing her miniature portrait curled in his hand, he lifted his fractured gaze and reached for his glass of brandy on the coaster atop the mute piano. He raised it and inspected the hue of the firelight glowing through it. The color of her hair, he thought. But, no, her long tresses had been redder than that, not strawberry blond, but glossy chestnut.

Who, what, where had he been before Lucy Coldfell had come into his life and sidetracked it utterly? he wondered. Ah, yes, he thought bitterly. Hunting for a wife.

He tossed back the brandy, remembering the first time he had laid eyes on Coldfell's young bride. He had certainly never reacted to Coldfell's daughter that way, which would have been a damned lot more convenient. *This is the woman I should have married,* he had said to himself.

Too late.

Too late to love her. Too late to save her.

He suddenly rose and hurled the glass with all his might into the fireplace. The glass shattered and the flames exploded up into the chimney from the last drops of alcohol.

Trembling with rage over what Coldfell had told him today, he got up and paced the length of the room, crushing the Aubusson carpet under his boots. Stalking toward the fireplace, he leaned against the carved alabaster mantel and rubbed his mouth with his fist in thought.

At some point in the past, he had been introduced to Coldfell's coarse, lusty braggart of a nephew, Sir Dolph Breckinridge. He had certainly heard of Dolph's reputation as a hunter. The baronet was known as a crack shot. He was also known as a Corinthian who liked to live beyond his means, and for that reason, Hawk surmised that

Dolph wanted very much to come into his inheritance as the next earl of Coldfell.

Hawk didn't know and scarcely dared wonder if old James was capable of siring a child in his advanced years— Abraham in the Bible had managed it, hadn't he? All he knew was that if Coldfell had gotten Lucy with child, then their son, and not Dolph, would have stood in line to inherit the earldom. Thus, with free access to his uncle's properties, Dolph had ample opportunity to confront Lucy alone; as a notorious hunter, he certainly had the killing skill; and with the threat of the countess's possible pregnancy, he had the unassailable motive to remove Lucy from his path to fortune and rank.

Hawk considered hiring a Bow Street Runner to investigate the matter for him, but decided it was too deeply personal to commit to a stranger.

After leaving her grave this afternoon, a brief stop at White's and a few casual questions had informed him that the Regent was throwing yet another party at Brighton. All the wastrels who chased after the Carlton House set would be following the prince there, Dolph and his companions among them.

Hawk burned to go immediately and call Dolph out, but as Coldfell had said, he did not *know*—he only suspected. He dragged his hand through his thick black hair.

He would go mad if he did not find out the truth, but he couldn't simply go on the rampage, hurling wild accusations with nothing to back them up—accusations involving another man's wife. Such rash behavior on his part would generate a whirlwind of gossip in the ton and scandal, by God, was the one thing he would not tolerate.

Always he had to think of his family's name, his own reputation and his young sister's. Jacinda would be making her debut in another year or so, and he wanted no taint of scandal whatsoever to touch her. The child was capricious and willful by nature, and secretly, as her guardian, he already feared their mother's famous wantonness ran also in her daughter's veins.

His political aims had to be protected, as well. The prime minister, Lord Liverpool, was keeping his eye on him for the next cabinet vacancy that arose. In the meantime, Hawk sat on the board of a dozen Parliamentary committees; his reputation for integrity translated to power and influence to muscle his bills through both houses. A loss of personal credibility could damage his efforts to see the penal code reformed, among other projects. Nor could he bear for Lucy's memory to be tainted with sly talk. Besides, he thought, if he made accusations prematurely, Dolph might slip through his fingers and he would only succeed in making a fool of himself.

Folding his arms across his chest, he stared at the rug, brooding. Reason commanded him to admit there was a slim chance Lucy's death could have been the accident it appeared. As a man of justice, he was bound by principle to give cool objectivity its due. He could not spend his waking hours fighting for justice in Parliament, then murder a possibly innocent man in a duel in a fit of rage.

He needed the facts before he could take action, but it was not as though Dolph would simply admit to murder. A subterfuge was necessary. He would have to study Dolph, he mused, perhaps even feign friendship until he found the way to back him into a corner. Every man had a weakness. He would find Dolph's and lean on it until he broke him. He'd get the truth out of him somehow.

Patience.

Wrath welled in him for justice now, but he checked it, letting his plan take shape in his mind. Though it would require a gargantuan effort of self-control to bide his time, with more information he could act more circumspectly . . . and more lethally.

Resolved on his course, he strode over to the door of the library and sent the footman posted in the hallway for his valet.

He would leave at dawn for Brighton.

The dim illumination from her tallow candle flickered over her single room as Bel finished up the shirts she mended for piecework.

At length she stood, stretched her aching back, then went to put on her gray wool cloak. She had promised the laundress that she would return the shirts tonight so that they could be starched, pressed, and returned to their owner in the morning. Smoothing the mended shirts over her arm, she locked the door to her room and pulled the red-lined hood of her cloak up. Its billowy folds floated behind her as she set off into the dark streets.

The moonless April night was black as pitch. The temperature had dropped ten degrees or more. Her breath misted, catching the light from the lone lamppost on the corner, but when she glanced around the intersection, she didn't see the night watchman. The Charleys were a nuisance during the day, always telling her to move on and sell her oranges elsewhere, but she was glad of their presence at night.

Drawing the tapes of her cloak closer around her throat, she hurried on. When she neared the loud, seedy gin shop, she crossed the street and padded along in the shadows on the opposite side. Sober men were indecent enough.

At last, with a sigh of relief, she safely reached the laundress's house and gave the woman the mended shirts. The laundress inspected her work with a nod of satisfaction, gave her several more to repair for the morrow, then paid her. Bel paused to hide the coins in the tiny leather purse at her waist inside her cloak. Drawing a deep breath, she pulled her hood back up, nodded good night to the laundress, and forced herself back out into the chilly darkness.

It was only a quarter hour's walk to the hovel she now called home. The greasy yellowish fog seemed to have thickened, throwing noises behind her like heavy footfalls, making her own steps ring strangely off the brick houses in the narrow, twisting alleyways of the rookery. She glanced over her shoulder and walked faster.

A striped alley cat glided by. Shrill laughter spilled from a lit window above. She looked up in its direction, turned the corner and, in that split second, the man grabbed her.

Her terrified scream was muffled by a rough, callused hand.

She immediately began fighting, blindly thrashing against an iron grip as she was swept into a small side alley.

"Shut up." The big man jerked her, then shoved her hard into the wall.

She barely caught herself in time from sprawling headlong. She looked up in wide-eyed terror to find the warden of the Fleet, clearly very drunk.

A sickening *knowing* promptly spiraled down to the pit of her stomach, paralyzing her. The carriage ride . . .

He had planned this.

"Hello, pretty," he slurred, harshly pressing her up against the alley wall as though she were one of his unruly prisoners.

Struggling for calm, Bel swallowed hard. She was shaking uncontrollably. Her chest heaved with fright. She tried to back away, sliding along the wall. He stopped her, bracing his meaty hand on the bricks to block her path. With his other hand, he touched her hair. He smiled. She sobbed.

"Told you we'd compromise, didn't I? Everything's going to be just fine, lass. Long as you give me what I want."

"No," she uttered.

"Oh, aye," he said hoarsely. He lowered his stinking mouth and tried to kiss her.

Wrenching her face away from him, she shrieked but he stifled the sound, clapping his hand over her mouth again. She fought against his brutal strength, her mind somehow refusing to accept that it was happening. Then his hand, hot and dirty, curled around her throat and he ground himself against her, his breath rasping at her ear. She grimaced in utter terror as tears welled in her eyes.

"Nice and easy now, girly, be still," he grated in a voice like rusty iron. "Ye knew ye had it coming." He pinned her hands above her head.

The details of the next few minutes she would never clearly recall.

The darkening world blurred and slowed and all she could hear was the pounding of her heart roaring in her ears. She sobbed and made herself stare up at the stars, tiny cold jabs of light like the heads of pins. Only the metallic clinking of the huge key ring he wore at his waist pierced her wild, black hysteria as he held her against cold cutting brick, tore her clothing, grabbed and hurt her. Then pain beyond horror, pain such as she had never known flashed before her stricken eyes, blinding her like lightning, sharp as a knife in her belly. The warden grunted and suddenly sagged against her, gasping, his grip slackening; she fought free with a scream trapped in her throat and ran.

"You tell anyone, and I'll take it out of your pa's hide!" he shouted weakly after her.

Blind with crying, clothes torn, hair disheveled, she flung into a crowded thoroughfare with street lamps. She didn't remember the Charley who found her and mistook her in a wild, incoherent state for a gin-drunk streetwalker, and apparently had escorted her to the magdalen house. She didn't remember the women there who helped her. She only remembered sitting for nearly three days on a cot against a barren wall with her knees drawn up, thinking over and over again, That's all I'm good for now.

Life as she had known it was over.

She—prim, respectable Miss Hamilton—knew better than anyone that there was a clear-cut line separating decency from disgrace.

Centuries had passed since she had been a refined country gentlewoman of Kelmscot, visiting with her neighbors, teaching Sunday school to the peasant children after services, attending the occasional Assembly ball. She was another sort of creature now, as lost and degraded as the prostitutes who came to this place seeking food and shelter from the cold, and mercury treatments for their horrid diseases.

She had nowhere to turn. Going to see Papa was out of the question. She couldn't even inform against her attacker because, as keeper of a major London prison, the warden would doubtless have friends inside the justice offices at Bow Street. There was nothing even to stop him from trying it again.

On the third day one of the streetwalkers who had taken shelter there tried to talk to her while she lay curled up, staring at the wall. Bel didn't recall much of the conversation until the brash, aging harlot had leaned toward her and offered in a shrewd tone: "If I 'ad yer looks and yer fine lady airs, I'd take me to Harriette Wilson's house and find me a rich lord protector, I would. Then I'd live in style!"

At that, Bel had looked up with her changed gaze.

She had heard that name before, spoken only in whispers. The divine Harriette Wilson was the greatest demirep in London.

She and her sisters were courtesans, Cyprians par excellence. They held infamous parties at their house on Saturday nights after the opera, which were said to be second only to White's Club in the hearts of London's richest and most powerful males. Rumor had it the Regent, the rebel poet Lord Byron, and even the great Wellington could be found in the company of these most sought-after diamonds of the Fashionable Impure.

Dolph moved in such circles. Why, she could become the mistress of his worst enemy, she thought as a faint, cold smile lit her face. How humiliated he would be, as she was now, how powerless and enraged, if he saw that she would rather become another man's harlot instead of his wife. For this, ultimately, was Dolph's fault.

Protector. Delicious word.

Someone to help her, take all her fears away. Someone who was kind and would not harm her. The idea, wild, destructive, burned like a fever in her brain. And why not? She was already irrevocably ruined. Not even Mick Braden, wherever he was, would marry her in her state of shame.

The thought of her childhood sweetheart filled her with disgust. How he had failed her. She could admit it now— he was probably right here in London somewhere, dallying with a tavern wench, getting his leisurely fill of bachelor-hood before sallying forth to Kelmscot, where he no doubt thought that she was still waiting patiently for him.

What a fool she was. If not for her fanciful hopes in him, she might have become another man's wife and none of this need have happened, she thought bitterly. Harriette Wilson could teach her how to fend for herself.

Her simmering anger grew potent, acrid, dangerous.

She had too much pride to throw herself on the notorious Cyprian's charity, but she could approach her as one businesswoman to another. If she promised Harriette Wilson a percentage of the proceeds from her future protector, she mused, the woman would surely agree to teach her the courtesan's arts. What else did she have to lose?

Moments later Bel was gathering up her few possessions, her hands shaking slightly with the brashness of her decision. She knew she wasn't thinking clearly but was too coldly, deeply enraged to care. She thanked the good people who had looked after her for the past three days and asked the streetwise jade where Harriette Wilson lived.

With her cloak wrapped tightly around her, she set out to find her fate on a day of mottled cloud and sun. It would be a long walk from the City to the clean, luxurious environs of Marylebone, north of Mayfair, where they were building roads and lavish terraces in the new Regent's Park. Anger was balled up tightly within her, keeping her warm. She hadn't eaten for a couple of days, but her physical hunger did not match her sharper one for revenge.

Protector. Sweet word.

He didn't have to be handsome. He didn't have to be young, she thought as she strode swiftly through the streets, not looking back, her arms folded tightly around her. He didn't have to shower her with finery and jewels.

He only had to be gentle and not make it too unpleasant for her, and he had to help her get Papa out of the Fleet and stand by when she faced that unspeakable brute.

If fate sent her such a person, she swore bitterly to the heavens, now that she was fallen, she would make it very worth his while.

"O 'Melia, my dear, this does everything crown!
Who could have supposed I should meet you in Town?
And whence such fair garments, such pros-per-ity?"—
"O didn't you know I'd been ruined?" said she.

—THOMAS HARDY

Bait the hook well! This fish will bite.

—SHAKESPEARE

⊰ CHAPTER ⊱
TWO

In the bracing sea breezes of Brighton Hawk found that he could breathe. Whether it was the distance from the crowds of London and all the places that reminded him of *her*, or the influence of the calm majestic sea, grief began to loosen its stranglehold over his heart.

The nights were relegated to his quest, but during the balmy April days he found solitude whenever he wished it, walking barefoot on the sand with his trousers rolled up around his calves. Far from the Promenade and the bathing machines, there was only the sough of the sea and the cries of the gulls. He felt himself healing, growing stronger.

Most mornings he liked to row straight out from the shore until England was hardly in sight. He fished. One day, warmed by the high spring sun, enticed by the placid, pale jade water, he took off his boots, pulled off his coat and waistcoat and dove off the side of his little dinghy.

The water was frigid and it stole his breath as he plummeted straight down through the tossing waves, shot like an arrow from a bow. The water was painfully cold, but it cleared his head to the point of an almost visionary lucidity. He swam deep, savoring the dull silence, the blue-green light below the surface. He thought of Lucy drowning in the pond and tried to imagine what that had been like.

Holding his breath until his lungs ached, he felt alone as always, yet free, floating, felt himself slowly coming untangled from her thrall, until at last he burst up to the surface, gasping, with no pearl in his clutches but the vague, strangely comforting notion that perhaps he had been more in love with his *idea* of Lucy than with the woman herself. It was both a virtue and a fault in him that he lived too much in his head, he knew.

Feeling more himself than he had in months, at length, he rowed back to shore with long, vigorous strokes, shivering in the brisk wind. He was staying at the Castle Inn on the west side of the Steine. Reaching his lodgings, he bathed, changed clothes, ate, then set out for the night's usual party. His new chum, Dolph Breckinridge, would be attending a concert in the Regent's garden, and so would Hawk.

Cultivating the baronet's rakish set had been easier than he could have hoped, though it was still too soon to broach the subject of Lucy without raising suspicions. Among the wastrels he had to put up with a good deal of ribbing about his superior morals, but they accepted his casual association as an enhancement to their own reputations. He bided his time, sensing that his goal was ever nearer.

The parties the Regent threw at Brighton were so vast that Hawk felt almost anonymous, strolling idly from room to room and out onto the greensward where the German orchestra was playing. To his satisfaction, he happened across Dolph standing alone at the corner of the terrace, staring out to sea in a pensive mood.

Maybe after ten days of cultivating the baronet, tonight at last he might unearth the key he sought. Hawk sauntered over to him at the balustrade, disguising seething hostility behind his impeccable facade of cordial reserve. "Breckinridge."

"Hawkscliffe," Dolph slurred, then sighed heavily and took a swig from his bottle.

Drunk, thought Hawk. *Perfect*. "Something wrong, old boy?"

Dolph sent him a sideward glance, his heavy-lidded eyes looking duller than usual. "Have you ever been in love, Hawkscliffe?"

Hands in pockets, Hawk looked judiciously out to sea. "No."

"No, I don't suppose you have, cold fish like you," he said, too drunk to heed his own insolence. "I'll bet you were born under Saturn."

Hawk lifted a brow. "Pray, are you in love, Breckinridge?"

"Hawkscliffe," he said, "I have found a diamond."

"Ahh, that brunette you had sitting on your lap last night after the theater?"

Dolph shook his head, gestured idly with his bottle. "That was just to pass the time. No, I have found the most beautiful, adorable, desirable, cleverest, sweetest girl. I know . . . such love," he said, pressing the bottle to his heart, "as you cannot imagine."

Hawk stared at him, taken aback. He had never till this moment heard the man speak of anything with much passion except the hunt, horses, and hounds. "Do tell."

"You should see her," Dolph went on. "No—no—on the other hand, no one is allowed to meet her until I have married her. I am keeping her hidden away from you all. God knows, you'll swoop down with your dukedom and your great name and try to steal her," he said, laughing drunkenly. "And if not you, then one of your intolerable brothers."

"Such a prize, is she?"

"More than you will ever know," he declared arrogantly, and took a drink.

"Has your angel got a name?"

"Belinda."

"When's the wedding?"

Dolph sighed again. "Won't have me. Yet."

"You're joking," he said mildly.

"She will, in due time," he assured him. "I'm thinking she will miss me so much while I'm away that she'll have reconsidered my offer by the time I get back to town."

"Well, I wish you great success with her," he said lightly, and turned away with a calculating gleam in his eyes.

Bull's-eye, he thought.

Having given his quarry plenty of time to ponder the misery of existence without him, Dolph Breckinridge returned to town with the buoyant eagerness of a hunter at the climax of the chase. The vixen was cornered. There was nowhere she had left to flee.

What a fine trophy she would make! he thought as he whipped his horses down the Strand. Belinda had led him a merry chase, but the enforced separation he had imposed on her had surely driven the defiance out of her. He intended to find her meek and willing to come to him at last. If not, then he would just have to devise some new way to block her foolish attempts to live without him.

Streaking down the street in his phaeton, he was heedless of the wrecks he almost caused and the pedestrians he nearly crushed under his whirring wheels. Impatient to find her, he scanned the faces of the vendors as his phaeton careened through the next intersection. He barked a curse at a delivery wagon going too slow in the road and curved past it, nearly colliding head on with a mail coach.

He shouted at the post driver and would have liked to stop and brawl, only he had more important things to do. Sulking angrily, he brought the whip down on his horses' backs and plunged on.

Where the devil was the chit? He couldn't wait to spar with her, for Belinda had been one of the few real challenges he had ever known.

Life had been easy for Dolph Breckinridge. Things

always seemed to fall out in his favor, like his inheritance of his uncle's earldom. His parents had never been any match for his strong will, even as a child. Eton and Oxford had been effortless because he had coerced the underclass bookworms into fagging for him. Thanks to the excellent physique and looks God had given him, women also fell in line—all but his dainty, indomitable Miss Hamilton.

Never had any woman so made him burn for conquest. What a feather she would be in his cap! With such a refined, obedient, beautiful wife, he would be the envy of his friends—among whom he now numbered the extremely powerful duke of Hawkscliffe, he thought in self-congratulation.

"Hang it all, girl, where are you?" he muttered to himself. His horses' ears swivelled nervously at the sound of his voice.

Failing to spy her in any of the usual locations, he took a break from his hunt and tore off in the direction of his club, knowing that a good repast and a drink would cure his bedevilment. Then he would resume his search and no doubt find the quarry in the open.

It was not long before he was drawing off his thick leather driving gloves and swaggering into Watier's. As one of the livelier clubs, the sight of a boisterous confab abuzz in the main saloon was not unusual.

About a dozen men were arguing good-naturedly on the subject of some new wager. Dolph strode into his club mates' midst, exchanging greetings with some while the discussion went on. He barely listened, more interested in ordering a good beef pie.

"*Prime* article. No one will get near her for anything less than carte blanche, you realize."

"That rules me out—at least until my venerated parent expires."

Snickers, idle laughter.

"Who do you think she'll choose?"

"Ten pounds says it'll be Argyll."

"No, Argyll belongs to Harriette."

"What about Worcester?"

"She doesn't fancy him."

"She fancies me!"

"Oh, please."

"She said I was witty!"

"She doesn't fancy anyone. That's what makes her so appealing. Ah, but to be the one to melt her ice . . . now, that would be something."

"Well, she's never given you a second look, nor any of us."

"What does she want? A demigod? Perfection? A saint?"

"I've got twenty guineas that says she's waiting for Czar Alexander to arrive. The women are half in love with him already. The *Times* says he'll be here any day—"

"No, no, she's a good English girl. She'll have nothing to do with a foreigner!" scoffed another. "I say it'll be Wellington, mark my words. Give me ten pounds on Wellington! And I daresay he deserves her more than any of us."

"With all due respect, Wellington could be her father," someone muttered.

"I think I shall hang myself if she won't have me," another said with easy cheer.

"All right, all right," Dolph declared, turning around, hands on hips. "I'll bite. Who are you talking about?"

They stopped abruptly, glanced at each other, and smiled slyly.

"Pardon?" Luttrell asked innocently.

"Where've you been?" asked another.

"Brighton, with the Regent," said Dolph haughtily. "What news?"

"There is a new Cyprian who has brought us all to our

knees," said Colonel Hanger. "We are placing bets on whom she will accept as her protector."

Dolph gave a short laugh, unimpressed. These fools thought they knew what beauty was.

"You doubt us?" one of the exquisites asked indignantly.

"What does she look like?" Dolph skeptically replied.

A collective sigh rose from their midst.

"Hair like spun sunlight—"

"Oh, spare us your poesy, for God's sake, Alvanley," drawled Brummell. "She's a blue-eyed blonde. In a word, stunning."

"Humph," Dolph snorted. "Those are easy enough to come by."

A trifle uneasy suddenly for reasons he could not name, he turned his back on them as the waiter came out and set his beef pie down before him.

"Has anybody heard where Miss Hamilton will be appearing tonight?" one of them asked behind him.

Dolph promptly choked on his bite of beef.

"I should think she'll be at Harriette's soiree."

Dolph washed down his cough with a swallow of ale, shot up out of his chair and whirled around, wiping off his mouth with his forearm. "What did you say her name is?"

"Who?"

"The Cyprian," he rumbled, lowering his head like a bull ready to charge.

Colonel Hanger smiled at him and lifted his glass in a toast. "Miss Belinda Hamilton."

He recoiled in horror.

"To Miss Hamilton!" they toasted cheerfully, but Dolph was already out the door.

He roared for his phaeton and in another moment was hurtling down St. James's toward Marylebone. He knew where Harriette Wilson lived, having attended many of the harlot's Saturday night parties at her house in York Place.

It was impossible. It was a mistake or a joke or a coincidence. She would not—*she would not!* She was a prude, a virgin, a lady. Damn it, she was *his* claimed property.

Almost too angry to concentrate on driving, he left a wake of chaos in the streets behind him as he thundered down on the reigning Cyprian's elegant, modest townhouse.

If it was true—if his Belinda really was in there, by God, he would break down the door and drag her out of that house by her hair. Drag her all the way to Gretna Green.

In front of Harriette Wilson's house, he leaped out of his barely halted phaeton and strode to the front door and began banging on it with his fist.

"Open up! Open up, Harriette, you slut! Damn it, Bel, I know you're in there! You will see me!"

The door abruptly opened under his beating fist. Dolph found himself eye to eye with one of the whores' bullies—a tall, bulky footman who looked like an ex-prizefighter. Treachery in livery. Harriette kept a couple of them around the premises as bodyguards, he recalled.

"May I 'elp you?" the menacing footman growled.

"I'm here to see—" He strove to calm himself. A bead of sweat ran down his cheek. "Is there a girl here by the name of Belinda Hamilton?"

"Miss Hamilton is entertaining guests right now," the brawny footman grunted. "You can leave your card."

So it was true.

Dolph stared at him in horrified disbelief until the footman snorted at him and closed the door in his face. He heard the lock slide home. He beat on the door, hollering, but no one answered. He staggered backward away from the house, across the pavement, into the middle of the street, where he threw his head back and howled in volcanic rage: *"Belinda!"*

Though the whole world was spinning sickeningly, he saw motion in the upper window. The curtain fluttered.

Panting with fury, the whites of his eyes wild and baleful, he fixed his stare there. The afternoon sun glared off the panes as the French windows swung inward and opened. Then *she* appeared—only somehow it wasn't her—his bedraggled little Bel in her threadbare woolen cloak.

It couldn't be her.

Dolph stared in awe at the beautiful courtesan stranger.

The woman in the window was a pale, elegant goddess. Her gleaming flaxen tresses were swept up in a sleek, sophisticated arrangement. She wore jeweled earrings and a rich gown cut too low for afternoon. The breeze billowed through her sheer long sleeves, sculpting her graceful arms as she placed her pampered hands on the windowsill and tossed a mocking twist of smile down to him like a thorny rose.

"Yes?"

"Belinda!" he bellowed in disbelief. "W-w-what have you done?"

She lifted her eyebrows coolly. "Sorry, I haven't the full honor of your acquaintance. *Au revoir.*"

Though the words were polite, Dolph knew she had just delivered him the most direct and thorough cut a young lady could give. She started to shut the window.

"Belinda, wait!"

She laughed blithely at him then looked over her shoulder into the room behind her. "Come and see this poor Caliban in the roadway," she called to her companions.

Two shadowy shapes of men came to the window, flanking her on either side.

Good God! Dolph thought, recognizing them. Argyll! Hertford! Those lechers were trying to seduce her! he thought. But they were powerful lechers, a duke and a marquis respectively, men of intellect and distinction. Dolph snapped his jaw shut to bite back a stream of curses, realizing he must watch what he said.

The Regent himself might be up there, for all he knew, or the royal dukes, or Wellington, for he could hear other people talking and laughing up in the drawing room.

"Belinda Hamilton," he said through gritted teeth, "I don't know what you think you're doing in this place, but you had better come down here at once."

She slipped her arms around both men's shoulders and smiled brazenly at him. "I know exactly what I'm doing, Dolph. I'm entertaining some very charming friends, as our servant already told you."

"I must talk to you!" he nearly wailed.

She laughed gaily, releasing the lords, who frowned at him in protective disapproval. She braced her elbows on the windowsill, then rested her flawless face in her hands with a smile of mock pity. "Poor Dolph, you look so distraught."

"Belinda, for God's sake, come down and speak to me."

"You're a boor, Dolph. What else is there to say?"

"This is unacceptable!" he screamed, throwing his head back.

Shutters and doors down the street opened and people looked out to see who was causing all the noise.

"Very well, I will give you a brief audience tonight at the party, but all I really want to hear from you," she said sweetly, "is an apology. Now go away before you rouse the constable."

With that she disappeared inside and closed the window.

Tears in his eyes, Dolph glared up at the empty casement, simmering, his mouth pursed in rage. He shouted for her again, but the glass panes merely reflected the blue sky back at him. Still barely able to believe her treachery, he spun around, jumped up into his phaeton and raced off down the street, his pulse thundering with the knowledge that this time, she had really bested him.

* * *

Bel's heart pounded with satisfaction after the long awaited moment of initial revenge on her mortal enemy. She would remember the shock on Dolph's loathed face for as long as she lived, but it was nothing compared to the suffering she had in store for him tonight.

"I told you they will soon be shooting themselves in the streets over you, Miss Hamilton," Lord Hertford said with a chuckle as she rejoined their company.

Harriette, her sister Fanny, and their friend, the *très* elegant Julia Johnstone, were scandal-mongering over tea with a handful of their favorites.

"Are you sure it's wise to let that rabid fellow come here tonight?" asked the duke of Argyll, glancing with a frown toward the window.

"All the better to torment him," Bel replied lightly as she took a round white tea cake from the tray.

"Cruel beauty," murmured Hertford, watching her eat it.

Bel shrugged, gave him a nonchalant smile, and settled into her place on the sofa once more, tucking her slippered feet under her.

Harriette sat beside her, a petite but voluptuous woman in her early thirties, with auburn curls and fine dark eyes that gleamed with wit. "Watch yourself tonight."

"I will, don't worry."

Perhaps it was rash to allow Dolph to come to the party, Bel thought, but she despised him enough to want him to see her in all her glory as the demimonde's newest sensation. Let him choke on his rage. He deserved it. She would rub her new fame in his face. With a house full of her admirers and Harriette's burly footmen to boot, there was not a thing he'd be able to do to her.

The amiable group resumed their conversation, but Bel was silent, nibbling her tea cake while her mind wandered back over the events of the past weeks.

On that April day when she had shown up on the Wilson sisters' doorstep, Harriette had expressed an immediate disinclination to help an obviously well-bred young woman ruin herself. Fortunately, her more tenderhearted sister, Fanny, had been there and had prevailed upon Harriette to help her.

Amy, the mean-spirited eldest, had taken one look at Bel, bristled with jealousy, and flatly refused to get involved. Between Fanny's pleading and Harriette's penchant for contradicting Amy, Harriette had inspected Bel—her looks, her carriage, the extent of her learning. Declaring her not a total disaster, she had given Bel to understand that the courtesan's trade was an expensive profession to break into when it was done right, chiefly because of the need to keep in step with their wealthy clientele. For example, she would need a supply of fine evening gowns and these had to be of the first stare. For a guarantee of twenty percent of the settlement from Bel's future protector, Harriette had agreed to sponsor her entry into the demimonde.

Bel had been promptly settled into the Wilson sisters' extra bedroom, where her first order of business had been to write a letter to her father explaining that she had been asked to chaperon a pair of her young ladies from the finishing school on a trip to Paris, now that the city was open to English visitors. She gave her letter to one of Harriette's big, burly footmen, who had delivered it to the Fleet for her.

From that moment on, Bel the teacher had turned into the student.

Warming to her project for the profit, the lark of it, and the fact that Amy was incensed, Harriette set out to mold her into the perfect courtesan. Having cast off the old self that had been so brutally shamed and disgraced, Bel was more than willing to be shaped into something beautiful and new . . . and fearless and hard.

Never again would she go hungry. The fortune she'd

earn would be her security. Why, Harriette got a hundred guineas for only a few hours' dalliance and it didn't always necessarily mean going to bed with her client. Sometimes the gentleman only wanted a dinner companion, someone to talk to. But the first thing Harriette taught her—the prime rule of the courtesan's creed—was: *Never fall in love.*

To love a man was to be in *his* power and power, to a courtesan, was everything.

A courtesan, Bel learned, was far more than a bed partner or even a skilled seductress. She must be a scintillating model of wit and gaiety, a connoisseur of pleasure to gratify all of a man's senses, physical, emotional, and intellectual.

Aside from making the most of her beauty, she must be a pleasing entertainer, an able hostess, a sympathetic listener, and a discreet confidante. It helped if she was a bold and spirited rider able to turn heads on Rotten Row. She must keep abreast of the political issues that obsessed the men and that meant reading the *Times* every morning as well as the Tory journal, the *Quarterly Review*. The Whig journal, the *Edinburgh Review*, was optional. Even though it had been founded by one of Harriette's lovers, the brilliant young Henry "Wickedshifts" Brougham, Harriette pronounced it too vexing and too hard to understand. The Tories had the majority, anyway.

She also had to learn how to invest her earnings, for a woman could not be a courtesan forever. Bel was mystified by the art of building wealth, especially after she heard that several of the grand, retired demireps like the Brazen Bellona and the famed White Doe had thousands in the funds. Never had she dreamed of a life of such untrammeled independence, for no wife, however respectable, owned her own money.

Harriette became her heroine. Harriette understood power.

Bel had not told her mentor of her ordeal in that dark alley. She had told no one. Indeed, she was convinced she had all but forgotten it. Only the nightmares still plagued her.

Halfway into the month of May, the world seemed full of endless possibilities as London grew crowded with dignitaries and war heroes, all flooding in for the Victory Summer. Bel had made her debut on the Town by attending the opera at the King's Theater in the Haymarket with the notorious trio known as the Three Graces—Harriette, Fanny, and Julia.

Throughout the entire performance, while La Catalani wailed in the melodrama of misplaced love, *Semiramide,* the Cyprians' theater box swarmed with men—old and young, handsome and plain, witty and dull, foreign and domestic, each one more grandly titled than the next, all paying homage to the Cyprians, sometimes in full view of their wives.

There were noblemen, officers, diplomats, poets, artists, pinks, dandies, and exquisites, Bond Street Loungers elbowing in next to high-minded men of science from the Royal Academy, and the one thing that they had in common was that all yearned for the sensual dream of voluptuous love that only a courtesan could give.

Wide-eyed with inexperience, Bel saw Harriette and the others treated like veritable idols, earthly embodiments of Venus herself. Harriette warned her to demand this homage as her due. It might seem haughty and rude, she had said, but it was the only way to be taken seriously. If she wanted to be seen as a prize worth having, she had to carry herself like one.

It was all a game, and Bel quickly learned to play it well.

There were several philosophies to choose from: Fanny found it easiest to devote herself to one well-chosen protector—in her case, Lord Hertford. Harriette frowned on this practice, for she didn't trust all her eggs to one basket, having been burned before by Lord Ponsonby. Instead, she regularly entertained a handful of favorites, among them Argyll, Worcester, and Henry Brougham, who loathed his wife: Harriette loved to brag with an air of nonchalance that Wellington had once been in her thrall.

Bel preferred Fanny's more modest strategy of finding one very agreeable protector to satisfy, but heeded Harriette's warning about wives' jealousies regarding these exclusive arrangements. Taking all this into account, Bel forged one guiding rule for herself in addition to the courtesan's creed of never falling in love: She refused to go under the protection of a married man.

Though this narrowed the selection considerably, oddly enough, Harriette concurred that her decision was wise. She wished she had followed that advice herself when she was younger, she said, for one could never rest too easy when one's keeper had a jealous wife at home. Bel had no wish to make enemies.

Besides, this was one small way of reminding herself that, harlot or no, she still had some clear notion of right and wrong. Rich widowers were fine; unmarried young bucks would do, as well. But *La Belle* Hamilton refused to be party to adultery.

She had met countless numbers of prospective keepers at the opera. In the nights that followed, she had gotten to know some of them better at Harriette's parties and at Vauxhall Gardens. The offers rolled in, directed to Harriette on her behalf, but although she still had met no one with whom she could imagine doing some of the shocking things Harriette and Fanny had described to her—all her erotic knowledge was theoretical to date. Indeed, she was hard pressed not to flinch when a man merely brushed past her in a crowd, nor to bristle with hostility if one presumed to take her hand.

Still, she pressed on in her reincarnation as one of the city's glamorous scarlet outcasts, ignoring her misgivings, relishing the thought of the fortune that would be her security. Then no one could ever hurt her and her father again. She would be free, independent. No one suspected that she was a complete fraud, but she did not allow this thought to deter her. Carefully, she continued building her facade as the perfect courtesan, blithe and saucy and carefree.

Julia had declared her too picky, but Bel kept waiting for the right one. Wistfully, she clung to her vision of a knight in shining armor, though she feared she was seeking a needle in a haystack.

Somewhere out there the ideal protector was waiting for her, she mused in a faraway mood, removed from the buzz of conversation in the well-appointed parlor. The perfect lover who would lead her through her fears.

Someone she could trust. Someone she could kiss without revulsion. Someone gentle and noble and good.

When I meet him, she thought, I'll know.

⅔ CHAPTER ⅔
THREE

It was Saturday night after the opera and the Cyprians' fashionable little townhouse was crammed nearly to the breaking point as Hawk made his way through the throng, feeling self-conscious and out of place.

The party was a garish kaleidoscope of feverish color and raucous laughter. He scanned the overheated salon for Dolph Breckinridge as he was jostled along through the inebriated, mostly male crowd. Somewhere a window must have been opened, for a cool, almost imperceptible ribbon of air threaded in through the crowd to trail against his cheek like a trace of sanity. He needed it at the moment.

He'd had no idea that when Dolph had spoken so longingly of his ladylove, this *Belinda*, that he had been talking about a demirep, for God's sake. Nor had he expected to come back to Town and learn that half of male London had made a bid for the girl. Three full pages of wagers were logged in the betting book at White's concerning who would win the incomparable Miss Hamilton for his ladybird.

Her kind had no morals, but Miss Hamilton, uniquely, could be said to possess *a* moral: She refused all offers from married men, Hawk had heard at the club. Such nicety of feeling, he thought dryly.

Gossip about Dolph's making a fool of himself in the street that day over the girl had traveled quickly. Hawk had known the moment he'd heard about the incident that she was the key to getting his enemy under his thumb.

There was only one problem, however. Hawk knew nothing about demireps and how they liked to be wooed, for their philosophy of profit from lovemaking had always rather revolted the romantic nature that lurked beneath his straitlaced exterior.

All he knew was that it wasn't the simple matter of flashing a fat purse before their eyes: Cyprians were not typical prostitutes. They had reputations of a sort to maintain, whims to be catered to, vanities to be stroked. A man was supposed to enjoy the chase and the hoops the elite courtesans made them jump through to win their favors.

Games and absurdity, he thought in disgust, heaving an impatient sigh under his breath. Even if this Miss Hamilton was as lovely as everyone claimed, he could never respect a woman who was no more than a glorified whore. Still, though his dignity was rather put off by it all, he was fixed enough in his quest to play along. He tried to look relaxed, but could scarcely hide his lordly disdain for the place and its resident harlots. His mother would have fit right in here, he thought in contempt.

Just then, he happened across a trio of his acquaintances, who promptly exclaimed with hilarity to find him in this house of lust. They clapped him on the back and pressed a drink into his hand. Feeling sheepish, Hawk drank with them, barely heeding their half-drunken ramblings. Furtively scanning the room, his gaze suddenly happened across a large gilt-framed mirror over the fireplace. In it, he saw Dolph Breckinridge.

Coldfell's nephew was tucked away in an alcove on the far end of the salon. At first, Hawk could not see the woman he had cornered there. Then Dolph dropped to his knees in pleading, and Hawk glimpsed her face.

His eyes widened; he froze; he stared. Abruptly, he tore

his stunned gaze away before anyone suspected he was spying. His heart was pounding.

My God, she is an angel.

He forced a taut smile at his friends, gripped his wine-glass so hard he nearly snapped the stem, and listened not at all to his companions' boasting about their success at Gentleman Jack's boxing studio.

A prickling sensation raced down his spine. He slanted another covert glance at the mirror and beheld the silvery gold vision of the elegant young courtesan, ruling from her alcove like a virgin queen of some arctic country. Ce-lestial and yet sensual, Miss Hamilton stared straight ahead, ignoring her kneeling devotee in cruel serene beauty. Her face was expressionless, as though her delicate features had been carved from alabaster. She had fine-boned cheeks, an aristocratic nose, and a firm, willful chin. Hawk's stare fol-lowed the graceful curve of her throat downward to her slender body.

Her white muslin gown had sheer long sleeves, a straight, pleasing neckline and a standing Elizabethan-style collar of Brabant lace that framed the back of her head. She wore her flaxen tresses piled and coiled in glorious chaos atop her head. Tendrils of it wafted like whispered secrets against the curve of her neck, precisely where he should have liked to taste her.

He quivered and forced his gaze away, his pulse ham-mering. Merely knowing she was expertly trained to plea-sure a man in every way sent ripples of unrest down into the hollow well of his soul. *God, it had been so long.*

Traitor, he said to himself in contempt.

One of his companions asked him a question, but Hawk had ceased paying attention, for as he watched the mirror again Dolph and Miss Hamilton began to argue. The baronet pushed to his feet, looming over her with a snarl. Still, she sat on her cushioned bench, staring up at him in taunting silence. Dolph began gesticulating wildly. Miss Hamilton's mouth curved in a slight smile of frosty mockery, at which Dolph shoved his hand into his pocket and flung a handful of coins in her face.

Hawk drew in his breath, fiery rage erupting through his veins. The young beauty flinched as the coins struck her, one catching her in the chin. The coins scattered all over her lap and rolled onto the floor.

Hawk whirled around, abandoned his friends without explanation, and began shouldering his way through the drawing room to go to her aid. He blasted his conscience for standing by and merely watching while a suspected rapist and murderer harassed a defenseless woman, demi-rep or no. He had certainly not expected an outburst of violence from Dolph in a room packed to brimming with Miss Hamilton's admirers. It appeared no one else had noticed the spectacle unfolding in the alcove, else there ought to have been a general hue and cry to lynch the blackguard.

Hawk glanced back at the reflection in the glass when the thick crowd slowed his progress. He could see Harriette's footmen, two big Cockney bruisers, surrounding Dolph in an instant, roughly herding him out. He was so intent on his purpose, shoving through the throng, that he bumped into someone and managed to spill the remainder of his wine on his formal white gloves. He'd forgotten he was even holding the wine. Muttering a curse, he passed off the empty glass to a liveried waiter and quickly pulled off his gloves and abandoned them on the servant's tray, as well. Heedlessly, he pressed on, then suddenly found himself face-to-face with Dolph, flanked by Harriette's footmen.

Instantly, he saw that Dolph was quite drunk.

"Hawkscliffe!" The baronet clutched Hawk's lapel with an air of desperation. "They are throwing me out! It's Belinda! She is driving me mad! You have to help me!"

He gritted his teeth against a surge of loathing. "What would you have me do?" He was sorely tempted to take Dolph outside and thrash him, but the man deserved so much more than that.

"Talk to her for me?" Dolph slurred. "Reason with her—tell her she has punished me long enough. All I want is to take care of her. And tell her—" His drink-reddened face hardened. "Tell her if she chooses anyone but me, she will be sorry."

The bodyguards snarled at his threat.

Dolph's grip on Hawk's lapel eased as they dragged him away.

Struggling to collect his fury, Hawk clenched and unclenched his fists by his sides. He pivoted on his heel and shoved his way roughly through the rest of the crowd. Men backed out of his path when they saw him coming, his face darkened by wrath. He arrived at the edge of Miss Hamilton's alcove just as she finished putting the last few coins that had been hurled at her on a servant's tray. Her hands were shaking, he saw, and it pained him.

"Get rid of it, all of it. Take it. Here. Go! Hurry, he'll be leaving in a moment," she said in a jittery voice, waving the servant off to return Dolph's money to him.

As Hawk stepped closer, suddenly unsure of what to say, Miss Hamilton frowned, reached into her bodice, and pulled out a silver half crown with a look of disgust. She handled the coin as though it were an insect that had fallen down her dress. She suddenly held the coin out to Hawk with an expectant look. "Please give this back to your friend," she ordered, the vulnerability in her eyes all at odds with her haughty command.

He grew a little dazzled as he held her gaze. The color of her eyes made him think of wild orchids, but no, they were bluer than that—the soft, deep, violet blue of meadow cranesbill. Shadowed under long dun lashes, her eyes were mysterious, guarded . . . and innocent.

"Hello?" she called impatiently.

Taken aback, Hawk held out his hand. She dropped the coin into his palm. He faltered to feel how the metal still held her body's silken warmth. A second ago, it had been pressed against her breast. His eyes glazed over.

"Go, won't you?" she insisted. "He'll be gone in a moment."

He snapped out of his daze. "Certainly, I'll give it to him later. I came to see if you were all right, Miss, ah, Hamilton, is it?"

"Oh, you're no help." She snatched the coin back from him and summoned another of her titled lackeys to deliver it—the fresh-faced young duke of Leinster. She gave him the coin and a caress on his smooth cheek, bestowing a smile as sweet as the breezes of the Blessed Isles.

"Thank you, Leinster," she murmured in playful, lilting singsong that Hawk was sure had the siren's power to mesmerize men. The handsome young Irish lord floated rather than walked away to do her bidding.

Hawk turned to her again in perplexed fascination, only to find he had lost his chance to speak to her. A couple of dashing youngbloods had swaggered over in front of him to pay their respects, oblivious to what had just happened.

All signs of Miss Hamilton's distress had vanished behind her flawless smile. The two youngbloods, with whom she was now blithely flirting, had no idea she had just been practically attacked by Dolph. Only Hawk knew. He stared in fascination.

Why, she was a consummate actress, he thought. Of course she was, he realized, then scowled, standing like a dolt outside her alcove, half fearing he was out of his depth. Never in his life had he expected to find himself a supplicant vying for the favors of some fine little twenty-three-year-old bit o' muslin. Who did she think she was? He, the duke of Hawkscliffe, had come to rescue her and she didn't seem to give a damn.

Miss Hamilton rose from her cushioned bench and parted the dandyish pair, flouncing off between them. With her nose in the air, she brushed by Hawk and strode toward the crowd that turned to adore her, calling out her name. She laughed gaily and lifted her arms out to them in an easy, natural acceptance of their worship. The dukes of Rutland and Bedford leaped to her sides and pulled her, all smiles, toward the green baize gaming tables while, to Hawk's astonishment, his chief political opponent, the gruff old Lord Chancellor Eldon pressed a fresh glass of wine into her dainty hand. The chit had half of Parliament fawning on her.

Hawk stood there, left behind, as perplexed, routed, and baffled as the two foppish lads. Never in all his memory had a woman on the game sailed right past him as though he didn't exist.

Obviously, she had no idea of his lofty name, his power and consequence—oh, shut up, he said to himself. Laughing suddenly for no apparent reason, he followed her.

Letting Dolph come to the party had been a mistake. She knew that now. She shouldn't have allowed herself the indulgence of gloating, but she had paid the price for her pettiness, hadn't she? He had certainly managed to frighten and embarrass her, Bel thought with a shudder, trying to put her stroke of bad judgment behind her and get on with the night.

Still, she couldn't help but browbeat herself for overestimating her ability to manage him. Soon after arriving at the party, Dolph had seemed near tears, begging her to hear him out. Crocodile tears, she thought. Rather than cause a scene, she had agreed to talk privately with him in the alcove, but when he had cornered her there, it had quickly escalated into an ugly confrontation. At least, thank God, no one but that tall, scowling man, Dolph's friend, had witnessed her humiliating moment.

Still a bit shaken by Dolph's violent outburst, but with her smile pasted in place, Bel put the baronet and his tall, dark, elegant friend out of her mind and sat down to play her favorite game, vingt-et-un.

She was not a true gambler, but this simple little game always proved profitable for her. The stakes were in her favor: if Lady Luck let her beat her present opponent, a well-heeled pink of the ton, she would win his jeweled cravat pin worth fifty guineas. If she lost, all that she had to give him was a kiss—but she never lost, perhaps for the simple reason that the gentlemen were drinking while she was sober.

Dozens of men had gathered around the table, cheering her on as she thwarted her opponent in the first of three hands. The young lord stroked his dimpled chin and frowned at his cards.

Though she watched her opponent, Bel was wholly aware of the tall, saturnine stranger—Dolph's friend—sauntering over to watch her play. A most august and imposing personage, she thought, studying him from the corner of her eye while she pretended to inspect her cards. Truth be told, she found him just a wee bit intimidating. Striking and cosmopolitan, he appeared in his mid- to late thirties, with the athletic physique and sun-bronzed complexion of an avid sportsman. His coal black hair was slicked back for evening, accentuating the stern, precise architecture of his face.

He stood with his chin high, his wide shoulders squared. With an imperious air of high reserve, he swept the crowd with a sharp, unsmiling glance. His cravat was starched and impeccable, his formal clothes austere black and white—and he wore them like the colors in which he saw the world, she thought in disdain, heedless of the colorfully dressed dandies all around her.

Unable to resist, Bel glanced over at him briefly just as he looked at her. He caught her gaze and held it frankly, sending her a faint, sly smile. For a moment, his velvety brown eyes utterly mesmerized her. She took one look into them and felt that she had known him all her life.

"Your turn, Miss Hamilton."

"Of course." Startled, she jerked back to face her opponent and smiled fetchingly at him while her heart beat rapidly. Arrogant blackguard! she thought, all her awareness focused on the stranger. How dare he stare at her? She didn't care how attractive he was, she wanted nothing to do with him. He was Dolph's friend. She knew because she had seen them talking briefly after Dolph had behaved so horribly to her.

Besides, no man that good-looking could be a bachelor. Life wasn't that kind.

"One card, please," she said sweetly.

She played her hand and soon gave a bright laugh to find herself the new owner of a shiny jeweled cravat pin. The young fop took his defeat with a grin, knowing he could go to the pawn shop and buy it back again tomorrow if he liked.

As Bel gave him her hand, he bent and pressed a gallant kiss to her knuckles, withdrawing with a bow. Suddenly, before she could protest, the dark stranger slid into the vacated chair, interlocked his fingers on the table and stared at her in placid challenge.

Narrowing her eyes, she rested her chin gracefully on her knuckles and gave him a dry smile of disdain. "You again."

"What's your game, Miss Hamilton?" he asked pleasantly.

"Vingt-et-un."

"I understand the prize is your kiss."

"Only if you win—which you won't."

A smile tugged at one corner of his beguiling mouth. He slid a thick gold ring off his pinky finger and placed it in front of her. "Will this do?"

Sitting up straight in her chair, she picked up the ring and examined it skeptically. The ring had an onyx medallion with a gold *H* emblazoned on it.

She slid him a calculating glance, wondering who he was and what the *H* stood for, but she didn't care to indulge his vanity by asking. No friend of Dolph's was a friend of hers.

"A pretty trinket. Alas, I already own a dozen like it." She gave his ring back to him. "I don't wish to play you."

"Dear me, do I have the look of a cardsharp?" he asked in a cool, cultured baritone.

"I dislike the company you keep."

"Perhaps you are leaping to conclusions—or maybe this is just an excuse?" he suggested with another sly smile. "Perhaps the *indomitable* Miss Hamilton merely wishes to back down?"

She sent him a ladylike scowl as the men around them laughed.

"Very well," she conceded in a severe tone. "Best of three hands. Face cards are ten points. Aces high and low. You'll regret this."

"No, I won't." He placed the ring once more between them, then coolly sat back, slung his arm over the chair's back, and propped his left ankle over his right knee. He nodded toward the deck on the table. "Deal the cards, Miss Hamilton."

"Giving orders, are we?"

"I am only answering you in kind, my dear."

Holding his taunting gaze, she realized he was referring to her earlier command to bring the coin to Dolph. She gave him a sardonic look. "I am your servant, my lord."

"Interesting notion," he murmured.

Under his penetrating stare she grew uncharacteristically flustered. Her hands trembled slightly, making her clumsy as she shuffled the deck, but at length, she dealt them each two cards, one face down, one face up. She set the pile down and picked up her hidden card, the king of diamonds. With her face-up six, she decided to take a third card, but she looked at her opponent first in inquiry.

He flicked his fingers, elegantly declining. She turned over a three for herself, hiding a smile of satisfaction as her total came to nineteen.

"Show me what you've got," she invited him with the mildest trace of flirtation. She couldn't seem to help it. There was just something about the man.

He sent her a knowing little smile and turned over a queen and a ten. "Twenty."

She scowled, sweeping her nineteen aside.

She dealt again, more determined than ever to beat the arrogant scoundrel, an impulse that had nothing to do with the small fortune she could get from pawning his fine ring if she won it. He was too smug and domineering by half.

This time Bel dealt herself a pair of knaves. Twenty. Marvelous, she thought, sure she'd get him this time. "Would you care for another card?"

"Hit me."

"Don't tempt me," she murmured, peeling an eight off the top for him.

"Hell," he said, tossing his cards down. "Went bust."

"I'm so sorry," she consoled him, her eyes sparkling.

As he brushed his spent cards aside with a lordly scowl of irritation, she picked up his large ring and slipped it on her finger, pretending to admire it on herself. He lifted his eyebrow at her. With the big ring flopping on her finger, she dealt the final hand. His face-up card was the two of clubs.

Obviously he would want another card, she mused, strategizing as she examined her own hand, a four face down and a nine face up, for a total of thirteen. She would have to be careful not to overshoot twenty-one.

She glanced across the table at her enigmatic opponent. He beckoned. She dealt him a five.

"Another," he murmured.

"The four of spades."

"I'll stay."

She looked closely at him, trying to read his blank expression, then turned over a third card for herself, a five. This brought her to eighteen. If she took another card, the chances were she'd go bust. Best to play it safe.

"Show, my dear," she said archly to him.

"You first," he countered with a dark smile.

That smile worried her.

"Eighteen." She turned her last card over.

He leaned closer and inspected them, then nodded. "A respectable hand."

"Well?" she prodded, unable to decide if she was irked or entertained by the man. "Are you going to show your cards or not?"

"Show! Show!" the spectators clamored.

He glanced at them then looked down and slid his cards forward one by one, the two, the five, the four, totaling eleven.

Oh no, thought Bel, her eyes widening.

He turned over a ten and smiled wolfishly. "Blackjack."

"A kiss! A kiss!" the men shouted in uproarious cheer, calling for more drinks.

Bel sat back, folded her arms over her chest, and pouted

for a second, then pulled off his ring and rolled it back to him with a scowl. He gave her an innocent smile.

Around them the men exclaimed and guffawed and hooted and drank.

Serenely ignoring them, her tall, arrogant opponent leaned forward and rested his elbows on the table, smug as any conqueror. He tapped his splayed fingertips against each other, regarding her in amused expectation. "I await my prize with bated breath, Miss Hamilton."

"Oh, very well," she muttered, blushing. "Let's get this over with."

"Tsk, tsk, sore loser," he chided softly.

She stood, braced her hands on the green baize table, and leaned across it to him, aware of the cheering growing to a thunderous volume. Her heart was beating rapidly, but for his part, he appeared thoroughly unrattled.

Bravely she leaned closer, pausing in hesitation as she hovered in front of him, her lips mere inches from his. "You could cooperate," she suggested.

"But why should I, when it's so much more fun to see you flustered?"

She narrowed her eyes. Ignoring their raucous audience by a surge of will, she closed the distance between them, kissing him resolutely on the mouth. A moment later, she drew back, glowing pink, and unable to hide the sparkle of triumph in her eyes.

He studied her skeptically, skimmed his fingers over the table, then drummed them boredly. "I thought you said you were going to kiss me."

"I—I just did!"

"No."

"What do you mean? I just did!" She turned from pink to red as the men around them howled with laughter at his matter-of-fact reproach.

He slid the ring across the table to her again. "Look at

this ring. It's worth ten of your new cravat pins. This is what I put into the pot. You can't give me a kiss like that and call it fair. Rules are rules, Miss Hamilton. I want a real kiss, unless you want to become known as an unsporting young lady."

Her jaw dropped with indignation. "That's the only kind of kiss you're getting from me."

He scoffed and glanced away, scratching his cheek. "And you call yourself a courtesan."

"What is that supposed to mean?" she demanded.

He shrugged, lounging in his chair. "I've had better kisses from dairy maids."

"Ooh!" cried the men, watching their duel in mounting suspense.

Bel folded her arms over her chest and glared quellingly at him. She would have thrown his ring in his arrogant face if his eyes weren't sparkling so playfully. She could see he did not intend to let her off the hook.

"Really, don't you owe these devoted gentlemen a true demonstration of your professional expertise, Miss Hamilton?" he drawled, toying with the ring, rolling it between his thumb and forefinger.

She glanced around uncertainly at her admirers, then glared at him. How dare the blackguard call her skills into question—threaten her livelihood? Little did he know he'd struck a nerve. Her chief worry, after all, was that her suitors, who had been offering such vast sums to take her under their protection, might find out that in fact she was terrified to go into a man's bed. If she didn't prove herself here and now, they might begin to suspect.

Most of them were cheering at his suggestion, though the more zealous ones looked genuinely offended on her behalf. The coxcomb would be lucky if he didn't get himself into a duel, whoever he was. No, she remembered a second later, men didn't duel over demireps, only over ladies. Her kind had no honor to defend.

Considering her next move, Bel tossed her head in haughty nonchalance and rested her hands on her waist. "The fact is, I don't give *serious* kisses to men whose names I don't even know."

"Easily remedied," he said as he flashed her a smile. "I'm Hawkscliffe."

"Hawkscliffe?" she echoed, staring at him in ill-concealed shock.

She knew of the duke of Hawkscliffe—Robert Knight— fierce young Tory leader on the rise, renowned in government circles for his courage, high character, and unyielding sense of justice. He was not merely a bachelor— he was the catch of the decade, with a hundred thousand pounds a year. So far, no young lady had quite measured up to Hawkscliffe's exacting standards.

She knew the major points of his family history and the rest of his title, as well—earl of Morley, Viscount Beningbrooke. She knew that Hawkscliffe Hall was a huge Norman keep standing proudly on a rugged hilltop in the Cumbrian Mountains. She knew all this because the intricacies of the aristocracy had been a large part of her girls' curriculum at Mrs. Hall's Academy for Young Ladies— where, disastrously, Bel had taught his hellion little sister, Lady Jacinda Knight.

Oh, dear, she thought, glancing uneasily at the rowdy, misbehaving peers all around the table, then looked again at Hawkscliffe. This man, whatever he was, was no friend of Dolph Breckinridge. Somehow this certainty, along with her connection to his little sister, made her feel a bit safer with him, as did his sterling reputation and the brilliant articles she had read by him in the *Quarterly Review* championing humanitarian views that she heartily applauded.

A girl could do worse.

Careful to hide her sudden interest, she folded her arms over her chest and regarded him in lofty amusement. "Pray tell, what is the Paragon Duke doing here, gambling and trying to coax unwon kisses out of a demirep?"

The men standing around them laughed at his expense, but not maliciously.

"Oh, just entertaining myself," he replied with a calculating smile. "You know full well that I won a *proper* kiss from you fair and square, Miss Hamilton."

"Well," she said archly, "no doubt you need it."

Laughter rippled around them at her tart rejoinder, but for the most part, the surrounding lords and dandies hushed themselves, a captive audience, waiting to see if she would kiss Hawkscliffe.

Now that she knew who he was, Bel decided she could not honorably back down. She would never allow herself to be intimidated by a self-righteous, renowned prude. He probably didn't know anything more about *serious* kissing than she did.

As she braced her hands on the table and leaned toward him a second time, her heart beat faster with anticipation and curiosity and undeniable attraction; the moment had come to see if anything Harriette had taught her had stuck.

Gently she cupped his clean-shaved cheek in her hand, catching a glimpse of his smoldering eyes before she closed hers, then she caressed his lips with her own, slowly gifting him with a kiss that left the rest of the noisy, clamoring party and the city and the world behind.

His mouth was warm and silky; his smooth skin heated beneath her touch. She stroked his black hair and kissed him more deeply, leaning further over the table. She felt him pull her toward him. His warm hand curled around her nape in firm, gentle possession as she parted her lips and

let him taste of her. He responded hotly yet still with re-
straint, entrancing her with his drugging kiss until she was
nigh trembling with pleasure.

At length he brought the kiss to a slow, soft end and released her.

Bel returned to sanity amid raucous cheers, feeling dazed.
Her lips were bee-stung, her cheeks glowed pink, and she
was breathing rather heavily. Hawkscliffe's slicked hair
was tousled and his starchy cravat was mussed and at the
moment, he looked anything *but* a paragon.

The glance he sent her, potent with desire, made her feel
for the first time thrillingly like a real courtesan rather than
just a silly, stiff girl pretending. She lowered her head, bit
her lip shyly, and glanced at him again.

With a sultry little smile the duke slid his expensive ring
toward her. "Take it," he murmured. "I insist."

By this gesture, she realized he meant to say that now
she had earned it. With a knowing smile, she slid it right
back to him.

"Keep it, Your Grace. The pleasure was all mine."

The men around them burst out laughing but Hawkscliffe merely smiled intimately and watched her walk
away with a promise in his eyes that said he would indeed
be back.

She had barely reached the other room when she heard
him loudly and thunderously applauded by all the other
men in the room.

She stole a glance over her shoulder and saw him laughing with easy good-naturedness as potbellied Lord Alvanley thumped him cheerfully on the back. Perhaps someone
had just told him she had never before shown such favor to
any of her admirers, for his suntanned cheeks were tinged
with a manly blush.

Charmed, she smiled to herself and turned away. The
hour was late, so she slipped out of the salon and went to

bed before any of her other admirers came seeking a chance to win a kiss of their own. She knew now just whom she wanted.

She was still smiling when her head hit the pillow, but though her heart beat with excitement and newfound hope, she forced herself to ignore the noisy party downstairs, shut her eyes, and willed herself to rest.

The hour was late and it wouldn't do to look haggard when her future protector came calling.

⇥ CHAPTER ⇤
FOUR

Hawk spent the night alone in his vast carved bed, tossing and turning in the satin sheets and staring up at the velvet canopy in a state of thrilled, thwarted, curious uncertainty.

A courtesan.

He had never kissed a courtesan before, never touched one, nor let one touch him. He had been careful of them. He had his prejudices, true, for a man in his position had to be cautious. And yet . . . how would it be if she were here now?

He closed his eyes, comforting his desperate solitude with candlelit visions of her, so mysterious and lovely, and all the while, her haughty, maddening little laugh echoed in his ears, taunting him.

He wanted more.

One kiss was not enough. He wanted to explore her every curve, taste her skin beneath his lips. . . . With a silent groan he turned his face to the wall, throbbing with guilty need. He couldn't stop.

He considered the fine texture of her hair as he dreamed of unpinning it, watching it fall in blond cascades around her shoulders. Then, in his mind's eye, they undressed each other and he drew her down onto his bed, where she used every inch of her silken young flesh to enchant him with her dream of love. *Fille de joie. Pleasure girl.* As his body ached and burned for her touch, he knew for a price he could make it happen.

Whatever her price, he could easily afford it. But he didn't dare.

A woman like that could take him for all that he had and walk away smiling. Or worse, bind herself to him forever with illegitimate children. She was dangerous.

But so damned alluring.

When Sunday morning came, he found that he must have finally slept, for he awoke to the sound of churchbells bonging for services. His mind was clear, his body invigorated, and his whole being eager to get back to Belinda Hamilton's side before Dolph Breckinridge slept off his hangover and heard about their kiss.

Judging by Dolph's behavior last night, his reaction to the news would not be pleasant. Hawk intended to be on hand to protect her when the baronet arrived.

Moreover, he had settled upon a solution. Miss Hamilton was obviously the fulcrum by which he could gain untold leverage over Dolph. First, he would have to test her a bit, gauge where her sympathies lay, but if she disliked Dolph as much as she seemed to, it was only a question of luring her under his protection.

The plan taking shape in his mind would mean associating closely with Miss Hamilton in the coming weeks, but by the sane light of morning, he saw no reason why he could not trust himself completely to his rigid self-control. He was the bloody Paragon Duke, was he not? The whole world knew he could easily deny temptation. He would treat *La Belle* Hamilton with courtesy and pay her for her time, but he would absolutely not get involved *that way* with a Cyprian.

He forced himself by sheer willpower to wait until afternoon to call on her.

It was quarter past four when he sprang out of his

curricle. He left it in the care of William, his able young
groom, a tall, red-haired, raw-boned lad of nineteen, then
strode up to Harriette Wilson's door and knocked.

He waited for someone to answer, squinting in the bright
May sunshine with the high wind rippling through his hair
and playing with the tails of his soft dun tail coat. He
glanced at the azure sky, enjoying the freshness of the air
and the fanciful array of meringue-puff clouds and the promise of summer splendors soon to arrive.

When a maidservant opened the door, Hawk handed her
his calling card and asked for Miss Hamilton. The maid
bobbed a curtsy then scurried up the narrow wooden staircase to see if her mistress was prepared to receive visitors.
He paced in the small entrance hall, his footfalls ringing
with an odd empty echo. It hardly seemed like the same
place that had been so thronged last night. His excitement
to see the lovely, impertinent, and most delicious Miss
Hamilton again was barely mitigated by the twinge of
guilt that endeavored to remind him he was only here because of Lucy.

The maid returned and asked him if he would wait a few
minutes more. He shrugged and continued pacing, tapping
his top hat idly against his thigh, curiously inspecting Harriette's sedan chair which leaned beside the staircase.

Miss Hamilton kept him, the mighty duke of Hawkscliffe, waiting a full quarter hour before she deigned to
allow him up into her rarified company. He didn't doubt
she had no other purpose in the delay than to teach him his
place—under her pretty foot. What could he do but sigh
and take it? Until he had her under his exclusive protection, the bit o' muslin held all the cards. Strangely, her
transparent machinations didn't touch his surprisingly
jovial mood. He couldn't help it. The chit amused him.

When Miss Hamilton finally sent her maid back to lead
him up, his heartbeat quickened absurdly as he mounted

the steps. The maid took him through the large, now empty salon, past the green baize card table, to the parlor in the back of the second floor. The maid curtsied and left him at the parlor's threshold.

He stepped closer and found Miss Hamilton arranged in demure perfection on a graceful Egyptian-style couch next to a round table that held a vase burgeoning with fresh-cut hydrangeas. She had a newspaper on her lap while her dainty slippered feet were displayed for him on an embroidered footstool. Even the afternoon sunbeam streaming in through the window seemed artful as it sparkled on her pale blond hair, which today she wore tumbling over her shoulders in flaxen waves and champagne-bright ringlets. All that bound her luxurious tresses in some semblance of order was a pair of ivory combs.

Hawk smiled as the fetching creature pretended not to notice him, letting him have his fill of looking at her. Her walking dress, with a wide scoop neck, was of sprigged muslin in muted yellow. The short puffed sleeves invited him to admire her slender arms. She looked for all the world like a soft, cuddly angel, he thought in asinine sentimentality. Though he knew the whole scene before him was the calculated result of mercenary feminine conquest, he was captivated nonetheless.

"Good day, Miss Hamilton."

On cue, she looked up, then beamed a warm smile at him. Her eyes shone with fresh brilliance. "Your Grace!"

"I hope I am not interrupting," he said in a rather wry tone.

"Not at all," she declared in pleasure, holding out her hand to him like a princess disposed to show favor.

Dutifully he strode forward and took her hand in his own, bestowing the expected kiss on her fingertips. Her large violet-blue eyes shone as she greeted him and if he was not mistaken, his young courtesan beauty was most decidedly blushing.

When he had kissed her hand, she did not let go of his light grasp, but curled her fingers around his and tugged him down to sit on the couch beside her, gifting him with a generous smile. His gaze lingered on her face, drinking in the sight of her.

"I wondered if you would visit me today," she said almost shyly.

He laughed softly. "You could doubt it?"

She smiled, blushing more brightly. They stared at each other in a charmed, relishing silence. He quite believed his heart skipped a beat.

"What's that you're reading?" he asked before he was tempted to catch her up in his arms and kiss her senseless on the couch.

"The *Quarterly Review*."

"Really?" Surprised that it wasn't some mindless serialized Gothic tale, he rested his arm along the back of the couch behind her and leaned nearer to inspect the volume she was reading. He caught a whiff of the soft, clean fragrance of her hair, a wholesome blend of rosebuds, sweet almond, and chamomile. It went straight to his head.

"I've just finished reading the most fascinating article entitled 'A Call for Total International Abolition of Slavery' by His Grace, the duke of Hawkscliffe. Ever heard of him?"

Startled, Hawk felt his cheeks flush. A wave of self-consciousness washed through him at her interest in his work. "Dull chap, eh?"

"On the contrary, Your Grace, I am finding your essays most expertly done. You are logical in your arguments, forceful in your style, and dare I say quite . . . *passionate* on your subject. I only wonder that your Tory colleagues aren't appalled."

"Why do you say that?" he asked in surprise.

"Some of your views verge on those of the Whigs."

He stared at her, torn between amusement and indignation. She was only a female, after all. What did she know of politics? "Oh, really?" he said in an indulgent drawl.

"Quite." She picked up a folded copy of the *Edinburgh Review* that lay on the table beside her. "You might enjoy meeting Harriette's friend, Mr. Henry Brougham. I've been reading both party's journals and your opinions on things are remarkably similar."

Hawk's left eyebrow rose. He could not decide if he was insulted, shocked, or merely amused to be compared so blithely to his great political rival and nemesis.

Miss Hamilton turned to him innocently. "Oh, do you know Mr. Brougham already, Your Grace?"

"Er, we've met."

All business, she cast the *Edinburgh Review* aside and flipped through the *Quarterly* again. "I've also been reading your essay 'Let the Punishment Fit the Crime.' Your ideas on penal reform are inspired. I don't claim to understand all the legal nuances, but I respect a man who knows right from wrong. There are so few of you," she added loftily.

Fighting perplexed laughter and rather embarrassed by her praise, Hawk lifted the journal out of her hands. "Come, Miss Hamilton, the day is too fine to stay cooped up indoors reading dull political essays."

"You're too modest," she scolded, but her eyes sparkled with pleasure at his invitation. She jumped up and strode off to fetch her wrap, bonnet, and parasol.

Abandoned in the parlor, Hawk couldn't stop smiling. He dropped his head with a puff of a sigh and raked a hand through his hair, casting about for his equilibrium. By Jove, he hadn't expected her to be as quick witted as she was pretty.

A few minutes later she returned, ready for their outing.

They bounded down the creaking stairs like high-spirited
children and burst outside into the glorious sunshine.

He lifted her up into his curricle then went around to the
driver's seat as William climbed to his post in back. Gathering the reins, he snapped them smartly over the backs of
his high-stepping blooded bays.

The horses' clopping hoof beats rebounded off the neat,
flat-fronted houses as his curricle rolled down the cobbled
street. Children playing ball in the road scattered as they
approached. Once they had cleared the rowdy tangle of
youngsters, he urged his team into a canter. Belinda laughed
with relish at the speed, her hair flying behind her and
whipping around the sides of her bonnet. He grinned, enjoying the rare treat of showing off at the ribbons for a
beautiful girl.

The drive to Hyde Park was not long. When they arrived, they found the Ring crowded with mounted riders
and open carriages, everyone out for a Sunday drive at the
height of the Season. The pace was fast and the park road-
ways muddy.

He quickly noticed the stares they drew. Young men
gawked at Belinda while matrons sent him appalled glares,
but this was only the beginning. Word would spread quickly,
he knew. Soon everyone—including Dolph—would have
heard that he was seen escorting the prize courtesan of the
day around Town.

Meanwhile he could only wonder how his fair companion felt when they passed society ladies who cut her dead,
or worse, when men who had paid boundless homage to
her the night before hurried past in their carriages with
their wives and children and pretended not to know her—
pretended she didn't exist. The hypocrisy of it all roused
his protective instincts with a fury.

Glancing at her, he knew she was upset because her
blank, forward stare had turned expressionless as it had

been last night during Dolph's tirade. Hawk's face hardened. Demirep or no, he would not let them do this to her.

Without asking her preference, he turned his curricle off of the West Carriage Drive of the Ring where Hyde Park gave way to Kensington Gardens. As it was a Sunday, the gardens were open. He drove until the curricle's whirring wheels had borne them away lightly from the hostile, jealous stares.

Nearing the Long Water, he slowed the trotting bays to a halt. He turned and found Miss Hamilton gazing at him in question.

"I thought we might walk by the water a bit," he said.

She nodded, visibly relieved to have been whisked away from the rude scrutiny of the Polite World. He set the brake, stepped down from the curricle, and went around to assist her down while William assumed his duties, going forward to hold the horses' heads.

They left the curricle with the lad and walked by the pond along the graveled path. A noisy band of ducks followed them, their squawking for crumbs the only language, for the two of them were silent.

Strolling along with his hands clasped lightly behind his back, he glanced at her, walking slowly beside him with her arms folded over her chest, her slim shoulders swathed in a shawl of filmy blue silk.

She had pushed back her bonnet so that it hung down behind her shoulders, the satin ribbons still tied around her neck. Her delicate profile was pensive as she stared at the glittering water.

"Your groom seems reliable for one so young," she remarked in a stilted attempt to break the pregnant pause.

"Would you believe he is a former chimney sweep?" Hawk answered with a half smile, grateful for the opening. "Years ago William's last employer sent him to clean out some of the fireplaces at Knight House, then my cook found him collapsed on the kitchen floor. We realized the child was in a state of starvation and exhaustion. Cook and Mrs. Laverty—my housekeeper—kept him and nursed him back to health. They took him on as the kitchen boy when he was well, but he soon showed a talent for working with horses, so we moved him to the stables. Give him ten years and he might well make head coachman."

"What a fine act of kindness," she said softly.

He lowered his chin, abashed by her praise. "It was all Mrs. Laverty's doing, I assure you. It would please me if you'd call me Robert."

She smiled at him. "As you wish."

They both studied the ground as they walked, letting their gloved hands graze and slide in a sensual, ever so subtle flirtation that aroused him more than he cared to acknowledge.

She cast him a tentative smile as they stopped behind a shady bramble of trees. "I fear after that jaunt down Rotten Row, your voucher to Almack's may be in peril."

"Almack's," he snorted, scoffing to think of the dull quadrilles he dutifully undertook with his colleagues' prim, marriageable daughters. He would probably marry one of them within a year.

Depressing thought.

More than likely, he would wind up with Coldfell's deaf daughter, more out of pity or chivalry than anything else. Lady Juliet seemed a good, obedient child from the few times he had seen her. As no one else would have the poor pretty creature due to her disability, it seemed to him the right thing to do.

"I almost went to Almack's once when I was seventeen," Miss Hamilton remarked with a sigh as she slipped her hand through the crook of his elbow and started them walking again.

"What happened? Didn't you go?"

"My mother died a few weeks before the long-awaited date of my entree there—"

"I am very sorry."

"Thank you, it's all right." She smiled at him wistfully. "Being in mourning, of course, I couldn't go anywhere."

"You should have gone if it would've lifted your spirits."

"Do you suppose they'd let me in now?" she asked with a wry smile.

"There, there, my dear." He chuckled softly and patted her hand where it rested on his forearm. "You're not missing much. The food is terrible, the punch is weak, the company's dull, and the dance floor is so uneven the whole building ought to be condemned. And they *don't* allow you to play twenty-one for kisses."

"Well, then, I am not a whit sorry to be forbidden there." Smiling mischievously, she squeezed his arm and leaned toward him with a confidential air. "So, tell me, Robert, where did a paragon like you learn to kiss like that?"

He raised both eyebrows and looked at her.

She dropped her hand from his arm and laughed. "Well?"

"I've been around," he archly assured her, then walked on.

"Oh-ho, have you?" She skipped after him. "Spill, Hawkscliffe!"

He laughed. "I shall never in my life kiss and tell."

"Oh, come on, you can tell me!"

"Well," he murmured, lowering his voice to a conspiratorial tone. "If you must know, there was a lady of my acquaintance once. A widow."

"A merry widow?"

"Very merry," he whispered with a grin. "I was younger than you are now. Ah, I was lovesick for two, three years," he said in short disgust. "Even asked her to marry me."

"The vicar's mousetrap, Robert? For shame!"

"I know, strange, but that's what I wanted." He shrugged. "I don't believe in idle dalliance."

She laughed at him as though she'd heard that before. "Oh, don't you? What *do* you believe in, then?"

He glanced at the glittering water, tempted not to answer at all, but the single word escaped his lips softly, foolish as it was.

"Devotion."

She stared at him for a long moment as though she couldn't decide if he was serious or jesting, then suddenly forced a blithe smile and walked on as though he had said nothing.

He realized he had flustered her and raised one eyebrow as she walked lightly ahead of him.

"Refused the duke of Hawkscliffe! How very singular! So, why wouldn't your merry widow marry you?"

Hawk's gaze slid after her, intrigued by her nervous reaction.

"She had done her duty, provided heirs," he said casually. "She had her fortune and wanted nothing to do with settling down a second time, not with me or anyone. God, how I wanted her. But she only desired to be free and independent."

"There's nothing wrong with independence if a woman can get it."

"Well, this particular lady has lived to regret her choice, I assure you."

She turned back and looked at him finally. "Came crawling back to you, did she? The merry widow wasn't so merry after she'd had her fun?"

"Rather."

"So you cast her off? Tossed her into the street?"

He smiled wryly as he gazed ahead down the path. He was too much a gentleman to admit that willing bed partners had never been in short supply for him. Still, though he preferred discreet, exclusive liaisons with sophisticated women, sooner or later, every lover he had ever taken ended up shrieking hysterical, baffling accusations at him that he didn't care about them, or was too absorbed in his political career, or something along those lines. When they threatened to leave him, he rarely argued, for in his experience, women could be neither pleased nor comprehended.

He jarred himself back to Miss Hamilton's expectant gaze. "Suffice it to say that people only get one chance with me, my dear. I am generally intolerant of the foibles of those around me; I cannot abide foolishness. It is a failing in my nature, I know, but I'm repaid for my lack of charity by laboring under an even higher set of standards for myself than those by which I measure others. Now, I'm sure that is quite enough about me," he declared, taking her hand. He led her gently off the graveled walk to the waterside. "I want to know about you."

"What do you wish to know?"

He steadied her as she stepped daintily from one large gray rock to the next, holding her soft yellow skirts clear of the mud. "Everything."

"There isn't much to tell. Born: Kelmscot, Oxfordshire, third September, 1791. Languages: French, some Latin. Accomplishments: plays the piano indifferently, can't draw. Loves history and cats."

"Cats, eh? What about dogs?"

"A little wary of dogs, I confess. Especially large ones."

"Hmm, I have six of them. Mastiffs and Newfoundlands. Each one weighs more than you do."

She shuddered. "His Grace lives in a kennel."

"They're not allowed in the house. Tell me something else."

"Such as?"

He looked straight into her eyes. "What's going on between you and Dolph Breckinridge?"

She stiffened, staring into his eyes for a long moment, looking utterly wary.

"Dolph Breckinridge is an ass," she said finally. "That is all I have to say on the topic." She looked away, pretending to gaze at the water.

"Do I detect a jilt?"

"Don't make me laugh."

"Well?"

She snorted with ladylike disdain. "Dolph has been the bane of my existence these past ten months. You saw the way he behaved with me last night. I know that you saw."

"Yes, but I wasn't sure what I was witnessing, a lover's spat or what."

"A lover's spat?" She wrinkled her nose in disgust. "Ugh, I'd sooner kiss a toad. Must we talk about this? The very thought of him spoils the day—"

"My dear Miss Hamilton, you know full well that Dolph is going to come after me in a fury the moment he hears that I kissed you—"

She held up one finger. "Excuse me, but it was I who kissed you."

"Either way, I deserve to know what I'm dealing with."

"It's your own fault. You're the one who insisted on a second kiss," she reminded him, poking him in the chest.

"Oh, you didn't like it?" he asked pleasantly.

She gave him an arch look, turned, and strutted on ahead of him.

Hawk stared after her, beguiled by her honeyed walk, then he suddenly followed with an odd rush of lusty exhilaration. God, she was a tempting minx. "I intend to win you, you know, so you might as well tell me everything," he said with deliberate breezy high-handedness.

"Do you really?" She turned and regarded him in wary

surprise. "Harriette says you look down your nose at our kind."

He lifted her hand and placed a gallant kiss on her knuckles. "I am no more immune to great beauty than other men," he deftly flattered.

"Do you always know just what to say?"

"Usually."

She heaved a sigh. "Oh, very well, but realize that I'm taking you into my confidence."

"I would never repeat what you tell me in confidence."

"I met Dolph last fall at a Hunt Ball. I had no desire to meet him, as I had noticed him standing all night by the wall making fun of us provincials, but he decided I was worthy of being asked to dance. He knew one of my neighbors and sought an introduction: I could not escape. It took me all of three seconds to discover how odiously obnoxious he is. Sir Dolph, however, took an unfortunate fancy to me and began pursuing me the very next day. When he realized I was serious in refusing his advances, his pursuit turned ugly."

"How ugly?" he asked, knitting his brow.

"He had my father thrown in the Fleet. That's how it began."

Hawk stopped and stared at her. "How did he manage that?"

She winced faintly. "I'm afraid Papa is rather an obsessed collector of illuminated manuscripts. You would have to know him to understand. Everyone who meets my father loves him. Even our duns were never very hard on him. They would come to collect and he would drag them into his library and show them the latest manuscripts he'd bought instead of paying our bills. The duns would become caught up in his enthusiasm and let him go with a warning to pay next month, but he never did. Then Dolph came along and bullied the shopkeepers to collect. He

promised to send them business from his London friends
if they would only press for what was due them from my
father. In no time, Papa was in the Fleet. He is there now—
and here I am."

"And here you are? What does that mean?"

She gave him a faint smile of dismay. "You know what it
means, Robert."

"Pray, Miss Hamilton, what is your father?"

"A gentleman—"

"A gentleman? A man buys old books and leaves his
daughter to sell her body or starve, and you call him a
gentleman?"

"Do not insult my father, sir. He is all I have," she said
sharply.

Hawk clamped his jaw shut, but he was not at all satisfied. Apparently he had also pricked her defenses, for she
looked riled and could not let it lie.

"My decision to become what I am is not my father's
fault. It's Dolph's fault for taking away everything we
owned. How dare you look down your nose at me? I had no
choice."

"And what does your father think of you whoring to
save his hide?"

"Papa knows nothing of this."

"Famous as you've become, don't you think it's likely
that someday he'll find out?"

"My father doesn't even know what century it is!" she
cried, throwing up her hands. Then she heaved a frustrated
sigh and turned away.

Hawk could barely contain his displeasure. "Do you
mean to say that your father could not be persuaded to part
with his cherished books even to save you both?"

"He no longer owned the manuscripts. He donated them
to the Bodleian collection."

"Oh, I never heard of such nonsense," he muttered, exasperated beyond any need to hold his tongue. "Begging your pardon, but your father sounds like a fool. That is just the sort of thoughtless, irresponsible idiocy I despise—"

Her jaw dropped with indignation; her eyes flashed like fireworks. "This visit is over." She pivoted, her bonnet swinging behind her, and began marching away from him, not in the direction of his curricle.

"Where are you going?"

"Home," she answered, not looking back.

"Don't you want a ride, Miss Hamilton?"

"I don't want anything from you!"

"So, you're just going to walk," he drawled.

"Yes!" She spun around to face him, her cheeks crimson with anger. "That's what people do when they don't own fancy curricles. You can drive that blasted thing into the Long Water for all I care," she shouted, then whirled and continued on her way.

Hawk stared after her in amazement, then clicked into motion, striding after her. "Miss Hamilton. Miss Hamilton!"

She turned in aloof query, looking haughty and impervious again, neatly shutting him out. God, that is a maddening trick, he thought. "Miss Hamilton, I'm sorry. It wasn't my place to say anything. Please. I tend to be opinionated. I can't help it."

She tossed her head and huffed primly.

Now that all his prying had uncovered the fact that she had almost as much reason to despise Dolph as he did, Hawk decided the moment had come to cast off the games. It was time to get down to the business at hand.

"The truth is I need to talk to you. Privately."

She folded her arms over her chest and gave him a dubious look, apparently unconvinced that it was talk he was interested in. "About what?"

"I'll explain everything, but this is not the place."

"Why, Your Grace, don't tell me you're going to offer me your carte blanche, too?"

Her audacity maddened him.

"Miss Hamilton," he replied in his starchiest tone, "I could not be persuaded to give my carte blanche to Venus herself. I am not that great a fool—though you may be the closest facsimile to the goddess that London has ever seen."

"A prettily worded recovery, Your Grace, but without an offer of carte blanche, we have nothing to discuss— privately or otherwise. Good day." She began walking away.

"Belinda!"

"Please don't waste any more of my time. I'm trying to make a living, you know."

"Be reasonable, you little cutthroat," he muttered, stomping down the path after her. "I can't give you unlimited credit to my accounts when I am responsible to my whole family for the management of our fortunes. You could be a gambler. A thief, for all I know. Besides—" He captured her hand and stopped her from walking on, holding her in place.

Her arm outstretched, she turned and scowled at him. "Besides what, you insufferable prude?"

"Prude, eh? Do you need another kiss to remind you what a prude I am?"

He tugged her closer with a gentle pull, smiling roguishly in spite of himself.

"Don't you dare."

"Then don't call me names."

"You started it."

Though her eyes sparked with defiance, she allowed him to pull her all the way to him until the tips of her breasts grazed his chest. She held his stare, both of them instantly swept up in the magnetic fascination that tempted their hungering bodies to touch despite their clash of minds and wills.

"I can give you something better than carte blanche," he murmured as he slid his hands around her slim waist, savoring the feel of her lithe, splendid body through the thin layer of muslin. He gloried in her lack of protest at his touch, but though she permitted it, she still clung to her air of defiance, tossing her chin at him.

"What could be better than carte blanche?"

He bent his head and paused, grazing his lips along her earlobe, barely able to resist, though he cursed himself for a traitor. He waited until she shivered with desire, then whispered, *"Revenge."*

She went motionless—glanced up at him warily. "On Dolph?"

"Interested?"

"Maybe."

"Shall we go somewhere and have a chat, Miss Hamilton?"

She eyed him warily, but allowed him to lead her back to his carriage. As he headed back to Harriette's house, he only hoped their mutual enemy wasn't already there waiting for them.

≼ CHAPTER ≽
FIVE

They found Harriette's house quiet when they arrived a short while later. Still incensed at the duke's imperious judgment over her and her father, Bel led him in cold, bristling silence into the parlor where their visit had begun. His tall, broad-shouldered physique radiated stamina and command, seeming to dwarf the dainty room.

She looked him over with a guarded glance from the corner of her eye and continued to stew. Bad enough that he had called her a whore, but he had no right denouncing Papa as an irresponsible fool, she thought as she removed her gloves with a resentful jerk. The worst part was knowing that the insufferable beast was right on both counts. Setting her gloves aside, she took off her bonnet and shawl.

Hawkscliffe had thrown his top hat on the round table and was drawing off his driving gloves. Tossing these on the table, as well, he began to pace. For a man of such imposing stature, he had an elegant way of moving in his expensive clothes, she thought as she sat down on the couch and watched him, waiting to hear him out.

With a musing expression, as though weighing each word before broaching his subject, he took off his excellently cut tail coat and threw it over a chair, shrugging the tension out of his wide shoulders.

Bel scowled. If she had been a lady, he probably wouldn't

have even considered such shocking informality as taking off his gloves, let alone his coat. On the other hand, she could not help but admire the perfection of his herculean torso, like the model for one of the Elgin marbles. She let her gaze travel over the sinuous curve of his strong back. His snug waistcoat accented the sweeping breadth of his shoulders and the tapered leanness of his waist and hips; his loose white sleeves only hinted at the sinewed brawn of his arms. She found herself wanting to touch him.

Scandalized by the impulse, she lifted her furtive study from his powerful body to his strong, square face. He went over to the bow window where the mellow, late-day sun illumined his bold profile, that aquiline nose that gave him a look of such stark, brooding intensity. His mouth seemed hard and grim, but she remembered his kiss—soft, satiny warmth. Devil take him, but he was a beautiful man, sleek and fierce as a bird of prey, with his raven hair and burnished skin.

Devotion, Bel thought with an inward snort of skeptical disdain.

Hands on his waist, Hawkscliffe glanced restlessly out the window as though waiting for someone to arrive. "I won't insult your intelligence by pretending I like your line of work, Miss Hamilton. Nevertheless, I consider myself a good judge of character and I find you sensible, strong willed, and capable of discretion. While I am not in the habit of exposing my jugular to anyone, it seems I have no choice but to confide in you and hope that you will help me. What I have to tell you cannot leave this room." Tensely he moved away from the window and sat down beside her. "Do you recall Dolph Breckinridge ever mentioning a woman named Lucy?"

Bel searched her memory then shook her head. "No."

"How about Lady Coldfell?"

"I know that Dolph's uncle is the earl of Coldfell, but he never mentioned the countess."

"Tell me this. Has Dolph ever threatened you with violence? Have you ever felt yourself to be in direct physical danger from him?"

"Not until last night." She hesitated. "He said if I don't quit my search for a protector, I would be sorry. Why do you ask about Lord and Lady Coldfell?"

A bolt of pain flashed through his dark eyes like lightning. "I believe Dolph might have harbored a similar obsession for her before he became fixated on you. Miss Hamilton, Lady Coldfell is dead. There are those of us who think Dolph may have murdered her."

Her eyes widened. She stared at him in shock.

"That is why I'm here. I want to hire you to act out a kind of charade with me. I need to find out the truth about Lady Coldfell's death, Miss Hamilton. You are the key to controlling Dolph. With you in my keeping, I can drive him to the breaking point and wring the truth out of him about what he did to her."

"And then what?" she asked faintly.

Lethal wrath smoldered in his gaze. "Then I will call him out and kill him."

Kill Dolph? Staring at Hawkscliffe in amazement, the first thing she realized was that this Lady Coldfell must have meant a great deal to him. Lovers, she thought. Of course. Then it registered in her mind that his sole motive in pursuing *her* was to solve his ladylove's death.

Disappointment nearly stole her breath. She lowered her head, careful to hide the twist of hurt inside her behind a faint, bitter smile. Of course. He had made his opinion of her clear enough.

Avoiding his gaze, she crossed her legs and smoothed her skirts over her knee. "Let me see if I have this right.

You want me to be the bait so that you can prove Dolph's guilt, then avenge your lover?"

"Lady Coldfell wasn't my lover—but, in essence, yes."

"Come, Robert, we need have no secrets between us. You can tell me the truth. She was your paramour."

"No, she was not, Miss Hamilton. Lady Coldfell was a chaste and virtuous woman. It wasn't like that between us. It was something higher, better than that. She was—pure."

Unlike me, she thought, somehow holding her taut, forced smile as she lowered her chin and gazed at her clasped hands. Roiling shame churned inside her.

"My, you really *are* a paragon."

"No, I merely saw how my mother's flagrant adulteries unmanned my father. I would never inflict that on someone, especially an old family friend like Coldfell."

"Admirable." She sat back, folding her arms over her chest. She had to commend his devotion to his dead lady, but didn't he see the insult he was giving her? Or did the insult not matter, since she was only a demirep?

"Perhaps you should have won me first before you told me your scheme."

"I would never thrust you into a dangerous situation without your fully understanding the risks."

"I'm sorry to say that Dolph didn't do it."

"What?"

"He didn't do it."

"Yes, he did."

Bel rolled her eyes. Hawkscliffe knew what he knew and that was it.

"He has the motive and is the only person outside of Coldfell's staff that has full access to the house and grounds, Miss Hamilton."

"I know Dolph," she explained in forbearance. "As much as I loathe him, even I can admit that he is brave. Insanely so. He prides himself on it. It's not his style to murder a weak, defenseless woman. There's no glory in that. He prefers bears and wolves and things that fight back. He prefers a worthy opponent."

"He also prefers to live beyond his means. If Lucy had become pregnant and had given Coldfell a son, Dolph would no longer have inherited the title and fortune that he craves."

She could not argue that point. Dolph was certainly fixed on coming into his rich inheritance.

"Or her death might have been accidental," he went on. "Dolph could have been trying to have his way with her, resulting in a violent struggle."

"Now that I could believe," Bel said quietly. She looked away, going perfectly motionless. A sickening, all-too-familiar knot clenched in her stomach at the mere thought of the topic of her recurring nightmares.

Hawkscliffe got up and went to stare out the window.

Bel rubbed her crossed arms briskly with her palms, suddenly feeling icy cold and clammy, though the room was warm. She could not bring herself to look at the duke as she struggled with his request. If Lady Coldfell had indeed suffered as she herself had—and worse—didn't she owe her fellow victim justice? Didn't she owe it to herself? But she was not sure she wanted to get involved in this. It wasn't good for her to think about it. The mere shadow of the memory made her feel dirty, battered, and ashamed. Best to forget.

"What if I refuse?"

"Refuse? Miss Hamilton, if Dolph did this to Lucy, doesn't it seem logical, even likely, in light of his obsession with you, that you could be next?"

She flinched, still studying the floor, though she could feel his tumultuous stare.

"I can protect you. He'll have to get through me to get to

you. Do you really think you'll be safer out there with some other man who doesn't know what Dolph is capable of?"

"What exactly is it that you propose, Your Grace?" she forced out coolly.

"Accept me for your protector. You will stay with me at Knight House, where I can keep you safe from any threat from him—"

"No, that is highly irregular. You can't have me living under your roof. There will be talk—"

"I don't care about scandal anymore!" he cried, raking his hand through his hair. "Who cares what they say? What right has anyone to say a word about what I do? I'm so sick of living under their tyranny and, by God, I will not let another woman die for the sake of my sterling reputation."

"What do you mean by that?"

Clearly torn, he lowered his head. "I was worried that people would talk about Lucy and me. People sense things, you know, and I . . . I could tell she was not indifferent to me."

What woman could be? she wondered.

"I avoided her at every turn. I wanted to do the right thing. But now I can't help but wonder . . . if I had given her a chance to speak to me privately, maybe she would have confided in me . . . something that would have allowed me to save her." His dark eyes were haunted when he looked at her. "Did she know Dolph was a threat? Did she know she was in danger? I ask myself these questions every night a thousand times, but I suppose I'll never know."

"Don't do this to yourself, Robert," she said softly. "Whatever happened, it's not your fault. You did what you knew to be right at the time. No one can expect more than that."

She watched him consider her statement then discard it.

"Maybe I wasn't virtuous," he said. "Maybe I was merely afraid."

She gazed at him in compassion, but he turned away, scratching his jaw.

"I realize you could have your pick of any man in London and that what I ask of you is not without danger, so I am prepared to make it very worth your while, Miss Hamilton. What do you say to a thousand pounds for the whole project? It shouldn't take more than two months at the most. You'll also have your own carriage and saddle horse, whatever servants you need, theater boxes, an allowance for your clothing and so forth, and in addition to all this—" His posture stiffened slightly as he clasped his hands behind his back and inspected the street through the window. "I shall not require you in my bed."

Bel stared at him, barely daring to breathe. "You're joking."

He bowed his head. "The woman I loved is dead, Miss Hamilton. I—just can't. I hope you'll understand."

"Of course," she breathed. He hoped *she* would understand? she thought wildly. A thousand pounds for two months of her time? It was a princely sum, a full third of Papa's debt—and she wouldn't even have to bed him!

Oh, to be exempt from the thing she feared most—and to see Dolph get his comeuppance to top it all off!

But then suddenly she noticed the grief so clear in his tanned, chiseled face and her triumph dissolved. Her heart went out to him. She rose and went to stand by his side. Taking his hand in both of hers, she gazed up at him in tender sympathy. "I'm sorry for your loss, Robert, truly. At least Lady Coldfell is with God now, and at peace."

He nodded grimly, looking down at their joined hands, his, large and bronzed, hers, small and pale. When he glanced at her his dark eyes brimmed with stormy sorrow and his voice was low. "Will you assist me in getting justice for her, Miss Hamilton? Please. You are the only one who can help me."

Bel gazed up at him, thoroughly melted.

Oh, to be loved by such a man. His lady was dead and still he loved. She hadn't known there were men like him in the world.

She hadn't the power to refuse him, even though she was only to be the expendable bait while Lady Coldfell's memory was to be held up as sacred. She longed to console him somehow, but he did not appear to want to be drawn out of his grieving.

"Two months?"

"If it makes you more comfortable, we can write in a date that our agreement will expire—say, the first of August."

"All right. And . . . you really won't ask me to come into your bed?" she ventured.

"I give you my word on it, but that will have to be our secret. The ruse is useless if Dolph or anyone else suspects the true nature of our arrangement. We'll have to be convincing."

"Well, then." Moving closer, she lightly grasped the lapels of his waistcoat and tilted her head back with a wry smile, hoping to cheer him. "In that case, Hawkscliffe, you've got yourself a mistress."

A rueful, almost shy smile spread across his face. "I shall be the envy of London."

No, I will, she thought with a little laugh, her heart beating faster.

"There is one other thing, Robert."

"Yes?"

"I understand you have a young sister who has not yet made her debut."

"Yes, why?"

"Don't let the girl come to the house while I'm there."

"Ah, right. I appreciate your discretion."

"We are paid to be discreet," she said with a tight smile.
There was a clumsy pause.

"Well, I suppose I should write up the agreement, then."

"There's ink and paper on Harriette's desk," she said,
nodding toward the escritoire.

He went to the desk and soon their bargain was spelled
out, signed, and made legally binding by his ducal seal.
Hawkscliffe blew the powdery blotting grit across the ink,
drying it.

"I hope you know what you're doing," she mused aloud
as she bent over and signed her name beside his.

"I always know precisely what I'm doing, Miss Hamilton. 'Tis the plague of my existence," he said wryly under
his breath.

Just then a sudden burst of noise startled them both.
They looked toward the closed parlor door as the sound of
angry bellowing reached them through the house, a flurry
of shouting and banging. Someone was pounding on the
front door downstairs.

"It's Dolph," Bel said as a tremor of uneasiness ran
through her. Instinctually she moved closer to Hawkscliffe.

"It's all right," he murmured. "Stay inside."

She nodded and stared after him as he prowled to the door.
Protector, her mind whispered.

"Be careful," she called after him anxiously, only then
noticing the menacing air of excitement that rippled through
his big, lean frame.

Hawkscliffe paused in the doorway and slid her a dark
smile. "Never fear, Miss Hamilton. Sometimes the bear
wins."

Hawk strode across the salon, perversely anticipating
the prospect of toying with the frenzied Dolph Breckin-

ridge. Dolph's voice got louder as Hawk neared the top of the steps.

"Where is she? Where is the little strumpet?"

Whistling, Hawk jogged down the steps to the entrance hall, encountering Harriette Wilson on the stairs, a diminutive package of red-headed feminine fury.

"Get out of my house before I call for the constable!" she was yelling at Dolph.

The baronet, in turn, cursed at her as he tried to fight his way in past the two hefty footmen struggling to keep him out. He had one hand hooked inside the door frame, from which he refused to be pried. His face was scarlet with struggle, his short-cropped sandy hair in disarray.

"I'll see to him, Miss Wilson," Hawk murmured, politely setting the haughty little queen of the demireps aside.

"Yes, please, do something, Hawkscliffe! He's making a spectacle in front of all my neighbors."

"Don't worry, he'll soon be gone. By the way, I believe Miss Hamilton would like to speak with you."

"Oh," she exclaimed, turning to him coyly. "Dare I hope you two lovely things have made an arrangement?"

Hawk gave her a narrow smile. "She'll fill you in."

"Splendid! Congratulations, Your Grace. I thought she would never make up her mind." Harriette whooshed off to talk to Belinda.

"You!" Dolph roared when he saw him coming. "Treacherous, backstabbing villain! Blackguard! Snake! Come out here and let me have at you!"

"My dear fellow, what seems to be the problem?"

Walking over to the door, Hawk nodded to the rough-looking footmen. They cautiously released Dolph and backed away. Immediately Dolph launched through the doorway, fists first, and tried to tackle him. Hawk, however, had not grown up as the sole disciplinarian of four rowdy younger brothers and raised them through their teenage years for naught. Innumerable sibling brawls, especially with Jack, who was bigger than he, had taught him to anticipate nearly every move in fisticuffs known to man.

He stepped nonchalantly out of the line of Dolph's charge, grabbing his opponent's right arm behind him and hoisting it up high and hard behind his back. Dolph barely had time to grunt before Hawk threw his left arm across Dolph's throat in a neat choke hold.

"Can't we settle this like civilized men?"

Dolph twisted and thrashed, to no avail. "Traitor! I knew you would do this! You told me you would talk to her for me, not court her for yourself! Today I wake up and hear about you *kissing* her!" he spat. "I suppose you were here all night?"

"Suffice it to say I've offered Miss Hamilton my protection and she has said yes, and that is the end of it as far as you're concerned."

Dolph howled. Hawk dodged the jab of an elbow aimed at his ribs.

"You can't have her!"

"She isn't yours to withhold or bestow."

"Yes—she—*is*!" Dolph tore free of his hold. "I'll kill you," he panted, trying to circle him.

Hawk watched him in wily amusement. "My dear boy, you'll do nothing of the kind. You really ought to learn to control your passions. They'll get you into trouble someday."

"You tricked me! You think you're so smart and that I'm a fool, but whatever I am, at least I don't go around pretending to be some kind of saint."

"My goodness, such venom. It's not good for the digestion, Dolph."

"Belinda Hamilton is *mine*. Belinda!" he yelled toward the steps. "Get down here! You're coming with me!"

"Why do you think that you own her?"

"I saw her first!"

"Do you even grasp the notion that she is a sentient being with her own wishes and her own will? She doesn't want you and she isn't coming down here."

"Belinda! Come down here now, you filthy little strumpet!"

"Now, that's really not very nice," Hawk chided, taking a menacing stride toward him, and another. "Shall we step outside?"

"Gladly," Dolph growled, missing Hawk's ruse merely to get him out of the house.

Glowering at him, Dolph warily backed outside, still poised to clash.

Hawk nodded firmly to a footman as he passed. The burly man in livery pulled the front door closed and locked it.

Only then did Hawk feel a modicum of relief, knowing Belinda was safe inside. He squinted as his eyes adjusted to the glaring afternoon sun. Dolph's phaeton crouched nearby in the cobbled street; the poor cowering groom had a black eye. *Bloody brute.*

"I did approach Miss Hamilton on your behalf, Dolph," he said, casually skewing the truth a bit. "When she assured me that you have no hope of succeeding with her, I saw no reason not to pursue her for myself. She's a pretty thing and I rather fancy her. A man in my position needs a hostess—you know, for all the political entertaining."

"A hostess?" Dolph asked with a bark of angry laughter. "Is that all you can think to do with her, you cold fish? Why am I surprised? You'll never love her as I do. No one can."

"Love, Dolph? Your actions toward Miss Hamilton bespeak anything but love. Considering all you've done to her, is it any wonder she detests you? Getting her father thrown in the Fleet? What were you thinking?"

"It's not my fault! I'm not the one who got the old fool into debt," he retorted, but his cheeks colored with embarrassment. "He did it to himself."

"And you've done this to yourself. I'll overlook your outburst and your stupid threats because you are young and hotheaded. But know this. Belinda Hamilton is now under my protection. Do I make myself clear?"

Desperation flashed in Dolph's eyes. "Just let me talk to her—" He took a step toward the door, but Hawk blocked him with a firm hand on his chest.

"Take your hand off me before I break it," Dolph snarled.

"I see you did not hear my warning." Keenly, Hawk held his stare. "Are you paying attention, Dolph? Keep your distance from my mistress. What do you suppose the chaps at White's and Watier's and every club on St. James's would say if they knew how you've abused their idol? Think, Dolph. Do you want the word to get out?"

"I'm not afraid of anyone! Besides, no one's going to duel over a demirep," he retorted hotly.

"Duel, maybe not, but you *will* be shunned. Cut. Ostracized. You offend Miss Hamilton again or bother her in any way, and you shall find Society a very cold place."

Dolph's hazel eyes registered the threat. His expression sobered, but he glanced again evilly at the barred door to Harriette's house, as though still mulling over how to get in.

Seeing that look, Hawk was glad from the bottom of his soul for the fortresslike construction of Knight House. There Belinda would be safe. He didn't dare leave her anywhere else.

"Now, then. If you really want to get back in Belinda's good graces, you may begin by doing everything in your power to get her old man out of jail," he smoothly suggested. "You put him there. Make it right. If I were you, I would find out the full sum he owes and pay it off."

"Pay his bills? Are you mad?" Dolph cried. "That daft old man owes nearly three thousand pounds and even if I wanted to pay off his debts—which I don't—I don't have that kind of blunt! I've got duns of my own to worry about until I come into my inheritance."

"Ah, well, that is unfortunate. But then—if you can't pay a trifling three thousand, you couldn't have afforded Miss Hamilton anyway. Good day, Breckinridge."

With that he walked back into the house, leaving Dolph standing there fuming.

The footman unlocked the door for Hawk, admitted him, and secured it once more just as Dolph flew up against the outside of it and began banging on it in renewed fury. Dusting off his hands, Hawk glanced dryly at the door as it jumped on its hinges. He looked at the two footmen.

"The man's deranged. Well done, both of you. You have my thanks for your quick work last night as well as today." He slipped them each a tenner. "If he's not gone in five minutes, come and get me."

"Aye, Y'Grace. Thank you, sir!"

He nodded and returned upstairs to collect his new mistress.

Little did he expect to come face-to-face in the hallway with Wickedshifts himself, Henry Brougham in his shirt-sleeves, scratching his chest and looking like he had just rolled out of bed. Harriette's bed, Hawk supposed, pursing his mouth in contained hostility.

"What the hell is all the racket?" asked the golden boy of the Whig party.

Henry Brougham was of an age with Hawk; in fact, he had been born in Westmorland, the neighboring county to Hawk's native Cumberland. The most brilliant lawyer and radical reformer in London, Brougham was feared and hated by the entire Tory government, perhaps second only to Boney himself. Hawk's party had cause to fear him. The man was a genius with unflinching moral courage. Apparently, however, he was no more above the lures of the demireps than any other man.

A smile of cynical amusement broke across Brougham's handsome face as he strolled down the hallway toward Hawk.

"Well, well, who have we here? A fine morning to you, Your Grace. Bit of a change of venue for you, eh?"

"Brougham," Hawk growled.

"What's all the noise?"

"Dissatisfied customer."

"Need help with him?"

Hawk's lips thinned blandly. "No, thank you."

"Well, then, if you'll excuse me, I am going back to bed." He turned around and headed for Harriette's room. "Lady Holland still wants you to come to one of her soirees," he called over his shoulder. "You know we are determined to bring you over to our side."

Hawk couldn't resist a retort. "The side of those who sit back and criticize?"

"No, Hawkscliffe, the side of humanity and reform."

"Thank you, but tell her ladyship I must respectfully decline."

"Suit yourself, but remember this—" Brougham stopped and turned to him. "What is old and corrupt and decayed must pass away. Change is coming, Hawkscliffe, mark my words. It is only a matter of time. I hope you know which side you're on by the time that day arrives."

"Marvelous cant, Brougham, but you might have noticed that it's difficult to do any good in the world if no one will put you in the government."

"I'm not worried. Justice will prevail."

"Only if one gives it a shove, in my experience."

Brougham smiled bitterly and shook his head. "Well, you just keep shoving then, Your Grace, right alongside those tyrants you sup with, Liverpool and Sidmouth and Eldon, and one day the people of England just might shove back. The lot of you will drive them to it, especially with the Regent's latest expense report. Your look tells me you don't believe it. Why not? If it can happen in France, why not here?"

"You'd like that, wouldn't you? Chaos, sedition, mob violence. Is that what you want?"

"Gentlemen," Harriette called, sailing into the hallway just then. She hurried past Hawk and went to Brougham, slipping her arms around his waist. "This is not the Parliament, my dears. No bickering in my hallway," she scolded. "Hawkscliffe, Bel awaits you in the salon and I have private matters to discuss with Mr. Brougham. If you'll excuse us?"

"But of course," he said coolly.

Harriette shepherded Brougham into her chamber.

Hawk stood there a second longer, shrugging off his vexation with the way the Whig party was continually wooing him. The dukes of Hawkscliffe were Tories, period.

The government was far from perfect, and it was true that the Regent was an embarrassment to them all, but anything was better than chaos. He ignored the gut feeling that haunted him, that every cause Henry Brougham had so far championed was right and just—ending the slave trade, educating the poor. Still, the man raised his hackles with his audacious free thinking. Whom did that uppity commoner think that he was? Why, Brougham's people had been raising sheep when his own had been defending the Northern Marches against the Scots.

Brushing off the matter in disgust, he walked down the hallway toward the salon, where he found Belinda waiting for him in the bow window, trying to look brave. When he came in she glanced over anxiously, her delicate profile limned in sunlight. Sensing her fear at once, he sent her a relaxed smile of reassurance.

"Breckinridge will be gone in a moment," he assured her. "He's having himself a little tantrum right now, but I believe I made him see reason."

Her reaction took him by surprise. She rushed to him in a flurry of light yellow muslin and slipped her arms around his waist, pressing her cheek against his chest. She closed her eyes fervently and held him for all she was worth. Taken aback, Hawk wasn't quite sure what to do.

He rested his hands tentatively on her shoulders. She tilted her head back and stared at him. The wretched gratitude, almost hero worship in her eyes abashed him. Though he had known her for less than twenty-four hours, he had a feeling he was seeing the true Belinda behind the cold distant star of the demimonde, and she was not the hardened professional she pretended to be.

Strangely moved, he wrapped his arms around her and pressed a kiss to her hair. "Hush, darling. Everything's fine. He can't hurt you now."

"Thank you, Robert," she choked out barely audibly.

"Nonsense, Belinda, it was nothing." He furrowed his brow. Lifting her chin with his fingertips, he searched her eyes. There were deep violet shadows in amid the blue, like smoke clouds across a silent battlefield concealing scenes of furious destruction and loss of life. What had happened here? he wondered as he intercepted her lone tear with his fingertip. He wiped it away. Her stare was soulful, as though she could not speak.

"Come," he murmured softly, "let me take you home."

She sniffled, nodded, leaned against him as he walked her slowly across the salon to the stairs.

"Robert, what about all those dogs of yours? I'm scared of dogs. I'm scared of everything," she said in misery.

He turned her by her slender shoulders to face him and

smiled tenderly at her. "I don't think you're scared of everything, Belinda. On the contrary, I think you've got quite a lot of ballast in your hull for someone so pretty. As for my dogs, they'll listen to you. I promise."

She looked away, her eyes red rimmed. "Devotion, eh?" she said almost too quietly to hear.

"Pardon?"

She smiled at him faintly. "Nothing." With a small nod as though to steady herself, she left him there and went up alone to pack her belongings.

Troubled by the secretive young beauty, Hawk leaned against the newel post and watched her climb the steps. An instinctual wave of protectiveness made his body clench. He had failed to save Lucy, but by God, he would not let Dolph harm a hair on this one's head.

Strange, fragile, wounded creature, he thought, momentarily forgetting his staunch vow not to get involved.

He had always been at his best when someone needed him.

❧ CHAPTER ❧
SIX

Night found Bel in the rambling oak-paneled library of her new protector.

The later grew the hour, the more nervous she became, wondering if Hawkscliffe would indeed keep his word or if the rules of the game would change now that she was all but imprisoned in his baroque vault of opulence and decorum. Trying to conceal the slippery fear that slid through her veins, she perused the bookshelves in a careful attitude of idleness while the duke worked at his desk by candlelight.

She had seen the smoldering potency in his eyes after dinner as he had stared down the glossy twenty-foot table at her, sitting back in his chair, sipping port after their lavish repast. She mistrusted it.

The uncertainty was nerve-racking, worsened by the fact that she had overheard the argument between him and Mrs. Laverty, the housekeeper, who presumed to give him a fine dressing down for taking a scarlet woman under his roof. She heard enough of Robert's tolerant answers to gather that Mrs. Laverty had been with the family for decades, if not generations. Only a servant rock sure of her supremacy in the household would have dared to speak so impertinently to her employer. Still, as a former Lady of Quality, well versed in the management of servants, Bel was appalled at the old woman's tirade.

"This used to be a decent house! I might have expected such behavior from Alec or Jack, but from you, Robbie? What would your father say?"

"Miss Hamilton is a friend of mine and she is in danger."

"Send her elsewhere or you'll have my resignation!"

Bel had fled out of earshot then, not wanting to hear the rest. The maids had regarded her in mingled fascination and scorn as she passed, the footmen with leering interest. After all, she was only a kind of specialized servant herself and their master wasn't there to rebuke them for their rudeness.

She marveled that supper ever arrived that night with the staff in such an uproar over her arrival. Fortunately, at least the terrifying brute dogs liked her. Now they were on duty, prowling the neat, green grounds, keeping watch within the high spiked walls of Knight House.

Trailing her fingertips over volumes of old history books that would have sent Papa into scholarly ecstasies, she felt safe from Dolph, but she wasn't entirely sure of Hawkscliffe. In the silence of the library, she could feel his stare on her body. When she turned her head, she found him watching her.

She lifted her chin indignantly. "Do you mind?" she asked in cool, haughty bravado.

Caught, he smiled and took a drink of his port, then licked his handsome lips. "Surely a thousand pounds buys me the right to look at you. I was thinking perhaps I'll commission a painter to come and make your portrait. You have a classical look about you that would well suit an allegory, I should think. Would you pose for Thomas Lawrence? Make your beauty immortal?" He grinned. "Nude, preferably?"

"Oh, you'd like that, would you?"

"I believe I quite would."

"An allegory for what?"

He stroked his mouth idly, letting his gaze travel over her. "Aphrodite, perhaps. Persephone." He snapped his fingers. "What was the name of the chit Zeus ravished in a rain of gold coins?"

"Danaë," she said, laughing despite her indignation, for the two of them were just such an odd pair, saint and magdalen. "Wicked paragon, are you insulting me again?"

"I'm only teasing," he said softly. That beguiling glow had come back into his eyes. Maybe it was just the port. But the room, the very air that stood between them was charged with tension.

She looked away self-consciously and sauntered toward the large piano by the corner window. "Do you play?"

"Not anymore. Do you?"

"A little."

"Play us a song, then, lovely," he murmured.

"Your servant, my lord," she said wryly as she took her seat at the bench, then sucked in her breath when she saw the gold-lettered insignia. "A Graf," she marveled. The proud magnificent piano was almost too beautiful to touch. "Oh, Robert, I don't dare."

"Of course you do," he said, smiling indulgently as he watched her.

"Mr. Graf makes the pianos of Maestro Beethoven," she said in awe. "My middling skills cannot possibly do it justice."

"But I wish you to play for me. Go on."

"I noticed pianos in nearly every room, Robert, but I am mystified by why you would keep a work of art like this in your library."

"Music is a personal affair to me, Miss Hamilton. Now will you play for me or not?"

"Well . . . if you insist." She rested her fingers lightly on the keys and explored, warming up her hands by playing scales, but then stopped abruptly and looked at him. "It's out of tune!"

He nodded and took another drink. "I know."

"Oh, you vex me to the point of fascination," she exclaimed. "How could you? You keep a piano like this here in your private library where only you can enjoy it, and then you let it go out of tune. Lord Eldon ought to make *that* a crime."

He smiled.

"In any case, I refuse to indulge you when I know full well my serenade will sound like cats fighting until this poor regal thing is tuned. I refuse to so thoroughly discredit my playing, which is bad enough to start."

"Well, you are a courtesan, you must be highly accomplished. What else do you do?"

"Nothing you have paid for." Resting her elbow on the top of the piano, she laid her cheek in her hand with a saucy smile.

"Little cutthroat." He laughed quietly, but she remained mistrustful of the beguiling gleam of desire in his eyes.

She glanced around the drafty library, trying to spy a distraction. "Do you have a picture of Lady Coldfell?"

His languid expression stiffened automatically, but he didn't move. "Why?"

"I want to see who it is we are avenging."

He veiled his eyes behind his long black lashes, and reached into his desk. She rose and walked over to him. Without a word, he handed her a miniature portrait in a small silver case with a gold clasp.

She opened it and beheld the likeness of a serene beauty with red hair, green eyes, and porcelain skin. She studied it, saddened by the world's loss of a young, vibrant life. "Did Lady Coldfell give you this?"

"Yes." He quickly took it back from her and locked it

again. He avoided her gaze; his strong, square face remained taut. Fingering the locket, he said nothing further for a long moment. "It was a self-portrait, actually. She was quite a gifted artist."

Bel perched on the side of his desk and studied him. "Did she know you were in love with her?"

"I don't know."

"You never declared yourself?"

"Of course not."

"How sad."

He shrugged, looking a trifle guilty about having accepted the gift of a married lady's portrait. If Lucy had been such a chaste and holy being, why had she given her picture to a man who was not her husband or relative? Bel wondered. It was hardly proper. Had it gratified the young countess's vanity, knowing that Hawkscliffe was in love with her? Had she strung him along, trying to tempt him beyond the bounds of his honor? "What was it about her that captured you?" she asked softly, keeping a close watch on his tense, sun-burnished face and chiseled profile.

He held the closed metal portrait case, still avoiding her gaze as he brooded. "Her simplicity. Her gentleness. Oh, I don't really know. It was just a dream, you see. I loved her in my head. I live too much in my head, that is my problem. Outwardly . . . why, nothing happened. Nothing at all."

"Do you regret that?"

"What good would it have done me to have reached for her? I would only have dishonored us both and hurt a friend."

"Do you always play by the rules?" she wanted to ask, but she saw her defensive tactic had worked. His mind was off of any amorous impulses toward her and mired in memories of Lady Coldfell.

The sorrow that the topic had brought into his soulful eyes filled her with such remorse that she reached out and stroked his silky raven hair, offering soft consolation. The wavy ends of it curled around the edges of his snowy cravat in back.

He allowed her to pet his head, but he didn't look at her.

She gave a sigh of nostalgia. "Courtly love. I think it's beautiful, Robert, even if it was just a dream."

"A dream is better than nothing." He placed the metal locket on the desk before him and just stared at it.

"I only wonder why you didn't build your dream around a woman you could have."

A faint, bitter smile curved his mouth, but he didn't look at her. "Perhaps I didn't want a woman I could have."

"Why not?"

"Because I *didn't*," he said curtly, slicing her a sharp gaze that flashed with warning.

She withdrew her touch, deeming it safe to quit while she was ahead. His stare dropped and shut her out like an iron portcullis, yet she had glimpsed the needy man inside the impeccable duke.

Masking a fond, almost tender smile, she eased down off his desk, "I shall say goodnight, then, Your Grace."

Automatically he stood and sketched a bow of lordly precision, hands clasped behind his back, his posture gone stiff and starchy again. She nodded and turned to go.

"Think about what kind of equipage would please you," he ordered in an imperious tone as she walked to the door. "I'm taking you to Tattersall's tomorrow."

She turned back to him in surprise. The candlelight from the lamp on his desk flickered across his tanned, rugged face and caressed his powerful form.

She just stared at him for a moment.

Slowly, profoundly, the realization sank into her mind that she was safe here in his care. She knew it. She could feel it. Even if he had flirted with her a little, he had no intention of breaking his word and forcing any advances upon her.

The amazement of her discovery was followed by a draining wave of relief—and then remorse. The man had meant her no harm and she had manipulated him, made him relive painful memories just to hold him at bay.

"I am sorry for mentioning Lady Coldfell," she forced out, but she couldn't bring herself to admit it had been a premeditated ploy. She didn't want him to think her a coward as well as a whore.

"Oh, it's all right," he said wearily. "I'm sorry I was short with you."

Her throat constricted at his simple decency, that he should apologize to her, when she was the one who had hurt him. The man was a godsend. He deserved more from her than this, she thought fiercely, vowing in future to be a better courtesan for him. She would not fulfill the prime function of her race, but a true Cyprian was much more than a bedmate; there were other ways she could make his life happier and more pleasurable. This big, showy house echoed with his loneliness; she could help him, she knew it. He was like her, though he didn't suspect it—both of them trapped within themselves.

"Is something wrong?" he asked.

The shine of tears in her eyes vanished as she looked up, forcing one of her arch, false smiles. "Imagine that—a man who keeps his word. How novel."

He dropped his chin and sent her a rueful smile. "You're too young to be such a cynic. Goodnight, Miss Hamilton."

"Your Grace." She dipped a quick curtsy to him, a token of respect offered more sincerely than he realized, then she slipped out of the library and headed down the corridor toward the staircase, her emotions in upheaval.

She had memorized the way to her room for fear of getting lost in the mansion. Knight House was a showplace designed to awe those who entered. Every vista down the marbled corridors proclaimed the high pomp and ancientry of the master's blue-blooded heritage. Everything was in a state of starched, orderly perfection. It was eerie, more like a great mausoleum than a home—as though Robert had entombed himself with Lady Coldfell.

At the top of the stairs she lifted a branch of candles from the fixture on the wall and made her way down the long dark hallway until she came to the beautiful apartment she had been assigned. She opened the door and entered.

Her feet sank into the plush Flemish carpet as she padded in and locked the door behind her. The light from her candelabra flickered over the intricately molded ceiling and the pale, silk-hung walls. She set the candelabra on the satinwood vanity then went into the connecting dressing room to change into her night rail. It was a fine, skimpy thing of pearly silk, no ordinary white cotton shift for the likes of her. She blew out the beeswax candles.

Climbing into the large four-poster bed hung with rich damask draperies, she lay awake awhile, heeding the unfamiliar smells and sounds. She had never stayed in so magnificent a place and probably never would again, once this was over. Knight House, its staff, and master still intimidated her, but now that she knew she was essentially safe under the duke of Hawkscliffe's protection, the strangeness of her new situation did not seem as threatening as before.

Maybe everything *would* be all right, she thought as the long locked tension in her limbs and shoulders slowly eased, then, for the first time in weeks, she drifted into a sleep without dark, violent dreams.

Hawk was beginning to discover the whole tenor of his life was changing with Miss Belinda Hamilton in it. She kept him in a perpetual state of delighted confusion. The next morning she was in cheerful spirits, seated next to him at the table in the pale-blue breakfast room. The east wall had high, arched windows through which the clear morning light streamed, weaving itself into her flaxen tresses, illuminating the rosy cream satin of her skin.

When Walsh, the butler, rolled in their breakfast on the wheeled cart, she turned to watch in curiosity and Hawk peered over the edge of the *Times*, stealing a covert glance at her. The sweep of her lashes, the mere angle of her nose did strange things to his insides.

"Oh, what have we here? Omelettes? How lovely," she exclaimed.

"Omelettes with leeks and morels, Miss Hamilton," the stately man intoned, fairly fizzing with disapproval of the girl.

"Morels?" She laughed gaily and sent Hawk a smile. "I prefer mine with no morals—but you had already guessed that, I'm sure."

Walsh started to remove her plate. "Beg pardon, miss, the kitchen will make it over—"

"I believe Miss Hamilton was making a pun," Hawk spoke up, fighting a smile of amusement. He lifted his tea and took a sip, then gave himself up to watching her. He set the *Times* aside.

"A noble omelette, tell your cook." She stabbed one of the little mushrooms with her fork, lifting it for Hawk's inspection. "You like yours with an abundance of morals, I wager?"

"Not always," he murmured as the butler served him his plate and removed the silver warming lid.

Walsh inquired if they wanted anything further, then bowed and withdrew.

"You're in high spirits today," Hawk remarked, reaching for the toast.

"Slept like a babe. Such comfortable quarters, I thank you."

"You're welcome. Eat up. We have a busy day ahead."

"I will!"

For some reason the same breakfast that he ate every morning seemed to him today like a feast, perhaps because his companion exclaimed with relish over every bite. The taste of things struck him newly; he supposed he had lost interest in food in recent weeks. Today he ate like a highlander. Besides the golden brown omelettes, whisked to feathery lightness, there was thick, pink, succulent bacon, glorious butter and raspberry preserves on white toast or warm Geneva rolls with a hint of saffron, and slices of fresh pears.

"Your cook is excellent, Robert."

He nodded, finished chewing, and took a sip of tea. "Thank heavens at least Cook is still here. We may have a bumpy ride for the next few days with the smooth running of the household. I apologize in advance for any inconvenience. It seems Mrs. Laverty has deserted us."

Belinda's eyes widened. She set down her fork. "She quit?"

"Not exactly. She has reassigned herself to Hawkscliffe Hall." He shook his head in irritation. "Temperamental old harpy, but she does a good job and besides, I can't fire someone who has been with me since I was in the nursery."

"Well!" she said indignantly, taking a little dab at the corners of her mouth with her napkin in ladylike determination. "Never fear. I will keep Knight House in top order for you in Mrs. Laverty's absence."

"Oh, and how do you propose to do that? The staff thinks you're some kind of lovely witch who has me under her spell. Besides, what does a courtesan know of domesticity?"

"Never you mind," she said loftily. "Just inform Walsh that Mrs. Laverty's authority has been transferred to me, and I'll take it from there. Such work is a mere trifle to me and it's the least I can do to give you, ah, satisfaction?" she said lightly.

He slanted her a dubious look, heartily ruing having exempted her from his bed, now that she mentioned it, but he kept his regret to himself. "You sound quite sure. Do you really know what you're doing? I detest a chaotic household."

She gave him a rather condescending smile and took a demure bite of omelette.

Hawk was too curious about her hidden talents to deny her. He called in Walsh and told him in a stern, warning tone of the domestic changing of the guard.

Miss Hamilton stared straight ahead in serene hauteur, sipping her tea, while the butler stiffened with silent horror at the order, then bowed and exited, charged with the unenviable task of breaking the news to the rest of the staff.

The courtesan sat there unruffled, as though she dealt with unruly servants every day of her life. She could carry herself like a veritable duchess when it suited her. Perhaps the little cardsharp has an ace up her sleeve, he mused, regarding her closely.

After the meal he herded her into his black town coach, which she proclaimed the pinnacle of supreme elegant luxury. The driver and grooms all were clad in sober dark-blue livery, complete with powdered wigs and tricorne hats. Drawn by four black geldings, the town coach had the Hawkscliffe coat of arms emblazoned on the door, with interior seats of soft, ivory-colored leather.

Their first stop was the Bank of England on Thread-needle Street, where he sauntered in with her on his arm and his ivory-tipped walking stick dangling idly from his other hand. Instantly he was surrounded by obsequious clerks who commenced groveling. Belinda and he were shown into one of the assistant manager's offices, where Hawk directed an account be opened in her name, to which he transferred the initial sum of five hundred pounds, per their agreement.

Her businesslike intensity as she signed her name to the documents made him smile to himself, then she stared at the deposit slip as though she half expected the numbers to vanish in a puff of smoke. Finally she tucked the little bill-fold of blank drafts reverently into her reticule.

She has known poverty, he thought, and something fierce and hot rose in him. He had to turn away from her, lest he catch her up hard in his arms. The result of his in-sight in the bank clerk's office was that he spent an utterly foolish sum for her horses and equipage at Tattersall's, their next destination.

Only the finest would do. Recalling the nasty stares she'd been dealt on Rotten Row the previous day, he was determined to give her the best, for style was its own re-proof to insolence. That much he had learned from his scandalous mother.

As they wandered the aisles and various barns, Belinda accrued an entourage made up of Hawk's various acquaintances, for the famed, stylish auction grounds were a fa-vorite male gathering place, usually devoid of wives and too much propriety.

Hawk wasn't sure if he was irritated or amused to be the protector of such a sought-after beauty. He was rather daunted by the realization that perhaps he wanted her at-tention all to himself, but she was too polite to ignore the odd assortment of amiable fellows trailing in her wake—a few sporting old squires and retired cavalrymen, a handful of horse-mad young bucks, even one of the minute-sized jockeys joined their company, giving Belinda shrewd opinions on the best horses for her carriage.

Hawk kept her close to him. Any onlooker would have thought she genuinely was his mistress and had him wrapped around her finger, but in fact it was she who protested the cost of the fine pair of high-stepping blacks and the elegant little *vis-à-vis* he selected for her. It looked like his coach in miniature, which she had said she adored.

"Robert, it is too dear," she protested softly, pulling him aside.

"Don't you like it?"

"Like it? It's the most elegant thing I've ever seen, but—"

He flicked a gesture at the agent and the equipage was hers.

Ah, Hawkscliffe, now you're showing off, he chided himself, smiling at the ground, hands in pockets, while she petted her new horses with childlike joy.

She looked dazed as he escorted her back to his town coach. When they were under way, he glanced over, pleased with himself, and found her studying him. He lifted a brow in question.

"If you are trying to make me feel overly indebted to you, you are doing a good job."

"Nonsense, I am merely carrying out the terms of our agreement. Don't you trust me?"

"At the very least, you must let me buy *you* something, then. A present."

"You want to buy me a present?" he asked in astonishment.

She nodded emphatically. It was an absurd, if sweet, impulse, but something in her eyes told him he'd better not refuse. He didn't want to hurt her pride.

"All right," he said guardedly, then agreed to let her buy him a few ounces of his favorite Congue snuff from Fribourg & Treyer.

Why it was so terribly important to her, he could scarcely comprehend. He congratulated himself privately when he managed to make her laugh by daring her to try a pinch. After all, even Queen Charlotte was a great aficionado of snuff and many grand dames of the ton considered it a respectable habit for ladies as well as men.

They loitered in the famous tobacconists' shop, both of them laughing a bit too loudly as he demonstrated the elegant hand movements which would assure that the vice was carried out fashionably. Following his instructions carefully, she tried, amid laughter, to copy him. Upon inhaling a pinch of it from between her fingertips, she began sneezing violently, her eyes watering.

"Vile! Vile!" she gasped out. "Blech!"

He cast a bland, apologetic look at the shopkeepers and handed her his silk monogrammed handkerchief. She continued to sneeze herself nearly senseless. When she had quite recovered, they left the shop in a spirit of jolly camaraderie. Hawk felt as though he had shed ten years of straitlaced self-repression.

Arm in arm they marched down Pall Mall, audacious allies in the face of the disapproving stares. Rounding the corner at Haymarket, they nearly collided with a trio of red-coated young officers. They apologized and he murmured an irritated, "Pardon," when suddenly he noticed Bel staring at the soldier in the middle.

Her face was turning ashen.

All swaggering soldierly charm, the handsome young officer had a tousle of wavy brown hair and a dumbstruck look on his face. "Bel?"

"Mick," she said faintly.

The young man's roguish face lit up with joy.

"*Bel!* There's my girl!" With a whoop of pleasure that resounded down the busy street, he grabbed her around the waist and whirled her in a circle. "I can't believe it's you! What in the world are you doing in Town? This is the lass I told you about," he cried to his friends.

"Put me down!" she wrenched out in anguish, backing up against Hawk the moment the young man released her.

Hawk didn't say a word, merely put his hand out and steadied her by the small of her back. Aware of the heated surge of jealousy that pulsed through him, he fixed an impaling gaze on the army fellow and bent his head to her ear. "Darling, shall I send for the coach?" he murmured—loudly enough for the other man to hear.

Mick—as she had called him—looked at Hawk in bafflement and the start of anger. He opened his mouth as if to tell Hawk to get away from her, then snapped it shut again when Belinda glanced up at him with her eyes full of silent gratitude and said, "Yes, Your Grace, please do."

Hawk gave her a bolstering nod then turned to give the quiet order to his footman. The coach was waiting for them just down the way. He glanced uncertainly at Belinda, then decided she probably wanted a moment of privacy with her friend—if this fellow was her friend. It was not easy to walk the few paces away, but one had to be a gentleman, after all.

" 'Your Grace'?" he heard Mick echo angrily. "Who the hell is that?"

Hands in pockets, Hawk glanced over darkly and saw understanding dawn in the young officer's stare. His boyish face turned pale as his gaze traveled over her fine, showy gown.

"What's happened, Bel?" he asked, panicking.

Hawk saw Belinda lift her chin, looking once more like

a marble Aphrodite, beautiful and impervious. "Where've you been, Mick?"

"Around—Bel, who is he?"

"He is the duke of Hawkscliffe, my protector. Good day, Captain Braden," she said coolly.

Hawk pivoted and stalked back to her side, thinking there might be trouble, but Mick only stood there looking flabbergasted. No fight seemed to be forthcoming. Having heard Hawk's name, Mick's two companions contrived to peer into a nearby shop window, making themselves scarce.

Just then the town coach rolled to a halt beside them amid a jingle of harness. The groom jumped down to open the door for them. Hawk offered her his hand to assist her inside. She laid her hand atop his, but she would not look at him.

"Bel, wait—" Mick took a step after her but Hawk blocked his path, staring him down in calm warning, his expression steel.

When the lad backed off, looking too bewildered to protest, Hawk stepped up into the coach, took his seat beside her and in a moment they were under way.

Belinda stared out the window, seemingly blind to the world passing by. Her face was an expressionless mask and he knew that she was locked within herself—and that he was locked out. He sat uncomfortably beside her, unsure of what he ought to do.

When they arrived at Knight House she got out quickly, mumbled an excuse, and fled to her room. His shoulders slumped as he watched her pound up the curved staircase.

Should he give her privacy until she had composed herself? he wondered.

Protecting her from overzealous admirers was one matter, but he wasn't sure he wanted to get involved to the point of giving her a shoulder to cry on. He was frankly unaccustomed to emotional displays, yet it seemed damned cold-blooded to pretend nothing was wrong. Perhaps he should check on her—merely from courtesy. He had no wish to be rude.

Somehow it was an exercise in courage as he climbed the steps and walked silently down the hallway to her door. He listened at it and winced to hear the sound of soft crying. He frowned; he scowled; he fought with himself; and then finally, certain it was a bad idea, he knocked.

"Belinda?"

He waited, but there was no response. Frowning with concern, he turned the knob and pushed the door open about a foot, peering in.

She was lying balled up on the bed, her long blond hair flowing over her shoulders. She didn't tell him to come in; then again, she didn't tell him to go away. Torn, he decided that chivalry demanded he offer help. He walked into the room and closed the door gently.

He went and sat on the edge of the bed. Her back was to him. Hesitantly, he touched her silken hair. "Poor sweet," he whispered. "There, now. It can't be so bad."

Her soft crying continued.

He petted her shoulder. "Do you want to tell me who that was?" he asked in the gentlest tone he possessed.

For a long moment she was silent.

"The boy I was to marry."

Hawk felt the pain in her quiet answer like a physical blow. He closed his eyes and shook his head as she started crying again.

"Everybody gets their heart broken sometime, love. You're young. You'll heal." He leaned back against the headboard then smoothed her hair behind her ear. Her sobs quieted a little as he continued to stroke her hair, his touch slow and tender. "You'll love again when the right one comes along."

"I will never love anyone," she said in a low, desolate voice, keeping her back to him.

"How can you know?" he murmured, aware that her youthful vow of sorrow echoed his own thoughts after Lucy's death.

"Because when a courtesan falls in love she is destroyed."

She turned onto her back and gazed up at him, tears clumped on her long dun lashes. He had never seen her look more beautiful.

Quivering with feeling, he could barely find his voice. "Belinda, your heart is too sweet to throw away."

"Everybody fails me, Robert," she whispered, staring at him—a young girl without hope, without dreams.

"I won't," he said without a second's hesitation—to his own vast astonishment.

In the silence that followed, he held her stare, wondering if he had just inexplicably promised more than he wanted to give.

But he realized that his lovely young cynic didn't believe him anyway, though her faint smile expressed gratitude for his good intentions. She sighed, closed her eyes, and nestled her face against his thigh. "You are a kind man."

Tenderly he reached down and caught her tear on his finger, brushing it away, his voice oddly gruff. "And you, Miss Hamilton, are too good for that thoughtless soldier boy."

He watched her fine lips curve in a wisp of a smile, but she kept her eyes closed.

"Robert?" she whispered barely audibly.

"Yes?"

"If I told you there was something—very important to

me," she said haltingly, "something I need to do—would you help me?"

"What is it?"

She opened her eyes. There were shadows in them the color of night. "I have to visit my father in the Fleet, but I'm afraid to go there alone. Will you come with me? Will you take me there tomorrow?"

"Well, certainly. That's no trouble."

"It's not?" she asked, seeming to hold her breath.

"We can go whenever you like."

He heard her slow exhale of relief. She grasped his hand, threading her fingers through his.

They were silent for a moment, merely being together. He stroked her hair with his other hand, marveling at its softness.

"Robert," she whispered more urgently this time.

He smiled faintly. "Yes, Belinda?"

She held very still with her hair fanned out over the mattress. She closed her eyes. "I think . . . that I want you to kiss me."

"You do?"

"Softly." She opened her eyes slowly and gazed at him.

He stared at her. Without a word, he leaned down and brushed her lips in a light, caressing kiss. He barely moved, cradling her head in his hands.

She let out a yielding sigh like silk.

They remained like that for a moment, an eon, a year, until, somehow, he dragged himself back, his senses reeling.

"Is that better?" he whispered, quite thrown off his equilibrium.

"Yes," she breathed. Her eyes swept open, long lashed and dreamy. "Thank you, Robert."

He could only stare at her for a moment, drinking in her beauty, then he smiled at the foolishness of it all and chucked her softly under the chin. "I know how to cheer you up. What do you say to an evening at Vauxhall?"

A small, innocent smile broke over her face. She let out a giggle and rolled away from him.

❧ CHAPTER ❧
SEVEN

Vauxhall Pleasure Gardens was not entirely disreputable, but could hardly be called genteel. A kind of gaudy year-round festival, it served as a singular place to see and be seen. Here spirits were rowdy, morals were loose, and courtesans were queens.

The very air seemed to glimmer with excitement and Bel felt frankly intoxicated to stride through the entrance and parade up the Grand Walk on the arm of one of the most eligible bachelors of the aristocracy, even if it was only as his mistress.

She couldn't stop stealing breathless little glances at him, tall and worldly and suave in his black and white formal clothes. His chin was high and he walked with a casual strut in his step, leading her past the artificial Gothic ruin and the Cascade.

People everywhere turned and stared at them, whispering and watching them pass. How she wanted to make Hawkscliffe proud to be with her! She knew they looked well together—she, a shimmering pale blonde, he, dark and elegant—but he could have made any woman feel beautiful.

She had adorned herself in a style of sophisticated understatement that she knew would please him. Her gown of white gossamer muslin flowed around her legs as she walked, filmy as the air. Her sheer crimson scarf draped behind her shoulders, matching the spray of miniature red roses tucked into her high-coiled hair. Beneath her gown, as a kind of irreverent joke, she had donned the professional harlot's trademark—white silk stockings with a red-clocked diamond at the ankles, accented with gold thread. She was deviously planning on letting the paragon catch a glimpse of them if the moment presented itself. Why not? His life could use a little spicing up.

Just then he touched her hand where it rested on his forearm. "Look."

She followed his nod. Ahead they could see and hear the bright blast of the balloon ascending from behind the trees that lined the broad walks. They could hear the orchestra's music tumbling out onto the grass from the pavilion, while paper lanterns lit the main walkways.

She glanced up at him with a brilliant smile and as they gazed at each other, it was as if the rest of the world did not exist, not even Dolph. Then he gave her a small tug and led her toward the bright, noisy main hall. Inside, Robert clasped her hand and began weaving through the throng.

One of the first people they met was Lord Chancellor Eldon, a tough old "Geordie" from Newcastle upon Tyne. Eldon's intellect and great force of character had gained him a baronetcy and allowed him to rise to one of the highest posts of office in the land, though he was not high-born, the mere son of a coal factor. Having caused a scandal or two himself in his day, Eldon was too powerful to care whom he offended among the Society ladies when he saw Bel.

Knowing the Lord Chancellor's ruthless views on maintaining the death penalty for minor offenses, Bel had not wanted to like Lord Eldon when she had first been introduced to him by Harriette, but she had been unable to resist his surprisingly warm and affectionate manner toward the people he liked—and he liked her very much, indeed.

Turning away from the appalled Society matrons, he greeted Bel in gruff delight, ignoring Hawkscliffe. She warmly shook his hand, then her protector and Lord Eldon regarded each other warily.

"My lord," said Robert with a nod.

"Your Grace," Eldon answered with a bit of a *humph*. "You'd best take good care of her," he warned.

"Oh, I will."

"And you, young lady, will save a dance for me."

She nodded graciously, fighting a smile. "My lord, it would be my pleasure."

He could not seem to resist the urge to pinch her cheek. "Such a pretty thing," he said with a chuckle. "Off you go."

They moved on through the crowd and Robert leaned slightly toward her. "Now I'm convinced you've made a deal with the devil."

She laughed. "Oh, it's not what you're thinking. Lord Eldon is in love with his wife—it's quaint, actually. We're just friends."

"Indeed? Well, I've been trying to get your friend's support on a certain reform bill for the past six months, but the man thinks it's perfectly fine to hang Englishmen for any manner of petty crimes."

"Well then, we shall have to give a dinner party, Robert. Let us see if we can't charm him."

With a low laugh he slipped his arm around her and pulled her against him, kissing her temple. "Little did I know you'd become my secret weapon in the political arena," he murmured playfully. "Did I mention you look delectable?"

Her eyes sparkled as she sent him a wily glance. "You're not half-bad yourself. I shall have to make sure no one steals you from me."

"I daresay." He gave his Obaldeston cravat a preening

tug in mock vanity. "Where's Brummell? Let's get his opinion of my coat."

She laughed and noticed that his gaze swept the room. His light hold around her waist stiffened slightly, but his tone remained elegantly droll.

"Our mutual friend is here."

Bel's heart sank, though she hid her reaction. "I suppose you knew he'd be here?"

"I had a suspicion."

She snapped her fan open like a shield. "Well, how do you want to play this charade of yours, Robert?"

"You know him better than I do. What do you suggest?"

"What would drive Dolph to distraction?" she mused aloud. The answer came to her at once. "I shall have to pretend to be utterly enamored of you."

"Pretend?" he exclaimed, feigning hurt, though his eyes danced.

She gave him a flat look. "That is, after all, what Dolph wants most for himself."

"This might be more fun than I'd anticipated."

"Enjoy it while you can, Hawkscliffe. It's only a ruse," she muttered, grasping his hand. She tugged him over to the group of supper boxes in the dimly lit corner where the Cyprians lounged, laughing, drinking, dining with their protectors, and looking gorgeous in their racy finery.

Chief among the merry crowd were the Three Graces— Harriette, Fanny, and Julia—and the usual gentlemen of their clique—Argyll, Hertford, Colonel Parker, Brummell, Alvanley, Leinster, and his passionate young cousin, the marquess of Worcester, who was hopelessly infatuated with Harriette.

Bel and Hawkscliffe were greeted with resounding good cheer. Their liaison was the talk of the town. When Harriette commanded the others to make room for them in the box, they slid in and ordered supper and wine. As Robert rested his arm on the back of her seat in a protective gesture, she smiled to herself, secretly relishing their charade.

Just then a chorus of friendly hails rose as a man whom she had never seen before joined their company. No woman could have helped but stare at the golden, dazzlingly beautiful young man; his naughty grin lit the pavilion as he came wading through a sea of ladies who doted and teased and propositioned him, slyly fondling him in the crowd as he passed. In his late twenties, he looked for all the world like a cheerful, rowdy young archangel who had tumbled to earth on a gust of wind.

He had a long mane of tawny gold hair pulled back in a queue and was extravagantly dressed in a royal blue velvet coat and skintight white trousers that clung to every muscular line of his legs. Hearty, suntanned, and broad shouldered, he swaggered over with the dashing air of some gallant, romantic highwayman.

Even Harriette blushed when he pinched her cheek in greeting.

"Oh, here we go," muttered Robert, noticing the young man.

"You know him?"

Scowling, Robert didn't answer, for at that moment, the golden scoundrel glanced over the heads of everyone else at the table straight at him, let out a loud laugh full of gusto, and started toward them.

"Ha! What's this? Calamity! Has the sky fallen? Has Hell frozen over? Can it be my stainless brother, here among the sinners? Surely my eyes deceive me."

"Oh, do shut up, Alec."

Bel lifted her eyebrows. His *brother*? The two looked nothing alike—they were like night and day—one black haired, dark eyed, and intense; the other golden, blue eyed, and droll. Still laughing, Alec, as he'd called him, swaggered over and clapped Robert heartily on the back.

"Oh, see how the mighty are fallen," he pronounced to all present like a born showman.

Everyone laughed, though Robert grumbled and scowled, looking not at all amused. Not nearly finished taunting his elder brother, the rogue leaned down, folding his arms on the back of Bel's seat.

"Hull-o," he drawled, quizzing her at close range in open male interest.

Bel raised one eyebrow at him and regarded him in boredom.

He dropped his monocle and turned to Robert with a grin. "So, this is the chit you've been squandering our rents on. Your Grace, I detect a definite improvement in your taste. Mademoiselle," he said with a courtly flourish of a bow, "my hat is off to you. I feared he was a monk."

She fought a smile. So, this rakish coxcomb thought to give her protector a hard time? Two could play at that game. She draped her arms around Robert's neck and smiled evasively. "Oh, he's no monk, trust me."

His golden eyebrows shot upward as she kissed Robert's cheek, clinging to him as though he were the only man in the universe. Then his rakish brother burst out laughing.

"Ahem," the duke said stiffly, shifting in his seat. She smiled fondly, detecting a slight coloring of his manly cheeks. "Miss Hamilton, may I present my brother, Lord Alec Knight. My *baby* brother," he growled with a measure of sarcasm.

"How do you do?" she said absently, not bothering to glance at Lord Alec, whom she instantly sensed was a born flirt, accustomed to stealing feminine attentions from any other man in his vicinity.

Instead she gazed only at Robert, languidly kissing his cheek and neck and ear while he and his brother conversed. Caught up in the charade, she was not sure herself if her seeming adoration was truth or trick. She could feel his pulse quickening in his artery when she kissed his neck. She closed her eyes and smiled sensuously as she gave his earlobe a light, nibbling kiss.

What would it be like if it were real? she wondered. What if she were his real mistress?

She glanced at Harriette—ever practical, ever solvent Harriette—and knew that only a fool would pass up a chance like this without at least trying to hang on to a protector like Hawkscliffe. Why shouldn't she? They got on well together. She could be of use to him and God knew he could afford her. He had no wife to be hurt by their affair, and she was certainly not looking forward to putting herself back out on the open market when their charade was done. Could he be persuaded?

Toying with his cravat, she nearly insinuated herself onto his lap as she entertained the possibility of making a true conquest of him.

Lord Alec chuckled. "You two look like you'd rather have privacy. Miss Hamilton." He nodded to her, sent his brother a twinkling grin, and sauntered off to talk to the others.

"Laying it on a bit thick, aren't you?" Robert muttered to her under his breath.

"Don't turn starchy on me, Robert. We *have* to be convincing," she purred, giggling a little as she caressed his chest.

"You're very convincing, Belinda. Trust me."

"How convincing am I, Robert?" she whispered.

He cast her a hungry look. "You tell me."

"Mmm, that sounds like an invitation." In a moment of exhilarating boldness, she slipped her hand under the table and grazed her palm over the pulsating evidence of his reaction to her display. He sucked in his breath when she touched him but made no move to stop her.

She watched his face and decided she quite liked being the one in control. "*Oh, Robert,* I'm *so* flattered. Too bad our agreement precludes my helping you with this big . . . hard problem you've got." She withdrew her touch with a wily smile.

"You had best behave, you heartless tease," he warned in a ragged whisper.

"Or what?"

"I don't know, but I will surely think of something in a moment when my head clears. Two can play at that game." He laid his hand on her knee beneath the table and slid a slow caress up her thigh.

An uncontrollable shiver of excitement raced through her, but she opted for a show of defiance. "What do you think you're doing?"

He sent her a private, hot little smile which beguiled her so much that she cupped his cheek and drew him to her for a deep, slow kiss. She didn't know what had come over her. She couldn't seem to get enough of the man. It was the honor in him, the trust she felt that helped her dare to spread her wings. If Dolph is watching, she thought behind her closed eyes, he'll have a fit of apoplexy. Then all thought fled as she reeled in a spiral of pleasure, ravished by the rhythmic satin stroke of his delicious mouth.

"Get a room!" someone shouted and only then, amid laughter and applause, did they part, flushed and breathless, self-consciously avoiding each other's gaze. Robert reached resolutely for his glass and took a long drink of wine while Bel, blushing, pushed her hair behind her ear and assumed her most aloof smile.

Lord Eldon came to claim his dance from her a short while later. She hesitated, unsure if it was wise to leave her protector's side with Dolph somewhere in the sprawling pavilion, but he gave her a firm nod. She realized Dolph would never risk making too great a fool of himself in front of someone like Lord Eldon.

"I'll be watching out for you," Robert murmured as she climbed past him out of the supper box.

"I know." She smiled at him, caressed his cheek, and joined the Lord Chancellor.

As they took their places for the ambling quadrille, she would've had to have been blind not to notice the countless women in the crowd who looked daggers at her. The censure of the Polite World filled her with a surge of angry rebellion.

As much as Dolph felt he owned her, likewise these Society mamas thought the duke of Hawkscliffe was their exclusive property, reserved for one of their daughters. Bel knew the type from her teaching days at Mrs. Hall's. She hadn't liked their pushy, conceited ways then; now she wished she could thumb her nose at all of them. Instead she turned on her most audacious, courtesanlike smile and blew Robert a kiss as she waited for the music to begin.

He smiled wryly, watching her. She was wholly aware of his stare as she danced. Moving through the figures with Lord Eldon, she stole a glance at the place where Robert sat. Lord Alec had joined him. The eldest and youngest of the Knight brothers sat together in identical poses, their muscled arms folded over their chests, their heads tilted together as they conferred, both looking out at the dancers, both impassive and rather sly. She surmised Alec was grilling Robert about his apparent conquest of her.

A short while later the quadrille ended. She curtsied in answer to Lord Eldon's bow. As the Lord Chancellor gave her his arm to escort her back to her table, Bel drew in her breath to see that while she had been dancing, the powder keg that was the situation between Robert and Dolph had given off a spark.

She should have known.

It appeared that Dolph had intended to intercept her when she returned from the dance floor, but Robert and Alec had come down to prevent him; seeing the dual threat to Dolph, his friends, in turn, had come to back him up. Now both sets of bristling males stood near the edge of the dance floor. Dolph was saying something to Robert. She could tell by Robert's fierce stance and taut, angry stare that the situation hovered on the brink of violence.

Murmuring an apology to Lord Eldon, Bel dashed off and shoved through the milling crowd to reach her protector's side, praying she would arrive before something terrible happened. Perhaps she could make Dolph calm down.

Argyll and Colonel Parker reached the scene at the same time she did.

Dolph looked at her in lustful hatred, but somehow held his tongue. Standing behind him, however, his friend was not so wise.

"Why, look, everyone, it's the new Hawkscliffe Harlot."

"What did you say?" Robert snarled through gritted teeth.

Alec took a step forward.

Colonel Parker pulled Bel back from going to Robert's side. As she turned to scowl at the handsome officer, the fatal words were uttered.

"Everybody knows the Knight boys are just a brood of mongrel bastards."

The music stopped. Every person within earshot froze and looked at the drunken, narrow-faced fop who had spoken to them.

Robert looked at Dolph.

Dolph raised his hands with an insolent laugh. "I didn't say it."

Then Alec moved, springing like a young lion on attack. He shoved Dolph aside, laid hold of the fop's lapels, and yanked him forward off his feet. He punched him across the face. The man went sprawling backward onto the parquet floor as though shot from a cannon.

Pandemonium broke out.

"Outside!" Argyll bellowed.

"Parker! See to Belinda!" Robert roared, turning to look for her in the crowd. "Go with Colonel Parker," he ordered, sending her a searing look through the mayhem.

She tried to protest, but he was already going after his brother, too late to stop Alec from picking his victim up off the floor and hitting him again.

"Take it outside, Alec," he yelled ferociously.

Bel could barely hear him in the chaos.

"Come, Miss Hamilton." Colonel Parker pulled her forcibly back to safety, where Harriette, Fanny, and Julia were looking on in astonishment.

"What's happened, dearest?" Fanny exclaimed, embracing her protectively.

"Dolph's friend called me Hawkscliffe's Harlot and now they're fighting," she cried as the glut of men surged slowly toward the exit.

"The Hawkscliffe Harlot?" Julia asked in apparent amusement.

Harriette glanced at Bel, looking not the slightest bit ruffled by the brawl. "My dear, if that's what was said, rest assured he wasn't referring to you."

"What?" she exclaimed, feeling like an hysterical amateur next to the Three impervious Graces. "Who else could he have meant?"

"You've never heard of the Hawkscliffe Harlot?"

"No! Who is that?"

Harriette slanted a nod in the direction of Robert and Alec. "Their mother."

"Their mother," she echoed in shock.

"Oh, yes," Julia agreed. "Georgiana Knight—the eighth

duchess of Hawkscliffe, you know. She lived for love. In her day she would have made *us* look like nuns."

"What?" Bel cried.

"They say she was a fantastic, passionate, indomitable beauty. She had affairs with all the great men of her day."

"From poets to prizefighters," Fanny chimed in.

"I am in shock," Bel gasped.

The brawlers had vanished out the door, leaving the hall abuzz with anxious chatter.

"Don't you know the story of the Knight Miscellany?" Harriette asked, taking her slyly by the elbow and drawing her closer for the tale, for the only thing Harriette liked better than a rich man was a good scandal.

"No! Tell!"

"Robert's father, the eighth duke, was too much of a gentleman *not* to acknowledge all his wife's offspring as his own, but only your keeper is his true son. The other four brothers all have different fathers—though the little girl is supposedly of the true blood, as well—the result of their reconciliation just before the eighth duke died."

"Oh, my dear heavens," Bel uttered, marveling. She knew she should be above gossip, but she could not possibly help herself. "Who was Lord Alec's real father?"

Harriette leaned toward, her eyes sparkling with glee at the delicious tidbit. "Supposedly, Alec was sired by a very notorious Shakespearean actor connected once with Drury Lane."

Bel's eyes widened.

Harriette laid her finger over her lips. "You didn't hear it from me."

"My goodness, how perfectly shocking!" Bel said, trying to take it all in. "Do they know they're actually half brothers?"

"Well, of course, they do, dear. But that doesn't matter

to them. You will never find full-blooded brothers more loyal to one another than that pack of gorgeous rogues."

"Robert's not a rogue, he's a paragon," Bel sighed.

"No such thing," Harriette snorted. "He can polish and shine and triple-starch himself if he likes, but underneath it—mark my words—he's still Georgiana's son, and her passion flows in his veins."

Defending their mother's honor was nothing new to Hawk and his brothers. They had been doing it since they were boys. They might fight like hellions among themselves, but whenever family honor was called into question, all five could be counted on to unite against the world if necessary.

Outside the general row continued under the stars and paper lanterns. Twenty or thirty men had gathered on the greensward between the Grand and South Walks to watch the brawl, if not to join in the free-for-all. Most were merely yelling cheers and making wagers, but anyone who had ever met the Knight brothers knew better than to bet against them.

With his flamboyant clothes skewed and long hair flown from its queue, Alec continued thrashing the fool who had insulted their mother, while Hawk guarded his brother's back, merely trying to keep things under control, with limited success.

Fortunately the summons bell rang across all of Vauxhall, signaling that the time had come for the Cascade to flow. In the distraction, Hawk was able to pull Alec off of the nearly unconscious fellow.

As the crowd dispersed, drifting over to view the marvel of the artificial waterfall, the manager of the Pleasure Gardens stalked out and ordered Alec to leave. The belligerent little man then commanded everyone else who had been involved in the fight to do the same.

Hawk saw that his brother appeared not much the worse

for wear after the tangle, except for the small line of blood that trickled from the corner of his mouth. A consummate dandy, Alec took out his handkerchief and wiped it away with imminently fashionable aplomb. "A good night's work," he lightly declared. "I believe I shall go visit some low gambling hell and take someone's fortune."

"I'm not leaving, I don't care what that runt of a manager has to say. Belinda was having too much fun to drag her away. It's only nine."

"That petty fellow won't make *you* leave, Your Grace. Enjoy your new toy. She's a hell of an improvement over Lucy Coldfell."

"Watch it," he growled.

Alec sent him an insolent look then sauntered off with a few of his raffish friends.

Just then Hawk noticed Dolph leaving. He was not done with the baronet yet. He smoothly bribed the manager of Vauxhall so that he might stay, then walked after his enemy. "Breckinridge!"

Dolph turned. His friends did, too.

"A word with you, please. Alone."

Dolph waved his followers on. They left, two of them carrying away the dazed instigator of the fight. Approaching in suspicion, Dolph jerked his square chin insolently in question. "What do you want?"

"I told you to stay away from her."

Dolph gritted his teeth. "I didn't go within ten feet of your slut, Hawkscliffe."

"Don't tempt me, Breckinridge. I'm not going to warn you again. Let me come right down to it. Obviously I have something that you want."

Dolph's spiteful gaze flicked toward the distant pavilion. Hawk followed his glance and saw Belinda standing by the entrance, illumined by the paper lanterns. To his relief she made no move to come closer, but remained there, watching and waiting anxiously.

"Beautiful, isn't she?" Hawk murmured.

"I've seen better."

Hawk laughed softly at the churlish reply. "As it happens, you have something that I want, as well, Breckinridge."

"What are you talking about? What do I have?"

"I think you know."

"I have no bloody idea what you mean."

"I may be willing to make an exchange of sorts," Hawk said, ignoring the shudder that rose up from his conscience as he made his cold-blooded proposal, even if it was only a false ploy.

"What kind of exchange?"

"Give me what I require and you shall have Belinda."

Dolph looked toward the pavilion where she stood, then glanced at Hawk nervously. "I don't know what you're after, Hawkscliffe, but Belinda is of no interest to me anymore. She's used goods."

"Maybe. Maybe not."

Dolph's nostrils flared. "What do you mean?"

"Maybe I didn't acquire Miss Hamilton for pleasure's sake, Dolph. Perhaps I had other reasons. Reasons concerning you personally."

"You bloody cold fish, you mean you haven't even managed to bed her yet?" he exclaimed.

"A gentleman never tells—but you know what the epicureans say. The sweetest morsels should not be gobbled up at the first possible moment, but savored longest, saved for last. You see, Dolph? There is still a shred of hope for you. If you follow my instructions precisely, you may still have her. If you botch it or attempt to cross me, then I will most certainly take her to my bed and press her skills to the limit."

"What do you want?"

"Information."

"About what?"

"I think you know."

"I don't know! Would you speak plain? God, you're worse than my bloody snake of an uncle."

"Mind your temper, Dolph. It will catch up with you one day."

"Tell me what you want! I want Belinda back. What do you want in exchange?"

"She was never yours in the first place, Dolph. I would hardly be giving her 'back.' "

"Hawkscliffe!"

"Ah, well, I can see the time is not yet ripe. You are not yet willing to own up."

"To what?" he cried.

Hawk began casually sauntering back to the pavilion, hands in pockets.

"Hawkscliffe!"

"By and by, Breckinridge. I'll be in contact with you."

Bel watched Robert striding toward her, hands in pockets, returning from his fight victorious. A quick dusting off of his black superfine tailcoat and a slight tug of his pearly white waistcoat and cravat sufficed to put him back into impeccable order. He smiled at her with a soft, possessive glow in his dark eyes and offered his arm. Together they went back inside.

Though Dolph, the main target of their charade, had left, somehow neither of them wanted to cast off the masquerade. They feigned mutual attraction very well, she thought. She even lured him out to the dance floor for a waltz.

Vauxhall wasn't Almack's, but their waltz together was glorious nonetheless. Her cheeks glowed and her head felt light with the dreamlike whirl of the dance as Robert swept her over the parquet floor in effortless athletic grace.

Adoringly she gazed up at him, turning and revolving about the floor in his arms until the disapproving world blurred into a smear of meaningless color around them and there was only him, his smile, his eyes.

At midnight they went out hand in hand and found a good spot by the river from which to view the nightly Vauxhall fireworks. Standing behind her Robert wrapped his arms around her waist to keep her snug and warm against the chill of evening, for there was a fair breeze along the Thames. She laid her head back against his chest and gazed at the exploding sky with a contented sigh. She looked up at him and watched the bright colors from the Chinese fire play across his aquiline features in red and silver and blue. The starlight seemed to dance on his lashes.

Even in the town coach on the way home, they both seemed unwilling to give up their charade. It all had felt so good. With the lateness of the hour, Robert took her into his strong, warm arms and held her, letting her drowse with her head on his broad shoulder. Neither of them broke the precious silence, as though one wrong word might clip the newfound bond between them, fragile as a golden thread.

When they arrived at Knight House they lingered at the top of the grand marble staircase, for the time had come to say good night. They gazed at each other longingly and both looked away.

Abruptly, she broke the nervous silence. "I—I think it went well," she said, her expression earnest.

He gave a stilted nod. "Er, yes."

"Robert?"

His stare homed in on her, flashing with desire like lightning, but he didn't move a muscle. He seemed to be holding his breath. "Yes?"

Her heart was pounding. Cowardice checked her.

"I—I had a wonderful time."

"Good. I mean, that was the idea. Me, too." He wet his lips and dropped his gaze, standing as rigidly as the gleaming suit of armor in the foyer. "Well—good night, then."

"Good night, Robert."

He bowed. She turned and began walking away, stopped and whirled around again. Hands in pockets, he was still standing there gazing after her, looking lonely, wistful, and a trifle forlorn, his cheekbones sculpted by the dim candlelight from the wall branch.

"What is it, my dear?" he asked softly.

"You will still take me to the Fleet tomorrow? Remember? You promised—"

"I never forget my promises, Miss Hamilton. Sweet dreams."

She offered him a tentative smile then whisked about and hurried to her room before she did something rash.

⊰ CHAPTER ⊱
EIGHT

The simple straightforward company of men this morning at his club had cured Hawk temporarily of desiring a woman he did not want to want.

His mood was a trifle irritable after another poor night's rest spent tossing and turning with wanting her. Charade within charade, he thought, determined to go on playing the plaster saint, beyond temptation. In a brisk, businesslike manner, he returned at one o'clock, as promised, to escort her to the Fleet. It was none of his business, but Hawk had half a mind to tell Mr. Hamilton precisely what he thought of his stupid folly.

Belinda had gone out shopping in the morning and had bought her father an assortment of gifts for his comfort, one of which was today's copy of the *Times*. As Hawk's town coach rolled down Faringdon Street toward the sprawling prison, she opened the paper.

"Just . . . checking," she murmured as she scanned the gossip page.

He had noticed that she had been tense throughout the drive as she sat across from him in the coach. She looked as pretty as the spring day in her high-waisted blue gown, light spencer, and white gloves. She paled, quickly shutting the newspaper again and throwing it away from her with a grimace.

"Bad news?" he asked.

142

"We're in there."

He snorted and shook his head. Why did the world care, anyway, who was courting whom? Was there no such thing as privacy? When they arrived at the Fleet, she left the *Times* behind and stepped down from his coach. She hooked her hand through the crook of his arm and lagged behind as they walked toward the great arched entrance.

To look at her ashen face, one would have thought she was being led to her execution. Her gaze climbed up the mighty, stone-block wall while her hands twisted the ribbons of her reticule so tautly that they nearly snapped. On the right the fortresslike walls of the prison yard loomed, spikes set in their tops to prevent escapes. These, too, she studied in shrinking trepidation.

"Come, Belinda, I'm sure there is nothing to fear," he said rather impatiently. He was not eager for this to take any longer than necessary. The place was unpleasant and he had to be at the House of Lords by two.

She glanced at him. The footman stared blankly ahead, standing behind her, laden with the presents for her father.

"We don't have to go in if you don't want to," he said more gently. "I can send my servant—"

"No. I have to see Papa," she forced out. "I'm all he has."

He touched her under the chin, realizing that it must be quite a humiliation for her to reveal her family's disgrace to him. "Your loyalty is very sweet. I only wonder if he deserves it."

"He is my father. Of course he deserves it. Robert, you said you would do this with me. Don't abandon me now—"

"I'm right here," he said softly, puzzled by her near-panicked countenance. And then it came to him that he was presently undergoing some kind of test, in her eyes. He stared at her, wondering just what was required of him. "I'll be right there beside you, Belinda. Are you ready?"

"Yes—yes. I owe you for this, Robert." Her smile was tepid at best as she pulled up her poke bonnet and took his arm again. "Remember, he doesn't know . . . about me."

"I'm aware of that," he replied tersely. Lord, how had he gotten himself into this? Never in his life did he imagine that he should have been forced to meet the father of his courtesan mistress. This was surely a bad idea, he mentally grumbled as he led her inside. Demirep or not, she was a gently bred young woman and had no business exposing herself to such a place. Still, he had to admire her sense of a daughter's duty.

He could feel her trembling slightly. She stayed huddled close to him as they walked in together, clinging to him when they passed the office of the warden of the Fleet. The door was ajar. Belinda was walking on the opposite side of him, her face hidden behind her poke bonnet, but Hawk glanced in curiously at the sound of rough shouting.

A scarred brute—obviously the warden—was dressing down one of his cringing subordinates. He shook his head. What a hellhole, he thought.

A guard led them through various corridors. Everywhere the prison was cramped and foul smelling, chaotic and noisy, with prisoners begging and cursing at them through the bars. Grimly Hawk clenched his jaw and put his arm around Belinda's shoulders, pulling her closer under his arm, wishing he could protect her from the filth.

On the far end of the corridor they were brought to a more decent ward. His defensive stance eased only mildly when they were led up a flight of stairs to where the more genteel debtors had private rooms.

When they stopped at a solid wooden door before one of the private cells, Belinda pushed back her bonnet. Her face was a sickly shade of white. Hawk pursed his mouth and hung back, not sure if she wanted him to follow her inside or wait. Belinda stared straight ahead. He saw her lift her chin; he saw her plaster on a smile. Something inside of him wrenched at the way her slender shoulders squared.

The jailer opened the door, and her face suddenly beamed.

"Papa!"

She threw out her arms and rushed into the cell with a laugh that sounded oddly brittle. Hawk stepped into the doorway and saw her throw herself into the arms of a white-haired, bespectacled man.

"Linda-bel! Oh, welcome back, dear, welcome back! You are looking better than when I saw you last. Must be the French food that agreed with you, hey, hey? So tell me— how did you like Paris?"

For no apparent reason and entirely without warning, she burst into tears. The old man pulled his spectacles up higher on his nose and peered at her. "What is this foolishness, you little watering pot?"

She was quite too hysterical to answer. Hawk decided it was time to take matters into his own hands. He cleared his throat to make his presence known and strode into the room, swept off his top hat and gestured his footman in with the goods.

"Mr. Hamilton, I presume?" He offered the old scholar his hand. "Robert Knight, at your service."

Her father shook his hand hesitantly, peering up at him. "Mr. Knight, you say? How do you do? Are you a friend of Bel's, and if you are, can you tell me why the chit's crying?"

Belinda hung around her father's neck. "It's just that I'm so happy to see you, Papa. I missed you so while I was in"—she looked pleadingly at Hawk—"Paris."

Hawk furrowed his brow and stared at her, then abandoned his attempt to make sense of it. "Your daughter has brought you a few trifles for your comfort, Mr. Hamilton."

"He's not a mister, Papa. He's the duke of Hawkscliffe. He's very modest. To a fault," she whispered, sniffling.

"Oh!" Alfred laughed with delight at his error. "I beg your pardon, Your Grace."

"It is of no consequence." Hawk knew he was turning imperious and curt, but he couldn't help but glare at the old scholar for the wretched look on Belinda's lovely face. What was the man thinking? Illuminated manuscripts over this precious girl?

"I'm sorry," she sniffled. "You're right—I'm being quite absurd. I just missed you, you old enchanter. Now have a look at what I've brought you." Wiping her tears away quickly, she moved to the cot where Hawk's servant had placed the gifts. "See here, Papa? A new pillow and blanket, brandy and some snuff—"

"Do I like snuff, Linda-bel? Why, I don't recall!" He laughed as though his empty head was the funniest thing in the world.

Hawk scowled and turned away.

"I don't know, Papa, but you can bribe the guards with it, if nothing else."

"Oh! Right. So clever, my girl! You didn't happen to bring me any, er . . . books, did you?" he asked, fidgeting like a child on Christmas morning.

"Of course I did."

Father and daughter proceeded to coo over the trio of new books she had brought for him, exceedingly dull treatises on medieval and classical history that made Hawk and his footman exchange a nonplussed look.

At last the old fellow turned to him. "Your Grace, why don't we open the brandy Bel has brought and give it a nip, hey?"

For his easy, gentlemanly manner, one might have thought they were standing in Hamilton's study rather than his jail cell.

Hawk smiled blandly. "No, sir, but thank you for the offer."

"How, er, do you know my daughter, by the by?" he asked almost gingerly.

Finally the man showed a glimmer of sense.

If it were his daughter showing up dressed in finery with a strange man by her side, that would have been the first question on his lips, after perhaps knocking the man to the ground. Hawk drew breath to answer but Miss Hamilton didn't give him the chance.

"His Grace has been the soul of kindness, Papa. His maiden sister, Lady Jacinda Knight was one of the students I chaperoned to Paris."

"Ah," the man replied, smiling cheerfully at Hawk. "How nice."

Hawk furrowed his brow. He could not recall telling her his sister's name.

"Bel, my dear," Alfred continued, "will you be teaching at Mrs. Hall's Academy again next year?"

Hawk's left eyebrow shot up. *Teaching?*

Belinda scrupulously avoided his gaze, moving about the room at a fidgety pace.

"I will if there's a need, Papa. I don't mind the work, but by next year, we shall surely be back in Kelmscot. I almost have all the money saved."

"Oh! Right, right. Right you are. Well done, daughter! Isn't she a clever thing, Mr.—I mean, Your Grace?"

Hawk stared at Belinda, feeling as though he were seeing her for the first time.

As though she could feel him mentally plodding through the nonsensical conversation, unraveling things she'd never told him, she shot him a glance full of mixed warning and plea.

"Did you convey the girls to Paris, Your Grace?" her father asked him hesitantly.

"Of course not, Papa," Belinda answered for Hawk with a scolding smile, flicking her father's arm. "His Grace is much too important a man to be carting little debutantes around the Continent."

With a nervous laugh that sounded nothing like the aloof, impervious star of the demimonde, she turned away again and began making up her father's cot with fresh linens, spreading the new quilt over it and plumping up the expensive goose-down pillow she had bought.

Hawk watched her with his heart breaking. It would have been easy, so very easy, to go to the magistrate and get her father out of debtor's prison, but he knew he would not.

The sum was a pittance to a man of his means, but the feather-brained fool deserved his confinement as punishment for his daughter's suffering. Besides, if he were to spring Hamilton from the Fleet, Belinda might no longer choose to stay with him and, hang it all, he needed her. Needed her to solve the mystery of Lucy's death. Needed her in his house, sitting at his out-of-tune piano.

When the jailer came back and said the time allowed for their visit was up, Belinda hugged her father good-bye and promised to come again in a couple of days. She asked him if there was anything he needed; old Hamilton said he should be delighted to have more paper and ink. Then he turned to Hawk with an ingenuous gaze.

"It comforts me greatly to know my daughter has a trusty friend in that large world beyond these bars, Your Grace. I'm in your debt." His artless words of thanks were spoken so disarmingly, Hawk nodded and shook his offered hand.

Turning away from her father Belinda sent Hawk a fleeting look of soul-deep gratitude as she passed him on her way to the cell door. That look made it all worthwhile. Huffing with irritation at his own softheadedness, he pivoted and followed her out of the cell. His now empty-handed footman brought up the rear of their trio as they followed the jailer back the way they had come in.

Now that he had met Hamilton, he could see why Belinda had taken such drastic measures to keep him in the prison's cleaner, warmer, and healthier upper regions. The old gentleman would not have survived in the crowded and violent mass cells.

Still, he didn't know what he was going to say to her when they were alone. *A finishing-school teacher?* The only sense he could make of it all was that she must have been teaching at Mrs. Hall's, waiting for her soldier boy to come home from the war to marry her, had eventually given up on both and decided on a more lucrative career to save her father and herself. Right now he didn't even want to think about her relationship with Jacinda.

Suddenly they heard the sound of fighting and furious shouts up ahead. As they turned the corner into the next dim echoing corridor, they came upon a brutal scene. The scarred warden whom Hawk had seen downstairs, a grizzly giant of a man with a huge key ring clanging at his waist, had thrown a defiant young male prisoner against the wall. The great brute was dealing out ruthless discipline with his bludgeon.

Hawk put out his hand, stopping Belinda. He knew the warden was only doing his rough and dangerous job, but he certainly didn't want her to see it.

"Halt, darling." He swiftly scanned the area with a glance. "Is there another exit?" he began, turning to the guard, but the man was already in motion, running to assist his superior officer.

Then Hawk noticed Belinda.

She was standing in a state of eerie calm, her face pale and expressionless as she stared at the graphic scene of punishment. In the dark corridor she was as pale and silent as a ghost, or an angel hovering by, looking saddened yet detached from it all. Blond tendrils of her hair waved softly in the draft down the corridor.

Hawk clenched his jaw, determined to get her out of here now. He would have to find another way out. He reached for her hand and clasped it.

"Come, darling," he murmured, but she didn't move.

"I'm not running from him," she said, and her voice fell as softly as rose petals over the screams of the prisoner.

Holding on to his hand like a child, she ignored his protest and began walking forward.

There were no cannons firing in her war, no bullets' blast. The armies that clashed in that moment were within her, fighting as though they would tear her soul apart, but she refused to run. She knew she must stand now, not cowering in the shadow of her powerful protector, but passing, look the monster in the eye and let him see she would no longer fear him. Perhaps he would not even comprehend, but *she* would know she had done it, and that would be enough.

I will not run. I will not run. ı will not run, she thought over and over with every step, though the jangling of his keys rasped through her consciousness like broken glass.

It was that sound that rang through her nightmares.

She was afraid—so afraid—and shaking, icy with fear down to her fingertips. But she had risen again after he had torn her down and now she had an ally, his hand in hers.

"Belinda—"

"It's all right," she heard herself say distantly, over the rushing of her blood in her ears. God bless Robert, he didn't understand, but he went with her.

Either the unfortunate prisoner had ceased to give offense or the warden became aware of their slow approach. In any case, he straightened up, moving with lumbering weight, the bludgeon in his hand—hard, cruel, smeared with blood.

And then he turned and looked straight at her.

Bel felt her throat close with panic. Everything moved slowly, like that night in the alley. Time bled to a trickle. She wanted to flee, bolt like a horse for the barn in a thunderstorm. But staunchly, she held her ground—nauseous, shaking, and freezing cold. Her body trembled with hatred, her jaw was clenched so hard that it hurt.

A slight, bestial smile thinned the warden's mouth and she could see him waiting for her to flinch or to betray what he had done. She did neither. Her stomach twisted in a hard knot, but her face remained impassive. She willed herself to find steely-nerved grit somewhere amid the pain that she had learned to live with. Robert said she had ballast in her hull. She'd remember that.

She advanced.

This surprised the warden, she could tell. His mean-eyed gaze flicked to Robert.

Bel suddenly wondered if she had just led her keeper into danger—but when she looked up at him beside her, she saw Robert deal the man a lordly look of distaste. She smiled faintly in cold satisfaction as it dawned on the warden that she now had a powerful friend. *Protector.* He came from a line of warriors and his name was Knight. Who could best him?

The warden glanced suspiciously at her again, realizing, she supposed, that they were at a stalemate—her silence of his crime in exchange for her father's safety. Little did he know he needn't have worried. The thought of Robert or any of her admirers finding out that she had lost her virginity to this ogre filled her with terrorized shame. Fine dresses and haughty airs had fooled them into thinking her such a prize. How she had duped them—she, the frigid courtesan, dirtier and less than a whore. Why, even to Robert, she was merely bait.

Without a word exchanged, her protector and she and the footman passed the crumpled prisoner, the warden, and the guard.

She knew she had won this battle, but the warden took the last jab at her in the form of a snicker that followed her down the corridor. He jangled his keys with jaunty nonchalance, and the sound of it was nearly her undoing.

She released Robert's hand and walked ahead heedlessly when, at last, she was just a few steps from the arched entrance of the Fleet. Gasping for breath, she pushed through the door. She looked up at the reeling sky, her head woozy, black rings exploding across her field of vision. She felt Robert's hands steadying her. She clutched his forearm, holding on to him and fighting not to faint. He slipped a supportive arm around her waist.

"Belinda, you look positively ill, are you all right?" His cultured baritone seemed to come to her through a thick wall of glass.

A wave of pain washed through her. God, how she wanted him to reach her—shatter the glass box she had sealed herself into and lift her out of it—and hold her to him, his naked chest to hers, nothing left to hide. But that would never be. Not love. Not for her.

"I'm—fine," she forced out, pulling away as she slowly regrouped. "Thank you."

She heard him mutter an order for the footman to go for the coach. He paced on the pavement while she waited in stony silence for the coach to come.

"Belinda, I don't want you coming back to this hellhole," he clipped out, giving her a fierce look of command.

Slowly she lowered her head. "Do you think that I want to?"

"Then don't."

She hadn't the strength to argue right now. She had to come back, of course. Her father was in there. For the barest moment it was on the tip of her tongue to simply ask Robert flat out to lend her the money to spring him, but her pride had taken too many blows of late. She was no charity child and his opinion of her was low enough without adding beggary to whoredom.

He paced nearer and stopped a foot or two away, his hands in his pockets. She gathered all of her courage and lifted her chin, coolly meeting his gaze. He studied her keenly. His dark, penetrating eyes seemed to stare right into the morass of her soul.

She couldn't speak a word or look away.

He shook his head at her, looking exasperated, but his voice was soft. "You should have let me take you out by a different route. You didn't need to see so much brutality, Belinda."

She nearly laughed aloud. The innocent. If only he knew. His simple gallant goodness brought tears to her eyes. "My paragon," she whispered.

"Why do you call me that? It isn't funny." He scowled and stepped back from her, looking so stuffy and pompous that she found the strength to smile as the elegant town coach rolled to a halt before them.

They climbed up and she sat beside him, laying her head on his broad shoulder. She knew he was peeved at her, but rather than protesting he shifted to make her more comfortable, putting his arm around her. She closed her eyes, exhausted after her private victory. He had the nicest smell and his arm around her was firm and strong, his hard, muscled shoulder a firm pillow for her head.

You helped me, she thought. You don't know it, but you gave me the strength to get through it.

"You should listen to me next time," he grumbled, trying to sound cross.

"I will, darling. Whatever you say," she whispered with the trace of a smile, thanking God for the man. *Just let me stay with you.*

≈ CHAPTER ≈ NINE

The temperamental English weather had gone unseasonably cold and had unleashed a torrent of rain by the time Hawk stalked out of the House of Lords that night at half past ten, hungry, tired, and grouchy. To make matters worse, he had a deuced headache from arguing through the supper hour with Eldon and Sidmouth and their ultra-Tory cronies, and then he had been too disgusted with their bloodthirsty views to eat.

All the while muddled thoughts of Belinda had churned in his head, troubling and confusing him and weaving themselves in with his starved libido until his brain was one big knot.

Riding home through Westminster he gazed out the window, watching the wind and rain buffet the plane trees as his rocking carriage rolled down the Mall. On a few of the wrought-iron lampposts, the feeble flames had been extinguished, leaving gaps in the lamp row that were as dark as his mulling brain.

This business about Jacinda and Paris and Mrs. Hall's Academy for Young Ladies—had it been truth or falsity, and could he afford even to care one way or the other?

The thought that a courtesan had been formerly molding the character of his already-headstrong maiden sister appalled him. For Jacinda's welfare, he had to find out the truth, only he wasn't sure he wanted to know anything more about Miss Hamilton than he already did.

He was trying, oh, Lord, how he was trying to keep a polite distance between them, not to get involved with her, but he felt himself being dragged helplessly into her orbit as if by some vast, cosmic magnet that women like her wielded and used to enslave rich, titled men like him. It wasn't bloody fair, that's what. Frowning out the coach window as the prickling rain blew sideways against the glass, he rubbed his throbbing temples and reviewed what he knew about Miss Belinda Hamilton.

There were troubling gaps in his knowledge. He wondered, for instance, how exactly she had become a courtesan. To have asked would have been shockingly bad form, so he supposed he'd never know unless she offered the information, but that seemed improbable. Unlike every other garrulous female he knew, Miss Hamilton was supremely unforthcoming with facts about herself. She was not telling and he was not asking. And why should he ask her questions about herself? he thought indignantly. There was nothing between them but a practical arrangement, useful to them both.

Yet, as he listened to the rain's drumming on his coach's roof, it bothered him to wonder, not for the first time, which of his acquaintances or club mates at White's had purchased her innocence. Hertford? He was debauched enough—or had she given it freely to that thoughtless soldier boy on his vapid promise of marriage at some future date? he mused as the coach pulled through the gates of Knight House. It is none of your business, Hawk. You don't care, it doesn't matter, leave it alone, he said to himself.

Fairly growling in irritation and suppressed lust, he got out and sloshed through the puddles between his halted coach and his front door, half-soaked by the time he stepped into the well-lighted entrance hall. He was barely through the door when Belinda walked toward him from the corridor, graceful and serene.

"Oh, look at you, you poor thing," she said.

God, she was lovely, he thought with a catch of longing in his throat. She was dressed with subdued elegance in a Manila brown silk gown with a choker of pearls around her creamy neck and her golden hair gathered up in a chignon. She glided toward him, her eyes dark as smoky as sapphires, glittering with sensuality as she swept him with an assessing gaze, taking in his wearied state.

"Welcome home, darling." She took his leather document box from his grasp and handed it off to the butler who had just closed the door. "Put this in His Grace's study," she ordered quietly.

Walsh bowed. "Yes, ma'am," he conceded, then went to obey.

Hawk stared after his butler, rather surprised at Walsh's civil tone toward her, then he looked warily at Belinda, instantly sensing that she was up to something. But as he studied her, his heart skipped a beat and his seething questions from the carriage fell into sand that scattered and blew away.

How could mere reason stand against the sensory power of her presence—her willowy walk, her pearlescent skin, her gardenia perfume, the gleam of candlelight on her moist lips from the chandelier above them? She was the most mysterious, alluring woman he had ever seen, devil take her, and it was all he could do to fight the fascination.

She gave him a soothing smile and stepped behind him, gently helping him out of his wet coat. "Let me take this, dear. Have you eaten?"

"I'm famished," he growled.

"Good. I kept supper warm for you. Come." She turned

and walked coolly down the hallway toward the dining room, her silken dress whispering around her long legs.

Rather baffled by her managing cordiality and the change he sensed pervading his entire household, he ran his hand through his damp hair and followed, too hungry to give it much thought. His mouth was already watering as he took his place at the head of the long mahogany table.

Belinda gave an order to one of the maids, who curtsied then scampered off to do her bidding. Wafting over to the side table where a bottle of white wine was chilling in a bucket of ice, she poured him a glass while Hawk wondered what the devil had happened here while he was gone.

What on earth had she done to his servants? This morning they had thought her a veritable Jezebel, so why tonight were they looking so sharp at her orders?

Bringing him his wine, she noticed his confounded expression and gave him a wry smile. "I called a little meeting of the upper servants while you were out."

"Pray, did you resort to witchcraft or was it merely bribery?"

"Neither. I simply reminded them of the honor they enjoy in serving at Knight House and how it is not their place to judge their master's actions, and I said—well, never mind what I said. Suffice to say, they have seen that I am not to be trifled with . . . Your Grace," she added with a demure bow, then she glided back and poured herself a glass.

"Is that is a warning to me, as well?"

Laughing softly, she came back to the table and quietly sat down on the chair to his right. "How was the session?"

"Maddening," he grumbled as he tore a piece of bread.

"Oh? What happened?"

She listened quietly, resting her cheek in her hand, nodding as, none-too-patiently, he recounted his argument with

Eldon and Sidmouth, then complained about his bloody miserable headache. By the time the footmen brought out his dinner, however, he had gotten much of his frustration off his chest and was ready to eat.

When the silver lid was removed from his plate, he discovered one of his favorite dishes—lamb cutlets *à la braise* with tender, butter-soaked asparagus. Belinda poured him red wine to accompany the meat and he dug in.

She sipped her wine, staring into the tongue of flame atop the candle. "We've got to set a date for our dinner party, Robert."

"Hm?" he asked, devouring his lamb.

"I'll need a guest list from you. The sooner we have these gentlemen over, the better. I won't be here forever, after all." She gave him a veiled smile and took a sip of her wine.

"Do you really expect these bullheaded old men to change their views about the affairs of the state just because you bat your pretty lashes?"

"Changing their views is *your* job, Robert. I can at least get them to listen to you. It will have to be a dinner for the gentlemen only. Their wives obviously won't come with me as hostess. For your reputation's sake, I daren't invite Harriette and her friends to entertain the men, either, or your house will become known as a brothel."

"Is this really a good idea?"

"Trust me. Write me a guest list. I'll take it from there."

"You scare me," he muttered.

She chuckled and touched his arm in fond affection. In spite of himself he smiled at her.

For dessert there was raspberry tart and almond cream to enjoy with his snifter of brandy. By the end of the excellent meal he was a new man. He stretched his arms above his head in sated contentment and quickly stifled a great yawn.

Belinda warmly took his hand. "Come, I have a surprise for you."

He gazed at her, intrigued. "What kind of surprise?"

"If I told you, would it be a surprise, Robert? Now be a good boy and come."

He picked up his brandy and let her lead him by the hand into the library. A low fire crackled, holding off the night's unusual chill. He sauntered in, looking around curiously. Another present? he wondered. His mood was greatly improved but his headache persisted.

"I hope you don't mind the fire. With the weather so miserable, I thought—"

"Fine," he mumbled.

"Sit in your chair," she ordered, folding her hands behind her back.

All too gladly he dropped into his large leather armchair by the fireplace. He waited.

"Put your head back and close your eyes."

He obeyed.

He heard her moving in the room, then it was quiet. A moment later the first slow, tender notes rose from the pianoforte. He opened his eyes and stared at her while she played for him. Obviously she had had the Graf tuned while he was out.

For a fraction of a moment he wanted to be angry at her presumption, meddling in his life, but he could not sustain indignation before the ripple of gladness that moved through him as he recognized the opening bars of "Voi che Sapete," Cherubino's sweet and graceful aria from the *Marriage of Figaro*.

A finishing-school girl's piece, he thought, smiling to himself as he watched her reading the music in most earnest absorption. She did not sing for him, but he knew the words:

You, who have master'd Love's gentle art,
tell me what ails me here in my heart . . .
Strange agitations, trembling desires,
blissful sensations, blistering fires?
Shiv'ring will seize me, then burning pain,
then in a moment, freezing again!
I seek for something charming and good,
never encounter'd, not understood,
a thing I sigh for against my will,
a thing I fly from, pursuing still,
a thing that haunts me, day and night,
and how perplexing, how sad my plight.
You who have master'd Love's gentle art,
tell me what ails me here in my heart.

He rested his elbow on the chair's arm and propped his chin on his loose fist, watching his mistress and savoring her playing in pure pleasure, more from the sweetness of her intention than for her skill.

This, he thought, was a beautiful gift. He closed his eyes and put his head back as she had directed and let himself unwind.

Life was good.

Her playing ended, but he didn't open his eyes, thoroughly relaxed at last. The library was a huge, black, echoing hollow behind him as he slouched in the large wing chair by the fire, the rounded snifter of brandy resting in his palm, the stem dangling between his fingers.

The dancing flames cast orange light over his face, steeped in shadow. His waistcoat was unbuttoned. He had been running his fingers through his hair to try to lessen the throbbing headache that plagued him, leaving his hair slightly tousled. His eyelids felt too heavy to lift as he heard the whisper of silk and smelled the wafting scent of Belinda as she approached him.

"How's the headache?" she asked, her voice soft and intimate in the black vast emptiness of the room.

"Alive and well," he murmured without moving or opening his eyes. "You play very tolerably indeed, Miss Hamilton."

"Not nearly as well as you do, I'm told."

"I'm rusty."

"Why don't you play anymore?"

"I haven't the time."

He heard her soft sigh. "Our souls need music, Robert, as our bodies need touch." He felt her take the brandy gently out of his hand, but he did not respond. She nudged his sprawled legs wider apart and stepped between them, bending down to untie his cravat. He opened his eyes lazily and stared at her.

He considered protesting. "Pray, what are you doing, Miss Hamilton?" he asked in a tone of mild curiosity.

"Making you more comfortable."

"Ah." He closed his eyes again, enjoying the peculiar sensation of her ladylike fingers plucking free the careful knot of his starchy cravat until, a moment later, she tugged on it and slid it off of him.

She caressed his bared throat lightly then unbuttoned the top of his crisply starched white shirt.

"Better?" she murmured as she ran her hand slowly down his chest.

He made a sound somewhere between a grunt of assent and a groan of need. His heart was pounding and his eyes were closed.

Laying her hand on his shoulder, she casually rounded his chair to stand behind him; he was savagely aware of her. His whole body quivered when she ran her fingers through his hair.

"Pray, what are you doing now, Miss Hamilton?" he asked stiffly.

"Easing your headache, my darling. Relax."

Vexed with want, he tried to obey as she petted his hair very gently. Had she no idea how she tempted him?

"Where does it hurt?" she murmured. "Here?"

"Mm," he admitted as she pressed her thumbs into two spots that pounded at the base of his skull. Her thumbs circled in gentle insistence over his bunched neck muscles until they began to loosen by degrees.

Moments passed.

"Belinda," he said gingerly at length, making his tone courteous for fear that one wrong word would make her stop giving him this glorious pleasure, "all that business at the Fleet today about Paris and your being a finishing-school teacher—was it true?"

Her kneading hands paused. "Robert, my dearest." Her tone was gently chiding with a hint of drollery. "What makes you think our arrangement entitles you to full disclosure of the particulars of my past?"

"Where my sister is concerned, your past *is* my business."

"Well, never fear, I did not corrupt your sister. Lady Jacinda is quite safe. Though I daresay the girl is impetuous and I hazard to guess it is for want of a mother's guiding hand."

"I've done my best," he said defensively.

She laughed very softly and ran her fingers through his hair. "I'm sure you have, darling, in all things. But *you* are a man," she added in a meaningful whisper.

"You are evading my question."

"Very well, if you must know, I taught French, music, history, and deportment at Mrs. Hall's Academy for a while. It was my final respectable position before—this."

Hawk closed his eyes and scratched his eyebrow, reigning in his vexation. It was one matter to have a courtesan rubbing one's shoulders, but a blasted finishing-school teacher was another affair.

"Dolph contrived to have me dismissed," she continued. "He came every day for a month, trying to see me, and finally convinced the headmistress that he was my lover— that I was neither respectable nor chaste, and a bad influence on the girls. Mrs. Hall concluded I was a threat to the students, that my 'conduct' would endanger the moral well-being of my girls, and I was fired."

"Didn't you tell her Dolph was lying?"

"Of course. But you know how stodgy Mrs. Hall can be, if you've had any dealings with the woman through Lady Jacinda. She was worried about the prestige of the school, but I didn't want any taint to touch my girls' reputations before they had even made their debut in Society," she added. "For their sake, I gave the job up without much of a fight."

"Then what did you do?"

"I went to Harriette and then I came to you."

"Ah," he said, sensing some subtle note in her voice that warned him he had trod onto dangerous ground.

"Now, Your Grace, would you kindly hush and enjoy your massage? Or shall I stop?"

He tilted his head back and smiled ruefully at her. "I won't say another word."

With a subdued answering smile, she caressed his cheek, roughened by his day's beard. "You're a handsome devil, Hawkscliffe. When you're not scowling, anyway. Put your head back."

He obeyed. She caressed, kneaded, and rubbed his neck and shoulders, silent at her work. To his surprise, her ministrations helped.

"Feels good?"

"Mmmm."

Gradually Hawk allowed himself to drift into the pleasure of her touch. Slowly the tension began easing from him.

"Yes, that's better, my love," she whispered, running her warm, sure hands up slowly from the sides of his neck to stroke his long-clenched jaw.

He grew lax and mesmerized by sensation. His body was hers, clay in her hands. Behind his closed eyes he imagined what he wanted to do to her. *Fille de joie. Pleasure girl.* Meanwhile, she caressed his temples carefully, then her fingertips feathered lightly over his forehead, pressing tiny hollows under the curve of his eyebrows, holding points there that only ticked dully now.

She paused—just long enough for a pang of disappointment to flash through him to think she was done with him—but he was mistaken. Brushing her knuckles silkily against both sides of his face and down his neck, she reached over his shoulders and unfastened a few more buttons down his shirt. Then she slid her hands inside of it, caressing his bare chest, exploring him.

Hawk tensed with want, his heartbeat slamming. He didn't dare open his eyes for fear that this was all a dream and he sorely didn't want it to end; he felt her unbutton his shirt the rest of the way until her silken hands brushed it open against his sides. The coolness of the air grazed his skin and the warmth of the nearby fire tinged his belly, warmed his groin.

As she reached over his shoulders, he felt her soft face beside his, nestling against his cheek as her hands glided across his chest and down his belly. His flesh raged with agonizing, craving life beneath her sweet, seeking touch. Anticipation swept through him like a fire, need such as he had never known with any lover in the past. *Touch me. Oh, God, yes, please touch me, help me.* His breathing pulled deeply. He gripped the chair arms, waiting to see what she would do.

He felt her kiss his ear, tonguing his earlobe lightly, and he fell thoroughly under her spell. But then he let out a soft groan of soul-deep gratitude and sprawled his thighs when she molded her hand over his hardness through his black trousers, petting him.

Perhaps she was waiting to see if he would protest, but he could not, being completely in her thrall.

His chest heaved; he was poised and throbbing as she touched him then unfastened his trousers and slid her hand down inside.

"Oh, *Robert,*" she whispered in approval as she grasped his smooth, rigid shaft and caressed him, base to tip and back again.

He moaned and lifted his hips, hungry for more. She gave it, freed him completely from his trousers and stroked him, lightly at first and then more firmly. His hands curled over the chair arms with a white-knuckled grip.

He could feel her watching his face, as though studying his reaction to every little nuance of her touch . . . learning the exact specifications of his pleasure like a true professional. The tip of her tongue followed the curve of his ear, driving him wild.

He turned his head, sought her lips, and kissed her in trembling greed as she gripped him, endlessly stroking. All of a sudden, her touch stopped. She ended the kiss and he opened his eyes, hazy and glittering. He looked up at her in shocked dismay from under his tousled hair. She couldn't possibly leave him like this. He'd pay her anything.

But she was not leaving, he saw in shameless relief, she was only walking around to the front of him. He stared at her in need and wonder and want, knowing that he had dreamed of this with her. She held his gaze, her beautiful face seductive and cool, her eyes dark orchid blue, shimmering with desire.

Laying her hands on his broad thighs, she slowly lowered herself to her knees between his legs. He waited breathlessly, entranced; he had never been so aroused in his life. Like some beautiful pagan worshiper, she ran her hands up his bare chest, kissing as she went. She raked her fingers through the wiry hair on his chest and flicked his nipples with her tongue while, lower, she cupped her hand to him and fondled his rigid cock.

Hawk could not believe his good fortune. He had not asked for this, hadn't bought this; she didn't *have* to do it—and that only meant that, right here and now, it wasn't his money that she wanted—it was him.

Then his amazement fled before the onslaught of ecstasy as she kissed her way back down his stomach. She licked a light, teasing circle around his navel then parted her moist lips and slowly, tentatively took the crown of his towering erection into her warm, wet mouth. He dropped his head back against the chair with a delicious groan and touched her silky hair. She sucked him lovingly, her warm, firm hands vigorously stroking all the while to the very root of him and gently caressing him everywhere.

Gasping heavily with need, he ran his fingers through her hair, lowered his chin and watched her, brushing her cheek with his knuckle in stormy tender lust. Why—how—wherefore he had denied himself this for so long, he could not imagine.

After several minutes of sheer bliss, she glanced up with a wicked little harlot smile, the stuff of schoolboys' dreams, running the tip of her tongue up the length of him. She caught his eye with her sultry, knowing gaze, then bent her head again, swirling her tongue around and around his ultra-sensitive tip.

If her movements and her wide, adoring eyes when she lifted her lashes and gazed at him, held a certain ingenuous naivete, this slight betrayal of inexperience did not lessen his pleasure, but only enhanced it. Too much expertise on her part perhaps would have been disturbing. He could not resist her as it was.

After he knew not how long, she moved back and met his stare in steamy seduction; he held her glance in fierce, animal want. He longed to lift her skirts and let her ride him right here in the chair. But she had other ideas. She stayed on her knees, clasping his hips, raking him with her nails. Suddenly he captured her around her nape and dragged her to him, kissing her in luscious savagery.

He heard her soft moan of welcome under his ravishing kiss. God, he had wanted to kiss her like this since the first night he'd seen her at Harriette's. Nothing tame, nothing controlled. He wanted to let it all go with her, until he had melted the last crystal of ice that made up her haughty facade, love her like fire until he had freed the angel inside her.

At length she stopped him, pressing him back into his chair. He caught her hand, threading his fingers through hers.

"Let me make love to you," he whispered.

She shook her head with a slight, cool, mysterious smile. "Just enjoy."

He had no power to protest as she went down on him again. Opening her sweet mouth wider, she took him into her very throat, nearly choking on the size of him, then she eased off, sucking him wholeheartedly with new, unmistakable intent. He closed his eyes in surrender.

Deprived as he was, it didn't take long. While his groans of ecstasy filled the room, his young courtesan beauty moved back and brought him to orgasm with her hot, silken hands, a shattering release that spurted high upon his chest and belly.

"Oh, *God,* Belinda," he finally gasped out, collapsing back in his chair, utterly spent.

He was barely even aware that several moments had passed and she had risen to her feet, but presently she produced the unfolded muslin square of his cravat and tossed it on his belly with a sultry, knowing little smile.

"Feeling better, Hawkscliffe?"

He laughed, a lone, haggard syllable, as she delicately downed the last of his brandy. Nonchalantly, she took back the now sodden cravat and tossed it into the fire with a casual flick of her hand.

Hawk merely stared at her in shocked admiration, too sated to move a muscle.

What a woman.

In silence she sauntered back to him and fastened up his trousers again, then lingered near him, idly stroking his chest and shoulder with her fingertips. Her lashes veiled her downcast gaze.

"Are you going to sleep here? Shall I get you a blanket?"

He grasped her wrist gently and tugged her down onto his lap, slipping his arm around her waist so she couldn't escape. He brushed her disarrayed hair behind her ear, noting the veiled look of uncertainty in her eyes.

"Why did you do it?" he asked softly.

"Because you needed it. Didn't you like it?" she asked, instantly on the defensive.

"Oh, God, yes," he declared with a husky laugh. "Did you mind it?"

"Don't be absurd. You have been calling my skills as a courtesan into question since the night we met, and I thought you should be put in your place," she said haughtily, tense in his arms.

He gave a soft laugh and pressed a gentle kiss to her cheek. "Well, you have made a believer of me, Miss Hamilton. Feel free to put me in my place whenever you desire."

She lowered her lashes, smiling. They lingered like that for a moment, she, stiff and wary, he, nuzzling her cheek and the crook of her neck, trying to ease her. She felt warm and wonderful to hold.

"Did I do it right, Robert?" she asked almost shyly after a long moment. "Honestly? You can tell me the truth." He started to laugh at the absurdity of the question, but he went motionless when she added, "Because you see, I—I never—"

Shocked, he stared at her.

"You didn't like it," she said, stiffening as she read his face.

"No, you were glorious, my angel. Come here," he whispered, taking her face tenderly between his hands. He silenced her fretful worries with a light kiss that deepened. Slowly she allowed him to part her lips and taste her tongue. God help him, he believed her. But why had she chosen to bestow her gift on him? He trembled as he kissed her. She was his entire world in that moment, as his mouth caressed the satiny cushions of her lips; he drew her breath into his lungs and caught her tiny sigh on his tongue and lost himself in mesmerized worship, savoring the mouth that had consumed him.

Luscious and deep, he gave her a kiss to tell her everything he could not say. She began to melt into his embrace, returning his kiss more urgently, running her fingers through his hair. He felt her desire blossoming like a tight rosebud unfurling for the sun's slow sumptuous heat.

He trailed his hand down her neck, longed to kiss her there, but could not tear himself away from her sweet lips. Plying her mouth with gentle insistence, he caressed her pale hair and thought, God, girl, what are you doing to me?

A few minutes later she ended the kiss, breathing heavily. Pulling back, she stared at him, her violet-blue eyes vulnerable and haunted. He trailed his finger down the curve of her cheek. "Sleep with me. Let me return the favor—"

"*No.* Good night, Robert, I must go." She squirmed in his arms but he held her more tightly, smiling besottedly at her half-hearted struggles.

"Stay, lovely. Sleep in my arms." He cupped her face and leaned to kiss her again, but she slid away from him and swiftly padded out of the library in a whisper of silk.

Hawk frowned as the door closed. He wondered if he should go after her, but no. Whatever her reasons, Belinda didn't want to be touched right now and he refused to blunder with her. She knew better than any woman he had ever met how to keep a man at bay. How was a knight to scale her walls, storm her citadel, take the ivory tower of her heart? he mused, feeling lonely now that she had gone. As his troubled gaze wandered the perimeter of the library, it settled upon the tuned piano and it occurred to him that there were other senses she possessed which he could gratify.

"Our souls need music as our bodies need touch." Wise finishing-school courtesan, he thought, smiling ruefully.

With a great heave of effort, he got up out of his leather chair. His shirt and waistcoat hung open down his bare chest as he sauntered toward the piano, cracking his knuckles.

He sat down wearily at the bench, lifted the lid. With an odd pang of nostalgia for some part of himself that had gotten lost along the way, tentatively he touched a key, feeling the lonely note echo down into the well of his soul. If she would not accept his touch, he would give her music.

The ivories felt satin smooth beneath his fingertips. He paused and closed his eyes, drawing the most beloved piece he knew from his memory and hoping, for both their sakes, that he still remembered how to pour out his heart through his hands. . . .

* * *

Shaken up, fighting tears of confusion, Bel changed
into her dressing gown then stalked over to her satinwood
vanity.

That kiss. My God.

Her hand trembled as she poured water from the pitcher
into the wash basin. She set the pitcher aside and leaned
down to splash her face before bed, scrubbing it a bit too
roughly, all the while reeling inwardly with the blind despair of one who fights an invisible enemy.

She could not believe she had done it. Like a true, dyed-
in-the-wool prostitute, she had performed fellatio on the
duke of Hawkscliffe and he had been so . . . beautiful. So
beautiful in his surrender, so beautiful in his release, the
luminous haze of satisfaction in his dark eyes afterward.
She wasn't even sure herself what her motives had been,
but it seemed she had needed to flex her power over him—
to show him that all the while he judged her a whore, he
failed to realize she knew exactly how to bring his holier-
than-thou facade tumbling down.

She had needed to give him a taste of what she could do
for him, so that perhaps he might cease seeing her as bait
and see her as a human being, or at least as a woman
worthy of a role as his real mistress. And she had needed to
show him that he was not as loftily high above her as he
liked to pretend. So she had all but seduced her keeper.
Why should she fear? Her position as his coddled, high-
priced mistress was probably sealed now. She would be
rich. He had liked it so much, he would probably want her
to stay on as his ladybird even after he had finished with
Dolph. But he was never going to respect her now. Not
after that.

She didn't even respect herself and she must have become a true whore by now because somehow she wasn't

even sorry. The feel of him under her hands, the strength and heat and velvet of him. The taste of him. The response in him to her kiss, her every touch . . .

She had set out to make a conquest of him, only to discover the terrible loneliness of her own heart, reflected in his vulnerable need—the emptiness inside her that cried out for his strength and tenderness. And in the end all questions of power were forgotten. To kiss him, to serve him, to give him such pleasure was pleasure enough for her, and that was a very dangerous state of affairs, indeed.

Robert. She shuddered, squeezing her eyes shut tightly as the water trickled through her fingers back into the bowl, impossible as love to hold. She abandoned the wash basin, doubling over silently, holding her stomach and fighting a gigantic wave of panicked loneliness for him that was like a physical pain.

He must not know. She must not feel this. A courtesan could not love or she would be destroyed.

She made her way over to her bed and lay down, throwing her forearm over her eyes to stop the tears from coming.

It was then that the first notes rose from downstairs, tentative, searching, like his first kiss that night at Harriette's. She held her breath, listening. The enchantment grew as his music spread, enfolding her. She heeded, holding on to every note as if her life somehow depended on it.

He played like a master. The sonata was intricate beyond anything she could have executed, tender, mournful and slow, then crashing into a grandeur and complexity that could only have been Beethoven and, as the moments passed, she knew that Robert was speaking to her, only to her, and a helpless laugh of joy escaped her lips as her tears broke free in a kind of separate release; for the first time, in this unforeseen way, with half a house between them, the frigid star of the demimonde finally allowed a man to touch her.

❧ CHAPTER ❧
TEN

More than a fortnight later Bel stood before the looking glass in her Bond Street mantua maker's shop. The brisk Frenchwoman checked the fit of the latest evening gown she had created for *La Belle* Hamilton, a resplendent concoction in ice blue silk with a heart-shaped neckline that plunged in the valley between her breasts. There was no mistake about it—this was a gown for a Cyprian.

Bel's gaze followed her hands as she smoothed the high, clean line of the gown's skirts over her waist and hips. She could not help but muse that by all appearances she was indeed becoming the thing she pretended to be, and yet, in this role, she had unearthed a richer joy than any she had ever known.

All she could think of was Robert.

"He love this one, mademoiselle," the woman murmured, her dark eyes gleaming with suave pride in her creation.

"Oh, yes," Bel agreed in admiration of the woman's skill. She could hardly wait to see the look on Robert's face when he glimpsed the daring decolletage.

"Spezial occasion?"

"The Argyle Rooms."

"I thought was for dinner party?"

"No, that will be the pink one. This is for the Cyprians' Ball."

Ever since the night of their interlude in the library, something new and miraculous had sprung up between them, lifting like a green, tender shoot of some as-yet unknown flower. She had forgotten what it was like to feel safe. To be happy.

Their charade continued—routs, concerts, soirees, Vauxhall, Picadilly Saloon, the theater, the opera, the park. Robert did not speak of Dolph or Lady Coldfell anymore. Bel avoided mentioning them, too, knowing that the first of August would come all too soon and, with it, the termination of the agreement she and Robert had signed. Before that date arrived, she wanted an invitation from him to stay on indefinitely as his mistress.

It was the perfect solution in her vastly imperfect world—perhaps it was the *only* solution. She could never return to respectability, nor did she relish the prospect of putting herself back on the open market when their scheme was done. How likely was she to find a new keeper whom she could trust half as much as her stuffy honor-bound duke? Besides, she dared to believe she was learning to make Robert happy.

She had heard through the gossip mill that he had laughed aloud for no apparent reason the other day in the House of Lords, right in the middle of a session. Then he had voted at the wrong teller's booth, to the amusement of his peers, and had to stand up before the Woolsack and recast his nay for an aye.

Last week Mick Braden had come to visit her, but Robert had refused to let him in—an incident which had made her feel protected rather than put upon, to her own surprise.

There had been no repeat of their intimacy in the library, but everything between them had changed. Slowly but surely she knew that they both were lowering their masks, dissolving each other's pretenses and becoming quite solid friends.

In addition to all this, she now had about seven hundred fifty pounds in the bank toward the three thousand she needed to spring Papa from the Fleet.

She snapped out of her musings, realizing her Parisian mantua maker had asked her a question. "How eez Madame Julia? So beautiful! I have not seen her of late."

"Expecting again," Bel murmured in a confidential tone.

The woman stopped and looked up, jaw dropping. "*Mon Dieu!* Is five children now?"

"Six—this one by Colonel Napier."

The mantua maker muttered under her breath and bent her head, speaking around a pin. "*You* be careful, mademoiselle."

"Oh, I will, believe me," Bel vowed. Harriette had instructed her thoroughly on the proper use and insertion of the small sponge tied with a bobbin of thread, her sole defense against pregnancy, along with the intelligent use of a calendar.

The method had been developed on the Continent and was assured not to impede the full pleasure of both parties. In England this mode of contraception was even recommended by wise accoucheurs to wives in delicate health for whom pregnancy would have been dangerous. Condoms made from the innards of goats were also available, but Harriette said no self-respecting peer deigned to use one, which was just as well, because Bel found the whole notion disgusting. If all else failed, there were home remedies that she had been taught to concoct which could end a pregnancy—ergot, aloes, lead preparations.

"*Les six enfants!*" the Frenchwoman was mumbling. "How she keeps her figure, *je ne sais pas.*"

When the mantua maker had finished pinning the gown

in a few places, Bel went back into the dressing room, gingerly took it off and changed back into her dashing military-inspired afternoon dress. Over a white muslin sheath, it had a dark blue broadcloth spencer with tight-fitting sleeves, brass buttons, and gold epaulettes.

She carefully made out her bank draft for the exorbitant ballgown, pleased with the knowledge that Robert had deposited another two hundred fifty pounds in her account—not, thank God, to pay her for what she had done to him, but simply because her clothing allowance was part of their agreement.

As she left the shop and walked out to her elegant black *vis-à-vis*, she thought with pride of the one hundred pounds she had already invested in the funds. It would grow slowly at the five percent interest rate, but at least it was begun. She did not forget to show her thanks to her protector, either, by buying him the occasional present, some small but thoughtful trinket. Before coming into the dress shop today, she had picked up an elegant silver hunt flask on which she had had the silversmith engrave a wry and risqué dedication:

> *To Robert with a kiss:*
> *That His Grace may wet his lips for future*
> *games of vingt-et-un.*
> *From your Belinda, happily conquered.*
> *June, 1814.*

This little token would go along nicely with the case of fine French black-market brandy that his privateer brother, Lord Jack, had just sent him, she thought, as William, the young groom, opened the carriage door for her. She handed him her small package of sundry things she had bought in the shops and asked him to stow it in the boot.

As she happened to glance across the busy street, she

saw Dolph Breckinridge sitting in his phaeton, smoking a cheroot and staring at her. He did not acknowledge her gaze with a tip of his hat or one of his unnerving smiles; he merely continued to stare, making no move to come closer. With the primal sensation of prey being stalked, she felt a chill run down her spine as she realized he had been sitting outside, watching her and her mantua maker through the shop window.

"We'd best get you home, miss," William said, bristling as he, too, noticed Dolph, but Bel shook her head, steeling herself. She hadn't run from the warden of the Fleet and she certainly wasn't going to run from Dolph Breckinridge. She refused to go scurrying back to Knight House. Her errands weren't finished yet.

"No, William. Take me to Harriette Wilson's, please." Robert's latest deposit meant she owed Harriette another cheque for twenty percent. She hoped her mentor was not entertaining a client at the moment, for it had been a while since they'd had time to chat.

Dolph sat where he was and just watched her ride away, making no move to follow. She heaved an uneasy sigh of relief and looked forward again, rather weary from so many late nights out. She needed a respite from the social whirl, but tonight they were scheduled to attend a party after the outdoor concert in honor of the visiting Prussian war hero, General Blücher. She shrugged off her weariness. The thought of going anywhere with Robert filled her with happy excitement.

She gazed out the window as the prancing black geldings drew her *vis-à-vis* through the busy city streets. She held an expressionless look as people watched her pass, their stares following her carriage as though they knew what she was.

They probably did.

She stole a wary glance behind and saw Dolph following

in his phaeton, though a delivery wagon and a barouche had slipped between them. Unnerved, she looked forward again. At length William brought the *vis-à-vis* to a smooth halt in front of Harriette's house. Dolph stopped his vehicle a short distance down the street and continued watching her. William jumped down from the driver's seat and went to the door to make her arrival known and to see if Harriette was free. Seeing one of the big, mean footmen answer the door, Bel felt safe enough to leave her carriage, though Dolph was not far off. She climbed out of the *vis-à-vis* and strode quickly to the door just as Harriette came out to greet her.

She didn't point Dolph out because it was embarrassing to be the object of an unstable man's obsession. Instead she forced a blithe smile as Harriette appeared in the doorway of her house. The petite queen of the demireps gasped, throwing aside her usual droll manner to exclaim in wild envy over Bel's carriage and horses.

"You haven't seen them?" Bel asked with a smile, crossing the pavement to her. "I thought I showed you already. Oh, I'm very fine, aren't I?"

"La grande cortesane!" Harriette cried with a tinkling laugh, giving her a fond embrace. "Oh, you and your carriage are so gorgeous I can barely stand it. Now, come right in and have tea."

Gladly Bel obeyed as Harriette tugged her inside.

"Ah, my little protegée, you have taken the Town by storm," Harriette exclaimed a short while later as they settled cozily across from each other on the couch, teacups balanced on saucers in their laps. It was the same room where Robert had made his bold proposition weeks ago. "Hawkscliffe, no less! If I were closer to your age I'd have to hate you. As it is, I feel an almost motherly pride in your achievements—Hawkscliffe and *La Belle* Hamilton! The world talks of nothing else. So, tell me," Harriette said, slanting her a shrewd glance, "how is your duke?"

"He's fine. I think he's in better spirits generally than when I first went to him—"

"No, you little simpleton, I mean, *how is he* in bed?"

"Harrie!" Bel laughed, blushing crimson, for not even Harriette knew the truth about the nature of their liaison.

"High stickler like him, I figure he's either a perfect bore in the sack or riddled with perversities. So, which is it?"

Flabbergasted, Bel opened her mouth to speak but no sound came out.

"Oh, come on, spill it, Bel! You know I won't tell a soul."

"Oh, yes, you will. You'll tell Argyll and Hertford—and the next thing I know, both houses of Parliament will be discussing my Hawk's masterful . . . performances."

Harriette laughed gaily and leaned back against the couch. "Well, perhaps he really is a paragon." She sighed and dropped her gaze musingly. "Ah, Bel. How cozy for you—he's rich, powerful, handsome as the devil, very generous, *and* a good lover. I must confess, I am worried about you."

"Why? You can see I'm in the perfect situation."

"Too perfect." Harriette shook her head. "I see how you gaze at him. It is all well and good to feel an attraction, even an attachment to one's protector, but I beseech you for your own sake, do not forget the primary rule."

They stared at each other.

Bel knew it by heart, of course: *Never fall in love.*

She looked into her tea. "Of course I won't, Harrie."

"Bel? Look at me, Bel. Are you sulking?"

"It's just—how did that rule come into being, anyway?" she burst out. "Why can't we?"

"You know why—because it forfeits the game! Whoever

declares first loses. You know that, Bel. Look what happened to me."

"What happened? You are the most sought-after woman in England—"

"I gave my whole heart to my beautiful, treacherous Ponsonby and he smashed it into a hundred pieces by returning to his wife. And now every other lover fills me with distaste—but I must continue to entertain clients because this is the only life I know. I am quite wretched, when one thinks of it." Harriette looked at the fireplace and gave a melodramatic sigh. "I don't want the same thing to happen to you. Be beautiful and gay and cruel, Bel. Never fall in love."

"But Harriette," she ventured, "Lord Blessington married Marguerite—"

"No, I will not hear of this," Harriette snapped crossly. "For every Marguerite, there are a thousand of us who end up penniless hags in the gutter."

"The gutter!"

"I am headed there, God knows, with all my duns."

"Bosh, Harrie, you know full well you could marry Worcester in a trice."

"Sweet foolish boy," she sighed in regret. "I am too fond of him to accept, for I know such a mésalliance would not be in my little marquess's best interest, or in mine."

"He may be younger than you, but everyone knows that he loves you."

"Love?" Harriette laid her hand on Bel's cheek with an expression of sorrow. "No more of this love nonsense. My heart is already uneasy with having brought you into this accursed life. I don't want to see it destroy you. I don't want to see you make the same mistakes I made when I was fifteen and just starting out. Magnificent as he is, your Hawk must fly away one day. Blessington was not a rising power in Parliament when he married Marguerite."

Bel said nothing, but studied the floor and stewed in rebellion.

"Bel?" Harriette prodded. "Do you think Marguerite's lot is so marvelous now that she's Lady Blessington? You're wrong, if you do. None of the other Society women will ever accept her—they won't even speak to her, though her behavior is faultless. If you lured Hawkscliffe into offering marriage, the scandal would wreck his career as a statesman. If you took that away from him, if you allowed him—especially him—to choose desire over duty, he would regret it and eventually come to despise you, and then where would you be?"

"I know what you say is true, but Hawkscliffe isn't like everyone else. He's so good and kind, so genuinely noble—"

"No more!" Harriette cried in exasperation, jumping up from the couch and clapping her hands over her ears. "You are going to destroy yourself. Do not get so attached to him. Take what you can get from the man, but be ready to leave him as soon as you detect any sign that he is growing bored."

"But that is so cold—"

"That is reality, dear heart. I'm teaching you how to survive."

Bel sighed in distress and reached to grasp her hand. "Don't be angry with me, Harrie. I'm doing my best. You know I will always listen to your advice," she lied merely to end the argument.

Harriette didn't know everything, she thought in rebellion. Maybe the prime rule was wise under normal circumstances, but her situation with Hawkscliffe was different.

Harriette remained miffed until Bel opened her reticule and wrote out her draft for fifty pounds, twenty percent of Robert's latest deposit. The cheque helped soothe her ruffled feathers. They talked of other things until Bel finally rose and bid her good-bye. By the time she returned to her *vis-à-vis*, she saw that Dolph had left. William reported no trouble from the baronet.

They headed back to Knight House. Several times she checked out the back window and searched the streets to make sure Dolph was not lurking somewhere nearby. Satisfied at last that she was rid of him for now, she propped her chin on her fist and stared out the carriage window, willing herself to believe that Harriette didn't understand. Robert was not like the idle, self-centered cavaliers who swarmed around the Wilson sisters.

Suddenly she saw a pair of small familiar faces in the hustle and bustle about the corner of Regent and Beak Streets. Her orange-selling days rushed back to her as she recognized her eight-year-old little rapscallion friend, Tommy, plying his charm on the corner, sweeping the crossing for a gentleman in a top hat, while, to her horror, she saw his nine-year-old brother, Andrew, a step behind, picking the man's pocket!

Bel hauled on the check string for all she was worth. William brought the *vis-à-vis* to an almost immediate halt. She didn't wait for him to open the door for her, but leaped out of the carriage and marched over to the corner and seized an ear of each boy.

She began pulling them none too gently toward her carriage.

"Hey, lady! Let go of us!"

"It's me, you little fools! Don't you recognize me?"

"Miss Bel?" Tommy cried, gaping.

"What are you trying to do, get yourselves hanged? Get in the carriage! This instant!"

"Yes, ma'am!"

"Yes, Miss Bel."

Paling and suddenly humbled, they scrambled into the *vis-à-vis*.

Glaring with anger while her heart pounded in dread, Bel wondered if anyone had seen Andrew's theft. She entered the carriage and sat down across from the children. The awful smell of the filthy creatures filled the carriage and they were so underfed that both could fit easily in the one-person seat across from her.

She folded her arms over her chest and glowered at them. "I am shocked and appalled at you boys. Hand it over." She put out her hand.

Andrew slunk down in his seat but produced a gold fob watch.

"You are a very naughty, wicked little boy," she told him. "Do you have any idea what could happen if anyone saw you steal this?"

The pair exchanged a dismal look.

"That's right," she said sternly, "you would go to jail."

"Do they feed you in jail, Miss Bel?" asked Andrew.

"Impertinence," she exclaimed, barely masking the twist of sheer pity in her heart at his question. Her impulse was to give him a hug, but she had to scold, for it would be fatal to give them any reason to pursue their guilty course. Good Lord, she couldn't just put them back out onto the street again.

Andrew hung his head. "We're sorry, Miss Bel."

"I know you are," she said sternly. "Now, you are not going to steal anymore, but you're not going to go hungry, either. Tommy, Andrew, I am taking you to a place where you will be cared for properly."

"What place?" asked Andrew, instantly wary.

"A school."

Tommy's eyebrows lifted. "School?"

Bel nodded firmly at them, resolved. She could cancel her order for her next evening gown. These two children would have a roof over their heads, clean clothes on their backs, and food in their bellies even if she had to take her money out of the funds.

"I don't want no school," Andrew said after a moment, scowling.

"I don't care," Bel replied.

"How come you don't sell oranges no more?" Tommy piped up.

"Look at her fancy drags, Tom. She's on the game," said Andrew like any long-suffering elder brother.

Taken aback Bel gaped at the boy, then wanted to die of mortification. She snapped her mouth shut and looked away, reminding herself that after life in the flash house, these children had seen it all. Still, she was heartily glad they didn't ask why it was all right for her to whore, but wrong for them to steal, for she had no idea how to answer. Guilt razed her conscience for having allowed herself to forget about the poor little wretches for more than a month, absorbed as she had been in her own problems.

She leaned out and directed William to take the Edgware Road out to Paddington. While teaching at Mrs. Hall's she had heard about a charity school there privately funded by the Philanthropic Society. Surely she could persuade the headmaster to accept her homeless waifs.

When they arrived Bel grasped each boy's hand to stop them from running off and marched them up to the squat brick school in determination.

She and her young charges were received with trepidation by the secretary. She asked to see the headmaster. The secretary agreed to keep an eye on the boys, who sat down obediently in the reception room, while she was shown into the headmaster's office. She waited in fidgety impatience for a couple of minutes then looked up in cool, aloof composure when in walked a pinch-faced, hook-nosed little busybody of a man.

"Sorry to have kept you waiting, miss. I am Mr. Webb. How may I help you?" he intoned in nasal pomp.

"Thank you for seeing me, Mr. Webb. I have come about two boys whom I would like to enroll as students in your school."

The corners of his mouth turned down. "We are full near to capacity, I'm afraid. Were they born in this parish?"

Bel hesitated.

"You did bring their birth certificates, Miss—ah?"

"Hamilton. Belinda Hamilton—"

His left eyebrow shot up.

Bel cursed herself the instant her full name was past her lips.

She knew she was famous—or infamous—in Town, but who on earth would have thought that the principal of a charity school would have heard of her?

He cocked his head, eyeing her like an ill-tempered little bird. "What relation are these children to you?" he asked in suspicion.

"They are friends. Mr. Webb, these children need a roof over their heads. They have been living on the streets. They've had nothing to eat—"

"One moment," he cut her off. "Living on the street? They do not sound at all suitable for our establishment, Miss Hamilton. I cannot allow them to corrupt the other children."

"Sir!" she exclaimed, taken aback. "They're not going to corrupt anyone."

"We have orphans here, but all come from decent homes of the *respectable* poor. I'm sure these urchins of yours are quite unfortunate, but if you cannot even produce their birth certificates, I am not obliged to take them."

"Perhaps I have not made myself clear." She forced a winning smile at him. "I am offering to pay for their enrollment and their keep. They are good, darling little boys.

They only need an education to make them fit for work one day, and a bit of discipline—"

"Miss Hamilton," he cut her off again, "their kind is not welcome here. Nor is yours."

Her jaw dropped. "My kind? You cannot condemn the children because of me."

"This is a decent Christian establishment, Miss Hamilton. I'm sure you'll understand."

"Is it? It doesn't seem very Christian to me. Didn't our Lord have a friend who was a whore?"

"Good day, ma'am," he replied coldly.

"Mr. Webb, you are condemning these children to the gallows."

"It is their parents' place to teach them virtuous conduct."

"They have no parents. I'm the only adult they know."

"Marylebone workhouse will take them—"

She suppressed an oath. "I wouldn't turn a stray dog in to the workhouse. I'll pay you extra—"

"We shall not accept your money, Miss Hamilton, considering its source."

"What do you suggest I do with them, Mr. Webb? Because I can't dump them back out onto the streets."

"Perhaps you should care for them yourself," he suggested, flicking a sanctimonious glance at her expensive gown then peering out the window at her lavish equipage. "It appears you can afford it."

Bel rose in fury, shamed beyond speech. She pivoted in a swirl of muslin and swept out of the small office.

"Andrew, Tommy, let's go." Her chin was high but inwardly she burned with humiliation as she marched out, pulling each boy by the hand. She felt the judgmental gaze of the headmaster following her. She herded the children into her carriage and in an icy tone of fury ordered William to drive them back to Knight House. Arms folded over her chest, she glared out the window while the two boys, frightened by her silent rage, watched her face anxiously.

"Didn't—didn't they want us, Miss Bel?" Tommy asked gingerly.

"It's not that, Tommy. It's just that they haven't got space for you," she forced out in a calmer tone. "Don't worry. Everything's going to be fine."

I don't know what I'm going to do with you.

Surely Robert would have a fit of apoplexy if she brought them to Knight House, but what else could she do? As she thought on it, she realized Robert didn't really even need to know that they were there. Each boy would have a job to earn his keep. Andrew could be in charge of the dogs and Tommy could serve as the kitchen boy. She saw no other viable options.

When they arrived at Knight House, she enlisted William's help with managing the boys. Considering his own brush with childhood poverty, the former street sweep was happy to help, and cheerful, easygoing Cook immediately took them both under her wing, as well. The big grandmotherly woman seemed happy to have children underfoot to feed and dote on.

Bel glanced from one boy's smudged, pale, wide-eyed face to the other as she explained to them their new situation and made it crystal clear that if either of them stole so much as a lump of sugar, she would personally tan their hides. Better a paddling from her than Newgate and a noose. They had bad habits to unlearn.

There was plenty of room for them in the servants' quarters. Two more cots were quickly made up near the hearth. The high-spirited boys began charming the staff from the minute they crossed the threshold of the stodgy mansion. One of the maids, all smiles, whisked off to find clean clothes for the boys. In a house that had raised five sons and countless male servants, there were trunk loads of boys' castoff clothes in the attic, some of which were still in acceptable condition.

All this while the duke was locked in his office in a meeting with someone, said Walsh. The butler watched these goings-on with a frown of trepidation, withholding comment on what His Grace might have to say about his mistress bringing home strays. Meanwhile, Cook began heating up some of yesterday's stew for the ragged pair. When at last the bewildered but happy boys dug into their meal, Bel gave Cook a smile of heartfelt thanks. The big, capable woman beamed a smile at her in return, her blue eyes twinkling.

Feeling much better about the children's safety, Bel retired to her rooms. She knew she shouldn't let it bother her, but she was still angry about that headmaster's rudeness. Feeling weary and a trifle grimy from traipsing around the city all day, she pulled the bell rope by the door in her room and asked the maid who responded for her bath to be drawn.

A bath and a rest were exactly what she needed to ready herself for the night's party. She wandered into her dressing room and looked around at the growing collection of gowns, trying to decide on what to wear tonight.

Within half an hour she was in heaven, lounging in a hot bath perfumed with milk of roses, her ankles crossed on the far rim of the tub. The thick steam curled up from the water, dampening tendrils of her pinned-up hair around her face. She had rubbed clear, precious balm of Mecca into her face and throat and could feel her complexion reviving. She took a sip of wine, sighed, and let her cares melt, resting her head back on the rim of the tub. She did not know how many moments had passed when a brisk knock at the door roused her from her state of deep relaxation.

"Belinda, it's Hawkscliffe."

She gasped, her eyes flying open wide. She sat straight up in the tub and without further ado, he breezed in, all business.

"It's about the dinner party—"

He stopped. She stared at him, hardly daring to breathe.

Then a sly, luxurious grin slowly spread across his face. "Well, well, well." He nudged the door shut behind him and locked it, casting her a charming little smile. "Hawkscliffe, old chap, you've got a real genius for timing."

Bel smiled nervously, blushing bright pink. She feared he had come to demand that she remove the boys from his house, but at the moment he only seemed interested in having a look at her. She sank down in the tub, gathering mounds of suds to veil her body from his curious glance. Supposedly a worldly courtesan, she didn't want him to notice her shyness, but in truth, she had never been naked in a room with a man before in her life.

"Was there something you, ah, wanted, Your Grace?"

"Not till now," he said with a roguish smile.

She gave him a ladylike scowl. He sauntered over, looking very pleased with himself. He must have been hard at work in his office, she thought. His waistcoat was unbuttoned and the sleeves of his white shirt were rolled up.

He walked up to the edge of the tub, bent down, and captured her chin, brushing her lips with a light kiss. "Hullo, bonny bluebell," he murmured. "Thank you for the handsome new flask. I shall treasure it"—he tapped the tip of her nose—"always."

She pulled back and smiled at him as relief poured through her. If that explained his visit, perhaps he didn't even know about the boys yet.

"Why are you always buying me things?" he asked as he sat on the edge of her bed a few feet away.

"It makes me happy."

He shook his head at her, looking mystified. "I wanted

to tell you we've got another guest to add to the dinner party list."

"Not the Regent?" she whispered in dread, her eyes widening. She already had a muddle ahead of her in trying to work out the proper seating order, what with lowborn men of stellar rank in the government shuffled in among dukes and a viscount. She dreaded wounding anybody's self-love by placing them at the table in incorrect rank and order.

"No, Lord Coldfell," he said.

"Oh?" Taken aback, she set her wine down on the little table next to the tub.

"Yes, the circumstances are a bit strange," he admitted, "but Coldfell has been a friend of the family for years. He knew I would never act on what I had felt toward his wife. You see, it was Lord Coldfell who first brought his suspicions of Dolph to me and gave me that lead to follow."

Bel nodded gravely. "And does he know the truth about our charade?"

"No, my dear. That is our little secret," he murmured with a beguiling smile, which she returned.

"I take it Lord Coldfell was the person you were speaking to in your study just now."

Eyeing the soap bubbles that floated, sparkling, on the water, he waved his hand dismissively. "No, that was Clive Griffon, Esquire, come to plague me again."

"Who's he?"

"A starry-eyed young idealist who has been begging me to put him in the House of Commons."

"Oh, really?"

"One of the boroughs I control has a vacant seat. Griffon wants to give it a go."

Bel raised an eyebrow at him. "A pocket borough, you mean?"

"So they are vulgarly called," he said loftily.

"I see." Put at ease by the neutral topic, she recrossed her ankles the other way, flexing her feet in contentment. "And how many of these boroughs do you have in your pocket, Your Grace?"

He glanced at her feet in amusement. "A gentleman never tells."

"Bosh."

"Six."

She looked over at him, gaping. "Six!"

"It is a lot, I know," he said sheepishly, though his eyes shone. "Well, Devonshire has seven."

"Must you dukes have your fingers in everything? Can't you confine yourselves to White's and the House of Lords? Commons is supposed to be an electorate."

He shrugged. "It's not my doing. I inherited them." Staring at her legs, he leaned back, bracing himself on both hands. Bel found that she no longer minded his leisurely perusal. "Truth is," he absently resumed, "I've been trying to shove Alec into office, but he won't take it. He's only interested in gambling and women."

"Your brother hardly seems the political type," she admitted.

"But this young Griffon . . . he's too zealous."

"Zealots usually are."

"He's got wild ideas."

"Not a Radical, I hope?"

"An Independent."

"You seem intrigued."

He shrugged. "Reform the penal code—yes, that I can see. But reform Parliament?" he said, shaking his head. "It'll never happen . . . though perhaps it should."

"They may make a Whig of you yet, my dear," she said, amused by his brooding frown. "Why don't you give Mr. Griffon a chance?"

"He's got the background for it, I'll give him that. He's a judge's son and he knows the law. But he's young."

"So's Alec. And so are you, for that matter—"

"Belinda," he interrupted in a low, intimate tone.

"Yes?" she asked, lazily washing her arm.

"I refuse to speak of politics for a second longer when there is a naked woman bathing in front of me. No man is paragon enough for that."

She draped her elbows on the rim of the tub and smiled archly at him. "Are you flirting with me, Hawkscliffe?"

"Trying to."

"Do you intend to just sit there and gawk at me while I bathe?"

"May I?"

"I'd prefer it if you made yourself useful. Come and scrub my back."

He sat up, lifting his eyebrows. "Is that an invitation?"

"More a command, actually."

"Aha." He pushed up from the bed and walked slowly around the tub behind her. Her heart began to pound as she watched him from the corner of her eye. "You . . . little . . . tease," he murmured.

"Who says I'm teasing? I believe I rather fancy you."

"Likewise, Miss Hamilton, and let me say I'm honored." He pulled up the ottoman from the nearby armchair and sat down on it.

She quivered as his hand delved into the water and chased the floating soap, grazing her side until he had captured it. She arched over, giving him her back.

His mouth hovered at her ear. "You are a naughty thing."

"Did I give you leave to talk?" she replied in a wanton purr. "Wash my back for me, slave. Now."

She felt him smile against her skin. He kissed her shoulder.

"How novel," he murmured as he ran the soap down her back. "I thought it was you who were *my* plaything."

"You have it backward, dear blockhead."

"No more talking, goddess, unless you want to lose your prize love slave."

She smiled and leaned forward so he could continue washing her back. His hands, expert and sensitive, began to glide slowly over her skin.

"Excellent work, Robert," she purred as he trailed his fingertips down her spine.

"Your servant, madam." He caressed her sides and squished the soapy bubbles through his fingers as he massaged her shoulders for many languorous moments. Bel could feel all her tension easing away under his touch. "Shall I wash your arms, Miss Hamilton?" he whispered at her ear.

Her head drifted back onto his broad shoulder. She smiled drowsily and shifted with languid pleasure in his embrace. "Say please."

"Please," he echoed hoarsely.

"You may."

He did. Crouching beside the tub, he was intent on his work.

His black glossy hair formed wispy curls in the rising steam. As he slowly smeared the soap down her arm, she reached over her shoulder and untied his cravat, leaving it undone around his neck. She unfastened a couple of his shirt buttons, touching his gleaming chest in admiration. She lifted her hand and cupped his cheek, gazing at him in heated yearning as she drew him to her for a kiss.

His firm mouth met hers in satin warmth; with a soft stroke of her tongue she parted his lips and kissed him hungrily. He moaned in his throat then reached beneath her arm and cupped her breast. Bel moaned, melting back against him. The feel of his hands on her skin was sublime.

His touch was exquisitely tender, kneading the weight of her breast, then his soapy fingers moved, slow and slick, around and around her nipple, dizzying her.

The pleasure so fascinated her that she lost track of kissing him, simply closed her eyes and savored it, her body going limp with spreading heat. He explored her body with his hands, kissing her hungrily all the while. Arching for his touch until her breasts thrust into his palms, Bel could find no fear within her, only trust and lush enjoyment, because this was *him*, this was Robert, her protector.

Kneeling behind her next to the tub, he plunged his arms up past his elbows into the water, soaking his rolled-up sleeves as he molded the shape of her hips and thighs with his large, gentle hands.

"My God, do you have any idea how perfect you are?" he whispered in her ear. "I've dreamed of touching you, but you're even lovelier than I envisioned and your skin . . . is the most heavenly silk."

"Oh, Robert, please," she uttered on a moan of breathless need. Closing her eyes in torment, she laid her head back on his chest.

"What do you want, sweeting? Show me."

She was beyond scandal as she captured his hand beneath the water and guided it between her legs, her heart pounding wildly at her own wantonness.

"Mmm, I thought so," he whispered as he lightly caressed her, igniting a burst of sensation that sent rainbows of delight arcing through her limbs. "But first Miss must have her bath," he murmured.

She moaned impatiently but let him do what he willed. Progressing at a leisurely pace down her left arm, he came to her hand, bent his head and kissed it. She turned her hand over, giving him her palm. He pressed a kiss into it then brushed his mouth against her wrist, staring hungrily into her eyes.

"May I wash your pretty legs, Miss Hamilton?"

"If you . . . take off your shirt for me," she countered, bold and breathless.

He gave her a narrow smile. "All right." Holding her stare, he pulled off his waistcoat and slid his untied cravat off his neck.

Bel bit her lip, watching the white lawn skim upward over his lean ridged belly, baring his broad, muscled chest as he lifted his shirt off over his head.

He cast the shirt behind him with a ripple of muscle all down his arm. She couldn't resist touching him. She molded her hand over the warm bulk of his shoulder, savoring the maleness of him, steely muscle and satiny skin. She ran her fingers through the lightly furred center of his chest, trailing her fingertip down the center groove of his chiseled belly until she came to the waistband of his trousers. She hooked her finger in the front and lifted a mischievous gaze to his face.

He was staring at her, his dark eyes stormy.

With a smile, her heart pounding, Bel sat back in the tub. "Very nice, Hawkscliffe."

He grinned at her, reaching under the water and curling his hand around her calf with a low, hearty growl. She laughed breathlessly, frissons of desire tingling all the way up her limbs from his touch. She handed him the soap, then watched him rub sprigs of bubbles up her calf. He kissed her bent knee.

"You really do have exquisite legs, Miss Hamilton."

She smiled, laid her cheek in her hand and gazed at him. Diligently working his way down her left limb, he took her foot in his hand and massaged it, squeezing and rubbing gently. He worked a point on the arch of her foot with his thumb that sent shockwaves of pained pleasure all the way up to her scalp. He did the same to her right. His fingertips stroked the soles of her feet until she writhed and giggled and squirmed at the tickling sensation. At last he rinsed her right foot with tender care, brought it up from under the water and kissed the top of it.

She widened her eyes. "My goodness, Robert."

He gave her a lazy, wicked smile and when he spoke, his words were soft, slow, and lulling. "Isn't that what you want, Belinda? A man who will kiss your feet? A man who worships the ground you walk on? Isn't that what you demand, what you deserve? Well, isn't it?"

She could only stare at him, enthralled. He sent her a smoldering glance and licked the inside of her ankle, then bent his head and slowly covered her feet in adoring kisses. Entranced, she watched the supple play of muscle in his shoulders, arms, and chest while he caressed her legs, his touch roaming higher up her thighs.

Her chest heaved with want by the time he lifted his smoldering stare to meet her gaze. When he spoke, his voice sounded husky. "Stand, Belinda, please."

She did not even think of disobeying. Every inch of her body sang with tingling sensation as she rose on rather wobbly legs, water coursing down her skin. Crouching beside the tub, he stared up at her body, roseate in the firelight. Her breasts jutted with full arousal in the chilly air. Her aureoles were dark and turgid, her nipples aching for his touch.

His stare was one of rapt awe. "There is no amount of money that could ever entitle a man to so much beauty," he breathed.

She moaned his name and reached for his shoulders to steady herself. He grasped her gently by the hips and kissed her stomach. She raked her fingers through his hair, vaguely astonished that she wasn't afraid. His hands glided back to her derriere and his lips skimmed the top of her lower hairline—neatly trimmed, as a courtesan's should be.

She could feel his warm breath deliciously penetrating her most sensitive core. She ached, wet for him between her thighs even as her skin dried from the bath. She struggled for sanity, knowing it was a losing battle.

"This is not in our agreement," she said faintly.

"I know. God, I know." He nuzzled her belly with his lips. "I want to taste you."

No longer waiting for permission, he dipped his head and pressed a bold kiss to her mound. She groaned. He touched her lightly with his thumb, then caressed with more pressure, and just when she thought the pleasure was too much, he followed with his tongue. She exclaimed aloud in wordless ecstasy.

His erotic kiss deepened, gently tracing her tiny rigid nub with his tongue. She raked her fingers through his thick black hair with a violent surge of want and steadied herself by holding on to his big, steam-slicked shoulders.

Harriette and Fanny had told her about this act, but never—*never* had she felt anything that even remotely resembled the bliss he now gave her.

At length he ordered her to lift her right foot up onto the rim of the tub. He moved between her spread legs and tongued her deeply. Caressing her with his open hand at first, he eased a finger inside of her and groaned against her belly.

"God, you're as tight as a virgin."

She almost smiled bitterly at his words, but then all thought lifted and flew like a flock of restless birds as he sucked hungrily on her clitoris, working two fingers into her passage until her moans rose to wild cries in a building crescendo. She moved with him, dropping her head back, holding on to his shoulders for dear life as she felt the swift advance of the imminent storm rolling through her. Thunderous joy tingled down her arms, prickled her very scalp. Shudders of ecstasy racked her and then the explosion of passion split through her like a lightning-clap, blinding in its glory. She cried out, gasping, delirious, nearly falling over his shoulders as he drank of her rain until every last droplet of strength ebbed from her body, leaving her weak and trembling.

She clung to him. *"Oh, God, Robert."*

As her climax dissipated, he stood and swept her into his arms, carrying her to her bed. He yanked back the covers and slid her under the sheet. Bel looked up at him in alarm, thinking that he would take his pleasure of her now, but he merely reached for the blanket and covered her.

He sat down on the edge of the bed, braced himself on his hands, and leaned down to kiss her softly. Then he closed his eyes and rested his forehead against hers. She felt the struggle in his powerful body to hold his burning need in check.

"God, what are we doing?" he asked in a ragged whisper.

"I don't know." She wrapped her arms around him.

He breathed her name, half a groan of want, and bent lower to kiss her neck. He skimmed her throat with kisses. "You knew this would happen to me, didn't you? You knew I couldn't resist. That all you had to do was wait."

She ran her fingers through his hair, closing her eyes in fervent rapture. "Is it a good thing, Robert? Are you happy?"

"So much it terrifies me." His lashes swept open and he stared into her eyes. "I've been alone so long, but when I'm with you, oh, when I'm with you, Bel, the earth sings and the stars dance and I don't loathe myself so much for a bore."

Amazed, she took his beloved face between her hands, smiling with a shimmer of tears in her eyes. "Oh, Robert. You could never bore me. How many times must I tell you?"

He pulled back with a slight, rueful smile, his dark eyes glowing like a sunset beneath his long black lashes.

I love you, she wanted to tell him. *You changed my life.* But she dared not.

With a final reluctant sigh, he pushed up, rose, and left her bed.

She came up onto her elbows, taking pleasure in the play of firelight across his smooth, muscled back. "Where are you going, lover?"

"To dress for Blücher's party. Will you miss me?"

"Terribly."

He cast her a half smile and threw his discarded shirt, waistcoat, and cravat over his bare shoulder as he sauntered to the door.

"Robert."

Reaching for the doorknob, he turned to her in question, his seductive face sculpted by the deepening shadows and flickering flame.

She mouthed a silent thank you and blew him a kiss.

With a sardonic smile, he bowed. "At your service, Miss Hamilton. The pleasure was mine."

⚓ CHAPTER ⚓
ELEVEN

A short while later Hawk waited impatiently while Knowles, his valet, put the final touches on his cravat. All the while he argued with his conscience over why he should not pay off the rest of Alfred Hamilton's debt and see the old fool out of jail. The more he came to care about Belinda, the more he wanted to help her in every possible way.

On the one hand, fulfilling her father's debts would have endeared him to her indefinitely, he knew, but the prospect carried serious risks. She had signed their agreement pledging her help, but how could he be sure she would not quit his company and abandon his scheme to snare Dolph the moment she no longer needed the money to free her father? Was it wise to make a gesture that would so openly admit how deeply attached to her he was growing? Moreover, he feared that if he paid off her father's debts, it would set a risky precedent that anytime she got into a scrape, never fear, Hawkscliffe and his millions would bail her out.

Lastly, and perhaps most seriously, if old Hamilton learned of his daughter's true profession, he might come to his senses and play the outraged papa, dragging her away from Hawk. With that realization he violently brushed off the idea of getting Alfred out of jail. No one was going to take that girl away from him.

"Very good, Your Grace," his valet said after a last firm adjustment to the white silk knot, then added slyly, "That should catch her eye."

Hawk raised an eyebrow at him.

Knowles politely masked his amusement and bowed. "A splendid evening to you, sir."

"Why, thank you, Knowles. I do look rather smart, don't I?" he added with a grin, then strode out of his chambers and jogged downstairs to wait for Belinda.

Descending the gliding curve of the staircase, Hawk heard a very strange sound, one he knew well but had not heard in decades: children's laughter. Indeed—with a particular note of mischief in it. *What the devil?*

The second the marble entrance hall came into view, he paused and squinted, sure his eyes were playing tricks on him. There, beneath the chandelier, two small boys were exploring the ancient suit of parade armor that had been given to an ancestor of his by Henry VIII. They were plucking at the jewels and running their grubby fingers along the dulled blade of the gleaming broadsword.

"Ooo, wow . . ."

"Look, this could *kill* someone!"

"Ahem," said Hawk.

Both children shrieked and whipped around, slamming together as Hawk lifted his chin, clasped his hands loosely behind his back, and proceeded the rest of the way down, eyeing them in displeasure. Probably relations of one of his servants, he thought.

"Pray, gentlemen, that is not to be touched. It is very old. What are you doing out of the servants' quarters?"

They didn't answer, staring up at him in awe. Their eyes were huge as he came to stand before them.

Folding his arms over his chest, he towered over them, glanced at the armor, and frowned. "You've gotten smudges all over it. Now it will have to be polished again."

"We're sorry," said the taller one, determined to look brave, suddenly.

"To whom do you belong?"

They conferred together in whispers over the question, reminding Hawk for all the world of the twins, his middle brothers, Lucien and Damien. As boys, the pair had shared a language all their own and to this day could almost seem to read each other's minds.

"Gentlemen, I asked you a question." Hawk bent down slowly to their eye level.

"Uh, what was it again?" asked the taller boy, scratching his head.

"Who is your mother and where is she?"

They shrugged. Hawk frowned.

The taller one seemed to gather himself, squaring his shoulders. "Is that yours?" He nodded to the suit of armor.

"Yes."

"Do you ever put it on?"

Taken aback, Hawk laughed. "No."

"Why not?"

"There hasn't been much occasion. Besides, I'm too tall."

"Could I try it?"

"No. You're too short. Children, how did you get in my house?"

"Miss Bel brung us 'ere," the littler one piped up.

"Miss Hamilton?"

The taller boy gave him a shrewd once-over. "You 'er fancy man, then?"

Hawk stared at him blankly. "How do know Miss Hamilton?"

"She gave us oranges."

"What?"

"Oranges," said the elder brother, rolling his eyes at the

smaller one's slight lisp. "She gave us oranges when she used to sell them in a basket."

"We don't get no oranges anymore," said the little one, looking crestfallen.

Bel walked down the curved marble staircase, marvelously dressed for General Blücher's party in a diaphanous tunic gown of a pearly Nakara color. A dashing plumed turban on her head, she swung her seed-pearl embroidered reticule from one gloved wrist, humming to herself. But halfway down the staircase, she heard Robert's exchange with the children.

She froze.

She gripped the banister with one hand and pressed the other to her midriff, feeling an aghast knot form in her belly as she overheard Tommy blurt out that humiliating piece of her past that she had never in a thousand years wanted her protector to know.

Robert's back was to her as he crouched before the children. "She sold oranges?" he echoed, sounding amazed, as well he might. In the eyes of a fashionable man, a costermonger was a thousand times more contemptible than a demirep.

Bel squeezed her eyes shut in mortification, then flicked them open again and stared down at the unlikely trio, feeling trapped. Before she could flee, Andrew saw her and his eyes lit up.

"Miss Bel!"

Abandoning Robert, they ran to her, pounding up the steps. Tommy hugged her around her hips and Andrew grabbed her hand, pulling her down to see the suit of armor, both boys chattering with excitement.

Robert slowly straightened up, folded his arms over his chest, and watched her with an unfathomable expression.

Bel saw that look and nearly threw up her hands in despair. Just when everything seemed to be going well in her life—just when Robert was finally beginning to see her as worthy of him—why now did he have to find out that his supposedly elegant mistress was a former orange girl? *Blast!* It wasn't fair!

Meanwhile, the children were tugging her every which way.

"Tommy, you're going to throw me down the stairs. Let go!" She looked down impatiently to pry the child's hug free, only to spy grubby fingerprints on her pearly gown. It was the last straw.

"Blast!" she cried in a thunderous tone above their giddy laughter. "Do you know how much this gown cost me? You've ruined it! Now I'll have to go back upstairs and change and we're going to be late for the party and I don't even want to go!"

"Boys," Robert ordered sharply, walking over. "Sit. Here." He snapped his fingers and pointed to the bottom step.

They slunk away from her and obeyed, staring up at him. They glanced at Bel anxiously. "It was an accident, Miss Bel—"

"I know, I know," she said more gently, already feeling the chagrin that followed inevitably in the wake of her outburst. "It's all right, Tommy. I didn't mean to yell." She wished the earth would swallow her.

Still bright red in the face, she forced herself to look at Robert, dreading to see the lordly disgust she would surely find in his stare. But when she dared glance at him, she found only patience.

"We don't have to go. Do you want to stay home?"

Home, she thought in misery. Is that where I am?

He took matters into his own capable hands, sending the

boys back to Cook for supervision. They didn't dare disobey him.

He walked slowly to her and examined the small fingerprints on her dress. "My valet can probably get this out with white wine. If not, we'll buy you another."

His soft tone was her undoing. She covered her face with her hands and sat right down on the step where she had been standing.

Robert eased down onto the step below her, giving her knee a caress. "Why didn't you tell me?"

"How could I? I didn't want you to know what I had been reduced to. I have my pride, Robert. I tried everything before turning to this life, you must believe me—"

"I don't mean the oranges, darling. I don't care about that. Why didn't you tell me you brought those children here?"

His question startled her. She lifted her head from her hands and gazed at him uncertainly.

"I will be solely responsible for them, Robert. I swear they won't make any trouble. I'll polish the armor myself—"

"Hush. Where did they come from?"

"God only knows. I met them when I was an orange seller, before I resolved to see if Harriette would take me on. I tried to look out for them. Today when I saw them, I tried to enroll them in a charity school, but the headmaster wouldn't take them. They'll earn their keep, Robert, I promise you that. It's just that I'm the only adult they know. They're good boys, if a little rambunctious, and they have nowhere to go. I feel it is my duty to take care of them—"

"And right now, it's mine, to take care of you," he said, gently catching her hand between his.

She stared at him. "You're not going to tell me to send them away?"

"Of course not. Why are you so upset, Belinda?" His voice was low and lulling. "I feel as though there's something else bothering you. What aren't you telling me?"

She gazed longingly at him. "I don't want my past to come between us, Robert."

"Miss Hamilton," he chided softly, "I happen to like oranges."

"You do?"

He cupped her cheek. "What's wrong, sweeting? Confide in me."

I can't possibly, she thought. Her heart wrenched.

"Didn't I make you a promise that I would never disappoint you? That first day I came to see you, you didn't want to tell me about Dolph, but I've protected you from him. You didn't want me to know about Mick Braden, but I was there for you then. You didn't want me to know your father was in jail or that you used to teach at Mrs. Hall's, but each time you trusted me with these things, did I ever let you down?"

"No," she whispered.

"Did I ever frighten you? Betray you? Make you angry?"

"No."

"I'm on your side, Belinda. Can't we put an end to the secrets?"

She thought she might well fall apart if he didn't stop gazing at her so gently and questioning her with such soft intent.

"I only want to help."

"I know. And you have helped me, Robert. More than you know."

He petted her knee, his gaze following his hand. "I wish you would let me understand why there is such sorrow in your eyes. I try to chase it away," he said, "but it always seems to come back."

She lowered her head, holding on to her composure for all she was worth. She did not know how much more of his gentle chivalry she could bear before she completely fell apart.

"I have seen sorrowful things, I suppose," she forced out stiffly.

"Like what?"

"Well—" She could barely speak past the lump in her throat. She cast around mentally for some ready excuse. "Those boys, for instance. There are thousands just like them living out there on the streets in direst poverty."

Suddenly she looked at him—Hawkscliffe—one of the most powerful men in Parliament, with the strength and resources to make a difference where mere mortals like her could not. It was so much easier to think about *their* problems instead of her own.

"Yes?" he prompted, waiting.

Her hand rested lightly in his, but now she wrapped her fingers around his and looked into his velvety brown eyes. "If you don't mind skipping General Blücher's party, there is somewhere I'd like to go—something I'd like to show you tonight—but it won't be easy for you to take."

"What is it?"

"A side of life I wager you have never seen. These children—"

"Belinda, we're talking about you."

"Yes—I know." She dropped her gaze. "And I thank you for caring about me and standing by me as you have. You've been one of the truest friends I've ever had, Robert. My problems are nothing compared to theirs. Please, won't you indulge me in this?"

He studied her, then nodded, looking mystified. "If it's what you wish."

She leaned to him and kissed his cheek lingeringly.

"Thank you. Best change out of those handsome clothes into something more workaday. Where we're going, there are people Andrew's age who would cut your throat for your watch chain."

"What?" he exclaimed.

"I'll meet you back here in ten minutes," she said, then dashed up the stairs before he could ask her any more torturous questions.

A short while later Hawk was mentally cursing his willingness to go along with this. They were riding their horses through the dark labyrinth of filth-strewn back streets that made up the rookery of St. Giles's. It was no place for a lady or for a civilized man. Astride his tall restless stallion, Hawk rode at a walk beside Belinda's docile gray gelding, one hand resting on the butt of his pistol while he scanned the street and the ramshackle buildings. William brought up the rear, astride one of the servants' hack horses.

The moist, musky stink of the river at low tide permeated the close alleys. No streetlamps pierced the unrelenting dark. Broken signs, creaking in the tepid breeze, hung from shops with cages over their windows. Potholes deep enough to cripple a horse yawned in the surface of the medieval streets.

"I hope there is a point to all this," he muttered.

Beneath her wispy riding veil, Belinda's face once again wore that haunting mask of serenity. Gracefully perched sidesaddle, she brought her horse to a halt with a slight pull on the reins.

"There," she murmured, pointing to a large warehouse with one gloved hand.

Hawk studied it. "It looks deserted."

"Would that it were." She urged her horse back into motion.

Hawk shook his head at her misguided courage and gave his horse a squeeze with his ankles, keeping abreast of her.

She halted again across the street from the dilapidated warehouse and dismounted.

"What are you doing, Belinda?"

"I'm going in there."

"Oh, no, you're not—"

"My horse, William?" She turned to the groom.

"Yes, ma'am." The lad jumped down with a grim expression and held her gelding's reins.

"Belinda!"

"This is what we came for, Robert. Let me go in first."

"You cannot be serious."

"They know me. I'll call you over in a moment once they've seen that you're no threat."

"Belinda Hamilton, you will not go in there. Get back on your horse," he ordered, but she ignored him, sweeping off her hard brimmed riding hat and hurrying alone across the street.

Muttering oaths, Hawk was already leaping down off his horse and following her when movement stirred in the gloom near the warehouse door. He drew in his breath and pulled out his pistol, but before his eyes, small shadows materialized out of the darkness and began gathering around her.

He stopped and stared.

Children.

He realized he was looking at a flash house. He had known such grim, lurid establishments existed, of course, but he had never seen one with his own eyes.

Belinda bent down and greeted the small, ragged shapes, silhouetted against the wall. Several hugged her. He saw her reach into her reticule and give away her money. He gazed at her, humbled by the grace and compassion she had dared to bring into this underworld of brutish squalor.

In a dawning wave of sorrow, he stared at the thin, wary, needy children surrounding her—budding thieves and prostitutes all, future fodder for Lord Eldon's gallows. As dismal a realization as this was, his concern for Belinda's safety was even greater. Lurking somewhere nearby was bound to be the pimp and his associates, no doubt grown and dangerous thugs, for these wraithlike children certainly weren't taking their profits for themselves. God only knew what kind of cutthroats roamed this rookery. He was glad he'd brought his guns and had armed William, as well. The three of them would be fortunate not to end the night floating facedown in the Thames.

Just then Belinda beckoned him over. He slipped his pistol back into its holster, glanced over his shoulder to assure himself that William was having no trouble with his temperamental stallion, then approached, feeling like a towering Gulliver in the land of the Lilliputians as the silent, hollow-eyed children backed out of his path.

At Belinda's urging he peered into the warehouse through the hanging door. Shock resounded silently through him and horror as his gaze traveled over the mass of youngsters inside.

By the time he drew her away, he was stunned into brooding silence.

"Are you all right?" she asked as they walked back to their horses.

He nodded. "You?"

"Oh, I'm used to this." She stared for a long moment at a nearby alleyway that yawned into pitch blackness like some corridor to Hell. Absently, she shook herself. "I only wish they hadn't seen me like this. It sets a bad example." Putting her riding hat back on, she walked away.

He followed her to her horse and gave her a leg up while William attempted to soothe the nervous stallion. In another few minutes they were on their way out of the St. Giles's maze.

"Something must be done for them," Hawk said quietly.

Belinda looked at him—looked into his very soul, it seemed. "I knew you would feel the same as I do. There are a small number of charities that offer these children aid, like the Philanthropic Society and the Relief Society for the Destitute, but from what I've seen, it's like trying to stop a flood with a bottle cork."

He reached across the empty space between them and took her hand. She looked over, her eyes wary beneath her half veil.

"You have never seemed to me more beautiful than you are right now," he murmured. "I will do everything in my power to help them, Belinda."

"I knew I could count on you." She squeezed his hand before she let it go to steady her horse.

When they reached Knight House, Belinda kissed him on the cheek and went to bed, murmuring that she was worn out by it all.

In a saddened mood at the ugliness in the world, Hawk drifted into his library, caressed his piano as he passed it on the way to his desk, and sat down to write out his thoughts and questions for future research about the flash houses, juvenile crime, and the concealed sickness that obviously infected London within a stone's throw from Carlton House and Buckingham Palace and every aristocratic great house like his own.

Time and again he caught himself staring at nothing, his mind drifting back to Belinda. He never would have thought he'd say it, but he was beginning to see that her decision to become a courtesan was not born of mercenary greed and vanity, as he had automatically assumed when he first met her. Through no fault of her own, but due to her father's incompetence and Dolph's predation, the gently bred Miss Hamilton had been steadily reduced to the level of a coster-monger. The humiliation she must have felt, he thought, cringing at the memory of the many small digs he had taken at her for her choice of occupations.

He had not fully appreciated that her choice had been a matter of survival. Tonight he had glimpsed the meaning of the word. And through it all, she had not lost her ability to notice and care for other people.

He put down his quill pen and rested his face in his hands, feeling like a damned hypocrite. All the while that he had been looking down his nose at her, judging her for a harlot, her heart brimmed with love for others and held a quiet, luminous, unsung virtue.

Good God, stop this nonsense, commanded the voice of reason suddenly in his head, sounding remarkably like his late father's cold, clipped tones. Indeed, he could almost envision the shade of the eighth duke standing glowering before him. *This is absurd,* it seemed to say. *You, a Hawkscliffe, are making an ass of yourself over a demirep. Stop idealizing this woman and tormenting yourself. Get control again before she makes an utter fool of you, for that is precisely what she'll do if you let this go any further.* At the single bong of the grandfather clock just then, the guilty vision of his father's anger fled, leaving Hawk alone with his fear of the things Belinda made him feel.

Nothing was solved. The tug-of-war between his heart and his head resumed with renewed intensity. Even now he yearned to go to her. He stared into the candle's tongue of flame, brooding.

I can't use her for bait, he thought. But he had to. And he knew that he would. His mouth curled in a bitter twist. His only option, after all, was to kneel at her feet and confess to the star of the demimonde that he had become her slave.

≼ CHAPTER ≽
TWELVE

In the gentle, undulating countryside of Leicestershire the mail coach stopped daily in the quaint market town of Melton Mowbray. A sturdy boy of ten, entrusted with a high duty, greeted the easygoing post driver every day and accepted from him whatever government mail had been franked to his employer, along with the master's daily edition of the *London Times*.

The boy then began the hour's walk on foot into the green, pleasant countryside, glad for the shady lanes, for the bright yellow sun shone hot. At last the hipped slate roofs of the stately manor house climbed over the rise before him. Reaching the top of the rise the boy paused to catch his breath.

The breeze rippled through his tousled hair as he viewed the ruddy brick manor house that nestled between the rolling hills, its reflecting pond glittering under the blue summer sky. He did not pause long, however, for the earl of Coldfell would be wanting his *Times*.

Heaving his leather satchel with the mail and newspaper higher onto his shoulder, the boy squinted in the sun. From the distance he could see the masons and carpenters up on the scaffolding, still fixing the east wing of the house that had been burned in the fire before the poor, pretty, red-headed countess had drowned.

Poor old master, thought the boy, spying his lordship hobbling out on his cane to inspect the workmen's progress.

Carrying his precious cargo, the mail boy jogged the rest of the way to his destination. When he approached, the kindly old earl rumpled his hair and smiled, taking the newspaper from him.

With the day's issue of the *Times* under his arm, Coldfell went inside to his study, closed the door behind him, and leaned his cane against the wall. He clamped his lined mouth and lifted his monocle, scanning the paper in grim eagerness for word of Dolph's death. After a few minutes' diligent search, Coldfell's eyes narrowed.

Nothing.

Glowering, he straightened up from the paper as the monocle fell from his eye. "Damn it, Hawkscliffe, what are you waiting for?" he muttered under his breath.

Robert had vowed to avenge Lucy and to destroy Dolph, but ever since Coldfell had left for the countryside, the duke had done nothing but parade around London with his flashy young ladybird on his arm. He could easily understand that Hawkscliffe was a virile man and perhaps had need of a woman's consolation after Lucy's death. Still, he did not like it. The duke clearly needed reminding about his quest. In another few days, Coldfell planned on returning to Town for this Tory soiree that Hawkscliffe's mistress was giving on her protector's behalf. Then he would see for himself just what the devil was going on between this courtesan harlot and the man he had privately earmarked as his future son-in-law.

As summer deepened, Dolph Breckinridge was awash in a despondency and a misery so complete he had never known such feelings could exist.

He could only sit in the bow window at his club, staring

bitterly at the Victory parade. It seemed to mock his defeat. *She will never be my wife now.*

Quaffing his glass of ale, he left and tried to elude the turmoil in his breast by driving. He slowed to leer into the shop window where he'd watched Belinda trying on her pretty gowns. *I hate her. I want her. I need her.* Damn it, what kind of exchange had Hawkscliffe meant that night at Vauxhall?

Tossing the spent stump of his cheroot into the street, he cracked the reins of his phaeton again with a sneer. He careened through the streets of London as though trying to outrun his own obsession. Why couldn't he forget her? He did not understand himself why she tormented him this way, made him so angry. It was either destiny or, he feared to think, there was something wrong with his mind.

He drove to all the places where he used to find her selling her oranges and the dingy tenement where she used to let a room.

Leaving the environs of the City, he drove north toward Islington until he came to the refined treed lane at the end of which sat Mrs. Hall's Academy for Young Ladies, the place where Belinda had worked, for he had divined a way to get back at Hawkscliffe, if he dared.

The finishing school was associated with a tiny quaint village from which it sat apart, aloof as an heiress at tea. Having come to see Bel here every day for a month, he knew the school's daily schedule; he knew the layout of the grounds.

Separating the stately brick school from the cluster of shops and the pub was a green stretch of field, an old commons that had been planted with flowers and turned into a little park. In the center of the greensward was a neatly kept pond with a gaggle of geese, some ducks, and one gorgeous swan vainly watching its own reflection as it drifted. The schoolgirls liked to feed the water fowl.

Dolph pulled his phaeton over to the side of the country lane and jumped out, leaving his vehicle in the care of his cowering groom. He checked his fob watch as he took a casual stroll across the cobbled village street to the bakery. Inside he bought a loaf of bread, then stepped back outside into the dazzling sunshine and walked to the pond to feed the ducks with the air of a man minding his own business.

As he bent down to toss the birds some crumbs, right on time, behind him, he heard the school bell ring. A narrow smile skimmed over his lips. Today was the day he would lure his quarry close enough to come and talk to him. He could feel it.

Behind him he could hear the fair pupils giggling and chattering as they filed out of the exclusive academy, two by two, for it was the hour of their daily constitutional. Slowly he looked over his shoulder at them.

Mincing with dainty propriety, the students, dressed in virginal white, proceeded onto the path that led down to the commons where he loitered. There were about thirty in all. He swept them with a practiced eye, but his gaze homed in on one young beauty who stood out from the crowd like the swan among the ducks.

Lady Jacinda Knight—Hawkscliffe's treasured baby sister.

She was the perfect means to teach Hawkscliffe that Dolph Breckinridge would not be trifled with.

While the other girls wore bonnets or had their hair plaited and coiled, Jacinda had a mane of wild honey gold curls that floated like a cloud around her apple-cheeked face. She was a fresh, bold, precocious little hellion with high cheekbones and sparkling brown eyes that had a sultry almond shape; she laughed more frequently and loudly than any of the other girls, was constantly in motion, and seemed to dance when she walked. All of sixteen, seventeen at the most, her body had a lithe, nymphlike grace that well suited her aura of high-spirited mischief.

Dolph wanted her.

He felt more than a stirring of lust, waiting with a hunter's expert patience for her to come near. Excitement pounded in him. Hearing a snippet of nervous, giggling whispers on the breeze, he sensed the girl's thrill to discover he had come back to admire her again. But how were they going to talk to each other?

He had hoped to prey upon her youthful naivete, but she knew she wasn't allowed to address a man without a formal introduction. Nor could he address her without breaking the rules of decorum.

Lady Jacinda approached on the footpath with her companion, a drab brown-haired girl with a tight bun in the back of her head, who looked as though she had already resigned herself to spinsterhood. Jacinda carried a frilly parasol, stepping as delicately as a vain filly on the parade ground when a stallion was near, while her plain friend read aloud to her from a book.

With the fetching, flirty glances Jacinda threw him from across the green, she seemed to Dolph more than willing to be seduced. He could well imagine she tormented boys her own age, but surely she had never received such pointed attentions from a man before—a man who knew how to satisfy the newly blossoming urges that no doubt filled her sweet teenaged body. The whole ton already prognosticated that the girl would have a lusty nature. After all, she was the only daughter of the original Hawkscliffe Harlot.

When Jacinda cast him another furtive look, he licked his lips and smiled at her.

She tossed her curls and looked away, blushing. Her spinsterish friend followed her glance and immediately frowned, pinched faced, scolding, and governesslike. They conferred in whispers. Dolph smiled to himself. Perhaps when he managed to get her alone, Jacinda would like to have a look at his scars, he thought. Women loved that.

He tore off some small pieces of bread and threw them to the ducks, feeling the girls' stares on him. Then, suddenly, in the blink of an eye, Lady Jacinda proved she had inherited her mother's genius for flirtation. Whether by feminine artifice or the interference of that still more coy female, Mother Nature, Jacinda's light silk parasol lifted out of her gloved hand and blew on a gust of wind, exactly like a kite, and landed in the center of the pond.

Dolph turned around just as she came barreling to the edge of the water amid the clacking ducks. She skidded to a halt beside him.

"Oh, no!" she cried, clapping her hands to her cheeks like Sarah Siddons on stage at Covent Garden.

Dolph nearly fell half in love with her for that.

"Miss," he said with a humble bow, biting back laughter, "allow me."

"Oh, good sir, I couldn't possibly impose upon your kindness—"

But Dolph stripped off his coat with a gallant half smile and began wading out into the pond to retrieve her bit of expensive frippery. Up to his muscular thighs in cold water, he reached the thing and grasped it, masking his irritation at having ruined boots that had cost him seventy guineas. Getting back at Hawkscliffe would be worth it, he assured himself. He turned around and found his little quarry beaming and blushing, the wind running riot through her sunny curls.

"It's a bit the worse for wear, I'm afraid," he said as he stomped out of the mud and muck and handed it to her.

A cascade of breathless laughter spilled from her lips. "Thank you, Mister—?"

"Sir Dolph Breckinridge, at your service, mademoiselle."

"Hello. I am Jacinda," she whispered, peeking over her shoulder.

Her friend was standing a few feet away scowling. A schoolmarm in an apron was on her way.

"You are beautiful," he whispered. "May I write to you?"

Her eyes widened, sparkling with excitement. "I'm sure that is not proper!"

"Nor's it proper when young ladies throw their parasols in ponds," he taunted softly. "Do you so like propriety?"

"Jacinda," her companion hissed. "Miss Alverston is coming!"

"Stall her, Lizzie," she shot back over her shoulder.

"Do you like driving? Come for a ride with me."

"Sir Dolph," she exclaimed, looking scandalized and unbearably eager at the same time.

"I'll teach you how to drive my phaeton. Won't that be fun? I'll teach you everything," he whispered, gazing at her rosy lips.

"Lady Jacinda! Stop bothering that gentleman this instant!" bellowed the monitor, arriving on the scene.

"She dropped her parasol, Miss Alverston," the spinsterish girl tried to explain.

Jacinda heeded neither of them, staring at Dolph, her big velvety brown eyes still wide with shocked fascination at his seductive words.

The older woman marched over and grasped her wrist. "Good day, sir, this is private property. You will have to read your paper elsewhere."

"Oh, I wasn't aware, sorry," he said blandly, looking down his nose at the woman.

"Thank you for saving my parasol," Jacinda called as the schoolmarm tugged her away by the wrist, then the young beauty turned and began skipping to keep up.

But her more prudent companion, whom she had called

Lizzie, stopped and glared up at him, hands on hips. "I remember you," Lizzie warned. "You're the Nasty Man who got our favorite teacher fired. You'd best stay away from here!"

"What are you going to do about it?"

"I'll tell on you!"

"Dear me, I might get my knuckles rapped by the headmistress."

"That's not who I'll tell, you—you rude person. I'll tell Lady Jacinda's brothers—all five of them! You'll be mincemeat!"

"Lizzie," someone called.

"Coming!"

"You'd better keep your mouth shut," Dolph growled.

"And you'd better stay away from my best friend," she huffed, then she turned on her heel and hurried back to the school.

Dolph sneered as he watched her, realizing he was probably foiled.

As sweet as that particular vengeance might be, pursuing Jacinda Knight would be suicide. Hawkscliffe alone was enough of a foe—he didn't even want to think about running afoul of that outlaw Jack or the war-hero Damien, who would no doubt soon return from the Peninsula.

He spit on the emerald grass and stalked back to his phaeton.

Perhaps he was biased, Hawk mused, but as the orchestra's music vibrated through the Argyle Rooms on the night of the Cyprians' Ball, he decided with considerable pride that *his* mistress was by far the most beautiful woman in the place. Her slender curves were draped in a shimmering ice blue gown, displaying so much cleavage at her plunging neckline that she positively made his mouth water. He would have liked to see her wearing nothing but the diamond-and-lapis-lazuli necklace that glittered at her creamy throat.

He had splurged for her again, surprising her with the gift just before the party. He gave a rueful sigh when he realized he was sinking fast into his folly and didn't even seem to care. Just looking at her lifted his heart.

She was chatting with three of the Unique Four, working the party, to his amusement, and charming everyone who crossed her path. She seemed to have a golden glow around her that made people gravitate to her and come away smiling—especially if those people were men, Hawk thought, beginning to get a trifle impatient with her social rounds. He wanted her back by his side where she belonged. God help him, he was besotted.

Scowling, he tossed back his sherry and set the small glass on the bar, wondering if he would end up as obsessed with the woman as Dolph was. With his stare fixed on her, he strode through the crowd, giving perfunctory replies to the greetings of his acquaintances. He ignored the flamboyant party in progress around him, all his attention focused only on her. Lewd stories, raucous laughter, cavorting and kisses and brazen fondlings were going on all around him. The Cyprians gave the men full leave to misbehave.

Belinda saw him coming and her eyes flared, their brilliance dimming the luster of the jewels. A trace of a bewitching smile curved her lips. He was transfixed.

She held his gaze as he parted the group of men who surrounded her. His spirit caught fire the moment he touched her. Staring at her in enthralled absorption, he took her hand and led her to the dance floor, deaf to the protests of the young men she had been talking to. Coaxing her with naught but a slight, private smile, he drew her into the minuet. Neither of them broke their challenging stare as they danced. Hawk drank in her every graceful movement, inhaling the scent of her perfume as she wove past him in the figures of the dance. She tipped her chin downward and sent him an alluring glance over her shoulder as she passed him. He reached out and put his hand on her waist, stilling her. She looked up at him in question.

They ceased dancing, though the minuet moved on around them. Inches apart, they gazed at each other, not moving, not even kissing, like two lovers in a porcelain statuette. The pounding of his pulse roared in his ears. And then, beneath the gay rhythmic clamor of the orchestra, he heard inside his heart another melody, free and wild and sweet as the piping of a solitary nightingale.

Belinda stared at him, her lips slightly parted, her eyes glistening with wonder as though she could hear it, too.

He knew then. He held her hand, trembling inside with awed reverence. It was no use. The impossible had befallen him. He was in love with her.

Bel wasn't sure what was wrong. Her protector was standing there staring at her and looking as though he had just been struck by some fiery celestial comet. She was about to ask him if he felt quite well, when Harriette sailed over to them and cheerfully hooked her arm through Bel's.

"Your Grace, so sorry, I need to borrow her for just a moment. I'll bring her back in a trice. Bel, if you'll come with me. There's someone who wishes to meet you—"

"No," Robert said harshly, grasping Bel's wrist harder.

Harriette and Bel both turned to him in surprise. He seemed to realize then that he had just uttered a most impolite syllable.

Harriette laughed and struck his arm lightly with her fan. "Oh, be a good sport, Hawkscliffe. She is here to entertain, you know."

Robert let go of her hand and looked at Bel imploringly. "She can do what she thinks is right, I'm sure."

Bel furrowed her brow. "Are you quite well?"

"I'm fine," he whispered.

"Come along, child. It's urgent." Harriette began tugging her away.

Bel went tripping along after her, but looked over her shoulder at Robert as Harriette pulled her away. He stood staring after her, his dark eyes blazing with intensity.

"Come, hurry! You'll never guess who wants to meet you. I'm so jealous."

"Who is it?"

"Czar Alexander!"

Bel gasped, stopped, and pulled her hand free. "You're jesting."

"Don't look now, but he's in the gallery with his entourage. He noticed you in the crowd," Harriette squealed in glee.

Bel glanced up at once toward the gallery and saw movement there, but the people at the railing were drifting away. "W-what does he want?"

"What do you think, dear? You caught his eye. I hope you are prepared to be accommodating."

"No!"

"No?" Harriette pulled her aside, turned to her, and set her hands pugnaciously on her waist. "What do you mean, 'no'?"

"I came here with Hawkscliffe."

"What is wrong with you?"

"Nothing—"

"Bel, you little fool, how many times have I warned you?"

"I'm sure I don't know what you're talking about."

"You're in love with him."

"No, I'm not," she shot back, but she could feel her cheeks heating with a blush.

"Yes, you are. You've forfeited, lost the game."

"I have not!"

"Really? Well, I'm glad to hear it. Because right now, the Czar of all the Russias is waiting to take you to bed. Come on. I'll not have you offending him and embarrassing me." Harriette grasped her by the wrist and began pulling her toward the stairs, but Bel planted her slippered feet and refused to budge another inch.

"No!"

"You can't say no; you are a courtesan," Harriette exclaimed.

"I choose my own lovers. I don't want him."

"Don't be a fool! It is the Czar! It's not as if he is repugnant. He's very handsome. Haven't you seen him?"

"Yes, I've seen him, but I am *not* going to leave Robert standing there alone all night."

"I'll send one of the others to entertain him—"

"Don't you dare," she warned.

"Belinda Hamilton, you cannot refuse the Czar of Russia. Do it for England."

"Oh, please! If he is such a gentleman as everyone says, then he will understand."

"I don't believe you. You are throwing away the chance of a lifetime! Treat him well and who knows where he can take you? Bel, he is an *emperor*. Don't be a fool!"

"If you're so impressed with him, you take him to bed, Harrie!" She pulled her hand free and pivoted, striding away on legs that shook beneath her.

"You ungrateful, arrogant little wench! How dare you embarrass me like this, after all I've done for you?"

"I've paid you twenty percent for everything you've done for me, Harrie, so forgive me if I fail to grovel sufficiently."

"What am I supposed to tell the Czar?"

"Tell him I am flattered, but my first loyalty must be to Hawkscliffe. I'm going home."

"Knight House is not your home, you little fool. You're

going to learn that the hard way. You're nothing but a servant there."

Bel hurried through the throng with Harriette's warning
still ringing in her ears. She was desperate to see Robert.
She prayed he wasn't angry at her for allowing Harriette to
drag her away. What had that stare of his meant? She burst
through a knot of people talking and suddenly came face-
to-face with him.

His dark eyes blazed with anger and hurt. She stepped
toward him, touching his chest in silent pleading. He lifted
her chin roughly between his fingers and thumb. He tilted her
head back and searched her eyes.

"What's this, changed your mind?" he growled.

Trembling, Bel clasped her arms around his neck in
reply and pulled him down to her, kissing him full on the
mouth. He wrapped his arms around her waist, kissing her
with hot, lusty abandon in the middle of the ballroom,
claiming her with an almost violent passion.

They were deaf to the raucous cries and whistles of the
people around them. No one noticed their furious desperation, taking it all in fun, but Bel was in an agony of longing
for him as she ran her fingers through his hair, opening her
mouth wider to accept his angry dominating kiss. She
could feel his intent—to teach her a lesson—teach her
that she belonged completely to him. She wanted only to
surrender.

Defiantly she hoped the Czar and his entourage and
Harriette were all watching. She ended the kiss but held
his face between her trembling hands and pressed her forehead against his.

"Take me home," she breathed.

He didn't need any urging. He swept her off her feet and
carried her out of the Argyle Rooms, all the way out to his
town coach.

She was barely aware of the driver and grooms whisking into their posts. When Robert and she were inside, they pulled down the shades and tumbled into each other's arms as the well-sprung coach smoothly bore them through the dark city toward Green Park.

He eased her back onto the ivory leather seat. Tasting and touching, fumbling with clothing, they groped and stroked each other, kissing all the while as if they'd never get enough. The coach was filled with the sound of their panting and the creak of the leather seats as Robert sat up and pulled her astride him, his hands hot and trembling.

"I've been wanting to do this all night. Give me those luscious—" He ripped the front of her bodice open, freed her breasts, and buried his face between them. "*Mmmm. God, I could devour you,*" he moaned as his hot, wet mouth captured her nipple.

Bel gasped then let out a low, breathless laugh of delirious pleasure.

Suckling her, he slid the torn neckline of her gown still lower, caressing her body everywhere.

She arched her head back and wove her fingers through his jet black hair as he moved to sample her other breast. Beneath her skirts, his hands crept up her thighs, spread in wanton invitation as she straddled his lap.

"Hmm, no petticoats," he panted.

She closed her eyes and smiled drunkenly as he slid his fingers between her legs. Kissing her neck, he indulged her until she thought her nerves would snap with her need for release. But at passion's edge, he stopped. She dragged her eyes open as he picked her up and set her down on the opposite seat. Staring at her, with a dark, sly half smile, he pressed her back gently against the luxurious leather and lowered himself to his knees.

"Robert—"

"Just enjoy," he whispered. "I know I will."

With a soft moan, she closed her eyes and yielded to his sensuous gift, twining her fingers through his silky black hair.

Soon her feet were braced against the edge of the opposite seat, her gown was hitched up around her hips, and she held onto the coach's looped leather hand straps for dear life while Robert took her with his fingers and consumed her with his tongue. She lifted her hips, moving with him, all her inhibitions melting in the steamy heat of the summer night. His rhythm quickened, matching her need, soaring her to new altitudes of wicked bliss.

He stopped, his hands shaking as he reached for his falls, his clean-shaved chin glistening in the moonlit dark. "I have to have you. Now."

Immediately a frisson of panic slid through her veins. *Not that.* She wasn't ready. She planted her hand on his chest, holding him back. She winced to deny him but prayed he wouldn't be angry. "Darling, n-not in the coach. Not for our first time together, please?"

He dropped his head back and let out a groan of agonized frustration.

"Oh, my sweet man," she whispered, enfolding him between her legs as she ran her hand down his body and cupped the swollen, steely hardness that strained against his snug silk breeches. "May I, Your Grace?" she asked with a coy glance at his face. At his low, lusty growl of desire, she shoved him back into his seat and took charge.

By the time the town coach rolled to a halt in front of Knight House, Robert and she climbed out, trying to reclaim a shred of dignity.

The smell of sex poured out of the coach when the footman opened the door. They had pleasured each other wildly and Robert's climax had been explosive.

Heating with a scarlet blush and holding back nervous laughter, Bel could not bear to look at the grooms and servants as they walked to the house. She had no doubt that every groom and even the horses knew what they had been doing during the drive home.

Carrying her shoes in one hand, her reticule in the other, somehow she walked inside with her chin high, her stare fixed straight ahead, knowing full well she was in a state of complete dishevelment, a rip in the middle of her already-low neckline and a high blush in her cheeks. Her whole body felt wonderful, however, and she couldn't wait to go straight to sleep.

Robert was somewhat worse off. Cravat undone, shirt hanging open halfway down his chest, he looked tousled and sated, a little savage and quite raw. He was silent as he walked beside her up the curving staircase. The marble steps felt cool under her stockinged feet.

At the top of the stairs, they stopped and looked at each other uncertainly.

Bel smiled at him and he returned it with a rueful chuckle, running his hand through his mussed hair. He dropped his gaze and for a moment there was a silence fraught with hunger and hesitation.

"Never been to a Cyprians' Ball before," he said.

"Neither have I."

Another awkward pause.

He slid her a questioning look. "I had a good time."

Her smile widened. "That was the idea." She took a step toward him and went up onto her tiptoes, placing a delicate kiss on his cheek. "Good night, Robert."

As she drew back he searched her eyes with a smoldering gaze. "When, Belinda?" he whispered.

Her caress smoothed the black satin lapel of his tailcoat. "Soon." Suddenly unnerved, she forced a casual smile and turned away, slinging her scarf over her shoulder, striding toward her suite as though she hadn't a care in the world.

"Good night, Miss Hamilton," he echoed and stood there, hands in pockets, with the lamplight sculpting his faint wry smile as he watched her walk away.

≈ CHAPTER ≈
THIRTEEN

The earl of Coldfell sat in Hawkscliffe's drawing room with the other Tory leaders, drinking port. The night of Miss Hamilton's long-awaited dinner party had come at last. Coldfell wore a taut smile on his lined face, but inwardly, he was a most disgruntled puppet master. His marionettes were not at all dancing to his tune, but soon, they would. Oh, they would.

Tonight he had come merely to observe the situation between Robert and his doxy. He could not believe he had so miscalculated Hawkscliffe's nature. The fiery young duke should have killed Dolph by now, but here was Hawkscliffe, cozily ensconced with his blond beauty, brazenly indifferent to the shock he had given Society and the scandal surrounding his name out there in the world.

As for his promise to punish Dolph, he seemed to have forgotten the matter entirely. Coldfell could only conclude that the fault lay with this blond enchantress, this *belle dame sans merci*, who had lured the knight off his vowed quest to avenge Lucy. Hawkscliffe was obviously in her thrall.

As a man who had always had a weakness for beauty himself, Coldfell could not begrudge the fair Bel Hamilton her living. What he did not approve of was the way she had clearly taken charge of Knight House, the servants, and even the duke himself to a degree. She carried herself like his duchess, not his whore, and Coldfell liked it not at all, determined as he was to see his daughter installed as the ninth duchess of Hawkscliffe.

Robert and Juliet would suit very well.

Coldfell knew he had his faults, but if he had one virtue, it was that he was a most protective and doting papa. Before leaving this world he intended to see his only child well married to a considerate husband who would take care of her. Who else but Hawkscliffe could he entrust with his sweet, flawed, fragile daughter? Who else would have the gallantry to wed the cloistered innocent, fully understanding that she was *not* feebleminded, merely that yellow fever had robbed Juliet in childhood of her hearing?

Unlike the worldly courtesan sharing the duke's bed, Juliet was an utter innocent in the ways of the world. It wasn't as though she could have a normal Season. Fate had robbed her of the grand debut that was every highborn miss's right. She couldn't dance; she couldn't hear music. Conversation with people she didn't know was nearly impossible for Juliet, though she could read lips easily enough with her father and her nurse. She was as shy as a little doe, and as lovely.

With his knight's chivalry Hawkscliffe would not be able to refuse, especially when he saw Juliet's blue, wonderfilled eyes and chocolate curls. Coldfell was counting on it. Their firstborn son—his future grandson—would inherit the earldom, then he could go to his grave knowing his daughter and his holdings were in good hands.

Let Hawkscliffe keep his harlot, he thought. It would minimize Juliet's wifely duties.

Just then the double doors that adjoined the drawing and dining rooms opened, and the stately, white-gloved butler appeared, bowing.

"Dinner is served," he announced in a dignified monotone.

"Wellington, care to do the honors?" Hawkscliffe offered, presenting his mistress to the Iron Duke with an elegant gesture.

Tall, stoic, and sternly erect of carriage, the great stone-faced general very nearly cracked a smile as he nodded and offered her his arm. "Miss Hamilton, I would be honored."

She accepted his escort gracefully.

Why, the courtesan was as thorough a conqueror as the general, he thought cynically, watching them go into the dining room.

She was, he admitted, a rapturous beauty. No male, however advanced in years, could have been immune to her charms. Her serene, secretive smile had them all quite fascinated. Eldon especially seemed to dote on her. The Lord Chancellor had sat right next to her on the sofa and probably would have tried coaxing her onto his bony lap if Hawkscliffe hadn't been there—and perhaps she would have accepted, for a price.

La Belle Hamilton had a sense of style and smooth graceful bearing. Her heavenly body was wrapped in a clinging muslin gown of palest pearl pink. If flame-haired Lucy, with her passion and lust for life had been fire, Bel Hamilton was ice, Coldfell thought, gleaming and multi-faceted, throwing light like a perfect diamond, but he could well imagine that she melted for Hawkscliffe.

Bringing up the rear, the darkly handsome young duke gave the others a smile of reserved, cordial warmth and held out his hand toward the dining room. "Gentlemen, after you."

Coldfell gave his host an amiable nod as he hobbled past him on his cane and went in to take his place at the table. He noted with an inward snort that the table was

excellently laid. The courtesan was a skilled hostess.
Every detail had been attended to. Beeswax candles reflected the high polish on every inch of carved mahogany
and gleamed in the rococo silverware and the great tiered
epergne in the table's center. Little delicate finger bowls of
orange-flower water awaited them on the impeccable
white linen tablecloth, and the bewigged, liveried footmen
stood at the ready in every corner of the room.

As Hawkscliffe took his seat at the head of the table, he
glanced down toward the foot at his mistress, a private
little smile tugging at his mouth. Coldfell saw them exchange a look of solid mutual understanding. They worked
so smoothly in tandem it was like watching a seamless,
graceful dance.

Coldfell glanced furtively from one to the other.

Admittedly, anyone could see that this woman was good
for Hawkscliffe. He looked far more relaxed and easygoing than Coldfell had ever seen him in the past; his
brown eyes were not so tormented. His mistress knew how
to handle him, too, smoothly breaking in with a charming
remark back there in the drawing room when Sidmouth
had begun to get the duke hot under the collar.

Miss Hamilton, in turn, had been visibly nervous early
on when the guests had begun arriving, but Coldfell had
seen how Robert's quiet support calmed her with little
more than a gentle touch to her elbow—a touch that bespoke a world of affection and trust. Full understanding hit
him hard as he witnessed their wordless, barely percep-
tible exchange of a glance.

They are in love.

The glow in Robert's dark eyes and the blush in Belinda's
pink cheeks betrayed them. And the magic that emanated
from them was having a contagious effect on the Tory
magnates, Coldfell thought, pursing his mouth. Their whole

party was in such merry spirits, it was as though Miss Hamilton had slipped some intoxicating powder into the sparkling wine.

As the elaborate first course was carried into the dining room—magnificent platters of goose and broiled trout, venison and succulent veal with countless side dishes like red stewed cabbage and Jerusalem artichokes—Coldfell lowered his gaze. He spread his snowy napkin over his lap and dipped his fingers in the scented water.

Very well, he thought tersely. Drastic measures might need to be taken.

Everything seemed to be moving along smoothly, but Bel was too nervous to eat more than a few bites of the roast turkey in the second course or to do more than pick at the lobster *à la braise* in the third. In the drawing room her mission had been to cultivate the Tory magnates for Robert, but now that they had moved into the dining room, she was more interested in her writers. One had to have poets at one's table, after all. Only Whigs talked politics at dinner.

She tried to get Walter Scott to give a hint of what he was working on, but all he deigned to talk about was not his delicious tales of chivalry, but Abbotsford, the grand mock-medieval house he was perpetually building in the Borders. On and on he rambled about the practical matters of building a manor house: timbers, additions, foundations, and turrets, reminding her for all the world of a great Scottish bagpipe, so full was he of gusty hot air, though amiable.

Smiling politely, Bel made a mental note to remember henceforth that novelists were long-winded creatures, then turned hopefully to Robert Southey. Surely the mild-mannered poet laureate would have something inspiring to say, but he turned out to be the soul of conservatism, a reformed romantic, and when the wine flowed, all he wanted to talk about was not the Muse, but that perverted hack pagan, Byron, whom he despised beyond all things.

Bel met her protector's gaze down the table and both fought not to laugh at the jealous writer's spleen. So much for poetry. Robert delicately asked Mr. Southey about his excellent *Life of Nelson* and a discussion ensued that even the taciturn Wellington joined, proposing a toast. They drank to Nelson.

"Lord Castlereagh," Bel spoke up, engaging the elegant and handsome Irish-born foreign secretary, "Hawkscliffe tells me you've entered a motion in Parliament that a monument be raised to Lord Nelson?"

"Who is more deserving than our fallen admiral?" Castlereagh replied, with a softening of the haunted melancholy she had noticed in his eyes. He was known as an unhappy man, too brilliant for his own good. "I only wish Nelson were here to see how his old friend Wellesley finally finished off Boney for him—oh, forgive me, *Your Grace,*" he teased the general, newly made duke of Wellington scarcely a month ago.

She smiled at Wellington's gruff chuckle as the others said, "Here, here."

"What style of monument is being considered?" she asked.

"Our architects have proposed a great column with Nelson's likeness at the top."

"Oh, that would be very grand," she said with a warm smile. "You will commemorate him in marble as Mr. Southey has made him immortal in prose."

"It was the man's deeds that made him immortal, Miss Hamilton. I was merely the scribe," Mr. Southey said humbly. "So, tell us, what is our fair hostess reading these days?"

"How kind of you to ask. Actually, I have lately found the most astonishing novel. I spend a lot of time in book-stores," she added, thinking of her many searches for Papa's beloved tomes, as well. "I found this little anony-mously written novel at Hatchard's. It came out last year. I read the first sentence and could not put it down."

"Anonymous, eh? Not one of those naughty French books?" Eldon teased her.

"No, my lord," she scolded while the men laughed.

"What's it called?"

"Pride and Prejudice."

"Hmm, sounds political."

She chuckled. "Not exactly."

Then she noticed Robert staring at her with an odd, loving little smile and she grew flustered, dropping the subject. She looked away, blushing brightly. "More wine, anyone?"

As the desserts were brought to table, apricot puffs, lemon torte, blancmange, a morello cherry tart, and a whimsical trifle of crushed Naples biscuits adorned with real flowers, Bel noticed the earl of Coldfell staring at her again.

The pale old man had cold, faded blue eyes and knife-hilt cheekbones.

She looked away, cringing inwardly in sympathy for the red-haired beauty in Robert's miniature portrait. Lady Coldfell could not have much enjoyed her marriage bed. With a gorgeous, virile specimen like Hawkscliffe in love with her, how on earth could she have resisted?

But then, Bel recalled, it was Robert who had resisted. The countess might not necessarily have been averse to a little dalliance.

At length Bel took her cue to withdraw, leaving the men to drink their port and get down to brass tacks. They all stood and bowed as she made her slight curtsy and thanked them for coming. They thanked her, in turn, for the marvelous feast.

From the head of the table, Robert gave her a slight bow of homage, his dark eyes aglow with promise.

The moment she walked out of the dining room, she leaned against the closed door and let out a long breath. She exchanged a silent look of flushed victory with Mr. Walsh, who waited in the hallway, his white-gloved hands folded behind his back. A smile twitched at his dignified face, then Bel hurried to the kitchens to congratulate the French-trained chef and his pastry cook and his assistants whom she had hired for the occasion.

The kitchens were in a state of controlled pandemonium, Cook busily orchestrating cleanup. An endless mountain of copper pots and cast-iron pans, silver and steel utensils had to be washed. Seeing the gargantuan effort that had gone into making her dinner party a success, she gave the whole kitchen staff the next day off.

Only after her generous offer was made did she recall that she had no authority to do so—she wasn't exactly the lady of the house. Too late. The servants took her word as her oath, cheering and instantly making plans to go to Hyde Park to wander the stalls of the Victory Festival and see the follies that were being readied for the even larger festivities to commence by the Regent's orders on the first of August. There were Oriental temples, pagodas, bridges. The hopelessly gaudy, hundred-foot-high Temple of Concord was also being erected just a stone's throw away in Green Park, for the purpose of shooting off fireworks.

She didn't have the heart to retract her offer. They were all so excited. To be sure, she had overstepped her bounds, but Robert was a kind master to his people. After they had worked so hard, she trusted that he wouldn't mind.

She discovered Tommy and Andrew playing quietly under the center worktable. Since it was nearly midnight, she took it upon herself to put them to bed. She shepherded them over to wash their faces and brush their teeth; neither boy was much pleased with the novelty of hygiene. Then they changed into their long cotton nightshirts and shimmied down into their cots. Bel read them a storybook from the library while she waited for Robert to finish with the Tory lords. Looking after the children calmed her from the frightening thrill of her decision to deny Robert no longer.

Tonight she was as ready to give herself to him completely as she was ever going to be.

By the time she blew out the candle, silently left the third-floor servants' quarters and walked downstairs with a small tremor of anticipation in her limbs, the men were all standing in the foyer bidding one another good night.

Coldfell was the last to go. Robert walked him to the door. "I'll see you at noon, tomorrow, then."

"Very good. I'll be expecting you. Thank you again for the dinner, Robert. Charming creature, your Miss Hamilton."

His smile widened. "Good night, James."

Coldfell hobbled out to his coach, assisted by his footman.

Robert waved adieu and, when the carriage had gone, quietly shut the door. He turned around, leaned against the closed door, and spotted her standing there, about halfway up the sweeping staircase, watching him. He flashed a white, wolfish smile and pushed away from the door, sauntering toward the bottom of the stairs.

"There she is. My secret weapon," he said. "My enchantress. Castlereagh and Wellington are won; Eldon and Liverpool have agreed to review my reports, and Sidmouth said if those two support my views, he won't stand in the way."

Bel shrieked with glee, lifted her long skirts, and dashed the rest of the way down the steps to him. He caught her at the bottom as she flung her arms around his neck. Laughing heartily, he swung her around in a circle, his arms wrapped around her waist.

"You were wonderful! Miss Hamilton, we are an unstoppable team," he murmured. "What do you say to world domination? Shall we try for it?"

"I can think of other things I'd rather try with you, sir," she said with a frisky half smile. "I've been dying to get my hands on you all night."

"Likewise, Miss Hamilton." Carrying her, he began strolling down the hallway. "I am so impressed with you."

"I told you so. The dining room, Robert?" she asked quizzically as he turned left into the chamber in question. "Really, you are a most depraved paragon."

"You barely ate a bite. Yes, I notice these things," he chided. "Somebody's got to take care of you. I've saved you a special treat."

"What is it?"

"The morello cherry tart . . . with whipped cream." He set her down on the table, which had been cleared but for the silver epergne, the cherry tart, and the little bowl of whipped cream, and farther down, a little pile of unused silverware that awaited Walsh to put it away.

The table was a huge expanse of snowy white linen, and on every wall, the big mirrors reflected the two of them, alone at last, wrapped up in each other.

"Robert, do you expect me to eat with my hands? Go fetch me one of those forks down there."

"How unimaginative of you, Miss Hamilton," he murmured, dipping his finger in the whipped cream. He offered it to her with a sultry smile.

With a low, wicked laugh, she accepted hungrily, sucking his finger clean.

He stood in front of her where she sat on the table; she parted her legs to let him move closer. Gently he took her face between his hands and kissed her with slow, drugging depth. As she clung to him, going weak with desire, she knew she had never felt so close to him, still flush with their shared victory.

She sighed with pleasure as he moved lower, kissing her chin, her neck. His hands moved in slow caresses up and down her back and then she felt a small tug and glanced askance at him, realizing he had just unhooked her gown.

"Pray, what do you think you're doing, sir?" she asked in mock hauteur.

"Having my dessert," he whispered, peeling her bodice down in front to her waist so that she sat on the edge of the dining-room table bare chested, with nothing but a diamond necklace around her throat.

She braced her hands back behind her and stared at him, waiting. He glanced at the bowl of cream. Then she laughed with lazy desire when he smeared her breasts with whipped cream and commenced licking it off. Her laughter died away as the hot, tugging sensation of his hungry, suckling mouth moved her into ever deeper waves of want.

She wrapped her arms around his wide shoulders, ran her fingers through his silky black hair. Caressing her breasts, he eased her back onto the table, cradling her head with one hand.

His hair tousled from her caresses, he glanced at her with a cocky half smile, whipped cream around his wet, wanton mouth.

"You have such a beautiful mouth," she whispered as she curled up and licked his lips clean. Her hands trembled as she undressed him.

Moments later his body was naked to the waist. She gasped softly at the blissful sensation of his velvety muscled chest against her bare skin, so intimate, so warm. She molded her hands to his powerful shoulders then ran them down his massive arms, entranced by every line of him.

He skimmed his lips across her brow, down her cheek, down her throat. "Are you going to let me make love to you tonight?"

"Possibly," she said faintly, her eyes closed in breathless sensation.

"Oh, I'll have to do better than that. *Possibly,*" he scoffed.

"You're welcome to try."

"That sounds . . ."—he kissed her, unpinning her hair—"distinctly like a challenge, Miss Hamilton."

She traced the ridges of his washboard stomach. "Hmm?"

"I think you've just thrown down the gauntlet. Now I shall have to seduce you in earnest."

She laughed and spread her arms out on the table, lying back. "Do your worst."

"I shall." His hands glided down her hips, following her curves. "God, you're beautiful," he whispered.

"Oh, Hawk, touch me," she breathed, chest heaving. Her wetness flowed in anticipation of his touch as his hand glided up under her skirts. She acquiesced, parting her thighs wider at his gentle push. Then his warm fingers eased into her soaked passage, his thumb circling lightly on her mound. She groaned in surrender. He kissed her breasts with leisurely enjoyment.

With his dark eyes gone hazy and heavy lidded, he watched her fall utterly under his spell. He pleasured her until she was writhing and riding his fingers on the hard table. Then he moved up, staring at her as he unfastened his black trousers. She waited in quivering anticipation. He guided his massive erection to her teeming threshold.

With a hot, roguish little smile, he sported with her, played the tease. He rubbed himself slick in her wetness until she begged for him and only then did he deign to give her an inch or so, tantalizing her.

"You are a wicked man," she panted.

"Yes," he whispered. "But let that be our little secret. Do you need me now, darling? Do you need me deep inside you?"

"God, yes, Hawk, please," she groaned, undulating beneath him.

He captured her hands, linked his fingers through hers, and caught her heaving gasps of awe on his tongue as he filled her, inch by inch, until he had driven in to the hilt.

Bel barely dared breathe. He slid his fingers through her hair, incoherently whispering his gratitude and bliss, but her mind was focused on the strange sensation of her body stretching to receive him. Why it didn't hurt, she couldn't say. It felt delicious, but he was so large she was sure he'd split her in two if she moved wrong.

"Ahh, Belinda," he moaned softly, "I've needed you for so long, my angel, *ma belle*." He began to ride her in a deep subtle rhythm. She was swept up in pure instinct, loving her ravisher and every moment of being, herself, the fulfillment of his need.

Yet, at the same time, she was aware, in the farthest reaches of her mind, of the distant whisperings of her most secret fear. She refused to heed it. She held him more tightly.

He slid his hands under her backside and began kneading her flesh in a hearty grasp. Robert was feverish, trembling. His skin glowed with a fine sheen of sweat in the candlelight and he seemed intent on simply devouring her.

He's being a bit rough, isn't he? her demons whispered.

She fought them in secret for all she was worth. *He's so big, so strong, if you told him to stop, he could ignore you.*

She touched his hair gently, trying to temper his fiery ardor, but she cringed inwardly at the thought of giving herself away. Robert thought he was making love to an experienced, worldly courtesan. If she could just play the part until he had found release, everything would be fine. The pleasure drained away as she tussled with her thoughts. She tried to blank her mind. Closing her eyes tightly, she struggled to hold on, letting him take his pleasure of her body, but in the next moment, her fate was decided for her.

As Robert drew her hands above her head, the stroke of his tongue in her mouth matching the rhythm of his big rigid member plunging into her like a battering ram, the table shook, and the little pile of silverware took up a soft, rhythmic clanking.

An echo straight out of her nightmare.

Bel's eyes flew open wide; *that sound*. Like the jangle of keys. She felt her hands pinned above her head, the hard table at her back like a stone-block wall.

And it all came back.

She cried out in a wave of irrational terror, tearing her face away from Robert's kiss, immediately trying to get up, but of course, she could not. He was too heavy, and that made her panic more. She shoved against his shoulders, thrashing and whimpering for him to stop.

"What?" she heard him say, panting. "What is it, Bel?"

"Get off of me!" she screamed.

Immediately he obeyed, fear leaping into his eyes. "What's wrong? Are you all right? Did I hurt you?"

She was already halfway to the door, pulling her dress up and crying.

"Bel! Wait!"

She kept going.

Catching up to her in the blink of an eye, he suddenly blocked her exit. "What the hell is wrong?" he demanded, hitching up his trousers.

"Get out of my way."

"Get out of your way?" he cried. "But we—we were—"

"We're finished now. Good night, Your Grace," she said through gritted teeth.

"Who's finished?" Looking flabbergasted, he dragged his hand through his hair in bewilderment. "What is this? Some kind of game?"

"Yes. It's a game. That's all you get. Now get. Out. Of my way, Robert. I mean it." Her whole body was shaking.

"Not a chance." He planted his hand against the door. "What are you doing to me?"

She swallowed hard, her gaze following the corded muscles of his arm, the sculpted brawn of his shoulder. She backed away from him a step.

"A game?" His voice was frighteningly soft, full of menace. "I finally let myself care for you and you think you can just toy with me?"

"I can do whatever I please," she said stiffly, dying inside, but she couldn't lower her walls now even if she had wanted to. "You don't own my body."

"Ohhh, I see," he whispered. "You want more money out of me, don't you? That's what this is. You greedy little cutthroat whore."

She let out a strangled cry and slapped him across the face as hard as she could.

He lifted his hand to his cheek and looked at her with hellish wrath in his eyes.

Trembling, she stared back at him, shocked and horrified that she had just struck him, but the damage was done. The cause was lost.

"I'll never pay for what should not be for sale," he ground out. "I'll never be that desperate."

With that, he walked out and slammed the door in her face.

⊰ CHAPTER ⊱
FOURTEEN

The balmy golden morning that followed did nothing to shake Hawk's anger, hurt, and disbelief. He should have been waking in his mistress's bed, but it was barely seven and he was already fully dressed in a gentlemanly brown riding coat, buff leather breeches, and impeccably blacked high boots.

Not a hair out of place, his cravat more starchy than ever, he stalked down the stairs, moving with cold, mechanical precision. He called for his stallion to be saddled and went for a short, reckless gallop in Green Park.

Serves you right, Hawkscliffe, drawled his smug better sense. I warned you of this but you had to have her, didn't you? Fool. Falling for a demirep.

Reaching the far end of the park all too soon, his disgust wasn't nearly spent. He scowled in lordly disdain at the gauche Victory decorations littering the formerly tranquil green spaces of the park, then urged his stallion across Hyde Park Corner onto Serpentine Road. The morning sun sparkled on the water to his left as he raced his stallion, pounding down the straightaway.

Hadn't he known all too well she was obsessed with money? She was constantly poring over her financial treatises, stock charts, and reports from the 'Change. Idiot that he was, he had thought this an endearing quality that bespoke her sharp intelligence. He had been too stupidly proud of her wit to consider the implications of her greed.

He couldn't believe she had slapped him, though perhaps she'd had every right to. He shouldn't have sunk to the level of calling her a whore, but he had been driven as far as he could go, inside her sweet body, moments away from climax, when he had been thrust off, pushed away as if his lovemaking disgusted her. He had never felt so used and rejected in his life, he thought bitterly, standing in the stirrups, riding low over the stallion's back as he swept onto the curving Ring in a cloud of dust.

He had been nothing but good to her. Never in a million years would he pay money to make love to Belinda Hamilton or any woman. Damn it, he had thought they were beyond that.

Perhaps their falling out was for the best. She was a courtesan. If he were wise, he would be relieved at the opportunity to distance himself before he got in any more deeply over his head. True, it hurt for now, but in the long run, it was safer to let her pass out of his life. She had certainly made it clear last night that she did not return his feelings.

Realizing his horse was getting winded, he slowed the animal to a trot.

The sight of the graveled path next to the Long Water, where he had walked with her on that first day, made him miserable. If she didn't want him, that was just bloody fine with him. He sensed there were things she wasn't telling him about her past, but how could he help her when she refused to trust him? She could keep her secrets for all he cared.

One thing was clear: The time had come to confront Dolph Breckinridge and bring this matter to its swift and bloody close. The sooner Miss High-And-Mighty Hamilton was out of his house and out of his life, the better.

Somehow that thought made his mood even fouler.

He returned to Knight House at a comfortable canter, barely aware of the traffic. He gave his trusty horse a loud pat on its gleaming neck and marched up to the door, drawing off his riding gloves. He felt his stomach rumbling, but when he strode into the breakfast room precisely at the usual hour, there was no sign of any omelette forthcoming, nor toast, nor juice, not so much as a cup of tea. His staff had vanished.

He searched in astonishment, going all the way to the kitchens without seeing a sign of life. Finally he pushed open the back door and found Belinda's two little street urchins playing in the flagstone delivery area with the dogs.

The dogs bounded over to him, but he shoved them off, irked with their bouncy, tail-wagging good cheer.

The two little boys shot bolt upright at his entrance, standing at attention like wooden soldiers.

"Where is everyone?" he demanded.

They looked at each other, then stared up at him, their eyes round.

"I'm waiting."

"Boat ride," the shorter one blurted out.

Hawk blinked in bafflement. "Pardon?"

They held a conference, whispering to one another.

"Where is Cook?" Hawk demanded. "Where is my breakfast?"

"Cook and her helpers went on a boat ride, sir."

"But—how can that be?"

"Miss Bel gave them a day off."

"Oh, did she? Ha!" he exclaimed with a short bark of outraged laughter.

One of the dogs whined and crouched down at his feet. The littler boy ducked behind the taller one.

Hawk growled and pivoted, marching back inside. If Miss Bel saw fit to give his servants the day off, then Miss

Bel could rouse her lovely arse out of bed and cook him breakfast. He ignored the two children sneaking along behind him, spying on him. He plowed up the stairs and stomped down the hallway, where he banged on the door of her apartment.

"Get up, you lazy wench," he muttered under his breath. "Miss Hamilton! I demand you open this door! Don't pretend you don't hear me," he said sarcastically into the crack of the door.

"She ain't in there, gov."

He whirled and found the two boys standing a few feet away. The littler one was sucking his thumb. Hawk scowled at the child.

"Aren't you a bit old for that? Where is Miss Hamilton?"

"She's gone."

"What do you mean, 'gone'?" Panic flashed through him. He tried the doorknob and it opened. He stepped into her bedroom and saw the boy was right. He checked in her dressing room and looked out the window, as if she might be hiding in the curtains.

He whirled back to them. "Where did she go?"

"Church."

"And well she might!" he declared indignantly, but the relief that flooded through him made his knees go weak.

With a frown, he inspected the children. "Did she make *you* any breakfast?"

They shook their heads.

Hawk pursed his mouth. She must have been in quite a state to have forgotten about her urchins. He sighed in vexation and walked toward them, taking charge. "Well, come on, then. We men will figure this out. How difficult can it be?"

Marching resolutely to the kitchen, the duke of Hawkscliffe took off his morning coat, rolled up his shirtsleeves,

and proceeded to burn half a dozen eggs while his two
young accomplices looked on in trepidation.

"Cook usually puts butter on the pan first," said Tommy
after a long, judicious moment of staring at the blackened
cinders that were to have been their omelettes.

Hawk threw down the spatula. "Now you tell me."

"I forgot."

"Give that to the dogs."

Andrew wrinkled his nose. "They ain't gonna eat it."

In the end Hawk discovered the leftovers from last
night's dinner party in the cold cellar. He and the boys
feasted on slices of cold roasted turkey with a crumbly
wedge of lemon torte on the side.

He was due to appear at Coldfell's villa in South Kensington shortly, so he left the children in William's charge
with the certainty that Bel would be home in time to feed
them their noon meal. Himself, he would eat at White's,
thank you, because he no longer wanted to see her. What
was there to say?

Before leaving to call on Coldfell, he marched into the
library. Willing away memories of his mistress on her
knees, he went to his desk and scratched out a terse note to
Dolph Breckinridge:

*I am now prepared to make our exchange. Eleven to-
morrow night at the White Swan Inn on New Row by
Bedford Street. Come alone.*

                                                    H

He franked the note to Dolph, then grimly took to his
horse again and set out for his promised meeting with the
earl of Coldfell. He supposed that in Coldfell's view, he
had some explaining to do. He was not looking forward to
it, but at least now he could assure the earl that he was
about to bring this matter to a close.

Just as he exited the wrought-iron gates of Knight House, whom should he meet on horseback but the annoyingly cheerful young idealist, Clive Griffon, come to plague him again. A boyishly handsome youth of one-and-twenty, Griffon had high color in his smooth cheeks and a tangle of guinea gold curls.

"Your Grace, well met! I was just coming to call on you."

"Ah, lucky day," Hawk grumbled. The lad always looked so enthused about life.

"Beautiful weather, isn't it?" he asked brightly as he turned his leggy white thoroughbred and began riding alongside Hawk.

"It'll rain soon enough."

Griffon laughed, then took it upon himself to escort him all the way to Coldfell's villa in the cultured, semirural gentility of South Kensington. The green and shady expanses had become a fashionable locale of quiet dignity for those who disliked the noise and the crowds, or who found the crescents and terrace houses too confining. Here were modest mansions, discreetly placed amid the trees, each surrounded by a few acres of grounds, and all within easy reach of Parliament.

Griffon prated all the way down Brompton Road. Hawk listened to the lad's idealistic enthusiasms today for the sole reason that it was better than thinking about Belinda.

"What do you say on the issue of women, Griffon?" he blurted out, cutting off the boy's speech against the corn laws.

"Women?" the lad exclaimed as they crossed Gloucester.

"Yes, women, Mr. Griffon. Females. The bloody un*fair* sex."

"Forgive me, Your Grace, I fail to see what women have to do with any of this. Were we not discussing the state of the nation's coffers?"

"My point exactly! That's all women care about—getting into our pockets."

"Right," he said hesitantly, casting him a strange look.

Hawk's attitude toward the boy softened from that point: all ill-used men needed to band together in this world of sly beautiful women.

"Look here, Griffon," he said sternly as they trotted their horses past George Canning's impressive new manor, "I'm going to give you a chance to state your case to Lord Coldfell. If he likes what you have to say, the seat is yours. Agreed?"

"Your Grace!" the lad said in awe, his eyes widening. "Yes, sir!" Then he began to gush with thanks at the opportunity to bring his views before the powerful earl.

"Humph," Hawk snorted, then nodded toward Griffon's horse. "That's a fine bit o' blood you've got under you."

Griffon grinned and gave the white horse's neck a hearty slap. "He's descended from Eclipse, I don't mind telling you. Want to see what he can do?"

"Not really."

Griffon laughed and made the horse rear up on its hind legs. It tossed its head, looking for all the world like some wingless Pegasus, eager to take flight. Hawk smiled in spite of himself as the white stallion crashed back down on all fours, then the lad streaked off astride him, the turf flying behind them. Ah, youth, he thought wryly. Hawk clucked to his horse and followed at an easy canter.

A short while later, they were admitted through the tall gates of the estate where Lucy had lived and died. The gray manor house stood proudly under the sprawling blue sky as they rode up the long straight drive, passing cultured grounds. Hawk looked around in approval. Not a blade of grass was out of place. There was no denying it; the earl of Coldfell and he were men cut from the same cloth. They shared the same values and unfortunately, had loved the same woman.

An image of a woman's face flashed in Hawk's mind, not a green-eyed redhead, but a flaxen blonde with eyes the gentle, dreamy shade of bluebells.

Reaching the house, they dismounted from their horses. Hawk turned to his young companion. "Wait where they tell you to wait. Don't wander off and don't make any trouble."

"Yes, Your Grace!" Griffon said with a breathless, eager grin.

Hawk sliced him a nod and marched toward the entrance as the butler opened the door for him. The earl received him in the bright parlor that overlooked the garden and the pond where Lucy had drowned. Above the fireplace mantel was a large portrait of her. Hawk glanced at it in a wave of pain.

Today, by God, he felt his loss doubled. Belinda hadn't left this world as Lucy had, but he had lost her all the same, and it was worse, possibly, because for a short while, he had felt that Belinda was *his* in a way that Lucy never had been. Little had he known that while he had been losing his heart, she had been making a living.

No doubt she probably expected him to capitulate, offer her carte blanche to stay on as his mistress, but that he would never do. No woman was ever going to make a fool of him. That was the one lesson he had learned from seeing his father slowly unmanned by his mother's every new fling.

"Your Grace, so good of you to come," said Coldfell, shuffling toward him in his house slippers, his dark silk banyan robe hanging open over his neat brown waistcoat and trousers.

"My lord," Hawk greeted him in reply, forcing a taut

smile. They shook hands, then Hawk took a seat across from the earl.

Coldfell crossed his legs and rested his interlocked hands on his knee. "Robert, I knew your father and I've known you since you were a lad. Now I invited you here today to ask you one simple question: What in heaven's name are you doing keeping that woman in your house?"

Hawk heaved a breath and dropped his head back against the chair.

"Take a mistress, yes, that is healthy for a man your age. Indeed, I compliment you on your taste, but—"

"I know."

"Do you? Do you know there is scandal afoot? Your reputation is in peril."

Hawk picked up his head and stared dully at the earl. "It's not what it appears. Suffice to say that Miss Hamilton is Dolph's obsession and I mean to make use of her in that capacity. It's just a charade."

"Well, it looked deuced authentic to me," he huffed. "Be careful with that woman, Robert. You know what she is."

Hawk didn't attempt to comment on that. "Rest assured, it will all be over very soon, my lord. Within the next day or two, I expect to deal with your nephew exactly as I promised."

"Good," he said in a lower tone. "I want to be there when the time comes. You'll send for me?"

Hawk nodded.

Coldfell sat back again with a satisfied expression. "Now then. If I may impose upon your patience, it would do my Juliet so much good to see you. She has no society and so few callers," he said, stiffly rising from his chair.

Hawk held a bland, cordial expression by ingrained politeness alone. "I'm sure it is no imposition." He resigned

himself to endeavor to be gracious despite his newfound
aversion to females.

"Good lad," Coldfell said with a twinkling smile.

The old man led him out into the extensive gardens.
Coldfell was scheming for a match between them again, of
course, but Hawk was in too dismal a mood even to
protest. Lady Juliet had excellent bloodlines, was too
meek, sheltered, and sweet tempered ever to give a man
any fear of scandal, and could not pass her deafness on to
her offspring since it had been brought about by yellow
fever, not born into her. Having met the girl before, Hawk
had already seen that the child was lovely enough to stir
his pity. He could well understand Coldfell's fear over
finding a considerate husband who would honor and protect his fragile young daughter.

Today, however, he found himself only wishing idly that
Alfred Hamilton had possessed one jot of the earl's pa-
ternal overprotectiveness.

Hawk held his hat in his hand, glancing around at the
beautifully designed, sunlit grounds with their man-made
ponds and fountains and topiaries. He tensed at the sight
of the placid green pond where Lucy had drowned and
looked resolutely away.

"By the by, I've brought someone for you to meet—a
promising young man ambitious for a seat in the Commons. I'd hoped for your opinion of him."

"I'd be happy to inspect him for the party," the earl conceded, leading the way as he leaned on his cane with every
other step.

"Thank you, sir." Hawk judged it prudent not to mention that Griffon was no party follower, but a staunch
Independent.

"What's his name?"

"Clive Griffon."

"Of the Derbyshire Griffons? Good old landed family."

"Yes, sir."

"Not the heir?"

"Why, yes, he is, as a matter of fact. He's got excellent prospects."

"Hmmm."

They came to the rim of a grove of small espaliered cherry trees, where, through the green lattice of leaves, Hawk beheld the very vision of sweet maidenly innocence.

Kneeling before an elaborately quaint dovecote, Lady Juliet had a white dove sitting on her finger and was gently petting it. She was seventeen years old and enchantingly lovely with rich brown curls, rosy cheeks, and milky skin. She was oblivious to their presence, cooing softly to her birds.

Hawk smiled askance at Coldfell, his heartstrings well tugged in spite of his mood. "I'm not sure we should disturb her. She seems quite absorbed in her pets."

The earl beamed with doting, fatherly pride. "Nonsense, she'll be thrilled to see you. You should get to know her better, lonely child that she is. I've told her all about you." Hawk looked askance at Coldfell, wondering what he could possibly have said: *Look, Juliet, here is the nice man who wanted to bed your stepmama.*

"Remember—speak slowly to her, then she can read your lips." Advancing on his cane, Coldfell started into the grove.

Hawk began to follow, but even before they arrived, the air suddenly rang out with a burst of young girl's laughter.

"What the devil?" Coldfell exclaimed, stopping as he stared into the ring of trees.

Hawk saw, and his heart sank even as his left eyebrow came up wryly. It seemed Lady Juliet had already found herself a companion in addition to her doves. What the cherry trees had previously obscured from their view was

Clive Griffon, upside down, standing on his head and waving his legs around to amuse her.

"Whooooaaa!" he yelled as he toppled head over heels to the grass, but he somersaulted and popped up like a clown in front of her, presenting the maiden with a white puff of a dandelion.

"Make a wish," Griffon said to her, speaking as easily to her as if he'd been out here with the girl for the past half hour.

She gazed at him, looking lovestruck, then blew on the silky white thistle globe. The bristles flurried, floating away; Juliet's lips were still pursed to blow when Griffon boldly leaned in to kiss her, but froze as the earl of Coldfell let out a yowl. Hawk's heart sank.

"That will do, sir!" her father bellowed, stomping toward the young couple with his cane. "Get yourself away from my daughter this instant!"

The meeting did not go well.

A short while later, Hawk and an undaunted Clive Griffon left the garden and went to their horses.

"I'm in love with her."

"Don't be an even greater ass than you already are. How could you kiss her, Griffon? Right in front of her father!"

"I can't help it, it's what my heart told me to do! Besides, she liked it."

"How do you know? How could you even talk with her?"

"She spoke worlds with her eyes. I have a favorite cousin who's deaf. It's no matter whatsoever if you're used to it. She's so beautiful!" Griffon clutched his hat to his heart and walked backwards to his horse, gazing at the house.

Hawk glanced in the direction of his stare just in time to see a crestfallen Juliet blow Griffon a kiss from an upper window. Griffon caught her kiss with an exclamation of joy, then laughed aloud. Hawk scowled, more from annoyance than from any thought of jealousy over his possible future bride. At the moment, he was quite content to remain a bachelor for the rest of his days. He thumped his beaver hat onto his head and swung up into the saddle.

"I shall marry her, Hawkscliffe. She's the one."

"Oh, you are the most absurd creature I ever met," he muttered as they turned back out on the road, riding at a trot toward Knightsbridge.

"Somebody's got to marry her, haven't they? I don't care that she's deaf. She's wondrous. . . ."

On and on he raved, until Hawk couldn't take it anymore.

"Griffon, I have decided to give you the seat," he interrupted impatiently.

The young man gasped. "Your Grace?"

"Miss Hamilton thinks I should give you a chance. Now, do shut up before you make me change my mind."

Dolph Breckinridge returned from his club to his bachelor lodgings in Curzon Street to find a small letter waiting for him. Seeing Hawkscliffe's ducal seal, he tore it open quickly and read the imperious summons with a sneer.

It was about bloody time.

Still, he was not about to dance to Hawkscliffe's tune. He took out a pen and paper and quickly scribbled his reply:

The White Swan does not suit me. I am known there and this matter concerns no one but ourselves and her. Head toward Hampstead Heath. Take Chalk Farm Road to Haverstock Hill. A mile past the intersection with Adelaide, on your right you will see a thatched-roof cottage

set back from the road. I will meet you there. Nine to-
morrow night is acceptable, giving leave for the added
distance. Bring Miss Hamilton.

D.B.

That night, surrounded by suitors, glittering with jewels, Bel sat in her two-hundred-fifty-pound-per-season opera box at the Royal Theater in the Haymarket, staring at the stage in a state of utter misery.

Now that she had wrecked things with Hawkscliffe and had broken the prime rule of courtesanhood to boot, she figured she might as well start looking for a new protector. Harriette had advised her to be always keeping her eye out for the next rich lover to be snared. Perhaps it was time she started taking her mentor's advice.

She couldn't believe she had slapped him. Did he really think she only wanted his money? Despair filled her to know that the only remedy for the damage she had done to the bond between them was to tell him the truth.

She had been lavishly enjoying his lovemaking, participating with an eagerness that made her blush now, but how could she ever explain the deep-seated terrors that the simple clanking of silverware had triggered in her? To make amends would mean having to tell him about the warden and she could not bear for him to know her shame. Robert had seen the horrid man with his own eyes. What if he thought she had invited it somehow? What if he thought it had been her ploy to lure the warden in the hopes of gaining some special privileges for her incarcerated father? She could not bear to trust him with her pain only to have him shame her worse by misconstruing the facts.

After all, he saw her as a whore, a woman who used her body to get what she wanted. And so she was. But she hadn't been then.

He would never understand.

Stealing a furtive glance at the faces of the men around her in the darkened theater box, she had no conception of how she was possibly going to get any further with them if she could not allow the man she adored to make love to her. She was unsexed, impotent—frigid.

When she returned to Knight House after the opera she stepped down from her *vis-à-vis* with William's assistance and steeled herself, walking up to the entrance. She wondered what Hawkscliffe thought about her going out alone at night, or if he had even noticed she was gone.

With a heavy sigh she picked up her skirts in one hand and started up the grand curving staircase, resigned to going to bed without having seen him all day. She slid her other hand along the smooth banister, her reticule dangling off her forearm. She was halfway up the steps when she heard the slow, heavy click of his boot heels echoing on the polished marble floor below, then his deep, cultured baritone reached her.

"One moment, Miss Hamilton, if you please."

She sucked in her breath and turned on the stairs. He stood in the foyer below, tall and urbane, clad in black, facing the door. His shoulders were squared with rigid hauteur, his elegant hands clasped behind his back.

"Yes?" she asked a trifle breathlessly.

He studied the door. "Tomorrow night at nine we meet with Dolph Breckinridge. I shall have some instructions for you pertaining to your role."

"Very well," she said faintly, chilled by his cool tone.

"Afterward you will be free to go at your earliest convenience."

She took in his words and a little part of her died to hear them.

How could she be shocked to realize that, indeed, he wanted to be rid of her as soon as possible? She stared

at his remote, brooding figure while the grand, high-
ceilinged room rocked and her heart broke anew. She
wanted to cry out to him, but instead tautly forced out, "I
understand."

"Good night ... Miss Hamilton." He stared at the
marble floor while the dim candlelight gleamed on his
black wavy hair.

She couldn't answer, her voice trapped in her throat.
She felt herself unraveling, but as there was nothing else to
be done or said, she gathered her wits, blindly lifted her
chin and proceeded with stiff, expressionless composure
to her rooms.

❧ CHAPTER ❧
FIFTEEN

The next night came all too soon.

As she and Robert cantered their horses along the dusky Chalk Farm Road north toward Hampstead Heath, Bel wanted nothing more than to reel her gray gelding around and bolt back for London, knowing that her loathed, lascivious enemy, Dolph, waited in the expectation of making her his own, but she would not fail Robert. Playing her part with courage tonight—helping him avenge his beloved Lady Coldfell—was her only hope of redeeming herself in his eyes.

Then again, perhaps he despised her enough to let Dolph have her.

They swept past Adelaide Road onto Haverstock Hill. Robert looked constantly to the right, waiting to spy the cottage set back from the road.

At length he slowed his pace, signaling her to do the same. They had found it.

The full moon hung low over the stone cottage, silvering the leaves of the great elm that arched over its thatched roof. The windows were dark, the doorway steeped in shadow. Dolph's thoroughbred grazed beside the cottage, but lifted its head and pricked up its ears as they rode up to the low stone wall.

Bel glanced nervously at Robert. His aquiline face was

expressionless, remote as ever, but his dark eyes gleamed with cold treachery. He was dressed all in black and wore two loaded pistols and a sword around his lean hips.

A flicker of motion in the gloom of the doorway materialized into Dolph. "Prompt as ever, Hawkscliffe. I see you've brought my prize."

Bel swallowed hard.

"Tonight she will be yours, Dolph, provided you cooperate."

"Does she agree to this? I don't want any tricks."

"I do," Bel forced out in a wavering voice.

"We're coming in." Robert swung down off his horse, then lifted her down from the sidesaddle. The fleeting moment of contact—feeling his arms around her waist—was misery. She wanted to hold him and beg him not to make her go in there, but she said nothing. He set her down on her feet.

She smoothed her riding habit and squared her shoulders, then they walked together through the little waist-high gate and up to the lonely cottage.

The front garden was overgrown and the thick tangle of roses that climbed the sagging trellis filled the summer night with cloying sweetness.

Dolph dropped back as Robert approached. Tall, radiating command, Robert stalked over the threshold; Bel followed him two steps behind.

Dolph leered at her like a satyr. "I'm hard for you already," he whispered as she stepped up to the doorway.

With a gulp, she hesitated, but she knew her role. Somehow she forced herself to touch Dolph. Brushing by him, she trailed her hand across his flat stomach and cast him a languid look, drifting inside. "Come."

She could not meet Robert's piercing stare as she walked by him into the adjoining small parlor. Bel turned in the darkness and waited as Dolph warily followed her in.

Robert remained, as planned, in the other room.

Bel stared at Dolph, slowly easing off her snug-fitting riding coat. Dolph's stare seemed to burn through her linen shirt as he sauntered toward her, his expression guarded. "You've changed."

"Yes."

"Ready for me at last."

"Yes, Dolph."

He looked like he wanted to devour her, but his eyes were full of feverish suspicion. "Why now?"

"Because I understand now that you're the only one who really cares for me," she said softly. In some twisted way, it was true.

"Bel," he whispered with a pained look. "I thought you'd never understand." Stopping inches in front of her, he stared down at her, brawny and towering. She could feel his deepening breath. Though she was scared down to the soles of her boots, she hid her fear and held her ground, biting back the protest that jumped up to the tip of her tongue when Dolph cupped her breast through her shirt.

Making no attempt to be gentle, he watched for her reaction, almost as if he wanted her to flinch. She merely stared up at him, emotionless and defiant. Smiling faintly, he squeezed hard—then harder.

Go in and tease him, Robert had ordered her earlier. Under his breath, he had added, You should be good at that.

She made Dolph's grip on her breast loosen by reaching up and slipping her arms around his neck.

His eyes flickered with hot, quick lust. At once he wrapped his arms around her waist and pulled her against the length of his body. Then he made a small moan and buried his face in the crook of her neck.

"Bel," he whispered. "Oh, Bel, you've been so bad. Bel, I would have done anything for you, but you had to run from me, and now—" His grip around her waist tightened suddenly so hard that it forced the breath out of her lungs.

With his other hand he clutched her hair and dragged her head back.

Bel stared at him, paralyzed with fear.

"Now that you're mine, I'm going to make sure you never get away from me again," he whispered.

She gasped for air as he picked her up off her feet and carried her for a few swift strides. The next thing she knew, her back was slammed against the wall and Dolph was suffocating her with fast, wet, savage kisses, leaving her no chance to breathe, let alone protest. Her eyes rolled with terror as she shoved against his shoulders, to no avail. His teeth cut her lips while he used his body to bruise hers, ramming his hips between her thighs. He was roughly unbuttoning her riding habit with a deft, ready skill she had not anticipated.

Oh, my God, she thought with crystalline clarity. He is going to rape me.

Her feet couldn't even touch the ground, but the most acute horror of all was knowing that the man she loved was in the next room.

Letting it happen.

Too damned quiet in there, Hawk thought, pacing with agitation in the kitchen.

He knew he had to give Bel enough time to work Dolph into a malleable state, but the silence in the next room sat like a knot in the pit of his stomach until he couldn't take it anymore.

His heart pounding, Hawk stepped into the parlor and saw how Dolph had her pinned against the wall. Crimson rage such as he had never felt rushed up from the depths of him at the sight—and sickening guilt.

With a low oath, he marched over and seized Dolph's arm roughly. "That's enough."

"Get out of here," Dolph ground out.

Hawk could not bear to look at Belinda, knowing the terror he would see in her eyes. With all his will he clamped down on his wrath. "Let's get down to business, shall we?"

"I said get the hell out of here!" Dolph roared, turning on him. He dropped Belinda. "I've had it with you, Hawkscliffe. What the hell do you want with me?"

Hawk pulled out his pistol and thrust it under Dolph's chin. Dolph froze; Hawk stared at him.

Belinda slipped free, crying, then fled. Hawk fought the impulse to go after her, help her.

"I'll tell you what I want, Dolph. All right? Let's quit the games." He thrust the gun harder against Dolph's throat. "I want to know why you killed Lucy, you son of a bitch."

Dolph stared at him in apparent shock. "Lucy? *You think I killed Lucy?*"

"All I have to do is squeeze this trigger. I suggest you start with the truth."

"Are you mad? Lucy drowned. Everybody knows that!" He glanced down nervously at the weapon. "Put the gun down, Hawkscliffe. What's the matter with you?"

"You drowned her. Just say it."

"I had nothing to do with her death—"

"Admit to it. Be a man for once in your life. You killed her for fear that if she bore a child, you'd lose your inheritance."

Dolph let out a scoffing, incredulous laugh. "And whose child do you think she would have borne if she had been breeding? Jesus, man, why would I kill her? She was my mistress."

Hawk stared at him, feeling the very earth fall out from beneath his feet. For a long moment he couldn't find his voice, then it came out as a snarl. "What did you say?"

"You heard me. We were bedmates, and trust me—she didn't want a brat anymore than I did."

Fury seized him. Hawk wrapped his fist harder around the butt of his pistol and used it to slam a brutal punch into Dolph's eye. The baronet cursed and tripped backward over a dainty footstool and went sprawling onto the floor.

Hawk aimed the gun at him with both hands. "Tell the truth now, Dolph. Or I'll blow your brains out, I swear to God."

"Calm down, Hawkscliffe! Jesus! I'm trying to tell you—"

"She was not your mistress. *She was not.* She was—pure." He was shaking with fury and some strange, terrible knowing that had begun to settle around his heart like molten metal cooling, hardening.

"Pure? Lucy? You're jesting."

"I am not jesting," he whispered. "You violated her, just as you would do to Bel if I gave you the chance."

"The hell I did. Look, mate, she was the one who seduced *me*—"

"She would never do that. She was—Lucy. She was—a virtuous woman."

"If you think that, then you didn't even know her—but of course, Lucy didn't want you to know the real her, because then the mighty Hawkscliffe wouldn't have wanted her anymore. She was playing you, Your Grace, sleeping with half the lads in Town while she angled to become your duchess. And I'll tell you something else, you poor noble *Dupe* of Hawkscliffe," he said with a malicious grin, "I'll tell you how pure our sweet Lucy was—she used to get undressed in front of her bedroom window just to torment the stable boys."

"I'll kill you," Hawk whispered as a bead of sweat ran down the side of his face. "You're lying. She was *not* your mistress and I know that for certain because for months you've been in love with Bel."

"Love?" he scoffed. "Since when do you have to be in love with a woman to accept an invitation to her bed? God, you're a prude."

He absorbed this, horrified. "She was your uncle's wife."

Dolph shrugged. "Yes, well, perhaps a tad perverse, but it was Lucy's idea. I was merely obliging her."

"You son of a bitch, *that's a lie*!" he bellowed, cocking the gun. He was going to do it, too. Kill Breckinridge here in cold blood. His finger alighted on the trigger just as a soft, firm voice reached him.

"Robert. Don't."

Bel had fled earlier, but returned once she had composed herself. She had been standing in the other room long enough to hear most of it. She was there now to watch Robert's dream of courtly love crumble. His face was harsh, streaked with moonlight, like a savage in war paint. He tensely gripped the gun, his aim fixed on Dolph's heart.

Bel took another step toward him. "I'm not going to let you do this, Robert."

"What do you care about him?"

"I care about you and this is not who you are."

"He's a liar."

"He is an unarmed man. Robert, please. You could hang. He's not worth it. Besides, he could be telling the truth."

"I *am* telling the truth," Dolph muttered, slowly sitting up.

"Prove it," Robert ground out.

"This cottage belonged to her. She left it to me," Dolph said. "This is where we would meet. I think she had other liaisons here, as well, but she always insisted on complete discretion so that my uncle would never find out."

Bel glanced at Robert. His mouth was pale, his eyes glazed. He looked like he was in shock. She turned again to Dolph. "Prove that any part of what you say is true, then we'll take it from there."

"I don't know—check in that desk over there." Dolph nodded to the left, not taking his eyes off Robert's gun. "Maybe you can find a bit of her personal effects in there that will convince you."

"Go," Robert ordered her.

Bel found a small oil lamp atop the desk and felt around in the dark for a tinderbox, finally lighting it. As the small flame rose, she opened the slanted lid of the writing desk, peered inside, and riffled through its contents.

"Shall I check for letters or something like that? Oh, there's a sketch book, drawings."

"Bring it here."

She obeyed, picking up the workbook of charcoal sketches. She brought it over to him and opened to the first page.

"Swans. Very gracefully done," she said dryly, then turned another page. "Daffodils. A picture of a girl."

Robert glanced over, his eyes tormented, his lips white. "That's Coldfell's daughter."

Bel started to turn to the next page, but when she glimpsed it, she stopped in shock. *Oh, dear.*

"Robert," she said gingerly, "*do* you believe this to be Lady Coldfell's work?"

"I'd know her hand anywhere. But that doesn't mean she used this place for trysts."

"Well, you'd better look at this, then." With a wince of distaste Bel turned the page to reveal a nude sketch of Dolph Breckinridge lying in bed in a sated sleep.

Robert looked over, stared in shock, then cursed. "Take this," he growled, thrusting the gun into her hands. "If he moves a muscle, pull the trigger."

Bel took the gun in dismay as Robert walked away with the sketchbook and went to lean against the arm of the sofa, nearer the lantern.

Dolph started to get up.

"Don't tempt me, you barbarian," she warned, drawing a bead with the pistol right between his eyes.

He sneered at her. "You wouldn't shoot me, Bel. I'm the only one who really cares, remember?"

"Shut up!"

"Breckinridge," Robert snarled in warning.

Dolph sank back down to the floor like an angry cur at its master's rebuke. Then Robert turned the page.

Bel glanced at his stricken face as he turned leaf after leaf, showing gracefully executed black-and-white sketches of not merely Dolph, but a carefully selected collection of the other young bucks of the ton, all in various states of undress.

"Oh, my God," he said in a hollow voice.

She looked over and saw his dark, stormy eyes fill with stunned sorrow as he came to a three-quarter foreshortened sketch of his own face.

Bel felt his bewildered pain as her own in that moment.

He turned page after page, staring at drawings of himself in a dozen different attitudes. Whatever games Lucy had played with his heart, clearly the woman had wanted him. Longing was clear in every fine, feathery stroke of her pencil. The countess must have studied him at great length, however furtively, to have drawn him so beautifully from her memory. She had captured the restlessness in him and the passion locked within his rigidity, and his integrity and high noble pride.

He lifted his fractured gaze to hers, at a loss.

"I think she was making a conquest of you and you didn't even know it," she said softly.

"Of course she was," Dolph muttered. "That's what I just said."

"If it was Hawkscliffe she wanted, then why did she seduce you?" Bel asked Dolph.

"Why do you think?" he retorted. "My uncle wasn't any use to her. She needed a man between her legs, unlike you, you frigid—"

"Recall that I'm holding a pistol before you insult me," she advised him even as she read the flicker of guilt behind his eyes. She studied him. Perhaps he had not killed Lady Coldfell, thank God, but she began to sense that he was definitely hiding *something*.

Robert pushed up from the arm of the sofa. "Breckinridge, you're free to go. I apologize for this debacle. Obviously, I was in error."

Bel looked from one man to the other in uncertain protest.

"Well, I daresay," Dolph snorted. He climbed cautiously to his feet and dusted off his flamboyant clothing. "I am tempted to call you out for this, Hawkscliffe, but lucky for you, I, too, can play the paragon. I *forgive* you," he said with a sarcastic snort.

"Robert, I think he's hiding something. I know this man—"

"He didn't kill Lucy," he interrupted sharply, disgust flaring in his dark eyes. "Beyond that, I don't give a damn."

"A wise answer, Your Grace. Now, you got what you wanted, so if we are quite through with this travesty, Belinda and I will be on our way."

"No!" she cried, holding Dolph at bay with the gun.

"A deal is a deal, my heart," he said with a leering smile.

"Robert!"

Hawkscliffe returned to her side and gingerly took back his pistol. "Go outside and mount up," he murmured to her.

"I'm not going with him!" she cried, appalled.

"Yes, you are," said Dolph.

"No, she's not."

Dolph's eyes narrowed to slashes. He stepped toward Robert in spite of the gun. "She's coming with me. That was the point of all this. You gave me your word—information for the girl."

"I lied," he said.

Dolph stared blankly at him. "You lied?"

"Yes."

"I don't believe this. I give you the truth and this is how you repay me? With trickery?"

Robert didn't move, holding his stare.

Bel backed away but could not bring herself to leave the room—she could feel it in her bones that something terrible was about to happen.

Dolph glared at him in outrage. "You—Hawkscliffe, the high stickler? Why, you're nothing but a damned liar! You fraud!"

Bel reached for her protector's hand, certain now of what was about to happen. There was only one possible outcome when a man called another man a liar. Honor had its price. "Come with me, please, he's not worth it," she whispered.

"You're a dead man," Dolph said.

"Please, Robert, let's go—" Dolph was a famous marksman and a crack shot.

"Yes, go, Hawkscliffe," the baronet spat in contempt. "Go home to your mansion, you false bloody hypocrite, and take your whore with you. My second will call on you shortly. Then we'll settle this like men."

"No!" Bel cried, but Robert lifted his chin without protest.

Dolph stalked out between them and slammed the front door as he left.

⚜ CHAPTER ⚜
SIXTEEN

They rode back to Knight House in grim silence, Robert brooding and taciturn, while Bel fought panic, knowing that at dawn that insufferable lecherous boor was going to put a bullet in the man she loved. Clutching her horse's reins, she stole frequent anxious glances at Robert, riding beside her. Moonlight limned his broad shoulders and sculpted his aquiline face, but his remote, dark stare remained fixed on the dusty road ahead. After an hour's ride south through the moonlit countryside back into Town, they rode down Regent Street and turned right on Piccadilly.

The crowds thickened as they neared Green Park, when suddenly a series of great booms and explosions echoed through the streets, spooking their horses. Robert brought his stallion under control then reached over and grasped her gelding's bridle, calming the animal. Once the horses were steadied, Bel and Robert, each in their own dismal worlds, looked up and saw fireworks exploding across the black sky over Green Park, opening the Regent's Victory festival.

August the first had arrived. The terminal date of their contract.

The bursts of color rocketed then bloomed, practically atop the roof of Knight House.

Bel felt a slow tremor of loss move through her body.

She looked at Robert, saw the red glare illuminate his rugged face. Neither said a word. Bel fought a surge of emotion, remembering the last time they had watched fireworks together on that deliriously romantic night at Vauxhall. Avoiding her gaze, Robert clucked to his horse.

They proceeded through the gates of Knight House, where the grooms took their horses. Bel dismounted, removed her riding hat, and wiped the sweat from her brow, watching Robert walk wearily up to the front door. The gold light from the lanterns that flanked the doorway cast a ruddy halo over his wavy black hair.

Her heart ached for him as she watched him disappear inside. After all his honor and gallantry, his shining ideal lady had been proved an utter fraud.

Amid her compassion for him, however, was guilt, for she knew that, in her way, she was as much a fraud as Lady Coldfell. How could she let him go on thinking she had pushed him away as a ploy to get more gold out of him? Unlike Lady Coldfell, however, she still had a chance to come clean with him, if only she dared. This might be their last chance to make peace.

She stared up at the grand, ornate house, half expecting its flawless facade to come tumbling down like everyone else's had this night.

Another tremble of cold fear ran the length of her body, but she squared her shoulders, knowing what she must do. As humiliating as this was going to be, he was her protector and she owed him the truth.

In the library Hawk dispatched two servants, one to locate his brother, Alec, to serve as his second, the other to ride to Coldfell's villa to alert him that the long-awaited duel was set for dawn.

When they had gone he sat down at his desk and slowly

pressed his eyes with the heels of his hands. He rested like that, feeling defeated and utterly alone.

He couldn't believe how wrong he had been. Good God, but Lucy had fooled him. He had gone into this thinking himself the righteous avenger and had come out of it looking like a blundering fool.

He couldn't blame Dolph Breckinridge for calling him out. Any man accused of so heinous a crime would have done the same. Hawk knew full well he was in the wrong and supposed his only honorable option, therefore, was to delope.

"Robert?"

He looked up at her soft call. Belinda stood in the doorway amid the shadows, her face tense and pale. Her beauty caught him like an unexpected blow to the chest. He picked up a quill pen and pretended to examine it.

"Is there something you require, Miss Hamilton? I'm afraid I'm in a bit of a rush. I have some business to get in order, as it appears there's a jolly good chance I'll be leaving this world with rather unforeseen haste."

She flinched and lowered her head at his words. He stared at her.

"Silent, eh? Let me guess—you've come to say 'I told you so.' And well you should. You knew from the start that Dolph didn't kill Lucy, but I refused to listen. Your point is well taken; I defer to your greater wisdom and shall remain to the bitter end Lucy's fool—and yours."

"God, but you know how to wound me," she whispered, lifted her head, and met his stare with anguish in her eyes. "Don't equate me with her. At least I don't hide the fact that I'm a whore."

He threw his pen on the desk and braced his mouth against his hand.

"I have something to say to you," she said in a brave, hushed tone.

No doubt, he thought, braced for a tongue-lashing, the way things were going.

Belinda shut the door. His veiled gaze followed her as she moved cautiously into the room where they had shared so many intimacies. Had her show of love been a delusion, like everything else? He couldn't tell anymore what was real, and was honestly tired of trying to figure it out.

She drifted toward his piano and rested her hand atop its glossy lid as she stood gazing toward the empty hearth. "I wanted to say that I-I've tried over the past two months to make your life happier in small ways. To make you more comfortable and to bring you—pleasure."

He clamped back the impulse to confess how well she had succeeded.

He was done with her and that was that. He was about to die for her, after all, for his refusal to hand her over to Dolph. Wasn't that enough? It was treacherous, this urge he felt to go to her and enfold her in his arms, to give comfort and to seek it.

He sat at his desk in stoic silence, waiting to hear her out and watching the complex play of emotions that chased across her fine-boned features.

"Robert, that night in the dining room, it wasn't greed that made me push you away," she said quietly. "The truth is—oh, Robert, please."

"What?" he asked prosaically.

Her graceful posture turned rigid and her small, delicate hand tensed where it rested on the piano. She closed her eyes but kept her face angled slightly away from him. "I know you look down your nose at demireps. Please try to understand. You are my f-first protector. The reason I pushed you away is because . . ."

Her words broke off as she struggled.

He waited, motionless, but made his tone bland and superior. "Yes?"

"I don't know how to make love," she said in a small voice.

He stared at her. "Forgive my indelicacy, Belinda, but let's be reasonable. Love is your trade. It's not as though you were a virgin when I entered you."

"No." Her voice dropped to an agonized plea. "There's something I need to tell you—something I've never told anyone. Something that happened to me." Her chin came up and at last she met his gaze with stormy yet weary intensity. "Robert, I didn't just get tired of being poor one day and decide to become a courtesan. I was a decent woman. When Dolph got me fired from the finishing school, I kept my head above water by selling oranges in the day and mending shirts at night, just as the children told you. The work was endless, but I had my honor. I saw these children—Tommy and Andy—and it was winter and their bare feet were bleeding, Robert." Her words were tumbling out faster and faster and a terrible foreboding was taking shape in his chest. "So I used the money for my father's chamber fees at the Fleet to buy them boots," she continued, her ladylike calm dissolving by the second. "Then I went to the warden to explain that I didn't have the money and would he give me credit for a fortnight and he said he would think about it and it was raining."

"Sit down, Bel," he whispered, rising, moving slowly around his desk, not taking his eyes off her. Her face had grown ghastly pale.

"No," she said vehemently, her orchid eyes feverish, her words exact. "Listen to me." She backed away from him as he approached her, but her words kept coming. "The warden knew it was raining so he made his coachman give me a ride home. I thought he was just being polite, b-but he just wanted to find out where I lived. He asked me if I had any brothers or a husband to help me and I was such a fool, I told him no."

"No, angel, please—" he begged her barely audibly, tears rushing into his eyes as something came into focus that he did not want to see.

"Yes. He came back in the nighttime, Robert, and he forced himself on me. Robert, I was a virgin. *Oh, God,* why did he do that to me?" she wailed as he took two swift strides and caught her in his arms, doubling over like a keening woman at a wake.

She clung to him, nearly gagging on her bitterness. "Why?" she cried. "I never hurt anyone. Robert, why did he have to do that to me?"

But all he could whisper was *"Jesus, sweetheart, no, no, no,"* as he held her, rocking her in his arms, horror and rage swimming before his eyes. His head reeled as if he had been struck with a sledgehammer. *I'll kill him.*

"That's why I became a courtesan, but Lucy was a fraud and Dolph called you a fraud and I'm a fraud, too," she sobbed. "I don't know how to—the other night I thought I could because I love you so much—but that sound of the silverware clanking . . . It's so stupid but it sounded like—his awful keys he carried."

Hawk recalled the huge key ring on that brute son of a bitch's belt.

"It all came back," she moaned, leaning against him as if she had no strength left. "I would never tell you no because of money. Robert, help me. It hurts so much."

"I'm here," he choked out. She was unsteady on her feet, so he eased her down onto the couch. He pulled her onto his lap and held her as she wept with pain. He hugged her hard, his own fierce, agonized tears of fury and remorse stinging behind tightly closed eyes.

Oh, God, if only he had known, he never would have made her go into that dark room tonight with Dolph. The warden of the Fleet. *Jesus Christ.* That scarred brute made Dolph look like a choirboy. But he hadn't known, for he'd been so careful not to get too deeply involved. He had been wrong about Lucy, wrong about Dolph, but with Belinda he had been willfully, blindly self-deceived. He had felt her innocence from the first time he had looked at her, but he had not trusted it, in light of what she had appeared to be.

"I'm so sorry," he whispered over and over again, kissing her tear-stained face. His apologies were not enough, but he couldn't stop their tumbling from his lips. She was shaking in his arms as she clung to him.

"I can't lose you, Robert. Forfeit this duel. Men don't duel over demireps."

He captured her face between his hands and stared fiercely into her eyes, tears filling his own. "You are more to me than that. I will prove it to you."

"By risking your life? I don't want to lose you!" She kissed him feverishly amid tears. "Stay with me. Love me, Robert. Make me whole again."

He closed his eyes and rested his forehead against hers, fighting the black chaos of his rage. "I will, my sweet," he said with measured calm, "but not tonight. Not like this."

"Tonight may be all we have if you go through with this duel!" she said angrily, pulling back from his embrace. "Don't do it, Robert."

Gazing at her anguished face, blotchy from crying, he cupped her cheek and held her stare in fierce tenderness. "Have faith in me. I don't deserve you yet, but after I've dealt with the men who hurt you, then maybe I'll be worthy of that gift." He stroked her face in anguish. "Oh, my sweet girl, who could ever hurt you?"

Fresh tears filled her eyes and he pulled her into his arms again, petting her hair and back as if to smooth away the pain. After a while, his touch calmed her, quieting her ragged breathing.

"I wish you would have told me this before you ever let me touch you."

"How could I tell you? All I've wanted since I met you is for you to respect me."

No reproach could have chastened him more than her meek confession. He lowered his head and closed his eyes, cursing himself to the deepest regions of Hell for his superior thrice-damned arrogance. How many times had he rubbed his disapproval in her face? What had ever made him think he had the right to judge her? Whispering another futile apology, he tucked her head under his chin and held her to his chest as though she was made of finest porcelain. They stayed like that until he could feel her tremors settle down into slow, restful breaths.

"Would you like some wine to calm you?" he asked softly.

She nodded.

Kissing her forehead, he set her aside and rose. He crossed to the liquor cabinet and poured her a glass of wine. He sent a shrewd glance over his shoulder at her, knowing she would try to stop him if she knew what he intended to do tonight.

Dolph was not the only one who would be punished before the dawn. Rage waited in his veins, quick and hot, savage. He veiled it from her.

Into her wine he slipped a drop of the laudanum that he kept in the cabinet for those nights when he couldn't fall asleep. It would calm her, help her rest.

For himself he reached into the liquor cabinet and took out the silver flask she had given him weeks ago, in happier times. He filled it with some of the French brandy his brother Jack had sent him, for there was dark work to be done this night and he would need its fiery resolve.

He capped the elegant flask and slipped it into his waistcoat for later.

He brought her the glass of wine; she murmured her thanks. Then he let his favorite dog, Hyperion, into the library to guard her and keep her company. The golden-coated Newfoundland curled up on the rug by the sofa where Bel reclined, tear stained and exhausted. Hawk leaned down and pressed a soft kiss to her clammy forehead.

She curled her fingers around his. "Don't leave me, Robert."

"I'm here." He sat down on the edge of the sofa.

For many long moments he remained by her side while she sipped her wine. He caressed her hair and held her hand. He took her wine for her while she loosened the tight collar of her white riding shirt, then gave the glass back to her.

"Thank you."

He smiled, feeling his heart wrench at her automatic politeness. "You were so brave tonight," he whispered, stroking her hair. "If I had known, I would have never put you through that, not in a million years."

"I know." A tremulous smile quavered on her lips.

"This whole plan to use you as the bait for Dolph . . . it was so wrong of me. Why did you let me do it?"

"I had to keep my word," she said. "I wanted to show you I was brave."

"You always do, Belinda. Ballast in your hull, my girl."

She smiled wistfully at his words, settling more deeply into the sofa's cushions.

He glanced toward the pianoforte. "Shall I play you a lullaby?"

"No, stay by my side," she pleaded anxiously, reaching for his hand.

"I'm here, I'm here. Poor angel, you've been carrying this burden on your shoulders all this time by yourself." He continued caressing her gently, brushing his knuckles against the soft feathery hairs that flowed back from her temple, but the thought of that scarred brute having his way with this gently bred innocent brought him to the brink of rage. It took all the self-control at his command to sit here quietly for another quarter hour and soothe her.

He remembered how coins had greased the palms of the prison guards and how the warden had been giving one of his underlings a verbal thrashing. Someone inside the walls of the Fleet would surely tell him what he needed to know, for a price.

Restless to be under way, Hawk glanced at the mantel clock. "I want you to rest, darling. Try to sleep," he said softly. "I'll be back in a little while."

"Why are you leaving me? Stay," she murmured, her eyes closed as the laudanum began to take effect.

"You rest now, my angel." He leaned down and pressed a whisper-soft kiss to her brow. "Know that I am your protector and I will never let anyone hurt you again."

"Mmm," she said, drifting away. Silently he rose, made the final preparations, then left the library and armed himself with his pair of Manton pistols, pulling on a plain black coat over them. As an afterthought, he took off his ring emblazoned with the family crest. Better if no one identified him.

Jogging down the curved staircase, he stalked out to the graveled courtyard behind Knight House and crossed it to the carriage house.

Down the row of shiny vehicles—Belinda's *vis-à-vis*, his town coach, traveling coach, and curricle—there sat an older black carriage that he had set aside years ago for his servants' use. It was perfect for his purposes tonight, sturdy but nondescript. He had William harness the team of four, then Hawk climbed into the driver's seat and took the reins.

William read his grim expression with worry and asked if he required his attendance, but Hawk didn't want anyone else involved in the matter of vengeance that lay ahead of him. He pulled his hat down low over his eyes and set out into the thronged streets, where the fireworks crowd had begun to disperse.

He must have looked the part, for a few drunken youngbloods leaving the festival mistook him for a hackney coach and hailed him, then cursed him and shook their fists when he didn't stop. His first destination was Faringdon Street and the Fleet Prison. He jumped down and called over a boy outside the Fleet to hold the horses, gruffly promising to return in fifteen minutes.

Hawk asked to see Alfred Hamilton and was admitted. He scanned the lobby as he strode through it behind the guard.

He noted that the warden's office was closed. "Warden off duty tonight?" he asked in a careful tone of pleasantry.

"Only works days."

"Ah," Hawk said with a nod, sizing the man up. "Must be a relief. He's a hard one."

"Aye, you're tellin' me. Bloody slave driver," the young guard grumbled.

When they reached the door to old Hamilton's cell, the guard turned to him expectantly, awaiting the fee for turning the key.

Hawk put ten gold sovereigns into his hand, probably more than the man earned in a month. "Know where I might find him?" he asked quietly.

"The warden?"

"I was hoping to speak with him."

The guard stared at the coins in his hand. His fist closed around them and he swallowed nervously. "The Cock Pit Tavern, I'd wager."

"And where might that be?" Hawk asked gently.

"Pudding Lane, stone's throw from Billingsgate."

"Are you sure?"

The guard cast a furtive look over his shoulder. "I'm sure. We just got paid and that's where he goes to wager on the cockfights. Plus the place serves liquor out of hours to serve the fish porters. Warden likes his drink, early and late."

Hawk nodded, satisfied. "It would be best if any record of my visit were removed from the log, don't you agree?"

"Could be arranged."

"Smart lad." Hawk smiled, gave him another few gold coins, then went into Alfred's cell to serve up the hard truth.

He did so without pity; the old man's anguished cry still echoed in Hawk's ears as he left the Fleet with a knot in the pit of his stomach. Whatever inclination he might have had to release Alfred Hamilton from debtor's prison had withered upon learning the consequences for Belinda of her father's irresponsibility. The old man could rot here as far as he was concerned.

He paid the boy the promised coin and climbed back up onto the coach, then drove east through the City to Lower Thames Street. A fog was rolling off the river. When the stink of fish from the sprawling riverside market of Billingsgate filled the air, he knew he was close.

In the distance the ominous hulking Tower of London loomed, shrouded in mist.

Hawk turned left onto the small side street called Pudding Lane and quickly found the Cock Pit Tavern, doing brisk business by the sound of it. He eased the coach into the shadows of an alleyway down the lane, then ducked into the mobbed pub, keeping to the wall as he searched the raucous crowd for the warden. Hawk spied him amid the knot of men clamoring around the blacklegs, who were busily jotting down their wagers.

Hawk slipped back out into the night and returned to his carriage. Climbing up onto the driver's seat, he sat back, folded his arms over his chest and waited in brooding, implacable silence. Occasionally he took a swig from the silver flask. The brandy kept him warm as the night sky began to drizzle on and off.

Each time the pub door opened, spilling a glow of warm light onto the wet cobblestone, he came alert, but the warden didn't appear.

After the first hour he got down from the coach and walked around the alley to stretch his legs. Something glinted on a heap of rubble by the wall of one of the buildings. He sauntered over, bent down and picked it up—a length of lead pipe. He hefted it in his grip with a narrow smile and went back to wait, biding his time. Another hour passed. He checked his fob watch. Quarter past two. His duel with Dolph Breckinridge was only two hours away; dawn came at four A.M. in the summer.

The drizzle turned into a more determined rain. He glanced in irritation at the sky from under the dripping brim of his hat, and then suddenly the door of the pub opened and out stumbled the warden of the Fleet.

Hawk tensed. His heartbeat kicked into a gallop. He sat forward slowly on the driver's seat as thunder rumbled in the distance.

The warden was with two other men, but they exchanged farewells on the corner and the others zigzagged away toward the river while the warden turned and started trudging up the street. Hawk waited like a predator in the gloom.

Silently he slid down from the driver's seat. As the warden lurched nearer, Hawk emerged from the shadows, walking toward the man. The warden saw him, then squinted through the rain toward the coach.

"Hackney! Take me to Cheapside," he slurred roughly.

Hawk was taken aback by the order, then gave a narrow smile. "Right this way."

Moments later the warden was sprawled on the floor of the coach with a gag around his mouth and Hawk's knee in his back. The warden had ferocious strength; they fought in the coach like two wild beasts thrashing in battle, but in the end, the man hadn't a chance. Hawk was too filled with wrath even to feel the blows the warden struck. Holding him down, at last Hawk bound the warden's wrists behind him, then went back up to his team.

His heart pounded with primal thunder as he whipped the horses through the tight, jagged streets of the rookery. After a wild run past the Tower of London into the rough dockside area of Shadwell, he brought the carriage to a halt between two abandoned warehouses.

The rain continued to drum steadily; there was not a soul around.

He jumped down from the driver's seat and walked back to open the coach door. He pulled the big, burly drunkard out, tossing him, bound and gagged, into the alley. Hawk picked up his length of lead pipe and walked slowly toward him. Fairness mattered to him not at all in this fight. Had it mattered when the man had overpowered a defenseless girl?

The warden glanced at the metal bludgeon, then looked up at him in horror.

"Recognize me?"

He shook his head.

Hawk sank down onto his haunches before the man. "I have only two words to say to you: Belinda Hamilton."

Spluttering with fright behind his gag, the warden tried to get up. Hawk kicked him in the chest and sent him flying back to the wet cobblestones again. As though watching himself from somewhere outside his own body, Hawk saw himself raise the lead pipe, then he struck him.

Again.

The contact as metal hit bone reverberated down into Hawk's soul.

Belinda.

The rain fell; the blood flew.

Cascades of rain poured from the eaves.

Nothing in his life had prepared him for the savagery that came out of him as he unleashed his vengeance on the man who had violated his woman. In the darkness, with his rain-soaked hair flying in his face and a snarl on his lips, he turned into something, someone he didn't know, and it was terrible and glorious. Hawk was talking to him between blows, circling him like a predator toying with its kill. The warden blubbered on his knees. Hawk kicked him again in the ribs and in the face, cursing at him, but then he stilled his brutal weapon, knowing that if he didn't stop now, he was going to kill the man.

Trembling, he threw the lead pipe aside and stood with his chest heaving, the rain plastering his black hair to his face, his blood-flecked shirt molded to him. Shaken by his own barbarity, he walked coolly to the edge of the dock while the warden writhed on the ground, groaning.

He looked out at the black, slick river. There was a ponderous convict ship moored at the final checkpoint, bound for the prison colony of Australia. Hawk's eyes glittered with satisfaction at the poetic justice of bribing the ship's keepers into taking the warden aboard and throwing him down among the convicts. No doubt a number of the prisoners in the hull would remember the warden and would repay him for his brutality from the Fleet.

At the foot of the dock stairs, a fisherman's little dinghy bobbed. He looked again at the convict ship. What the name of the duke of Hawkscliffe could not accomplish among these underworld river rats, that of Lord Jack Knight, his privateer brother, easily could. If all else failed, he could simply dump the warden over the side of the dinghy and let the Thames take him.

He returned to the warden and dragged him across the dock and down into the rowboat, then unwound the line that moored it to the post. He set out, rowing hard against the sweep of the current.

By the time he got back to shore, the rain had already washed away the blood from the cobblestones.

Still feeling the jittery intoxication of pure wild instinct in his veins, Hawk tilted his head back, closed his eyes, and let the rain fall on his face.

"Gentlemen, you have two minutes," intoned Dolph's second, checking his fob watch.

Bel watched Robert confer with Lord Alec a short distance away.

In a remote grove in Hyde Park, amid the gray predawn mist, they met for the duel.

Dolph was pacing by his coach. The physician and surgeons whom Lord Alec had obtained waited impassively, leaning against their carriage. The earl of Coldfell had arrived, too. He sat in his luxurious black coach, shrewdly watching everything while his bony fingers slowly drummed upon the head of his cane.

Alec left Robert with a nod and went to Dolph's second to make sure the foes' bullets carried equal charges of powder.

Bel was distraught as she stared at Robert walking toward her. She hated every minute of this ordeal but would not have missed being here with him for anything. At least this was one advantage of being a fashionable impure; a lady could never have attended a duel. It was small consolation also that the seconds had agreed that the duelists should fire at the same time. She didn't know how she could have borne it to watch Robert stand there and offer himself to Dolph as a target, only waiting for his turn to shoot.

She couldn't bring herself to ask where he had gone while she slept; deep down, she knew. He had returned with flecks of blood on his clothes. As he sauntered toward her now, he slipped the flask she had given him out of his waistcoat and took another swig from it. He offered it to her with a little, teasing smile meant to coax a smile out of her, in turn, but she shook her head. He put the flask back in his waistcoat, then captured her hand and led her beneath a large oak tree.

He gazed down at her, holding her hands in his. They stared at each other.

"Robert," she uttered, willing herself not to cry nor to beg him again not to do this. She knew he really had no choice.

He raised her hands to his lips and kissed them, one by one. "No tears, bonny blue. Just a kiss for luck."

She threw her arms around his neck and drew him down to her, kissing him for all she was worth, trying to hold him when Alec came and told him it was time. She clung to him. Bel felt her tears brim and rush hotly down her cheeks as she tasted him, savoring the brandy on his tongue, memorizing the silk of his ebony hair and the scratchy texture of his cheek in need of a shave. He ended the kiss, caught her face between his hands and stared fiercely at her, his dark eyes ablaze. "You are my lady and I fight for your honor." Releasing her almost roughly, he withdrew.

Stifling a cry Bel watched him walk away, her body trembling. That one small word—*lady*—he had to know it meant the world to her. The sky was beginning to pale in the east and Venus gleamed blue-white above the trees.

Robert went to the center of the grove where Dolph waited. Lord Alec came to Bel and tucked her hand in the crook of his arm, escorting her over to the coach. She couldn't fathom how the blond archangel managed to look so cool headed at a time like this.

"Rob's going to be just fine, Miss Hamilton, I assure you. He's too bloody minded to bow out knowing Jack would inherit his title."

Pistols in hand, Dolph and Robert stood back-to-back in the center of the grove as the first blood red rim of the sun showed through the black trees.

Bel felt sick to her stomach as the first notes of the morning's birdsong lilted through the grove. She began to pray again very hard in her mind.

Lord Coldfell hobbled forth on his cane, having been chosen to do the honors of dropping the white handkerchief to mark the start of the duel. Standing on the edge of the grove, he held it in his bony hand and waited.

Dolph's second gave another signal and the two men began walking off the measured distance, twelve paces each.

Dolph and Robert turned. Both stood sideways to present the slimmest target. They raised their pistols like cruel mirror images of each other.

Then the earl released the white silk handkerchief. Bel stared, stricken, the blood roaring in her ears. The white silk square seemed to take an eternity to flutter down gently to the wet dewy grass.

The split second it touched the ground, their fire exploded. Bel could only stare in horror, her hand clapped over her mouth. She couldn't seem to move, bumped and jostled by the flurry of doctors rushing by her.

He's hit.

Chaos broke out on the field of honor. Dolph's curses of pain filled the air along with the shouts of the surgeons. Both men were down. Suddenly in motion, Bel ran to him, her breath stuck in her throat.

"Robert!" she screamed.

"Belinda!" He was conscious, looking for her through the crowd of doctors around him.

She hurtled into their midst and dropped to her knees by his side just as the surgeon pulled back Robert's coat, seeking the wound. Everything was a blur. She kept asking him if he was all right and he kept saying he was fine; she blocked out the sound of Dolph's groaning and calling for her, then suddenly the surgeon exclaimed.

"Look!"

The surgeon pulled Robert's silver flask out of his waistcoat. It was grotesquely bent, but it had stopped the bullet. Bel and Robert both stared at it in disbelief.

Then he looked at her incredulously. "I knew that shot didn't sound right . . ."

"A ruined flask and a button shot off your waistcoat, Your Grace," the surgeon said with an astonished grin. "Somebody was lookin' out for you."

"Let me see!" Bel wasn't satisfied until she had bared Robert's chest and seen with her own eyes that he had suffered nothing more serious than perhaps a bruised rib from the impact of the flask intercepting the bullet.

She stared at him again in utter shock, then threw her arms around his neck and flattened him back onto the wet grass with a giddy screech of relief.

Pulling her atop him, he wrapped his arms around her waist and kissed her as the light from the rising sun began filling the grove. Heedless of the surgeons and others present, they jettisoned propriety, kissing in joyous abandon, but Bel ended their kiss with a soft, scratchy laugh when she felt his manhood stirring beneath her.

"Some paragon you are," she whispered, running her fingers through his hair. "Duels and demireps and black-market brandy. What ever would the Patronesses say?"

"Devil take the Patronesses, sweetheart. Let's go home."

They pulled each other up. Robert put his arm around

her shoulders and they began walking wearily toward the town coach. Beaming, Bel held onto his waist and gazed up at him.

Lord Alec fell in step beside them. "You should take up gambling, with your luck."

"How's Breckinridge?"

Alec glanced toward the other end of the grove. "He's dying, actually."

Bel stopped. "Dying?" She became aware then of Dolph calling for her in a voice that was truly too pitiful to ignore. Hesitantly she paused and looked back at him.

Dolph was on the ground in a pool of his own blood, resting back against his friend's steadying embrace. His face was deathly pale.

"Robert, please give me a moment," she said.

"Belinda, don't—"

"I have to do this," she murmured, releasing him. She walked over to where Dolph lay.

Dolph's eyes filled with tears when he saw her, but his mouth was dry and pale. He wet his lips weakly. "Bel."

The surgeons had opened his waistcoat and shirt to expose the chest wound. His scar from the bear's claw was overrun with his life's blood. Bel felt slightly faint at the sight.

"I don't want to die until you have forgiven me," he rasped. "I'm sorry I put your father in the Fleet. I did it because—you know why. Here." He lifted something in his blood-stained hand. Bel went down on one knee beside him and accepted it—his necklace with a tooth of the bear who had scarred him. "I do love you, in my fashion."

"I know, Dolph." She laid her hand on his forehead. "Try to relax."

He gripped her other hand. "I'm not scared," he ground out, shaking as he attempted to look scornful. "Uncle! Where is my uncle?"

"Is there something you wish to say to me?"

Bel looked up and saw Lord Coldfell step forward with his cane. He looked entirely unmoved by his heir's imminent demise. She exchanged a wary look with Robert, who had joined the small assembly around the dying young man.

Dolph's grip on Bel's hand tightened as if for strength. "The fire at Seven Oaks. Uncle, I started it. It was I."

"Yes, Dolph, I know," the earl said in cool satisfaction.

Dolph suddenly began to wheeze and choke.

His second cried out and looked in panic at the doctor. The head surgeon swept to Dolph's side, but there was nothing to be done. Bel stared at her tormentor as the spark of life vanished from his eyes and his grip on her hand slackened.

He was gone.

She stared, frozen, for she had never been this close to death before. Robert parted the crowd and came to get her, drawing her to her feet. He slipped his arm around her waist and steadied her as he led her away from the crowd. She leaned her forehead against his chest, taking shelter against him.

"Hawkscliffe!"

They turned and found Lord Coldfell pursuing them. Bel felt Robert's posture stiffen beside her.

"Well done, Robert," the old man said in a low, hearty tone when he reached them. His pale blue eyes gleamed. "You've done justice this day, Robert. Your father would be proud. I won't forget it. There's a great deal I can do for you."

He shook his head wearily. "It's not necessary."

Bel tightened her hold around Robert's waist, appalled by the earl's satisfaction at the death of his own heir. "My lord, if you'll excuse us, His Grace needs to rest. Come, darling," she murmured.

Robert nodded farewell to the earl and draped his arm

over her shoulders. Together they walked back to the
coach, but when she stole a quick look over her shoulder,
Lord Coldfell was still standing where they'd left him,
staring at Bel with a sharp, calculating look of displeasure.

❧ CHAPTER ❧
SEVENTEEN

About an hour later Hawk lay holding a scantily clad Belinda in his arms as they both attempted to rest after the night's ordeal. The morning sun filled her bedroom and danced on her warm, silky skin, which he stroked as he pondered the events of the past twelve hours. Her right arm was thrown across his bare chest; her head nestled in the crook of his neck. The fragrance of her hair wafted up to his nostrils and every now and then he kissed her head, breathing her scent, savoring her softness.

His body was weary but it was his heart that was emotionally exhausted after the extremes of rage and anguish, guilt and love that he had experienced within the past twelve hours—her shattering confession, the uneasy aftermath of the barbaric violence he had unleashed on the warden, the sharp taste of his own mortality left over from his battle with Dolph. Yet the vengeance he'd exacted could not erase what Bel had suffered and all of it left him feeling rather empty and sad, but for the treasure of her in his arms.

The fear that surged through him at the thought of any future harm coming to her made him enfold her lithe body more snugly in his embrace. Their agreement was complete, but he could not bear to think of her leaving him. He could never let her go back to that courtesan's mode of life with all its dangers, but who was he to tell her what to do? She was, as ever, "free and independent."

"Robert?" she spoke up, breaking into his tangled thoughts.

"Hmm?"

"I've been thinking." She came up and braced her elbow under her, propping her chin on her hand. He gazed at her in silent, mystified delight. "I'm still a little confused about Lady Coldfell. *Was* her death an accident, then, like the coroner said it was?"

He shrugged. "That's the best that I can make of it."

She frowned with perplexity, her eyebrows knitted. "I still don't understand why she seduced Dolph, if it was you she wanted."

"Having judged her so completely wrong, I daren't even venture a guess as to her motives," he sighed as he toyed with a length of her pale flaxen hair.

"Well, I have a hypothesis, though you're not going to like it." At his questioning glance, she continued. "Dolph said Lady Coldfell aspired to become your duchess."

"Yes."

"But what about Lord Coldfell? He's advanced in years, but aside from his limp, his health appears good."

He lifted his eyebrow skeptically.

"I know it's farfetched," she continued, "but suppose Lady Coldfell was genuinely desirous to be rid of her elderly husband as quickly and expediently as possible so that she could snare *you* for a husband before you turned your attention to someone more eligible. At the same time, she has Dolph at her beck and call—an expert killer, eager to come into his inheritance. Now, I'm sorry, but I simply don't believe Lady Coldfell wanted Dolph merely for her pleasure. Women aren't like that. When we seduce a man, it is for a purpose."

"Are you suggesting . . . that they conspired together to *kill* Lord Coldfell?"

"Just think on it for a moment. With the earl laid to rest, Lucy would have been free to marry the man she truly wanted—you—while Dolph would have come into his title and fortune. Didn't Dolph mention something just before he died about setting a fire at Seven Oaks? Perhaps Lucy put him up to it."

He shook his head, chilled by the ruthless scenario she posed. "If you had known Lucy, you would realize how impossible it is, what you're suggesting. She was no murderess—"

"Yes, she was virtuous and demure, too, for all you knew," she retorted. "With all due respect, my dear, I don't think you knew Lady Coldfell at all."

This silenced him briefly. "Lucy might have had a secret life of conquests and affairs, but I cannot believe she would even contemplate murder. As for old Coldfell, *I'm* certainly not going to tell him the truth about Lucy's affair with Dolph. Some secrets are better taken to the grave."

"What if he already knows? That's what I'm saying, Robert. Coldfell is the one who started all this, by coming to you for help, as you told me. Frankly, I don't trust the old schemer."

"Belinda, Coldfell has been a friend of my family since I was in leading strings. He knew my father. He wouldn't lie to me."

Sighing away her exasperation, she reached up and gently petted his hair. "Darling, you have so much honor in you that you can't believe anyone you care for would be capable of wickedness. You are too generous with your trust. You saw how happy the earl was today when Dolph died of his wound. Didn't it strike you as unnatural?"

"What was unnatural was Dolph's bedding his aunt, even if she was only an aunt by marriage. Coldfell's behavior today was perfectly consistent with his belief that Dolph had killed Lucy. You're the one whose judgment is off in this matter, Miss Hamilton—your problem is you don't trust anyone." He waved off the subject. "Now, I don't want to talk about this anymore, especially if we can't agree. It's *over*. Lucy and Dolph are both dead. Neither of them can come between us anymore, so let's just put all this behind us and concentrate on you and me."

"Oh, Robert," she sighed, giving him a chiding smile.

"That's better. If you don't mind, I've had a bit of a brush with death today and it tends to put matters into perspective." He leaned closer, cupped her face in his palm, and kissed her lips. "Stay with me," he whispered, stroking her sunlight-colored hair. "I want to take you to my home in Cumberland. I want to show you the lakes and mountains and fells and all the places that I love. They are almost as beautiful as you. We'll leave first thing tomorrow morning."

She stared at him in distress then looked away. "Oh, Robert."

"What is it, bluebell?" he asked with the gentlest possible smile.

"I'm confused."

"About what?"

"You."

"Why? There's nothing to be confused about." He cupped her chin, staring into her eyes. "Stay with me. I'll take care of you for the rest of your life."

"What do you mean?" She held very still, staring at him with fathomless violet shadows in the depths of her eyes.

Instantly Hawk realized his appalling mistake. *Dear God, she thought he was offering marriage.* Paling, he stared at her without knowing what he could possibly say.

He watched her absorb his silent, helpless stare and

draw her own conclusions. Her lips were parted slightly as if to speak, but whatever she might have said, she discarded it and merely gave him a wry half smile.

He suppressed a groan of remorse, sliding down her body to kiss the pale silken skin between her breasts. "Oh, angel, the last damned thing I want to do is hurt you," he said miserably as he laid his head on her chest and clamped his arms around her waist to prevent her angry exit, which he expected within seconds.

"I know," she whispered, draping her arms softly around his shoulders.

"If it were possible—"

"I know."

"There are limits to what I can do."

"I *know*, Hawk, it's all right," she snapped, blushing red with angry embarrassment as she started to get up. "Speak of it no more. God's teeth, I never presumed you would marry me and if you think I have been angling for it, I will leave now and you shall not see me again—"

"Stay!" He held her down beside him, his heart pounding fiercely at the threat of losing her. "I don't think that. Don't go. Bel—stay."

Warily she eased back onto her elbows on the bed, holding his gaze in guarded hostile warning. His heart clenched at the world of vulnerability behind the blue blaze of her eyes. God forbid he give offense. Such pride, such fire beneath your ice, he thought.

"Truly, I have never known anyone like you, Miss Hamilton," he said softly.

"No, you have not," she agreed, then tossed her head. "I have no use for marriage, anyway, not even to a duke. I control my own life—I make my own decisions, and I wouldn't give up my independence for the strawberry vines on your ducal coronet even if you begged me to."

He smiled at her, chastened. A very brave speech, he thought, loving her. He touched her hair. "Will you stay?"

She held his gaze, her tone and expression both softening. "I'm sure it's not that simple."

"Yes, it is." He laid his hand on her hip, gripping her gently through her whisper-soft satin peignoir. "Damn your courtesan's rules, Bel. Don't I deserve a chance?" His hold on her hip became a caress. "I'll never leave you. I'll never mistreat you. I think you know that by now. Try with me. Let us find what we may find."

"What do you expect to find, Robert?"

"How should I know? I've never experienced anything like this before in my life."

Tears shone briefly under her graceful long lashes before she blinked them away and glanced at him again with a reluctant twist of a smile. Sitting up, she wrapped her arms around her bent knees and sighed. "You are asking us both to set ourselves up for great hurt when it comes time for me to leave."

"Leave? Don't speak of leaving, angel. You must stay forever." He smiled at her, a little shocked himself at his words.

"As your mistress."

"As my love," he countered insistently.

"I don't know what to do. I've grown so fond of you and . . ." She ran her hand through her hair, then lowered her face into the crook of her elbow, resting her forehead on her bent knee. "When I think of how I almost lost you today . . . well, it's like being given a second chance, isn't it? You know I want to be with you, it's just . . ."

"It's what?" he asked, gazing patiently at her as she struggled with herself.

"Unprofessional."

"Is it the money? If you want me to pay off your father's debts, I will—"

"No! It has nothing to do with money." She shot him an appalled look. "As for Papa, maybe he deserves to suffer a bit for what's happened. Perhaps then he'll learn. He got himself into it, let him get himself out of it. That's what my mother would say."

He touched her shoulder comfortingly, then caressed the smooth, sinuous line of her back. "Bel, I think you should know that I told your father everything."

She seemed to weigh this news for a moment, not turning to him, her delicate shoulders hunched self-protectively around her bent knees. "How did he take it?"

"About as well as you might expect."

She buried her face against her knee again as if to hide from the world.

"He'll be all right, sweeting."

"I have a feeling you did something terrible to the warden," she said, her voice muffled by her stance. "I don't mind that you did, but what if the authorities come after you for it?"

"They won't," he said gently. "You need never fear him or even think of him again. You're safe now . . . and I love you."

She lifted her face and turned to him, her eyes wide at his words, her lips soft and trembling. "I love you, too, Robert," she said very quietly. "I shouldn't, but I do."

A wide smile spread slowly over his face. Ignoring her fussing frown, he gathered her into his arms and pulled her back down onto the mattress. "Shouldn't? Yes, you should, you little cockle-brain. Shouldn't love me," he snorted, his voice soft and scratchy. "What bad form. Why shouldn't you love me?"

"Because you'll never really be mine."

He scowled at her without menace. "I took you for a smart woman until now." She laughed. He traced the curve of her cheek, gazing at her. "Stay with me. I am yours already and have been for some time, if you haven't noticed."

"You were going to throw me out the night before last. That's what I don't like about this, I've no security."

"Ahh, now I understand," he whispered, staring into her eyes. "Security."

"Yes. You can toss me out on the street whenever I begin to bore you."

"What would make you feel secure enough to believe that I will never toss you out into the street? Perhaps this." He reached over to the side table by her bed and picked up the crushed flask, which he had placed there earlier upon undressing. He handed it to her. "Here's your proof, love."

She took it and stared at it as she turned it this way and that, studying it. He watched her profile, saw her eyes fill with tears.

"You could have died for me," she whispered.

"Yes. And I would do it again to protect you if there were ever a need. Gladly."

She turned to him without a word and wrapped her arms around his neck, holding him tightly. He slipped his hands around her waist and heard her sniffle, felt her tears drop onto his bare shoulder.

"I had no right to doubt you. You're such a strong man and you're so patient with me—you don't deserve all this suspicion. I'm sorry, Robert. I don't mean to seem ungrateful. I'm not used to this, I guess, but I think—I'm going to trust you now."

"Now that's good news to start this day," he whispered, catching her tear as it broke and careened down her creamy cheek. It sparkled on his fingertip like a jewel in the morning light. The ice is melting, he thought. He brought his fingertip to his lips and tasted the salt of her tear as her expression turned wistful and still, then, slowly, he leaned toward her and kissed her.

With a soft, needy groan, she parted her lips for him. He tasted her mouth in a tender, searching kiss that silently pledged everything within himself, a kiss that sent radiant illumination into the farthest, darkest reaches of the universe, as though a new celestial star were being born from their love.

She lay back in soft yielding. He moved atop her; she wrapped her long legs around his hips. He closed his eyes more tightly, dizzy with need, but ended the kiss when he felt the flames of temptation begin to sweep over him through the urgent contact of their bodies.

Now that he understood the invisible scars she bore in the very heart of her femininity, he knew to treat her with a lover's most exquisite gentleness. The time was not yet ripe, but soon it would be.

A splendid idea came to him. He bent his head to kiss her neck and came up smiling with his brilliant inspiration. "Rest, Miss Hamilton. I have something wonderful in store for you tonight."

"What could be more wonderful than this?" she murmured, gazing up at him with a dazzling, dreamy gaze.

He twined a length of her golden hair around his finger and kissed it. "You'll see." Then he kissed her eyelids and ordered her in a whisper to sleep.

Later that day Robert busied himself at his desk in the library, dispatching notice of his departure to his country house to the chairmen of his various Parliamentary committees, drawing up instructions to his gentleman of business, and seeing to various other details while Bel readied the household to repair to the country. She was briskly going from room to room on the first floor, helping the maids drape the furniture in brown holland for the duration of the master's absence, when she crossed the entrance hall and happened to intercept the hall porter on his way to give Walsh a letter that had just come by special messenger for His Grace. The butler would then do the honors of delivering it upon a silver tray to the duke, but Bel brushed off the formalities of procedure, smiled at the hall porter and whisked off to deliver the missive to Robert herself. It was as good an excuse as any to look in on him. Glancing down at the letter, she frowned to read it had been posted in Islington, then turned it over to see that the return address was Mrs. Hall's Academy for Young Ladies.

For a moment she hesitated just outside the library door. What could it mean? Some new attack upon her character? But Lady Jacinda was still at school there. Maybe it had nothing do with her. Suddenly fearing that something was wrong or that Jacinda had fallen ill, Bel strode into the library, crossed to Robert's desk and tossed the letter before him, leaning across to kiss his forehead.

"You might want to give this your immediate attention. It just arrived by messenger."

"Lord, what now?" He picked it up and slit the seal.

Bel moved back and waited anxiously for the news. Robert's stern face darkened as he read, then he crumpled the letter in his hand.

"What is it?" she asked quickly.

"I am advised that my sister is being suspended from school for speaking to a strange man in public. A man by the name of Dolph Breckinridge." He threw the balled paper with a low oath.

Bel covered her mouth in shock. "How could he dare—?"

"No doubt he thought to strike at me through her. Thank God Lizzie Carlisle was on hand to keep a shred of sense in my sister's head."

"He didn't hurt her—"

"No, thank God. Lizzie called for the schoolmistress directly. Apparently Breckinridge had been trying to lure my sister into his carriage."

For a moment Bel was silent and sickened with shock. If Dolph had done anything to that innocent child because of her—the thought was too terrible.

"I'm afraid my sister and her lady's companion are just going to have to come to the Hall with us," he said, resting his fists on the desk. "I hope you don't mind, though *I* sure as hell do. Playing the chaperon was hardly what I'd had in mind."

"Of course I don't mind, Robert, but what of the girls' reputations? Perhaps I shouldn't come." She held her breath and braced for disappointment.

"Don't be absurd. You're the reason *I'm* going." He scratched his square jaw in thought. "If you have no objection, we could simply pass you off as their governess. Nobody knows you up north."

"Another charade?" She sighed wearily. "Jacinda will know there's something naughty going on. She's too clever for us even to *try* to hide the truth from her."

"Then she's just going to have to be an adult about it. She's very grown up, in her way."

"Lizzie will be scandalized. By the by, I didn't realize you were familiar with Miss Carlisle. What a dear, shy, unassuming girl."

"She's my ward."

"She is?" Bel exclaimed. "Goodness, Robert, is anyone in London not under your keeping?"

"Miss Carlisle is the daughter of my former estate manager. The man died a decade ago and Lizzie was his only child, with no relatives to turn to. She has been Jacinda's companion since they were very small—not to mention the little hoyden's conscience. Thank God she was there when Dolph attempted to introduce himself."

Bel shook her head, clasping her hands behind her back.

"I feel responsible for this. When I think of what could have happened, what he could have done to her—"

"Belinda," he cut her off softly. "Don't. It accomplishes nothing and no harm was done. Put it out of your mind. Now, run along. I've got a lot of work to finish before it's time for your surprise."

Bel smiled shyly at him, feeling her heart soar. He sent her a sardonic little smile and picked up his quill pen to write his answer to Mrs. Hall.

They left Knight House at eight o'clock that evening.

Robert had advised her to dress with particular formality, but gave her no hint of where he was taking her. In the town coach he pulled down the canvas shades to keep her from guessing their destination.

Her anticipation climbed when she felt the coach glide to a halt and heard the footmen leap down, coming to open the doors.

"Close your eyes, lovely. Your surprise is at hand."

"But I can't bear to, when you look so handsome."

"Flattery won't get you anywhere," he drawled.

Laughing, she obeyed, but his stunning image was imprinted on her mind. Robert had donned richer finery than she had ever seen him wear, foregoing, for once, his gloomy black in favor of a dark plum-colored tailcoat of velvet, gorgeously embroidered down the front. It had a stand collar that pressed the tips of his gleaming white shirt collar against his jaw just so. His white silk cravat was a work of intricate perfection, while his satin waistcoat was sprinkled with small paisleys in a muted gold tone— reserved and terribly fashionable. His fawn-colored breeches molded every line of his powerful thighs, while his flawless white silk stockings accented his excellently muscled calves. He was virile male beauty incarnate, right down to his low-heeled black pumps with their small flat bow. For all the care that had gone into his attire tonight, somehow she wanted nothing so much as to begin undressing the delicious man at the first opportunity.

"I can't stand it," she exclaimed, squeezing his hand with her eyes pressed tightly closed. "Where are we?"

"You'll see," he teased. "No peeking."

She heard the carriage door as it swept open and a metallic clank as the footman pulled down the step. Robert took her gloved hand in his, got out first, and guided her to the step of the coach.

"Smells like horses," she declared, wrinkling her nose.

"All right," he said. "You can look."

Slowly she lifted her lashes. Robert stood to the side, beaming at her and supporting her by her hand as the footmen waited at attention.

Bel's stare climbed up the long, plain, dignified building before her. Recognizing it, her jaw dropped.

"Almack's," she breathed.

He grinned. "Surprise."

Almack's Assembly Rooms! Her fond girlhood dream come true! But she snapped her mouth shut and turned to him in fright. "I can't go in there! I'll be hissed out of Town!"

"By whom?" he asked softly, his boyish smile full of mischief. His dark eyes twinkled. "We have the place to ourselves."

She stared at him in shock. "You rented Almack's for me?"

"Mm-hmm."

"The whole thing?"

"Even the orchestra."

"Oh, *Hawkscliffe!*" She launched herself off of the coach step into his arms.

A manly blush crept into his cheeks as he kissed her, laughing, and set her down on her feet.

"No one has ever done anything so thoughtful for me in my whole life! Oh, but this is terrible extravagance—"

"You're worth it." He swept a gesture toward the double doors, a world of tenderness in his eyes that did not match the wry, worldly twist of his mouth. "Go have a look."

With a shocked laugh full of outrageous glee, she dashed ahead of him, disappearing inside. Chuckling, he followed.

"Oh, Robert, it's . . . *Almack's*," she said in hushed awe as he joined her, for she had gotten no farther than the entrance hall. She stood staring reverently at the towering grand staircase that led up to the assembly rooms.

She longed to go up, but she felt like a trespasser on hallowed ground. She could almost hear the Patronesses' hissing their disapproval. When Robert walked over and stood next to her, she turned to him in distress.

"I don't belong here."

He said nothing, but smiled chidingly and offered her his arm. Taking courage from his calm steady strength, she slowly rested her hand on his arm, then he escorted her up the famous staircase where, for the twelve Wednesday nights of the Season, only those of the most pristine reputation and most graceful refinement were admitted.

She felt him watching her fondly as she marveled at every trifling detail, though Almack's simple elegance was no match for the opulent grandeur of Knight House. There was a vestibule at the top of the staircase; on either side of it were card rooms that Robert told her were also used for suppers and banquets, but straight ahead lay the holy of holies—the ballroom.

Nearly breathless with amazement, Bel walked in and stared all about her. The ballroom appeared about a hundred feet long and half that width, with a flat white ceiling that soared thirty feet above them. A cream-colored frieze, much gilded, circled the room; below it were pale celadon-green walls and enormous arched windows, regularly spaced. The moldings and carvings all were in white, medallions and festoons. There were benches against every wall, and an elevated bandstand at one end with a gilded latticework. Her eyes widened as she noticed the musicians waiting politely, standing at her entrance.

Bel nodded to them uncertainly. "Good evening."

"Good evening, miss," said the conductor with a genial bow. "Is there anything in particular that the young lady would care to hear?"

"W-whatever you usually play, thank you." She turned to Robert in amazement as the gentlemen of the orchestra sat down and picked up their instruments.

He smiled as their charming divertimento spilled through the ballroom.

She walked into the center of the ballroom and laughed aloud, twirling this way and that, merely trying to take it all in. There were dazzling mirrors and glittering chandeliers and two life-sized classical gods holding candelabra.

"I can't believe you did this for me. Robert, it is the most wonderful gift!"

"I remembered how wistfully you spoke of this old place that first day we walked in Hyde Park. Besides, I want this night to be perfect for you," he said in a low, intimate tone, then he lifted her hand and gave it a kiss. "Won't you do me the fair honor of a dance, Miss Hamilton?"

She let out a cascade of starry-eyed laughter. "Oh, good sir, let me ask my chaperone!" she trilled, playing the debutante.

He laughed at her and led her out to the middle of the vast echoey ballroom and ordered the orchestra to strike up a waltz.

They turned and faced each other. He bowed to her; she gave him a low and very correct curtsy, both of them fighting smiles.

Bel laid her right hand upon his left; he placed his right hand on her waist, and the music began.

They danced until she could not remember any reason in the world not to laugh. They finished a bottle of finest champagne and danced again, their revolutions around the uneven floor like the hands of the clock passing two, three hours, until, in the middle of a turn, Robert caught her up against his chest, cupped her chin, and slowly lowered his mouth to hers.

Bel closed her eyes, slipped her arms around his neck, and accepted his tongue into her mouth in warm, loving invitation. She ran her gloved fingers through his hair.

Her head was so light, her blood so hot, it seemed minutes before they were back at Knight House, kissing endlessly as they progressed by fits and starts down the hallway to her chamber, stopping frequently to savor every touch. Their gloves were off. His cravat was untied.

He felt around for the doorknob, not breaking their kiss, then opened her bedroom door, sweeping her inside. She pirouetted past him into the room, kissing him with feverish urgency all the while.

A path of moonlight led straight to her canopied four-poster bed, but they lingered by the door. She pressed him back against it, grasping the lapels of his velvet coat. He spread his legs wider and she stepped between them, for his kisses had made her boldly impatient.

"You taste like champagne," she giggled, then stroked his luscious tongue with her own in another soul-deep kiss. She pulled his undone cravat off his neck and started on the buttons of his waistcoat.

He hooked his finger inside her gown at the shoulder and followed her décolletage down to the front, grazing her aureole as his touch passed over her breast.

"Mmm," she panted, feeling her nipple instantly harden. He stroked her throat upward in a feathery caress. Rounding her chin, he touched her lips. She closed her eyes and took his fingertip into her mouth, kissing and sucking it with lavish care. He watched her, his breathing deepening in the dark.

With his other hand, he grasped her hip and pulled her closer against his big, quivering body. She could feel the pulsating length of his hardness against her belly and knew he was holding himself in check; she took rich pleasure in his obedience, his almost passive obliging as he let her have her way with him. More brazen still, she cupped him through his formal knee breeches. He moaned and dropped his head back against the door.

Her hand climbed up the length of his arousal, then up his flat belly to his chest, and then she curled her fingers around his nape and stared at him. He looked at her in tormented ecstasy.

"Come and teach me the pleasure you promised," she whispered, "because I am so ready to learn."

He gave her a half smile so seductive, it sent a thrill all the way down to her toes.

He sauntered over to her bed, leading her by the hand. She sat down on the edge of it and waited, leaning back on her hands. He bent down and stole her breath with his kiss, petting her breasts gently through her gown, then he kissed her chest and withdrew with a suave bow to light the candles.

She smiled at that, feeling cherished as he chased away the darkness, lighting every candle in the room. Her chamber blazed with warm, orange light from the candelabra on the mantel, the taper on the vanity and the one on the little table near the bed, then Robert drifted back to her, smiling softly with the low, intimate glow of the flames molding the beloved sculpture of his face with mysterious shadow.

Standing in front of her, he slowly pulled off his unbuttoned coat and dropped it behind him. Bel's admiring gaze took in the breadth of his wide shoulders, the clean sweep of his taut waist. The gold buttons on his waistcoat winked in the candlelight as he popped the last few open and shed it, as well.

His loose white shirt of fine lawn had a small frill down the front, which Bel parted as she came up off the bed, baring his muscled chest and kissing the V of bronzed skin. She trembled with anticipation as he gathered his shirt in his hands and slipped it off over his head.

Their eyes met. He stared tenderly at her, his moist lips swollen with kissing, his hair tousled.

She stroked and kissed his fine velvety flesh, exploring his powerful chest and sculpted belly. His eyes were closed as he just stood there, languidly enjoying her exploration.

She rested her hands on his broad shoulders and indulged herself with a leisurely caress down his arms, savoring every elegant, rock-hard curve of his biceps and strong forearms.

"You are a . . . magnificent specimen, Hawkscliffe."

He laughed softly, lifted his lashes and captured her hands when her touch reached his wrists. He wove his fingers through hers and bent down, kissing her.

For the longest time, they stood like that beside the bed, holding hands and kissing.

"I want to see you," he whispered at last.

A blush rose to her cheeks, but, though shy, she was eager to proceed. She turned around and lifted her hair out of the way; he unfastened her gown in the back and unlaced her light stays.

Her heart beat faster as he gently slipped the gown off her shoulders. The soft muslin sliding down against her skin felt incredibly sensuous. It was followed by his hands, lightly skimming her body. She shivered with desire as he sat down on the bed behind her, grasped her hips, and kissed the small of her back again and again through her nearly transparent chemise.

When her gown was naught but a pool of white silk on the floor, he sank to his knees and reached under her chemise. His warm, sure hands moved up her calf to her lace garter and he applied himself to removing her stockings.

He peeled them down and she stepped out of them. He stood again, his magnificent chest heaving with desire. Under his long black lashes his eyes had darkened and glittered like the stars at midnight.

She touched his chest gently. "One moment," she whispered. "We don't want you to wind up an accidental papa."

She started toward the chinoiserie screen so she could make use of the small round sponge with the thread, just as she had been taught, but Robert stopped her with a soft tug on her wrist. He looked deeply into her eyes. "Would that be so bad?" he asked.

Her heart skipped a beat. "N-no."

"Are you ready for this, Belinda?"

"Yes, I-I'm ready now." She held her breath nervously and went with him, hand in hand, to the bed, where they finished undressing. He slid under the sheets while she sat beside him uncertainly for a moment, her heart pounding.

She watched him as he touched her midriff in awed tenderness. She drew in her breath sharply when his wandering hand cupped her breast.

He curled upward in one graceful motion and kissed it. Bel closed her eyes. He opened his mouth and suckled her—and then it was begun.

Their hands ran all over each other, gliding, stroking, kneading. He drew her down between the sheets with him and she discovered the powerful aphrodisiac of his nakedness against her. He aroused her almost unbearably as their bodies entwined.

For one fleeting instant she felt a shadow of fear upon her heart, but all she had to do was open her eyes and gaze at him to make it pass. There wasn't one moment when he wasn't exquisitely gentle, patient, kind.

"I love you, Belinda," he whispered as he eased her onto her back, kissing her throat.

Transported with amazed joy, she breathed her answering vow of love as she wrapped her legs around his hips. Now, yes, she thought, holding him tightly as he guided himself to her threshold, but he wasn't nearly ready to satisfy her need so soon.

He rose onto his hands above her and watched her face while he teased her to the edge of distraction with the tip of his cock, moving in short, provocative little strokes.

She lifted her hips, moaning for more, but he smiled wickedly at her and took it out. Moving down over her body, he bent his head and delighted her for a while with his clever tongue, laving and flicking her rigid nub, sucking it as she moved with him in the most intimate of rites. Again he brought her to pleasure's sheerest edge, but when her cries reached the verge of release, he stopped, returned, and slipped the tip of his hardness inside her yearning liquid passage. He gave it to her just a little bit deeper than before, but she craved so much more. He alternated this torment several times until she was in agony or ecstasy or both at once.

"Please, please," she heard herself begging breathlessly.

"Are you sure it's what you want?" he whispered. "I need you to be sure, Belinda."

"God, yes," she groaned, arching wildly to feel his body against her, his hard chest chafing against her breasts. "I want you inside me. All the way inside me, Hawk, please, please."

He kissed her forehead and slowly acquiesced, inching inside of her.

"Ohhh," she murmured in awe, closing her eyes at the feel of him filling her so carefully. She wrapped her arms around him and held him, felt the light dewy sweat on his chest when he came down onto his elbows and returned her embrace, barely moving within her.

They were both quite still, only feeling and savoring their glorious union after wanting it for so long.

He kissed her lips and resumed loving her until they had built to a nearly frenzied rhythm. He paused, panting hard.

"Give me a second," he whispered. He slipped her a luscious smile, his lips plumped and thoroughly kissed. He lay back, pulling her atop him, and his voice was a seductive growl. "Take me, lovely."

Slowly sitting up astride him, Bel obeyed. "Oh, my love," she breathed, reveling in it. He was inside her to the hilt, his bronzed, strong hands gently grasping her white hips as she began to ride him.

"You are so beautiful," he gasped, watching her with dark, glittering eyes.

When he touched the pad of his thumb to her throbbing center, she shuddered and dropped her head back, quickening her rhythm. A few moments later he sat up with a ripple of stomach muscles and caught her bobbing breasts in his mouth. The feel of his taut belly chafing against her mound was her undoing.

Pleasure surrounded her on all sides—inside her, around her—his hands, his thick member, his mouth. She abandoned herself to her shattering climax, heedless of the loud, wrenching cries that tore from her lips. She was conscious only of him enfolding her body in his wild loving bliss.

Even as the throes of her passion started to ebb, he let out a low breathless cry that was muffled against her neck. His chest heaved as he rolled her onto her back and possessed her. Again and again he pulsed within her—he shuddered—and then his straining muscles began to go slack. She felt his heartbeat pounding wildly against her body.

"God, I love you," he uttered. He sounded almost shaken.

She pulled him down gently; he laid his head on her bosom, his body still sheathed inside hers. Heavy and spent, he pressed a single, tender kiss to her breast and slowly caught his breath.

"I love you, too, Robert," she whispered, kissing his forehead. *"I love you, too."*

◄ CHAPTER ► EIGHTEEN

Two days' journey on the Great North Road had brought them through the gentle green farmlands of the shires where Bel saw quaint flatboats bearing their loads along the canals and white smoke puffing from the bottleneck kilns of busy potteries. With the harvest so near, the patchwork fields burgeoned with barley and wheat.

The weather held, with good breezes and skies of intense blue above them; beneath them, the macadamized road was excellent, so the endless hours of riding in Robert's sturdy traveling coach turned out to be very tolerable.

When they rolled over the bridge into the ancient city of York, where they would spend the second night of their journey, the late summer light still danced in gold spangles on the Ouse River. They collected Jacinda and Elizabeth and went for a stroll through the Shambles to stretch their limbs, stopping to take a turn inside the huge, silent medieval minster. Bel marveled at the towering great east window, depicting the Creation. The field of exquisite stained glass seemed to stretch all the way up to heaven, richly detailed from the imaginations of artisans who had been dead for centuries.

She took Robert's hand and together they stared up at the great west window, through which the last rays of sunlight beamed in splendid color. They left the minster with regret, for Jacinda was whining and both girls were tired, hungry, and cranky. They retired to the warm hospitality of the coaching inn across the square on High Petergate.

The hearty fare that Robert had ordered to be brought to their rooms consisted of steaming cottage pies with Yorkshire pudding. Bel took an inexplicable satisfaction in watching Robert eat and wash down his supper with a good dark ale from the tap room. It seemed that the farther they traveled from London, the more invigorated he became.

After the good country meal, Jacinda hugged them both good night and Lizzie made her shy curtsy. The girls retired to their room and Robert leaned back in his chair, watching her with a gleam in his eyes that she had come to know.

He left the candle lighted on the table and soon had coaxed her into the bed. She hit the mattress with her arms around him, smiling to think of how quickly she was overcoming her fears. Then he went about furthering her education.

In the morning they were refreshed and ready to strike out west through the Yorkshire Dales and over the broody moors, arriving in Westmorland County by the end of the day.

"We're practically in Scotland," Bel declared, to which His Grace and his sister took offense. She laughed at their indignation as they promised her she had not yet seen the most beautiful scenery in the world. Even the famous painter, Mr. Constable, had said so, Jacinda boasted.

The third day consisted of weaving through the hills and fells and among the sparkling breezy meres. Bel could smell the hint of magic in the air; the hills turned to an emerald so green it made her heart ache. Broad rippling peaks soared around them on every side. The air felt thinner as their elevation rose. Perhaps this was the simplest explanation for the presence of the poets' muse in these windy haunts, she thought, but beauty greeted her wherever she turned, from the towering magnificence of Saddleback, to the sheep drowsing contentedly next to blue water in the valleys.

When they stopped to admire Lake Grasmere, she glanced at Robert's hard profile, etched in sun, the breeze riffling his black hair. The rugged hills, brown and green, cloud mottled, were flung out in a panorama behind him, and she realized then that this was his world, his true element—not the stilted opulence of Parliament and Knight House, nor the crowded streets of London under Society's watchful eye, but these free ranging vistas with their moody skies and rustic comforts.

And when they arrived at sunset before Hawkscliffe Hall, shimmering in the distance, he was the fitting master of the castle they beheld, looming above a mirrorlike tarn. For a long moment, they all stopped and stared at it.

Hawkscliffe Hall possessed such an air of timeless permanency that she recalled again Robert's whisper on the morning after his duel, *Stay forever*. For the first time since he'd spoken them, it gave her pause to consider what he had meant by those words. Forever was no idle fancy to a man who dwelled in a castle that had stood for centuries, she realized. For a moment her certainty faltered; however romantic, the arrangement between them was temporary. Wasn't it?

The only answer that came to her was the cry of a circling hawk far above them, soaring on spirals of air.

Robert squinted against the sun, looking up at it.

The fields around them waved with wildflowers and the dusty road ahead curved around the water.

"You didn't tell me you live in an actual . . . castle," Bel said as her wondering stare followed the sweeping blue-gray curtain wall that defended the steep hill crest, about a half mile off.

Robert looked askance at her, smiling faintly.

Hawkscliffe Hall had crenellated battlements and high

round wall towers at regular intervals and a tall square keep, from which she could not help but imagine ancient archers firing their long bows, knights charging out on their war horses. Yet the whole scene was idyllic, like a daydream.

The hawk screeched again triumphantly.

Bel looked up at the majestic bird, shading her eyes with her hand. "It's beautiful."

"They thrive here. I'll show you the mews, if you like falconry. Come. It's been ages since I've been home."

She followed him back to the coach, mystified. In London, he had seemed to her the ultimate man of the world, almighty in his wealth and influence, possessed of smooth cosmopolitan power, a man whose innate finesse and diplomacy paved the way in the world for his high ideals. Yet here, in the home of his ancestors, she could not help but see him as a kind of strong, rugged warrior overlord in the prime of his manhood.

The castle came complete with dragon, Bel discovered, as once more her path crossed that of the termagant chatelaine, Mrs. Laverty, but this time, she was not about to let the woman intimidate her.

Inside, Hawkscliffe Hall was a maze of rambling passages and nooks and crannies in which she could well imagine Robert and his siblings had loved to play hide-and-seek when they were children. While Jacinda told her excitedly about their resident ghosts, Robert led her on a tour through the whimsical, strange, unpredictable place.

Their mother's gilded, frothy rococo tastes overlaid earlier, darker, and sturdier Jacobean styles, all within a medieval shell.

Jacinda could barely contain her enthusiasm as she rushed to and fro, touching everything and reacquainting herself with beloved familiar objects in every room. There was a Venetian saloon, a Chinese drawing room, a ballroom and a billiard room that all bore the stamp of the Duchess Georgiana's Versailles-inspired decor.

The most recent section of the castle, airy and tastefully redecorated, led back into a much older, dim refectory gallery, with a long somber dining table. The great hall and the tapestry rooms were the oldest of all. Bel could almost imagine Robert's forebears making their battle plans against the Scottish border clans. Her imagination ran riot as she stared all about her. She wished Papa could have seen the place.

Attached to the back of the castle was a winter garden with an orangery. Beyond the graceful glass walls lay topiary terraces with a small knot garden in the center. She realized that beyond the gardens, the thousands of acres of sweeping turf and sloping woodlands belonged to Robert, as did the deep indigo lake, inky where it lay in the shadow of the screes.

They went outside into a graveled courtyard where Robert pointed out the chapel, the servants' hall, the estate office and carriage house, and the huge stables and mews set farther back.

Jacinda and Lizzie dashed off to visit their favorite horses while Bel and he strolled back inside.

"Your home is a marvel, Robert, truly, a wonder. It is like something out of Walter Scott's tales," she said, shaking her head in amazement.

"And you are most welcome here," he answered softly, lifting her hand to his lips.

At a footman's inquiry, he ordered her things to be deposited in the bed chamber adjacent to his own. He delivered this brazen command without blinking an eye. She looked askance at him, startled but happy with his open attitude about their affair. It seemed they were in accord at last—she had abandoned the safety of the courtesan's prime rule, and he seemed to have finally, genuinely accepted her into his life.

That night he took her into the state bed where he himself had been conceived and possessed her with a vigor rooted in the strength this land gave to him.

In the days that followed Bel discovered that even though Robert had been absent for months, he was one of the pillars of local life, called upon almost daily by people who would come from miles around to ask for his advice or assistance. He always made time for them.

She occupied herself minding the young ladies. They looked up to her, though she was only Robert's mistress. Their affection and need of her helped her to heal almost as much as Robert's love. Each sunny afternoon they went vagabonding across the countryside under wide-brimmed bonnets, in search of scenes to sketch.

Though Jacinda and Lizzie were both nearly grown girls, neither had known their mothers. Bel was touched by their eager need to be loved and their willingness to accept her guidance. On successive days, over tea and cakes, she soon learned that Jacinda was frightened of making her debut, knowing that the Patronesses and their ilk would be watching her with eagle eyes, looking for any sign of her mother's flagrancy in her behavior.

Lizzie, in turn, confessed that her status as a penniless ward had long been a great trial to her pride. She worried what would become of her when Jacinda had her Season and married. Moreover, she was hopelessly infatuated with Lord Alec.

On Monday of their second week in the country, Jacinda promised Bel a magical surprise. "Today I'm going to take you to see the most spectacular place of all. We've been saving it for last, haven't we, Lizzie?"

The two girls exchanged a look and giggled.

"Why, what is it?" Bel asked, as she piled their picnic hamper and sketch pads into the arms of their long-suffering footman.

"Pendragon Castle," Jacinda announced in a reverent hush. "Many ancient years ago it was the castle of Uther Pendragon—the father of King Arthur!"

"Oh, Jacinda, you are full of fairy dust."

"It's true! The place is eerie. Some say that the enchanter Merlin is locked up in the great yew tree that stands over the ruins."

"Balderdash."

"She's telling the truth, Miss Hamilton, honestly," Lizzie attested with a solemn, wide-eyed nod.

"My brothers used to play knights of the Round Table there when they were small," Jacinda said with a wide smile, then skipped out into the sunshine.

They set out on foot and met a number of local people along the way—a trio of shepherd children managing their flock, an old peasant driving his cart of chickens to market, and two weathered, capable-looking men, whom Jacinda introduced as the gamekeeper and the land agent. They said they were on their way back to the hall for luncheon.

Bel looked on with amusement as Jacinda questioned them about the surrounding fields and woodlands with all the seriousness of the rightful lady of the manor. Their eyes twinkling, the two kindly men indulged her, but Bel sensed their manly interest in her, the "governess," and shied away from it, saying little.

The sun-bronzed land agent could not praise the duke highly enough for the prosperity he had brought to his tenants by his forward-thinking uses of agricultural improvements. The big, soft-spoken gamekeeper confided that he had been instructed to turn a blind eye to a certain amount of poaching on His Grace's lands, which had added to Robert's reputation as a benevolent landlord.

Finally they parted ways, with the footman trudging behind them, laden down with their supplies. As they approached Wild Boar Fell they spotted a herd of wild ponies drinking at the River Eden. They stopped and watched the ponies in delight until the herd decided their party was not to be trusted and stampeded off over the rise. Exclaiming happily over the unexpected encounter with the fell ponies, they made their way to the looming, craggy ruins of Pendragon Castle.

Bel stared in fascination at the ancient stone shell of the fortress. A living fragment of a timeworn myth, Pendragon Castle stood tall on one side, where a great, blighted tree hung over its ragged pinnacle, but the other half of its ramparts had crumbled away.

She walked nearer, exploring it while Jacinda ordered the footman to lay out their picnic. Bel could almost imagine a roguish band of boys playing here at being knights of King Arthur's Round Table. She heard a shuffle of rock behind her and turned to find Lizzie carefully picking her way through the fallen, mossy stones.

"I was just thinking that I never did hear about the rest of Lady Jacinda's brothers," Bel said to the girl. "I only know Hawkscliffe and Lord Alec."

"Well, the second-born is Lord Jack, but he is not discussed in good company." She sneaked a glance over her shoulder. "I'm afraid he is quite the black sheep."

"Is he really one of the Gentlemen?" Bel whispered, invoking the euphemism for smugglers.

"I wouldn't put anything past him, oh, but he has a good heart, Miss Hamilton."

"Why did Lord Jack become a smuggler?"

Neither of them saw Jacinda hopping over to them from rock to rock, but apparently, she had heard them. "Because he wanted to rebel against Papa for being cruel to him," she declared. "My papa wasn't *his* papa, you see. Only Robert and I are of the true blood. Robert's the heir, Jack was *supposed* to have been the spare, and I'm the kiss-and-make-up baby."

Bel gasped and Jacinda let out a peal of laughter. "It's all right. I don't mind telling *you* about my family, my dearest Miss Hamilton. You're one of us now." She hugged Bel when she reached her side, then laughed and pirouetted on a rock. "Everybody knows my mama had lots of lovers—and so shall I when I'm grown up," she said defiantly.

"Jacinda!"

She shrugged off Bel's horrified look nonchalantly. "The only one of my brothers that Papa liked was Robert."

Bel debated for a moment on lecturing the girl, then decided Jacinda was only testing her for a reaction. "It's not unusual for a man to lavish all his attention on his heir and overlook the others."

"Papa died just before I was born, so I wouldn't know what his reasons were, but you must admit it wasn't very nice of him. All I know is that one day Jack got fed up with it, dropped out of Oxford, and went to sea. After Jack are our identical twins, Damien and Lucien."

"They're unbearably handsome," Lizzie whispered.

"Damien is a colonel in the Infantry and a very great war hero, I don't mind telling you," Jacinda said proudly. "He once took a French eagle in battle. The officers in his regiment had a copy of it made for him and it hangs in Knight House."

"Oh, yes, I've seen it," Bel said, mystified. "And what of Lucien?"

"We're not exactly supposed to know where he is," Lizzie started.

"But now that the war is over, I'm sure it doesn't signify anymore if we tell you!" Jacinda looked at Bel with a streak of mischief in her grin. "Lucien's in Paris. He's a *spy!*"

"Observing officer," Lizzie corrected, but Jacinda snorted at the polite term.

"A spy, really?" Bel asked in amazement.

"Yes, but you must never tell a soul. We're all supposed to think he's on an archaeological dig in Egypt for the Royal Society."

"Why are we supposed to think that?"

"As an explanation for his absences from England and the main body of the army. Poor Lucien, I think he really would have preferred to be an archaeologist, but duty called. He tried the army at first with Damien—they asked him to design weapons and work with the military engineers—but he was quite perfectly miserable. He hated taking orders."

"Lord Lucien is a scientific gentleman, Miss Hamilton," Lizzie stated knowingly. "Everyone says he's a genius."

"If you say so, Lizzie. Lord knows I can never comprehend a word he says. I'm hungry," Jacinda suddenly whined.

"Then let's have our feast," Bel said with a bright smile, still fascinated by the exotic menagerie of Knight brothers, but uneasy at Jacinda's brazen words about taking lovers when she was grown up. Even if the girl had only said it in an adolescent attempt to be shocking, it did not bode well.

As they sat down to a repast of sliced ham, cheese, and fruit, Bel passed a searching glance over Jacinda's pert, elfin features. "Tell me about your mother, Jacinda. Do you remember her?"

"Some. She was ever so beautiful and clever and fearless," she said, looking away wistfully toward the babbling river. "Everyone was jealous of her, that's why people hated her—because her spirit was too big for the little box the world would put her in."

Lizzie looked uneasily at Bel.

"Robert is ashamed of our mother, but only because Papa deliberately turned him against her."

Bel knit her brow. "Is this true?"

"Alec says it is," Jacinda said, her wide, dark eyes unusually somber. "Robert won't even let me ask him questions about Mama, though he's the eldest and knew her best. It's not fair. People talk about her lovers and her salons and her scandals, but did you ever hear of how she died, Miss Hamilton?"

Bel shook her head, not certain she could bear it. There was something so grim in the girl's fresh, lovely face.

"Our mama's involvement with the French emigres began at the time of the Terror. She received a plea from her bosom friend, the Viscomtesse de Turenne, with whom she'd studied at the Sorbonne. The lady begged Mama to take her children and get them out of France—her husband, the Viscount, had already been killed by a mob. Risking her life, Mama went straightaway to Paris and from then on became involved in helping the children of the aristocrats escape to England. Over the years that followed, she made several trips back to France, bringing more of the nobles' children to safety each time. Though the Jacobins finally put away their guillotine, emigres were still considered traitors to France and aiding their escape was illegal. Mama was arrested in the fall of 1799 in the final months of the Directory. She was charged with being a royalist agent and an English spy and then taken before the firing squad and shot."

Bel stared at her. "It's true," Lizzie murmured with a grave nod.

Bel couldn't seem to absorb it. For several moments no one spoke. This was the woman of whom Robert was ashamed?

"Jacinda," Bel said gently at length, "your mother was a

true lioness. I never heard of anyone so brave. I know you want to be like her, but for her sake, I hope that you will try with all your might to follow the rules of decorum, at least until you are married, because in truth, my dear, it's very painful when the whole world disapproves of you. I feel she would want me to warn you of that. I don't want to see you hurt, and I also hope you'll remember that if you get into a scrape with a young man, it may well mean that one of your brothers will have to duel to defend your honor. Sweetheart, to see someone you love put his life at stake for some foolish mistake of you own—that is a very dark thing indeed. Take it from me."

This, Bel saw, sank in. Jacinda stared at her and nodded, wide-eyed. Abandoning such grim topics, they finished their picnic and then sat for a while, sketching the ruins of Pendragon Castle with the tree hanging over and the river snaking by. Bel was drowsy with relaxation by the time they gathered their things and trudged back toward Hawks- cliffe Hall.

She was lulled by the twittering of the thrushes in the field, when suddenly she heard hoofbeats drumming down the road. The girls and she turned, while the footman got out of the way of an open landau drawn by a team of grays.

"Oh, Lord," Jacinda groaned under her breath. "It's Lady Borrowdale and the milksop sisters."

"Jacinda!" Lizzie scolded, fighting a smile.

"Who is it?"

"The Marchioness of Borrowdale, our most bothersome neighbor. She's determined to snare a couple of my broth- ers for her awful daughters. Poor Robert. He bears the brunt of it."

Bel heard this and stiffened as the liveried driver pulled the team.

At once a large matron in a plumed hat leaned out of the

carriage and called in a thunderous voice, "Yoo hoo! Lady Jacinda! Hallo! Hallo!"

Jacinda heaved a sigh. Lizzie followed her over to the carriage to greet their neighbors.

"We were just coming to call on you, my dear! How lovely you look! Why, you are nearly full grown!"

"Thank you, your ladyship," Jacinda said in a long-suffering tone.

"Miss Carlisle," said the marchioness in begrudging acknowledgment of Lizzie.

"Lady Borrowdale. Lady Meredith, Lady Anne, how nice to see you," Lizzie replied obediently, offering them a small curtsy.

With an air of brisk self-importance Lady Borrowdale turned back to Jacinda and tried to start an exchange of pleasantries between her and her two daughters.

Bel shook her head to herself. She could spot a matchmaking Society mama at twenty paces. This was without doubt the most unpleasant aspect of her existence as an outsider. Every marriageable daughter of the northern nobility likely burned with ambition to become Robert's duchess, and there was not a thing she could do about it.

He had kept their arrival quiet and had simply gone about his business, but word had obviously spread that one of the most eligible bachelors in England was at home. Bel had the dismal feeling that this trio was just the beginning. Fortunately there was no way either of these pasty-faced girls could pose any threat to her place in Robert's heart. With tense, unpleasant expressions, the girls showed no glimmer of wit, sympathy, or amusing conversation to make up for their lack of looks.

They just sat there in the landau across from their overbearing mama, sullen, staring at Jacinda as though they despised her for her beauty and spirit and fire. One had a weak chin and lackluster eyes; the other had a pointy nose and looked, in all, like a sly little baggage.

"And who," the woman warbled, eyeing Bel mistrustfully, "is this?"

Having been singled out, Bel approached cautiously, wondering what sort of wicked rejoinder Harriette Wilson would have had for the marchioness of Borrowdale.

"Lady Borrowdale, may I present my governess, Miss Hamilton," Jacinda said.

Bel inclined her chin. "Lady Borrowdale."

"Governess?" Lady Borrowdale looked her over from the brim of her bonnet to the tips of her kid half boots. "Mm-hmm. I thought you were attending an academy in London, my dear," she said, turning again to Jacinda.

Apparently only those with a title were worthy of Lady Borrowdale's address.

"I've been suspended," Jacinda announced, grinning proudly.

"Ah, not exactly suspended, my lady," Bel corrected Jacinda in a chiding tone as Lady Borrowdale's eyes flew open. Bel contrived to laugh at the girl. "You are such a naughty thing." She turned to the marchioness with her most charming air of management. "The child is jesting, of course, your ladyship. His Grace merely felt that Lady Jacinda could do well with some country air after so many months in Town."

"Ah, how nice that the duke of Hawkscliffe consults you on his sister's well-being, Miss, er, what was it?"

"Hamilton," Bel said coolly, taken aback by the note of innuendo in her words.

"Of course, so sorry. I marvel that His Grace has not provided additional chaperonage."

"Miss Hamilton is a highly qualified governess," Jacinda retorted staunchly, her golden eyebrows knitting together. She moved closer to Bel.

"I'm sure she is, but she looks as though she is barely out of the schoolroom herself. You know, my niece's governess is looking for a new position, now that her charge has married. Swiss, don't you know, most efficient. She would be very suitable for you. I'll be sure to mention the matter to His Grace when we go up to the Hall. After all, what do bachelors know of the proprieties?"

Lady Borrowdale's eyes darted to Bel again with quick, gleaming malice.

Bel just looked at her. Did this self-important creature really think that the Paragon Duke would fool around with his little sister's governess? Of course, it was all a charade, but whom did this woman think she was, to question the duke of Hawkscliffe?

"Lady Borrowdale," she said, unable to hold her tongue, "I assure you His Grace's sterling reputation is constituted by a keen observation of all the proprieties and a more than ordinary measure of honor."

There. She had defended her employer like a loyal servant.

But then she saw that if her intention had been to put Lady Borrowdale's mind at ease about her presence at Hawkscliffe Hall, her words had had the opposite effect. The matron's small eyes blazed at the challenge to her authority, but Bel stood her ground.

"What extraordinary impertinence!" she gusted. "Is *this* to be your example of ladylike behavior, Jacinda? A London miss with haughty London airs? It will not do, I say. It will not do!"

"A refusal to grovel to your ladyship is hardly arrogance," Bel replied, amazed at how easy it was to put down overblown women. It was as easy as setting down overly amorous peers.

Lady Borrowdale gasped. "I will not be talked to thus by a governess! Young woman, apologize."

"For what, ma'am? I am merely reminding you of His Grace's excellent good name."

"I need no reminding from you, miss! Reminding me? Oh, you are bold. His Grace will hear of this."

At this threat, Bel did the one thing she should not have done.

She knew better. But after so many months of taking hateful stares from women like the odious marchioness, this time she could not help herself. She answered Lady Borrowdale's glare with a half smile of cool, knowing amusement, as if to say, "Tell him anything you want, he'll not get rid of me."

It was the smile of a courtesan.

Lady Borrowdale stared at her, flustered and taken aback.

"Your ladyship," Jacinda broke in gingerly, "perhaps now isn't *the best* time for a visit."

"We've been out to see the ruins today and we're all a trifle tired," Lizzie offered anxiously.

"Won't you come tomorrow for tea?"

"Humph!" said Lady Borrowdale, looking suspiciously from Jacinda to Lizzie to Bel. "Tomorrow I'm engaged. Will His Grace be at home on Wednesday afternoon?"

"It's hard to say. My brother has been extremely busy of late—"

"Tell him I wish to speak to him," she ordered Jacinda.

Even the free-spirited Jacinda looked cowed. "Yes, ma'am."

"Driver!" Lady Borrowdale barked. She shot Bel one last pointed glance as the driver and postilion worked to turn the carriage around.

They stood by the road and watched as the marchioness and the milksop sisters rolled away in their landau. Jacinda turned and stared at Bel, her eyes sparkling with incredulity. Bel returned her gaze uneasily, but Lizzie was the first to give way to a giggle.

"Oh, the look on her face! I thought she'd fall out of her carriage on the spot!"

"It was wrong of me," Bel started, but both girls began laughing uproariously and even the footman chuckled.

"She deserved it! She's deserved it for years!" Lizzie cried, wiping away a tear. "My dearest Miss Hamilton, please, will you teach *me* how to fight back like that?"

Robert smiled at the story of what had happened with Lady Borrowdale and assured her he would smooth it over, but Bel had been right—the marchioness and her daughters were only the first of many, and not all were as plain as the milksop sisters.

Demure and beautiful innocents from around the district came calling on the pretext of visiting Jacinda, meanwhile poking their noses into every room they passed like curious kittens, always trying to catch a glimpse of Robert. He had all but evacuated the first floor in order to avoid them.

That night, as Bel lay awake watching him sleep, his profile limned in moonlight, she found herself brooding on the knowledge that he had to marry someday. Then what was she going to do? Stay? Leave?

She had no idea. It was a subject they never discussed; there was no reason to discuss it, for his choice of brides had nothing to do with her. Marriage for men of his class was based on power and property, and it was as simple as that. She did not begrudge him his duty; she had known that so highborn a lover could never offer her his name and she had never expected it.

Still, it hurt.

She consoled herself with the knowledge that though

she'd never share his name, she had what mattered—his passion, his fire, his heart.

All she had wanted, starting out, was to be free and independent with a fortune of her own for security, and now, she had that. She was on her way. He had given her back so much of herself, reclaimed from the darkness and shame that had nearly swallowed her, that she did not see how she could betray her earlier vow never to become entangled with a married man. Every hard-won ounce of her integrity meant too much to her to throw it away again. If and when Robert married she would have to find a new protector in order to be able to live with herself.

She banished the chilling knowledge by reminding herself that he had shown no interest in any of the young ladies who had come in the hopes of snaring him. There was no need for panic yet. If he had any plans for marriage, perhaps they were still years off. A wave of need for him rippled through her. She stared at him in the darkness.

Moving closer to his warm, powerful body, lax in sleep, she woke him with a possessive caress down his chest and beautiful ridged belly, a touch meant to entice. His skin was so warm, so smooth. He was such a beautiful man. She kissed his cheek, his chest. She needed to make him know in this moment that he belonged to her.

She kissed his neck, stroking him softly until he began to stir. He moaned, waking, and surrendered to her will as she coaxed his sex to roaring life. She eased atop him and kissed him. Holding him down, owning him, she took his stiff member inside her and rode him awake, making love to him in tempestuous devotion.

"God, you are my fantasy," he breathed as she used every trick she knew to heighten his pleasure, ravishing him until he spilled her off of him and pressed her down onto her belly. His heavy breathing filled her world as she felt the hard wall of his chest against her back. He slipped his arm around her waist and held her still as he penetrated her from behind.

She arched with pleasure, reveling in his dominance. She forgot her fears in the primal joy of their coupling. He entranced her with each deep, powerful stroke; she grew drunk on his groans. The rest was a blur of need and pleasure and passion as they strove to have their fill of each other, but when they came together some time later, Bel felt tears rise up behind her closed eyes—tears of release that left her empty with despair.

It was all for naught. He was in her arms—he was in the very palm of her hand, she knew, but she would never really possess him, as he possessed her.

When you love a man, you are in his power, she thought, forlornly musing on the Cyprians' rule which she had so confidently discarded. *When a courtesan loves, she is destroyed*.

She was completely in this man's thrall and she knew it. It was only a matter of time before she must pay the price for her folly.

Robert stroked her back in long, tender caresses. With her head resting on his chest, she listened to his strong, slow heartbeat. He kissed her forehead.

"I love you," he whispered.

I hope so, she thought, staring off into the darkness.

⅍ CHAPTER ⅍
NINETEEN

Perhaps it was the duel and his brush with death that had given Hawk his newfound lust for life. He felt invigorated and alive; he was happy and in love, and knew himself to be loved in return by the one woman who made him feel complete. The only flaw that marred his satisfaction and his peculiar new sense of belonging was the niggling guilt that this situation was unfair to Belinda, and now, the new complication of the letter he had just received from Lord Coldfell, on which his destiny seemed to hang.

It lay, discreetly folded, on the desk before him. Pondering the offer, weighing the risks, he sat with his crossed heels propped on his desk, his hands carefully whittling a sharp point on his writing quill with a penknife.

Months ago he had heard about Bel's quaint rule against involving herself with married men. As surely as he knew that it was his duty to marry according to his station and produce heirs, he knew with equal certainty that, when the time came, he would go to any lengths necessary to make her stay with him. He was never letting her go back to that courtesan life. It was for her own good.

All that remained before answering Coldfell's letter was to make sure that Belinda's love for him was such that she would not be able to say good-bye when the time came for him to marry. Perhaps it was cruel of him to strip her of what she saw as her last surviving moral, but he knew full well she needed him, damn it, and he was never letting her go. If she really loved him, she would bend to the necessity of his marriage with her usual dignified grace.

What could be done for it? he thought with a sigh. His sole answer to the uneasiness of his conscience had been to work diligently on the promise he had made to her about doing something to mitigate the plight of the flash house waifs.

Days ago he had written to the major London relief societies, surveying them for information, statistics, a report of the conditions of their facilities, and so forth. When he had his findings in order and returned to Town, he meant to sit down at the club with Lord Sidmouth, the home secretary, and rally him for a promise of support.

For a moment his mind drifted back to her waking him in the middle of the night with her delicious lovemaking. He savored the memory of her sweet demand, especially since he alone knew how far she had come, once fearing to be touched. What mortal man hadn't dreamed of being ordered to service so luscious a beauty? He never knew what she was going to do next. No wonder he found her so exciting. God help him, but he had fallen hard for her.

The sound of footsteps in the corridor snapped him out of his hazy reverie, then a knock sounded on his study door.

"Yes?"

The door opened and one of Jacinda's latest visitors peeked in, an insipid young miss with auburn side curls framing her face. "Oh, Your Grace, I'm so sorry to disturb you! Your servant said I might find Lady Jacinda in here."

"Ah, no, only me, I'm afraid," he said, rising to his feet, wearily polite.

The chit lingered, inching in, hanging on the doorknob. "What a happy accident. You are well, I hope." She gave her curls a flounce.

"Er, yes, thank you." Brazen little thing, he thought in

irritation, recognizing her as the daughter of the baron of Penrith. *Accident, my foot.*

"Did you hear I've just come back from my first Season?" she said with an affected, fashionable lisp.

"Congratulations. I'm sure you were quite a toast," he said cordially.

She twirled a curl around her finger, mincing closer. Hawk glanced around for an escape and saw none.

"I was so sure I would see Your Grace at Almack's or somewhere, but you were nowhere to be found."

He froze and stared at her, wondering if she'd heard the rumors in Town—more than rumors—about him and his famous mistress. Surely her elders had not permitted this young miss to hear such talk. But, good Lord, what if she had *seen* them together somewhere? What if she recognized Bel?

"Don't you enjoy Society, Your Grace?" the girl simpered, inching ever nearer.

"Well, it's been a very busy time for the government," he said, donning his smoothest smile. "What with the sessions and the war finally coming to an end."

"Ahh," she said, then she started chattering about Society as if she were one of the Lady Patronesses in the making.

Hawk's whole body was tense.

Not only did he fear what might happen if she laid eyes on Bel, but he also knew he had to get out of this room. Knocking along in time with his heartbeat, he could feel that great etiquette clock ticking—the one that signaled the timing when a young miss's reputation began to be compromised by a visit alone in a room with a gentleman—even if she was uninvited. Even if it was all a sly feminine ploy.

Rules were rules, and dozens of the ambitious young schemers and their parents had already tried to slip the noose around him by this means in the past. They had failed and so would she. Marriage was bad enough without being tricked into it.

"The country seems monstrous dull after Town, don't you think? Lonely, too," the baron's daughter sighed, inching ever closer.

"Well, I'm sure a charming young lady like yourself has innumerable friends. Like Jacinda," he said pointedly. "Let me go get her for you—"

"Oh, don't trouble yourself, please, Your Grace—"

"It's no trouble," he interrupted with a taut smile. "I'll just . . . go get her and send her on."

He heard the girl stamp her slippered foot in frustration as he strode out, clearing the room with seconds to spare.

Hearing the baroness and some other women talking in the drawing room, he was forced to sneak by like a burglar in his own house lest they accost him. The mothers were always in on it, he knew from experience. He took the stairs two at a time and barely felt quite safe from their predations when he reached the upper floor, mentally grumbling about his sister making these appointments and then forgetting about them.

Had the girls gone out? he wondered, for he found them nowhere when he searched the upper floor. Bel would have told him if they were leaving for one of their daily excursions through the fells.

Seeing Jacinda's maid, he asked if the woman had seen his sister. The maid paled, nodded, and confessed their whereabouts: "They've gone into the duchess's old boudoir, Your Grace," she said, cringing as she bowed.

His eyebrows drew together and his face darkened. "Pardon?"

"Yes, sir. They're in the duchess's chamber, sir."

Glowering, Hawk pivoted and stalked down the hallway. He couldn't believe his sister had directly defied this longstanding taboo. He marched stiffly up the stairs to the fourth floor. He clenched his jaw at the sound of girlish laughter from inside a room down the corridor, and when he flung open the door, fiery wrath leaped into his eyes at what he saw.

Jacinda was seated at their mother's gilded vanity, looking utterly ridiculous under the towering white wig woven with jewels that their mother had once worn. She was dabbing the little brush from the glue pot on her cheek and pasting on another of their mother's silk patches.

"*What* are you doing?" he ground out in a menacing snarl.

All motion stopped.

Jacinda jumped up off the cushioned bench and whirled around, quickly whipping off the tall wig. "Nothing."

Lizzie Carlisle slipped off the feather boa she'd thrown around her neck and went to stand behind Jacinda, looking frightened.

"You know you are not allowed in here," he said in a deep voice, crisply enunciating every word.

"M-Miss Hamilton said we could," Jacinda stammered.

"Robert, what's the matter with you?"

He looked over at the sound of Bel's voice.

She had been curled up reading in the window seat. She presently snapped her book shut and got up, coming toward him with a frown. "There's no harm in it."

She could not know, obviously, what a nerve this had struck in him. "*No one* is allowed in this room, as these girls are perfectly well aware."

"Why?"

"Because I said so. Jacinda, take those hideous patches off immediately and hie yourself downstairs. The baroness of Penrith and her daughter have been waiting for you for a quarter hour."

"Why are you so mean?" she cried. "You're just like Papa. She was my mother, too!"

"Look at yourself. You look like a slut. Take those things off your face!" he roared.

"Robert!" Bel stepped in front of him. "Don't shout at her. She's just a child playing dress up."

"Stay out of this. Jacinda—"

"I'm going!" She peeled the last silk patch off her cheek and scurried past them, looking frightened and hurt. Lizzie silently rushed after her. Robert gave his ward a severe look of reproach, as well.

"What is the matter with you?" Bel demanded when the girls had gone.

He slammed the door and turned on her. "I thought I could trust you with them!"

"What is that supposed to mean?"

"I've been trying for the past sixteen years to make a lady of that little hellion. You had no right bringing them in here!"

"Robert, the girl has a right to know her mother—and so do you."

"But for the accident of her womb, the woman who bore us was no mother, Miss Hamilton. Mrs. Laverty was more a mother to me than the Hawkscliffe Harlot ever was."

"So you think. She tried. Your father wouldn't let her."

"You know nothing about my parents."

"Neither do you." She held out the book she had been holding, offering it to him. It was an old clothbound tome with a blue ribbon that could be used to tie it shut. She gazed at him in compassion. "Take it, Robert. It is your mother's diary."

He looked from it to her in wary shock, but made no move to take it. "You've been reading her diary? How could you?"

"I know she'd understand, especially if I can make you

see how much she loved you. Darling, I'm beginning to understand why you are so angry at her."

"*Angry?* Who said I'm angry? I'm not angry. Why should I be angry?" he bellowed. "So I have to spend my entire life making up for her whoredom, what is there to be angry for in that?"

"Robert, be fair to her. Surely you realize by now that your father tainted your perception of her before you were even old enough to know better—"

"My father was a good father! He taught me right from wrong—you don't understand." He struggled to leash his emotions and calm his sharp, thunderous tone for he didn't want Bel to know how volatile this topic made him. "I was all my father had," he forced out. "Maybe he drank too much, he was a three bottle man, yes, but he had the honor to stay with her rather than drag our name through a divorce scandal after she had given birth to Jack. And how did she thank him for that? Tupped a Welsh marquess and gave us the twins. Now, I'm glad to have my brothers in the world, but don't you think it's strange that she kept dropping these children when she never even wanted them in the first place?"

"Is that what you think? That she didn't want you? She suspected as much. Robert, look in these pages—" Again, she tried to give him the diary, but he brushed it off and stalked toward the door, feeling like he would fly apart if he did not get out of here. "This is absurd. I'm leaving." He reached for the doorknob but her voice stopped him.

"Hawkscliffe thrust Morley into the role of father again today—" Bel paused.

He stopped, facing away from her. Earl of Morley had been his courtesy title as a lad, before he had inherited the dukedom. He did not need to turn and look at his mistress to realize she had opened his mother's diary and was reading a passage from it to him.

" 'My poor son. He's so consumed with guilt that he alone has his father's love that he tries to be a father, in turn, to his little brothers. It is too much for a boy of thirteen. So serious and proper, he barely ever smiles—and never at me.

" 'I could forgive Hawkscliffe all of his coldness, all his unfeeling stale indifference to me, but how am I to forgive that he has robbed my child of the carefree boyhood he ought to have been given before he faces a world of responsibility so far beyond that of common men?' "

Hawk closed his eyes, pained.

" 'To be sure, our Morley is equal to his destiny, but sometimes when I see him, stiff brave little man-child, I want to take him in my arms and say, "It's not your fault that Papa doesn't love your brothers. It's mine." ' "

"Enough," he whispered.

His chest felt like there was a bonfire in it, churning with feelings that would tear him apart. His shoulder blades felt like steel pins from standing up straight for too many years, always bound with the duty to set the example, behave beyond reproach. Be perfect. That was the duty with which Father had charged him. Nothing less would do. Don't make a mistake. Don't look the fool.

He swallowed hard. He could not bring himself to turn around, but there was a mirror on the wall by him and, in it, he could see Belinda gazing at his back, looking so compassionate, so loving.

He looked away from her quickly and his gaze roamed the cluttered, dusty, half-forgotten room in the reflection as he fought with himself. He saw the velvet pillow where Mother's favorite cat used to sit and the rush of memories that came back with it nearly reduced him to tears.

He lowered his head. Bel came and caressed his back.

"Talk to me," she said very gently.

"I . . ." He drew an unsteady breath. "I wasn't allowed

to love her, you see. I was just a boy, I needed her—but if I showed any love toward her or need for her, my father saw it as a betrayal. I was all he had. He told me so every time he got drunk. He said everything depended on me. She could have the others—she could keep her bastards, he said, but I was *his* son. It wasn't fair to my brothers—it wasn't fair to me—and I knew it wasn't fair to her either."

She whispered his name and put her arms around him. He clutched her hard as he felt walls of anger, walls of stone toppling silently inside of him.

"When that French firing squad killed her, oh God, Bel, I wanted to . . . burn down the earth. I'd been such a cold bastard to her for so many years, just like he had wanted me to be. Don't you see? I drove her to it. It's my fault she's dead."

"Robert—"

"If I hadn't sat in judgment over her with my heart closed, looking down my nose at her as though I had no faults of my own, she wouldn't have felt compelled to redeem herself with her foolish heroics. If only I had told her what I really wanted to say, she'd be alive right now!"

"What did you want to say to her, Robert?"

"That I did love her, Bel. Please tell me that she knew that."

"She did," Bel whispered, holding him tightly. "Don't be ashamed of her anymore, Robert. She gave you the best of herself: the heart in you that loves so well."

His composure shattered at her softly spoken words. The loss was too deep, too intricately woven into what he was. "Oh, Bel, the only one I'm ashamed of is myself."

He sat down and put his head in his hands, grimacing with the effort to hold back tears. He lost the battle with a ragged curse, shuddering as grief overwhelmed him. Bel put her arms around him, pulled his head down to her chest, and comforted him like the mother he had never known.

Days passed.

The melting away of ancient walls in him had literally expanded his ability to love, as if his heart had swelled beyond the boundaries which for so long had been his defense, but his devotion to Belinda had begun to torment him, knowing what he risked, knowing what he had to do, the suicidal choice he had to make—his honor or his heart. He knew he could not hide his torn emotions from her much longer.

Presently he stood on the battlements of the keep, surveying his lands and busy fields on the first day of harvest, doing his best to hold guilt at arm's length. He pushed it away yet again, suddenly noticing a lone mounted figure on the road. He squinted against the high afternoon sun.

He stared, sure that his vision deceived him, but as the solitary figure rode nearer astride a plodding, thick-bodied white horse, he could just make out the book tucked under the man's arm, the glint of sunlight on spectacles, and he realized it was indeed Alfred Hamilton—riding toward Hawkscliffe Hall like Don Quixote come tilting at windmills.

"Well, I'll be damned," he murmured into the breeze.

He strode inside and sent his servants to go out to the road to greet him, others to make a bedchamber ready for him. Bel was out with the girls observing the harvesters, but he did not expect her to be out long in this heat. For his part, he went out to the courtyard and waited to welcome the old man personally the moment he arrived. Though he still felt stern disapproval for Alfred Hamilton, good breeding and loyalty to Belinda dictated that he at least receive her father graciously.

But when Hamilton arrived in the courtyard, to Hawk's wary surprise, he got down stiffly from his horse, poked his spectacles up higher on his nose, declined refreshment and glowered at Hawk.

"Mr. Hamilton, you are welcome to my home—" he began.

"A word with Your Grace, if you please," he cut him off in a severe tone.

Taken aback, he gestured toward the Hall. "At your service, sir. Do come in."

He had a feeling he was in for it as he showed old Hamilton inside. The moment they stepped into his study, Hawk sat down, beginning to feel like a schoolboy back at Eton caught at some very serious mischief. The gentleman scholar clasped his hands behind his back and stared at him. The footman withdrew, closing the doors.

"Let me come straight to the point," said Alfred. "I have come to demand, sir, that you do right by my daughter or give her up directly."

Hawk felt his mouth go dry. "Pardon?"

"*Marry* Belinda. The last time we met, you gave me some very hard truth to swallow. I have come to return the favor. You style yourself a man of honor; do, then, the honorable thing."

Hawk absorbed this, weighing his words carefully before he dared speak. "With all due respect, sir, Belinda is quite happy as my mistress. She is protected, cherished. She wants for nothing. I make sure of her happiness daily—hourly. We are, both of us, happy."

"You are, no doubt, but not my daughter. Belinda is a gently bred young lady. She could never be happy as any man's fancy woman. She needs more than that from life."

Hawk rose from his chair, peering down his nose at Hamilton with lordly indignation. "My good sir, I have protected your daughter and have been absurdly generous with her, while you left her in penury to fend for herself. So please forbear from lecturing me on what Belinda needs."

"You will not prostitute my daughter!"

"Frankly, sir, Belinda prostituted herself and had done so before I met her. Don't look at me as though I've wronged her; I've been her rescuer in all this."

"For a price, Your Grace. For a price."

Hawk dropped his gaze to the floor, his heart pounding with anger and guilt. "I'm afraid it is impossible. We are comfortable as we are."

"And what kind of life is Belinda going to have when she no longer makes you 'comfortable,' you arrogant fool? When you are done toying with her—when she is big with your child?" he asked harshly. "I know the ways of men like you, sir. You will pay her off to leave you alone the moment some new pretty thing catches your eye. My daughter is no whore and, by God, no one knows that better than you! She was an innocent girl when she was attacked. She did what she had to do to survive!"

"I am not toying with her," he said quietly, staring at the floor. "I happen to love your daughter."

"Yes, young man, I believe that you do." His manner turned searching. "You risked your life to strike down her enemies. But how can you stop there? You must go to the end of the line, Hawkscliffe. You must marry her. I think that, deep down, you know that as well as I."

"It's not that simple."

"Why?"

"Because of who I am."

"Oh, yes, who you are—the paragon—the model of manly virtue. Mr. Duke, battling your way to the top of the heap, are you? And what is one young girl's life, one heart to trample on your way?"

"No matter what happens, I intend to take care of her."

"Until it becomes inconvenient. Until you marry some spoiled Society chit who will forbid you to see Belinda. You love your good name more than her. Honestly, Your Grace, after all I've heard about you, I expected more from you than this. Just like I have—just like young Mick Braden—you have let Belinda down."

"No, I haven't," he said hollowly, feeling as though he had been punched hard in the gut. He could still hear her little whisper ringing in his ears: *Everybody fails me, Robert.*

I won't, he had vowed.

"My sphere of influence is wide and there are countless responsibilities riding on me," he said hotly, hating it that this happy-go-lucky fool had managed to put him on the defensive. His own excuses sounded petty in his ears. "I must marry for the good of my family. For God's sake, I can't marry my mistress. The scandal would rock the whole party. It simply isn't done!"

"Is this the paragon, the man of principle—bowing down to the dictates of some etiquette book instead of acting on truth?"

"Pray, do not insult me under my own roof, sir."

"I don't wish to insult you. Nor do I have the power to compel you to do what is right. All I can do is tell you what I learned sitting in my cell all those nights since you visited me and opened my eyes to the hard, hateful truth—that we cannot pick and choose what part of reality we will deign to see and which part we will ignore. We must be willing to look at the whole picture, the difficult and the good together. I ignored that which I did not want to see, and the person that I love most in this world suffered a wound that I can never undo." Impotent tears filled his old eyes. "I have to live with myself, with this monstrous failure. I would take Belinda away from here today if I could, to stop you from hurting her, but I've lost the right to interfere in her life. I know that. I know she won't leave you, even if I plead with her. She is in love with you. I knew from the first day she brought you to the Fleet that she was in love with you. After all she has been through, if you harm her, I swear on my wife's grave—"

"I would sooner lose my life than harm a hair on her head."

"I hope you think on those words." Alfred stared at him, his book tucked tightly against him.

Hawk noticed it was not an illuminated manuscript, but a weathered Bible.

"Your Grace, I am not an important man," the old scholar said. "On the whole, I am a fool. I can only exhort you to prove your much-vaunted honor now and warn you that if you let true love escape you, all for the sake of your worldly fame, one day you will wake up and realize you are no better than I—a blind, bloody fool."

Bel found Robert in an odd mood when she returned; he seemed distracted and a bit distant as she and Jacinda told him about the wild fell ponies they had lured with apples. Jacinda and Lizzie whisked off to wash up for supper, then Robert told Bel that her father had found his way to Hawkscliffe Hall.

"What?" she stared at him in amazement, joy, and a certain measure of trepidation. She had not faced her father since he had found out she was a courtesan. "How did he get out of the Fleet? Is he here?"

"I don't know, we didn't get into it. He has elected to stay at the inn in the village. He'll be back to have supper with us."

"Oh, no." Bel's heart sank. "That can only mean he disapproves."

"That was the impression I got, yes."

"Did he say anything to you?"

He shook his head and looked away. "Belinda?"

She had started to leave to tidy herself for supper, but at his soft call, she came back to him.

He looked at her slowly over his shoulder, his square face forlorn. "You know I love you?"

She smiled, caressing his shoulder. "Yes, as I love you. Is something wrong?"

He laid his hand over hers on his shoulder and turned to steal a pensive kiss. "I only want you to be happy," he whispered.

"I'm happier here with you than I ever have been in my life."

He embraced her and she rested her head on his chest, forgetting her worries momentarily about seeing Papa. At length Robert kissed her forehead and sent her on her way.

Fortunately Papa arrived with enough time before the meal for them to have a heart-to-heart talk. In the garden there was a great yew tree with a seat built around the trunk. They sat there in the shade as the rays of daylight stretched long across the bowling green.

Bel had expected the scolding of her life, but instead her father apologized to her with such an air of grief and regret over her attack that he moved her to tears. It took some convincing to make him understand that Robert's love had done so much to heal her.

"But he is not your husband, my dear," he protested gingerly, holding her hand.

"I know that, but I . . . trust him, Papa. I love him. If he were to marry me, it would damage his political career and his reputation—not to mention Jacinda's—and there's so much good he can do in the world. What is more important—my personal convenience or the thousands of people whose lives could be improved by Robert's work? I know it must sound horrifyingly unconventional, but in all honesty, what does a piece of paper matter to say we are man and wife? I know in my heart that he loves me."

He furrowed his brow, pursed his mouth, and shook his head with so troubled a countenance that her firmly cheerful facade almost crumbled and she nearly blurted out the truth—that, more than anything else in the world, she longed to be Robert's wife.

What choice did she have? She was a courtesan; she was his mistress. That was her role and she must accept it. The last thing Robert would ever want was a duchess who would carry on the scandal of the Hawkscliffe Harlot—though, from all Bel now knew about Georgiana, she would have worn the slur with pride.

"How did you manage to get out of the Fleet?" she asked, anxious to change the subject.

He gave her a glum look. "I called in a few favors that my colleagues from the university owed me."

She didn't have the heart to ask him why he had not done that in the first place, but although she held her tongue, his rueful glance seemed to read her thoughts.

"I didn't ask them for help straightaway because I was worried about my reputation, just like your duke," he admitted in remorse. "I will never forgive myself."

Bel sighed and patted his shoulder in affection. "Well, I wish you would, because I forgive you. Besides, that is one strong advantage of being ruined, Papa—I for one haven't got a reputation to worry about anymore."

He scowled at her quip, but she laughed to assure him she was fine.

Supper was served soon after.

Bel sensed the tension between Robert and her father, though both were too well bred to act rudely. Luckily Jacinda's running chatter filled any awkward silences and kept everyone amused. When Lizzie finally got a word in, Alfred realized a fellow bookworm was at the table and took great delight in drawing the shy girl out.

Jacinda looked momentarily nonplussed at not being the center of attention, then seemed to decide she loved her friend too dearly to mind and cheerfully ate her supper and listened to the talk of books.

From the corner of her eye, Bel noticed Robert looking at her strangely. She sent him a questioning look, but he just reached for her hand at the table and held it, gazing at her while the others discussed *Gulliver's Travels*.

That night after Papa had left and the girls had gone to bed, he led her up to the top of the keep and seduced her under the stars, coaxing tears of surrender from the deepest reaches of her heart with his whispers of eternal devotion.

His sweetness was so perfect, his tenderness so exquisite, it was almost as if he had known that the very next day he would break her heart into a thousand pieces.

Bel stood in the corridor outside Robert's study, listening in a sudden state of foreboding. He had summoned her for some reason, but by the sound of it, he was not expecting her yet.

"I know you are very fond of Miss Hamilton, girls, but things are much more complicated in Town than they are here. If you so much as nod to her in the park, you risk damage to your reputations."

"You want us to cut her, Robert?" Jacinda cried.

"It's not 'cutting' her. She understands. It's not the way I want it, girls, it's just the way it is."

"But it will hurt her feelings—"

"And we love her!"

"Of course you do. We all do. Girls, I am only concerned for your future."

"Are *you* going to cut her, Robert?" Bel heard Jacinda ask.

"Of course not. The code is different for men, as you well know."

Abandoning her brief moment of eavesdropping, Bel judged that moment a good one to go in. They all fell silent and turned to her, looking a trifle guilty to be caught discussing her, but she smiled at them in forgiving reassurance.

"He's quite right, Jacinda, Lizzie. You won't hurt my feelings a bit. We can have a signal. How's that? If you see me, open your parasols or your fans, and I'll take that for a cheerful hello, and I'll do the same."

"Oh, Miss Hamilton!" they cried, hugging her. "We're so sorry!"

"Don't be silly, it's not your fault. I'm still a finishing-school teacher at heart, you know, and if you are not on your very best behavior in public places, I shall be very cross."

Robert sent her a chastened smile of gratitude as she laughingly hugged the girls.

"It'll all be fine. Now run along and start packing your things, because it seems we are going back to London?" She turned expectantly to him.

He nodded their dismissal. "If you ladies don't mind, I'd like to speak to Miss Hamilton in private."

After Lizzie and Jacinda had slipped out, Bel folded her arms over her chest and turned to him curiously. "What's going on?"

His dark eyes shone with triumph as he strode over to her and clasped her arms, giving her a light squeeze. "You're not going to believe this. Sit down."

"We're going back to London?"

"Yes, yes—but we won't be staying there long."

She gave him a puzzled look. "Where are we going? That is—am I coming with you, wherever it is?"

"Of course," he scoffed. "I don't go anywhere without my political secret weapon, my lovely, sparkling, ravishing hostess!"

"Well? What's the news? You look like the cat who ate the canary."

"Bel, I have been chosen to go with Castlereagh's British delegation to the Congress of Vienna."

She gasped and clapped both hands over her mouth.

His hands turned to fists of victory. "Isn't it incredible?" He paced in jittery excitement. "Do you realize this congress is going to be the most important international gathering since the time of Charlemagne?"

"Oh, Robert, you will be in the history books, just like so many of your ancestors!"

He grinned, blushing slightly. "We still have to get the Regent's approval of my appointment, but I have the prime minister's recommendation, thanks to Coldfell. Wellington, of course, will also participate."

"Wait one moment—what was that about Lord Coldfell?"

He turned to her, hands in pockets. She noticed a flicker of some vague uneasiness in his dark eyes. "He was the one who put my name before the committee."

"Robert," she stared at him, flabbergasted.

"What?" he asked a trifle guiltily.

"If this came from Coldfell, then there's *got* to be a catch."

"Well, of course there is," he muttered, rubbing the back of his neck as he let out an uncomfortable little laugh. He glanced at her with pleading emotion in his dark eyes, then he dropped his chin almost to his chest. "God, this is hard to tell you."

She paled. "He's not asking you to risk your life and limb again—"

"No, nothing like that." He swallowed hard. "I want you to know straight off that it doesn't mean anything. It's just—" He faltered.

"Robert?"

He drew a deep breath, visibly steeling himself. "He wants me to marry his daughter, Juliet. And I have agreed."

Hawk could barely bring himself to hold Belinda's shocked stare. Her eyes had gone glassy and the color had drained from her face. She sank down into the nearest chair, staring at nothing.

He took a step toward her. "Please—don't misconstrue this. You're the one I love. I have to marry sometime."

Her eyes seemed huge and they grew darker and darker, but when she spoke, her voice was barely a whisper. "The little deaf girl?"

"Yes. Coldfell hasn't got any more heirs. His daughter must bear a son before he dies or his title will revert to the Crown." He crouched down before her chair. "Coldfell merely wants someone who will keep the girl protected. Belinda—"

The silky rustling of her skirts twisted his heart as she rose and glided past him, momentarily stunned into silence. "She is Jacinda's age."

"It doesn't matter. My relationship with Lady Juliet will be scarcely more than fraternal. You're the one I love, the one I need. The one who inspires me. You're my equal. I know you understand my position, Bel. Please, say something."

"I think I shall be sick," she whispered.

"I don't want this to hurt you, Bel. You know I have to take this opportunity."

"A son, Robert? What am I to say? The stork isn't going to bring it. How can I share you?" she cried.

"You can't possibly be jealous of her."

"Why can't that cunning old man leave you alone? What if it's a trick?"

"It's not a trick. I just received Lord Liverpool's letter confirming my appointment."

"Confirming it? Then you've known of this for—how long? And you said nothing? How long, Robert?" she demanded angrily.

"A few days," he forced out.

Glaring at him, she stalked over to his desk and sifted angrily through its contents until she found the communique from the prime minister. He saw that her hands were shaking and he lowered his head.

" 'Castlereagh verging on another depression,' " she read aloud. " 'We need someone steady and cool headed on hand. . . .' "

Seeming to lose interest suddenly, she tossed the letter back onto his desk and went to stare out the window with her arms folded tightly over her chest. "I knew this would happen," she said. "I was waiting for it."

He took a step toward her slim, bristling silhouette, then thought better of it.

"Do you have to marry her to keep this appointment?" she asked in a tone made carefully neutral, still keeping her back to him.

Pain washed through him as he stared at her in misery and when he spoke, his words came heavily. "I think we both know it's more than just the appointment, darling. Even if I were to pass up this opportunity, the problem will not go away. Eventually I must marry according to my station. Might I not just as well do the country some good, if they're going to give me the chance?"

There was a long and hollow silence.

"It is the chance of a lifetime for you, Robert," she said, finally. "Perhaps it is even your destiny. Congratulations.

I'm sure you will serve your country with your usual skill." She turned around, her refined features fixed in a white mask of serenity. "Beyond that, all that's left to say is good-bye."

"No," he uttered, taking a lurching step toward her.

"What, then?" Her facade crumbled with anger. "What are we even doing here? Hiding away from Society and the Patronesses? Good God," she exclaimed, nearly laughing with pain, "I am in love with a man who is ashamed of me!"

"That is not true—"

"It is true. You are as ashamed of me as you were of your mother. To you, I have always been a whore and that's all I'll ever be."

"That is a lie," he bellowed so wrathfully that she flinched. "I've said a thousand times that I love you."

"Yes. That is what makes your decision so odd." She stared at him piercingly for a second, then brushed him off with a dismissive gesture and began to stride across the room toward the door. "Good-bye, Hawkscliffe. I'm going back to London."

He captured her arm as she passed him. "No," he ground out.

Her gaze flicked to his hand wrapped around her elbow, then up to his eyes. She glared at him with feverish wrath. "Don't . . . touch me."

"You're not leaving."

"You are not my lord and master." She wrenched her arm free of his grasp. "I'll call to collect my belongings from Knight House when you're not at home. I earned them, after all."

"Where will you go? What will you do?" he demanded harshly, towering over her, purposely intimidating her, as if he could frighten her into obedience. "You have nothing to go back to without me."

She continued glaring up at him defiantly, her eyes snapping blue sparks. "Harriette will take me in. I'll find a new protector—"

"Over my dead body."

She gave him an icy smile. "Does that hurt you, the thought of me in another man's arms? How does it feel?"

"You will not go back to Harriette's," he said through clenched teeth. "Leave me if you must, but I forbid you to return to that—that whoredom. I'll give you all the money you need—"

"I don't want your money!" she nearly screamed, shoving him back, though he barely moved a step. "How dare you? Don't you ever learn?"

She whirled on her heel toward the door, but he caught her again. She turned and punched him in the chest in futile fury, and he grasped her by her shoulders, talking gentle nonsense to her as he tried in desperation to still her.

"Listen to me!" he finally cried, giving her shoulders a shake.

"Let go!"

"I need you," he pleaded in a low, trembling voice. "Don't go. You're the only one who understands me. You're my best friend, Bel—"

"Then how can you treat me this way?" she whispered, tears in her eyes. She stopped fighting all of a sudden and looked away, lifting the back of her hand to her mouth to smother a small sob.

"Oh, Jesus," he breathed, unable to believe she was slipping through his fingers. Amid seething terror, he somehow persuaded his hands to loosen their hold on her soft shoulders, though everything was spinning out of his control. Now that he had begun to lose her, he couldn't seem to make it stop. When he reached to touch her hair, she jerked away. "Come on, Bel. Stop this."

"Let me go. I understand, you can't marry me, I'm not

asking it of you. But in turn, you mustn't ask me to dishonor myself any more deeply. Please, if you love me, Robert, let me go. I may be just a demirep, but I have a few principles myself. I have to draw the line somewhere or I'll lose myself. I finally got myself back, thanks to you, your love. I would rather lose what we have than turn it into something sordid. I can't go back to being ashamed. I'm sorry."

"I thought you loved me."

"If you're going to marry her, do so honorably. Do your best to love her, if she is to be your wife."

"I love *you*," he said angrily.

"Well, I'm leaving you," she whispered before stepping past him almost briskly.

He grabbed her wrists, stopping her again. "No!"

"Have pity, Robert! Before we get in any deeper—before it is impossible to say good-bye—let me walk away from you with a shred of my pride intact. Please, please—"

"Belinda, I love you—"

He reached to touch her, but she pulled free of his grasp and rushed out of his study, stifling a sob.

"Belinda!"

Hawk strode out of his study and saw her running down the corridor.

"Belinda!"

She didn't look back, hurrying up the stairs. He could hear her sobbing over the rustle of her silken skirts.

He started to go after her, but then her piteous plea to let her leave with dignity sank like a hook in his heart, pulling until it bled. He stopped himself, blind with confusion and loss and disbelief. He howled her name one more time, but when she did not appear, he slammed his fist into the wooden door, cracking it with a splintering thud. He leaned back against the doorframe and ran both hands through his hair, squeezing his eyes shut tightly.

Everything inside him raged to go after her—make her stay even if he had to lock her in her room till she obeyed. But if being his mistress would injure her fragile self-opinion, then he had no choice but to let her go.

❧ CHAPTER ❧ TWENTY

Harriette welcomed her back with open arms. Their reunion was a tearful one as Bel sobbed out her story to the Three Graces, all of whom went out of their way to comfort her.

And so *La Belle* Hamilton was back on the game. Business was booming under Harriette's roof. Bel allowed two types of men to court her—those who were far too old for her and those who were too young to be taken seriously. Then, on her fifth night back in Town, she went to the King's Theater in the Haymarket and he was there.

She was holding court in the opera box that he had paid for, surrounded, as usual, by sex-starved men, whom she laughingly abused with her wit, newly sharpened to a razor's edge, when a strange prickling sensation descended upon her. Everything seemed to move slowly and the sound blurred into the background. Fluttering her fan, she looked across the great colorful vault of the opera house and saw him.

He was sitting with his elbow on the chair arm, his fingers obscuring his mouth. He appeared not the slightest bit interested in the spectacle on stage. His eyes intense and fiery, he was staring only at her.

The breath left her lungs in a whoosh. Her heart twisted and her fan went still. Her body flashed hot then cold, and she began to shake. She tore her gaze away, suddenly fanning herself frantically. She did not hear a word that anyone said to her.

For about a minute and a half, she tried to sit there calmly and pretend nothing was wrong. She suddenly rose, making excuses as she fought her way free of the theater box. Men offered to escort her as she went striding haplessly down the hallway.

"Leave me alone!" she cried to those who followed her, wrenching the showy plume out of her hair so hard that tears sprang into her eyes.

In the lobby she sent one of the attendants for her *vis-à-vis* and fled the moment her capable new driver brought it round. She went home and cried herself to sleep. But when the morning came, she knew what she had to do.

Harriette and the others were still in their beds after their late night. By the cool white light of morning, Bel gathered up the majority of her fancy gowns, packed them into her carriage, and brought them to the pawn shop, where they garnered her a fortune of nearly fifteen hundred pounds.

She then directed her driver to Tattersall's, where she dismissed him with his pay and sold her elegant black little *vis-à-vis* and fine-blooded horses back to the auction house for another enormous sum—two thousand guineas. But she could not bring herself to part with the diamond-and-lapis-lazuli necklace Robert had given her as a gift on the night of the Cyprians' Ball.

Hiring a hackney coach to the bank, she deposited the drafts from the pawn shop into her account, along with the proceeds from the sale of the carriage. Signing her name to the deposit, she stared at the scribble of numbers, taken aback.

The total came to thirty-five hundred pounds. She rolled

three thousand of it into the funds, did a bit of figuring, and suddenly found herself in possession of a decent living. At five percent interest, the three thousand would yield her a hundred fifty pounds a year.

She sat back and stared at it in amazement. She need only live a quiet, modest, simple life—the kind she had wanted in the first place—and she need never depend on anyone again. Not her rich admirers nor Harriette nor even Papa. It was poverty compared to what she had grown used to, but worlds above selling oranges. She would have this living and she need answer to no one. She wouldn't be able to keep any more servants except perhaps a chambermaid, but for the first time in her life, she suddenly *was* . . . free and independent.

She looked up in amazement toward the graceful dome of the bank and closed her eyes, silently blessing the friend who had made her small fortune possible.

Oh, Robert, how I miss you, she thought, misery overtaking her moment of hope. But she gathered her reticule and left the bank, for there was still more to be done.

Later that day, she parted ways with the Wilson sisters and took up lodgings in a quiet boardinghouse in Bloomsbury, not far from the Foundling Hospital. A couple of the all-female establishments she would have preferred to take rooms in had refused to accept the likes of her, but she had walked away from the matrons' rudeness strangely at peace with herself.

In the days that followed she forged yet again a new life from the ashes of the old. She spent her nights reading to escape her broken heart; during the days, she devoted herself to volunteer service at the Foundling Hospital and the Relief Society for the Destitute, seeking to forget her own cares in attending to the plight of the street children.

She wondered often how Tommy and Andrew were faring at Knight House.

Though the people associated with the charities allowed her to help there, they kept a wary distance from her. None of them seemed interested in becoming her friend. If she had one regret, it was that she had no place anymore in any level of society. She was neither respectable nor fashionable—in the past she had always been one or the other. As a courtesan she had constantly felt crowded; now she was all too alone, haunted by her thoughts of Robert. Her former protector was never far from her heart.

She was glad her father had stayed in London to do research, for these days he was her only companion. He could not help but be overjoyed about her discarding the Cyprians' life. His eyes filled with tears of pride every time she visited him, which was frequently, since they supped together most nights.

She had held on to her theater box at the Royal Haymarket for Papa's sake. Once a week she took him to a play. After all, her subscription to her first-rate theater box was already paid for and would expire at the end of the season. Might as well enjoy it while it lasts, she told him. They both laughed that, however much he disapproved, he was not above enjoying the excellent seats that had been a perquisite of her previous employment.

Then, about a week later, another friend resurfaced. Bel came strolling home one early September evening, her back aching from her work with the children all day, to find Mick Braden sitting on the front steps of the boardinghouse waiting for her, just like he used to when they were young.

He stood as she came through the gate and when she walked toward him, she could see the anguish written in his boyishly handsome face. They stared at each other for a long moment.

"Hello, Mick," she said at length.

"Your father told me where you were."

"Would you like to come in?"

"Please," he said hoarsely.

When they reached her small sitting room, he slowly took her into his arms and held her as if she were made of the most fragile glass.

"I'm so sorry. Your father told me everything." He released her and took her hands in his. "I hold myself accountable, Bel. I want to make it up to you. Marry me."

She closed her eyes and turned away, heaving a sigh, then she looked at him again. "I don't love you, Mick."

"I know. It's all right. But, you see, there should be an appropriateness to marriage, Bel. You and I are appropriate for each other. Your feelings for Hawkscliffe will fade in time, but I'll still be here because I am a part of you. We've known each other all our lives, haven't we? I care for you, and I have an obligation to you. I am not a man who shirks his duty."

"Is it duty that prompts you, Mick? You don't love me, either?"

He brushed her hair gently out of her eyes. "How do you define love? I care for you, I feel responsible for you. I even find you passingly pretty on occasion," he teased softly. "You and me—it just makes sense. Call it what you want. All I know is that you can't live by yourself forever. Not you. You should be a wife and a mother. It's in your nature and it's what you've always wanted."

She flinched, lowering her head.

"I can give you that life," he said. "I owe you that. I don't care about your past. I know what the circumstances were, and I'll never judge you for it. We can leave London and make a new start. I know I failed you once, but if you'll give me another chance, I'll never fail you again."

She closed her eyes in distress. *Right words, wrong*

man. She opened her eyes and gazed at him again. "Oh, Mick, I don't know. So much has changed. I'm no longer the girl that you knew."

"Yes, you are, deep down. But even if you have changed—" He smiled and chucked her gently under the chin, "I'll still adore you like I did when you were nine."

She smiled at him fondly. "You threw a worm on me when I was nine."

"Evidence of my devotion."

Devotion . . .

The very word made her unsteady. She forced a smile, tears threatening. "I'll need to think this over."

"Take your time. I'm here for you, anything you need. Good night, Bel." He bent and kissed her hands, then gently released her and marched out.

It had been two weeks since he had seen her at the opera. Three, since she had abandoned Hawkscliffe Hall and stormed out of his life. Hawk had gone through the preceding days in a fog of desolation.

After escorting his sister and her companion back to Town, an endless round of meetings and committees ate up his time. He attended them all, going through the motions with his usual aloof, cordial reserve.

"Hawkscliffe is back," everyone said, and they meant more than his return from the country.

The men at the club toasted his health as his star continued to rise. The Patronesses welcomed him back into the fold. Though disappointment at his rumored nuptials appeared universal among the female half of the ton, women had taken to sighing when he walked past. It seemed his admirers were touched to the core by his gallant choice of poor, gentle, lovely Lady Juliet Breckinridge. Taking the flawed beauty for his bride had sealed his fame as a knight in shining armor.

He felt like hell. He felt like a fraud and his soul was dying.

Every time he saw Coldfell, he had the strange, brooding, angry feeling that he had unwittingly sold himself to the devil.

He got through each meaningless, dragging day by pretending with all his might that Belinda Hamilton didn't exist. It was difficult when Knight House echoed with images of her everywhere he turned. There was no escape from the whisper of her memory in every room. She was in his blood, under his skin, haunting him like a pitiless ghost. The smell of her still clung in his clothes, the taste of her still lingered on his tongue, and sometimes when he tried to fall asleep, he could still almost feel her touching him and he hurt so badly that he wanted to die. *Forget.*

He would forget.

Every day when he strode into White's he braced himself for the blow, knowing that one of these days, the gossip was bound to reach him about whom she had chosen for her new protector. But thankfully his club mates were careful not to talk about her around him.

All but one. Lord Alec returned from some house party where he had been languishing in his usual decadence for some time. His blue eyes blazing with anger, he walked into White's, strode straight over to where Hawk sat studying a primer of German phrases for his Austrian trip, silently forming the awkward words on his tongue.

Alec braced his hands on the table and glowered at him. "You're an idiot. Do you know that? An idiot, you pompous ass."

With his chin angled downward over his book, Hawk slanted him a dark warning look.

"You killed for her. You would have died for her. I saw how you were together. She's the one, Hawk, and you let her go. For what?"

He didn't answer.

"I know why, you imbecile. One word—fear. Go after her."

"No."

"Why?" he cried.

"She left me. What am I supposed to do?"

"Whatever it takes! Anything is better than just sitting there like some cold, righteous prig! Do you want me to talk to her for you?"

"*No.* Jesus, Alec, keep your voice down." He glanced around at the stares of his club mates. "As you can see, I'm trying to work here, so would you leave me the hell alone?"

"Alone is exactly what you're going to be, Your Grace— and exactly what you deserve. You know something? She's better off without you. Because you, my friend, are just like your cold-hearted father." Alec shoved away from the table and stalked out.

When he was gone Hawk looked blankly at the page of German phrases. As he sat there slowly rubbing his mouth in agitation, he felt an indescribable panic rising in him. His pulse roared in his ears.

He observed himself closing the book before him. He slid a piece of fine linen paper toward him and dipped his quill pen in the inkpot to his right. His hand trembled as he paused, searching for the words in his reeling brain, then wrote:

Notice of Carte Blanche

By my signature is hereby granted full fiduciary au-thority to the holder of this certificate, Miss Belinda Hamilton. All debts incurred herewith should be for-warded to me at Knight House, St. James's Square. Signed this 12th day of September, 1814.

                                    Hawkscliffe

He dripped a dab of wax below his name and pressed his signet ring into it. When the wax hardened he folded the note and put it in his waistcoat. Then, filled with a strange sense of careful detachment, he rose in measured control from his chair. The next thing he knew he was in his curricle, driving hell-for-leather through the streets of the City, whipping his horses to Harriette Wilson's house.

He jumped out of his carriage in front of the Cyprians' door and pounded on it. When the mean-looking footman answered, he stood in amazement as the servant told him Miss Hamilton was no longer there.

Harriette came down and after much pleading on his part, coldly gave him Belinda's new address.

Though the worst of her inner scars were healing, Bel still got nervous whenever she had to walk through the city streets after dark. Tonight she had stayed later than usual at the children's relief house. She set out walking with the intention of flagging down a hackney coach, but none passed her. Fortunately it was only a little past twilight when she rounded the corner past Russell Square, walking swiftly toward the boardinghouse.

Looking down the street ahead of her, she suddenly stopped in her tracks. Parked out in front was a sleek, black, shiny town coach that she knew all too well. Her heart leaped up into her throat. Her head suddenly felt light.

Somehow she forced herself forward. She caught a whiff on the balmy evening air of Congue snuff; she heard his deep, cultured baritone giving an order to William on the box, and her heart lurched again.

He's come back for me! He's going to make it right—

She picked up the skirts of her simple cotton dress and strode faster for fear that having found her not at home, he was leaving. She began to run.

"Robert!"

At once he stepped around the coach and blocked her path, starlight gleaming on his black hair. His face was shadowed, his eyes luminous, so dark with mystery that they appeared almost coal black. He seemed taller than she remembered, bigger and more splendidly dressed, more magnificent.

More intimidating even than on the first night they had met.

She slowed to a walk and approached him in awe, humbled all over again by his lordly grandeur. His broad shoulders were tense.

"I have been waiting for you," he said, his tone short, imperious, as though in reproach.

I've been waiting so long for *you*, she thought, her heart beating crazily. She couldn't believe he had come. Had he had a change of heart? She barely dared hope. "I was out."

"May I ask a moment of your time?"

"Of course."

He gave a curt slice of a nod. "Thank you."

"This way."

William sent her a bolstering smile as they passed. Bel led Hawkscliffe through the gate and up the stairs to her lodgings. Inside her sitting room she lit the table lantern, illuminating her modest but homey quarters.

As the light rose she turned to Robert and drank in the sight of his drawn, taut face. His mouth was a firm, grim line and there were shadows under his dark, tumultuous eyes. She dropped her stare, pained by the change in him and a fleeting memory of the feel of his bare skin against hers.

On that last day at Hawkscliffe Hall he had glowed with healthy vitality and excitement. Now he was stiffer than ever, brooding and remote as he turned away, his impeccably gloved hands clasped behind him. "You are well, I trust?"

"I'm fine. Yourself?"

"Never better," he growled.

"How are Jacinda and Lizzie?"

"Back at school."

"How did you find me?"

"Through Miss Wilson. Why, are you in hiding?" he asked in a razorlike tone.

"No. What do you want?"

He looked away. "I am here because I did not foresee the need—" He faltered. "My new position requires a good deal of politicking and entertaining which my wife-to-be is quite incapable of carrying out, due to her disability. I require a hostess." He turned and stared forcefully at her. "Come with me to Vienna."

Disappointment burst like the Vauxhall fireworks in her solar plexus. So, he was still set on his course. Lady Juliet was still his wife-to-be.

"I'm not going anywhere with you," she forced out.

He clamped his jaw shut and tore his frustrated gaze away, fairly steaming. The haughty, wary look he gave her clashed with the desperation in his eyes.

"I'm not about to make a fool of myself over you, Belinda Hamilton. Now, we've both had time to step back and think this over. Perhaps you lost your temper in the country when you walked out on me. I'm willing to overlook that but, by God, I will not crawl for you. Come back to me and let us be as we were, no questions asked. I'm willing to give you this, if it will soothe your vanity." Reaching into his waistcoat pocket, he pulled out a folded piece of parchment.

He handed it to her with a glower, but as she passed a suspicious glance over his aquiline features, she could have sworn she read fear in the depths of his eyes.

"What is it?"

"Open it."

"Giving orders again. Very well," she muttered loftily under her breath as she unfolded the single sheet of paper and read it.

Hawk watched her read it with his heart in his throat. He was terrified of her reaction. It was all he could do to hold himself back from pleading with her on his knees to come back to him. His stare greedily consumed every lovely, familiar curve and plane of her face as she read and reread his missive.

I need you, he told her silently. *I'm dying without you.*

She took a deep breath on which, he knew, hung his fate. The orchid blue flash of her eyes dazed him when she glanced up and met his brooding stare.

"Carte blanche?"

He nodded, frightened because there was a hard note in her voice that he did not understand. "It's what you wanted from the start. It means I trust you as I trust myself," he wanted to say, but somehow he could not.

"Didn't Harriette tell you that I am no longer a demirep?"

Suddenly alarmed, he furrowed his brow. He recalled Harriette mentioning something along those lines, but it had passed through one ear and out the other in his wild haste to win Belinda back.

"She didn't tell you?"

"Yes, but—this is *me* asking for you, Belinda. Not Worcester or Leinster or God-knows-who. Surely you will come back to me. I—make you happy."

"Look around you, Robert," she exclaimed angrily, sweeping a gesture at the humble room. "Does this look like a harlot's boudoir to you? Am I dressed in finery? No. You see? I did what you said, in the end. I'm just an ordinary woman now, living a private and independent life, and I happen to like it. You have your earl's daughter and your glorious name to comfort you; I have my work with the poor children. You don't need me anymore and as you can see, I don't need you."

"I do need you," he uttered wretchedly.

She held up the paper in a hand that trembled slightly. "And this is how you show it? You offer to buy me? Who's idea was this? Lord Coldfell's?"

He swallowed hard. "Take it, Belinda. Nothing I've won means a damned thing without you."

"I am no longer willing to be anybody's whore, Robert. Not even yours," she replied and with that, she tore his carte blanche up into a dozen tiny pieces and threw it in his face.

Hawk stared at her, rather dazzled, as the shreds of paper fluttered to the floor around his polished Hessians like so much confetti.

Belinda lifted her chin and marched to the door of her apartment. She opened it for him and waited for him to exit, but all that he could do was stare as it slowly dawned on him that she was in earnest.

He studied her in shock, feeling as though he were seeing her for the first time, devoid of the gaudy trappings of her former trade, bereft of the icy facade that she no longer needed. This was who she had been before Dolph Breckinridge had singled her out for his prey, he thought, amazed.

"Please go, Your Grace." She stood there, proud and strong, healed because he had loved her and shining like an angel in her anger, hair of gold gleaming in the lamp-light.

"Bravo, Miss Hamilton," he wanted to say. But he just stared at her in awe and thought, *I will love this woman for as long as I live.*

He walked dazedly to the door. "By the way," she said with a haughty toss of her head, "wish me happy—I am marrying Mick Braden in a fortnight."

⊰ CHAPTER ⊱
TWENTY-ONE

Marrying Mick Braden?

The next morning came and he was still in a state of shock over her announcement. The sick knot in the pit of his stomach had not gone away. He sent his breakfast back to the kitchen, unable to eat it. Presently Hawk marched through the opulent foyer of Knight House, his nerves raw and eyes red from another sleepless night. Hasty and frayed, he hurried outside into the blaring sunshine and waded through the crowd of his tail-wagging, barking dogs, indeed, in a less-than-impeccable state.

He was late for his meeting at the club with the home secretary. White's was just around the corner and down St. James's Street, so he always walked there. He did so now, fumbling through his leather folio of documents on the flash houses, cursing under his breath at having to chase one of his pages of notes when the wind took it.

Mick Braden, he thought bitterly as he strode up the front steps of No. 37, absently nodding to the doorman who let him in.

Mick Braden was not fit to tie the ankle ribbons of her sandals! Then the thought of that scurrilous soldier boy anywhere near the vicinity of her ankles darkened his mood even further. Damn it, she was *his*. He knew every inch of her legs and her body like the back of his hand.

God help you, he said to himself. *You're more obsessed than Dolph Breckinridge ever was.*

He hurried through the club until he spied the bald pate of the home secretary shining over the back of a rich leather chair. He joined him.

"My lord, sorry I'm late."

The powerful ex-prime minister peered over the edge of his *Times* and passed a disapproving glance over Hawk's face. "Hmm," he replied, lowering his newspaper. "Something the matter, Hawkscliffe? You look a trifle out of sorts."

"Er, no, sir." He forced a thin smile. "Things have been a bit hectic, is all, preparing for Vienna and so forth." Hawk cleared his throat and sat down.

"Ah, of course. Congratulations on your appointment. You will serve with your usual skill, I'm sure. Let me also wish you happy on your nuptials, Your Grace."

"Thank you," he mumbled, but the reminder of his impending doom so routed him he lost his train of thought as he took out his notes.

Viscount Sidmouth glanced at his fob watch. "What was it you wished to see me about, Hawkscliffe?"

"Of course, er—let's see. A situation has come to my attention, which I believe would be of some concern to you as home secretary, my lord."

Sidmouth folded his hands and regarded him with interest.

He began to explain the plight of the flash-house children, the awful wheel of poverty and crime that led the young wretches straight to the gallows, but he saw within moments that it was no use.

Lord Sidmouth politely heard him out, resting his elbows on the smooth leather arms of his chair, but the expression on his long narrow face was utterly closed.

It was not merely that he botched the presentation. Sidmouth, who was in charge of dealing with matters of social unrest throughout Britain, clearly did not want to hear it. Hawk gave it his best, but Sidmouth shook his head and talked instead about their limited resources, which must needs be spent to deter the constant threat of insurrection.

The whole government was still secretly terrified of an outbreak of mob violence like that which had happened in France, what with the machine-breaking Luddites and the Regent constantly outraging the people with his lavish spending, and now with so many veterans on their way home and no work for them. Unfortunate, of course, but the government's energies could not be drawn off into trivialities, et cetera. Besides, he said, to turn soft on child thieves would tempt them in even greater numbers to commit crime, with the hope of getting away with naught but a slap on the wrist.

At length Hawk left White's in sheer defeat, Lord Sidmouth's refusal ringing in his ears. He was thoroughly disillusioned with his party and his government.

Shoulders slumped, he walked back to Knight House in a fog of misery.

He did not know what to think of his colleagues anymore with their repressive legislation and their phobia of the peasantry and the poor. He happened to know for a fact that Henry Brougham of the Whigs was crusading for the education of poor children, but Hawk's arrogance had prevented him from joining forces with the man. Disgusted with himself, he decided to send his carefully compiled information to Brougham. Maybe it would do the cause some good, and to hell with the personal glory of having been the savior. "They may make a Whig of you yet," Belinda had once said to him.

Maybe so, my darling. Maybe so, he thought as he walked slowly down the busy street and turned in at St. James's Square. He dragged himself into his house, handed off his leather folio and coat to Walsh, ignoring the butler's solicitous frown, then wandered upstairs, drawn in spite of himself to the bedroom that Belinda had occupied. Heart aching, he lay down on the bed where he had taught her the mysteries of love. Despair throbbed through his body.

He pulled her pillow across his eyes and tried to sleep. Whatever dark fugue that Castlereagh suffered, he thought, it couldn't be worse than losing the love of one's life.

As dismal as his day had been, the social event that Hawk faced presently assured him the night was going to be worse. If he had been another sort of man he would have gotten very drunk, but instead he closed himself off and continued going through the motions, donning his formal evening clothes, climbing up into his town coach, and setting off for King Street.

He was scheduled to socialize publicly tonight for the first time with his bride-to-be. Lady Juliet, the earl of Coldfell, and much of the ton awaited him—the new favorite, the bridegroom—at Almack's. He did not know how he would force himself to go in there, as the coach rolled to a halt and William smartly opened the door for him. Hawk stepped down onto the street and stared up in brooding spite at the elegant building.

This was all wrong.

But in he went. With the weight of the world on his shoulders, he climbed the grand staircase, saw visions of Bel everywhere, her lovely face flushed with love and excitement. He wanted to die, but he donned a hollow smile of cordial reserve and walked into the ballroom.

The assembly rooms were crowded with the elite of Society—peers and their pampered wives and debutante daughters, venerated elders, and wisecracking rakes in studied poses of boredom. Hawk could not think how he had once fit in so perfectly here. He hated everyone he saw, the man coming toward him most of all.

Coldfell walked lightly on his cane, beaming as he showed his daughter off to the world. Juliet looked like a life-sized doll, with huge china blue eyes and porcelain skin against her dark mink curls. She really was a pretty thing in her simple pink dress, but she looked terrified. Hawk realized he was scowling at her and made himself stop.

"Robert, here we are," Coldfell greeted him.

He gritted his teeth in a strained grimace of a smile. "My lord." He nodded to him then turned to the girl with a most formal bow. "Lady Juliet."

She watched his mouth, curtsying carefully.

After a few minutes' terse chat with her father while Juliet's gaze kept bouncing worriedly back and forth between them, Coldfell gently placed Juliet's hand on Hawk's arm.

"Why don't you two young people get acquainted?" he said genially.

Hawk fought not to scowl again as Coldfell hobbled off to mingle with his cronies. He stifled a guttural growl and looked askance at Juliet. He thought of asking her to dance, but of course that was impossible. He thought of offering to get her punch, but he didn't dare leave her alone when she looked so frightened.

Instead, he spied an empty bench by the wall, well out of the way. He led her over to it and they sat down. They looked at each other without hostility, but also without the faintest trace of correlation. He did not know how to communicate with her or if she even had the wherewithal to understand him. She offered him a miserable smile, which he returned. For the next ten minutes they sat there in their own separate worlds. People glanced at them and whispered and no doubt thought them an adorable pair.

Everywhere Hawk looked, he saw visions of Belinda from that spectacular, magical, unforgettable night he had brought her here to free her from her feelings of shame and exclusion. A pensive smile played at his lips to recall her tipsy with champagne, spinning impishly across the crooked dance floor, thumbing her nose at the Patronesses.

How he had underestimated her, undervalued her—so supremely arrogant, handing down his rulings and opinions as if they were God's own truth on stone tablets. He had been blind, but he could see it all so clearly now— what he had lost. By Jove, she had put him in his place. Obviously trying to lure her back with an offer of material gain had been the perfectly wrong thing to do. His bad judgment had probably driven her all the more gladly into her thoughtless soldier boy's arms. But when he thought of her throwing his carte blanche in his face, he wanted to applaud the magnificent creature.

No, she could never be any man's mistress now, he mused. She had recovered her pride entirely and knew now that she was worth more than that. She had healed, and for that, he was grateful.

He suddenly felt Juliet tense beside him. In a mood of utter depression, he realized he was ignoring his fiancée. He turned to her in dutiful resolve only to find her staring across the ballroom. He followed her gaze and found the object of her anxious expression: Clive Griffon, MP, had just walked in.

Oh, hell, thought Hawk as Griffon spotted them and began marching in a straight line toward them, shoving his way amid the dancers with an air of wild tragedy. His boyish face was flushed with anger and, by the look of it, a bit more drink than the lad was accustomed to.

Hawk's expression turned cool and aloof. He tried to pretend not to notice him while Juliet shifted in her seat, looking trapped. Griffon came and stood before Juliet, trembling with tempestuous romantic emotion. Juliet stared at him in sorrow, then glanced nervously at Hawk.

"You are a fool," Griffon said to her, enunciating every word clearly as she read his lips. "He loves another, and you love me and I adore you. Juliet, how could you betray me?"

Juliet whimpered and reached for Griffon's hand, but he pulled away bitterly.

"Never fear—your secrets are safe with me."

"Secrets?" Hawk knit his brow and turned to Juliet. Another woman with secrets was the last damned thing he needed.

"As for you, sir, even if it costs me my seat I'll tell you to your face Lady Juliet is only marrying you because her father is forcing her to. Ask her if you don't believe me!" he shouted as Mr. Willis and his assistants arrived on the scene to eject him.

"What secrets?" Hawk demanded.

They seized Griffon's arms as Coldfell came hobbling quickly through the crowd. "Get him out of here!"

"Out with you!" Mr. Willis bellowed as Griffon fought him.

"Ow! Juliet, I love you!" he cried as the attendants began pulling and half dragging him away.

"How dare you attack my daughter?" Coldfell thundered.

"How dare you force her into a marriage she doesn't want?" he roared right back at him.

The whole place stopped. Hawk's eyes widened. He had never heard anyone dare address the earl of Coldfell that way. Apparently, never had the earl of Coldfell.

His lined face turned a mottled crimson. He jabbed at Griffon with his cane. "I demand this knave be removed! I've warned you a dozen times to stay away from my daughter—"

Hawk rose and went to help restore order, reaching the

two men just as Coldfell lowered his voice, glaring, inches away from Griffon's face. "I will see you out of office," he said in a low tone.

"You, sir, are the last man in the world who should be threatening me," the lad growled quietly at the earl, "unless, of course, you would like all these people to know the truth about how your wife died."

Hawk and Coldfell were the only ones close enough to hear his softly uttered words. Hawk stared at Griffon in shock.

Griffon gave his mussed coat a jerk, righting it. "Lucky for you, Lord Coldfell, I am not a man who stoops to blackmail."

Coldfell was a sickly shade of white as Hawk grasped Griffon's shoulder. "Come with me," he ordered, turning the lad toward the exit. "I'll take it from here," he said briskly to Mr. Willis and his attendants.

"Hawkscliffe!" Lord Coldfell protested weakly.

Hawk ignored him, steering Griffon out.

People backed out of the way with appalled whispers as they passed. "You knew I love her, Hawkscliffe! How could you betray me? Both of you—"

"Would you shut up until we get outside?" Hawk muttered angrily, his heart pounding. He pulled Griffon out the door and turned left, ducking inside the entrance tunnel to the adjoining livery stable. "Tell me what you know about Lady Coldfell's death—or were you bluffing?"

"I wasn't bluffing!" Griffon pulled away, rubbing his forehead, looking young and tormented. "I promised Juliet I would never tell a soul . . . but if you are to be her husband, then perhaps it is best for you to know, in case you ever need to protect her."

"From what?"

"From the truth. Hawkscliffe, will you be sworn to secrecy?"

Hawk just looked at him in warning.

Wearily Griffon shook his head. "Lady Coldfell's death was no accident. Juliet was there. She has been frightened out of her wits since the woman died. We have been writing to each other secretly since the day we met, when I went to Coldfell's house with you. I suppose I won her trust. She poured out her heart to me in her letters. She's so frightened of anyone finding out. Do you swear you will not use this information against her?"

"Yes, damn it, tell me! You have my word."

Griffon glanced over his shoulder uneasily. "When a fire started at the earl's Leicestershire estate, Juliet suspected that her cousin, Sir Dolph Breckinridge, Coldfell's heir, had set it. Dolph was supposed to have been in London, but she smelled his awful cologne on the air in her room and in the hallway before the smoke overcame the scent. She woke her father and they both escaped the fire, then she told her father she suspected Dolph had been in the house."

"Go on," he said, recalling how Dolph had admitted to setting the fire before he had died.

"In the meantime," Griffon went on, "Coldfell had learned that his wife had been having an affair with Dolph. His suspicion of Dolph setting the fire led him to suspect that his wife might have somehow been in on it. About a week after the fire, they all returned from the ancestral pile to Coldfell's South Kensington mansion. Merely sordid up to this point, here is where the story becomes bizarre. According to Juliet, Coldfell took Lucy into the parlor and confronted her. At first Lucy tried to deny everything, but Coldfell kept badgering her until finally, when he asked her point-blank if she and Dolph were trying to kill him, she said yes and picked up the fire poker and swung at him with it."

"You're not serious."

"Oh, yes I am. Juliet said Lucy followed him around the parlor with the fire poker like some kind of madwoman until she had struck him in his bad leg. The old man was on the floor and Lucy could have killed him with one blow, but Juliet came up behind her and struck her out cold with a vase."

"Juliet killed her?"

"No, Juliet's blow didn't kill her, it only knocked her unconscious," he said hastily. "Coldfell ordered Juliet to help him drag Lucy out to the garden. Neither of them are very strong, but between the two of them, they threw her into the pond. Since she was still unconscious, she drowned. It was self-defense, Hawkscliffe. I personally find Lord Coldfell a reprehensible schemer, but Lucy and Dolph would not have stopped until the earl was dead. Even worse, Lucy's plan for Juliet was to lock her in an asylum once her father was dead."

Hawk stared at him in amazement, barely able to absorb it. His heart pounded impossibly fast. He felt something inside him breaking free of its shackles—a power, a rightness, an audacity such as he never had possessed. He knew in an instant what he was going to do.

He gripped Griffon's shoulders. "Listen to me. You must marry Juliet."

His eyes widened. "What?"

"You love her. She belongs with you."

"Your Grace!"

"Don't argue. It's what you both want."

"But her father has forbidden me from going near her! I'm not going to resort to blackmailing him with this knowledge. I promised Juliet—"

"You won't have to. Come with me." He let go of him and pivoted, striding out to the front of the building, where he sent for his town coach.

Griffon hurried to keep up. "I don't understand."

"Just wait."

In a state of quivering exultation, Hawk waited for William to bring the coach. He turned to Griffon. "I'm going back inside. When I come back, I'll have Juliet with me. You must take her away and marry her before her father can send anyone after you. Once you are married, there's not a thing he can do."

Griffon let out a wordless exclamation of wonder.

"That is what you want, isn't it?"

"Yes! With all my heart! But—it'll never work. And Coldfell will sue you for breach of promise! You hate scandal—"

"Never mind that. Come and stand below the window of the mezzanine. I'll bring her out that way."

"Your Grace, if you help us run away together, Lord Coldfell will surely take the Vienna Congress appointment away from you! The Prime Minister takes his word as gospel—"

"It doesn't matter. Just take your place and be ready."

Griffon nodded anxiously and slipped back into the shadows around the side of the building, while Hawk jogged up the stairs and went back inside, drawing a deep breath. His heart pounded wildly with thrill at his own mad recklessness.

The truth shall set you free, he thought. For the first time in his life, he would shake off the tyranny of his class.

The moment he walked in Coldfell greeted him, all apologies. "Your Grace, I am most humbly sorry for this scene that young rapscallion has made. It is really unpardonable. He has plagued my house since he first laid eyes on my daughter."

"Why, then, that young Romeo has been a plague on both our houses, I daresay, hasn't he, Juliet?"

Juliet stared at him, wide eyed, looking quite terrified

that he had done something dreadful to her true love. Hawk grasped Juliet's hand as he turned to Coldfell feigning a look of regal displeasure. "If you don't mind, I would like a brief private word with your daughter to sort out this most embarrassing predicament," he said in his stuffiest, most paragon tone.

"Of course," said Coldfell. He poked his daughter's arm in stern reproach and pointed for her to go with Hawk.

Hawk coolly offered her his arm, playing the affronted bridegroom. Even her father seemed to feel he was entitled to sit Juliet down and chasten her. She looked frightened and overwhelmed as she put her hand on his arm and walked slowly by his side.

"No need to gawk, my good people," Hawk declared, still in a high and mighty countenance, but he felt a gigantic, secret laugh building inside of him. How shocked they would be at his final, ultimate defection! By God, he'd go over to the Whigs, to boot! How delicious the scandal was going to be! He could almost taste the air of freedom, climbing toward it. "This way, Juliet."

He tugged her by her hand toward the modest doorway and small staircase that led down to the mezzanine. The moment they were out of everyone's sight on the stairs, he pulled her more firmly, hurrying her. He turned and mouthed the word to her, "Come!" She furrowed her brow in question, but he shook his head and led her toward the arched French window that overlooked the King's Place courtyard to the back of Almack's. He opened it and pointed below. Obediently she peered out, then her face lit up with joy as she saw Griffon waiting down there for her. She waved.

Hawk turned her by her shoulders to face him, willing her to understand. He enunciated each word as clearly as possible. She stared at his mouth, waiting. This time they were determined to communicate.

"Juliet."

She nodded anxiously.

"Do—you—love—Griffon?"

A dreamy look came over her face and she nodded with her young heart sparkling in her eyes. Then she gave him a wince of pure apology, but Hawk laughed.

"It's all right. Do you want to marry him?"

Her eyes widened. Another breathless nod.

"Climb up and I will help you escape."

Her eyes widened. She hesitated—stole another glance down at her beau—then nodded eagerly.

He whistled for Griffon then helped Juliet climb out the window. Hawk slowly lowered her by her hands into the young man's waiting embrace. He followed her out the window, dropping from the ledge by his hands. He landed agilely on the cobblestones below and turned to the beaming young couple, beckoning them impatiently. They ran out to the front and Hawk rushed them both into his coach, but Griffon turned back to him and shook his hand, pumping it in both of his.

"I'm sorry for my outburst, Your Grace. I don't know what to say."

"There's nothing to say. I trust your judgment—I trust your situation that you can provide for a wife."

"She shall want for nothing."

"Good. Now I'm going to trust you with my coach, as well, so mind you don't scratch it. Go. William—Gretna Green!" he ordered. "And drive these bloods as fast as they can run! It won't be long before Coldfell's on your trail."

"Yes, sir!"

"Hang it all!" Griffon said suddenly. "What about my stallion? You remember him? The big white one? He's tied up in the Rose and Crown yard!"

"I'll see to the horse. Inquire at my house when you get back—"

"No, you must take him as a gift for what you've done for us tonight."

Hawk waved off the generous offer. "Just go! You'll never get a second chance, Griffon. Coldfell will never let you near her again. Her son will be an earl with four seats in the Commons, and you will be his father."

"Your Grace," he whispered in awe, holding Juliet near him, "I don't know how to thank you."

"Have a long and happy life together, and stick to your ideals when you use the power you'll gain. That will be thanks enough." He pushed the coach door shut, then William urged the team into motion.

"Hawkscliffe!" Griffon shouted down the street, waving out the window as the town coach rolled away. "You have the heart of a poet!"

Hawk waved, praying that he might be given a poet's eloquence as he ran into the livery yard, swung up onto Griffon's pearl-white stallion and charged off to win his lady's heart.

"A horse! a horse! my kingdom for a horse!"

Bel and her father sat enthralled in her theater box while the astonishing Edmund Kean, playing as Richard III, tore across the battlefield stage crying out the history's most famous lines at the climax of the fifth act. Though she knew the play well, both she and her father stared, thunderstruck, as King Richard did battle with his nemesis, the earl of Richmond, and was slain.

Kean delivered a death scene not to be equaled in Christendom. There was a moment of cathartic silence as the audience, trampled by the poet's pen, could only gaze at the dead villain-king in lingering shock. The theater was perfectly silent. Then, before Richmond could speak his triumphal piece, all of a sudden, the center doors at the back of the theater creaked open.

Bel felt a flicker of annoyance at the interruption as she gazed at the stage, still spellbound. Suddenly a ripple of gasps moved in a wave through the audience, starting in the back. Whispers and wordless exclamations whirred. Shouts followed.

How rude, Bel thought, turning indignantly, then her jaw dropped as a huge white horse bearing a magnificent black-haired rider clambered into the theater and down the center aisle. Even Mr. Kean looked up from his demise upon the stage.

Bel stared in disbelief. The duke of Hawkscliffe urged the shying horse to the front of the theater, heedless of the amazed cries that filled the air.

"What is he doing?" Bel breathed in shock, gripping her father's forearm.

"I have no idea," Papa murmured.

The horse whinnied nervously and tossed its head, flipping its white forelock. The audience was in an uproar. The stage manager and his assistants rushed out to try to stop him, but Robert reeled the horse away in a graceful pirouette, its long plume of tail dusting the stage, then he made the stallion rear up.

"Stand back!" he shouted in a voice of thunderous command. "I have come on the most urgent business. You shall have your show!"

"Leave him be!" someone in the audience shouted.

"Is that Hawkscliffe?"

"It can't be," people were saying.

Edmund Kean said something to the stage manager, who in turn threw up his hands then called his assistants back before the horse kicked anyone.

With a slight, devilish smile, Robert guided the tall white horse back to a vantage point just below Bel's theater box. With a sweeping gesture, he produced a gorgeous red rose and lifted it, holding it out to her. The courtly gesture won him cheers, whistles, applause. Even Mr. Kean laughed.

The roguish smile Robert sent her made her heart somersault with crazed, incredulous joy.

Her heart beating wildly, Bel reached over the railing and accepted the rose, abashed to be brought to the public's attention, because everybody knew who she was—"the Magdalen," the papers now called her—the penitent whore.

"Come away, my lady," he said softly.

"Have you gone completely mad?"

"I was mad ever to let you go. Take me back. You won't be sorry, I swear," he said. "Marry me, lovely."

"Robert!"

The whole audience leaned in as he turned to her father.

"Sir, I love your daughter more than anything in this world," Robert loudly announced, his rich baritone ringing out across the theater. "Do I have your blessing to ask for her hand?"

"You do, Your Grace," Alfred said with a fond chuckle.

"Papa!" Bel protested.

There were ripples of laughter at her mortification; people stomped their feet on the floor and cheered.

"Robert, you are making a fool of yourself!"

"Yes, my darling, that is the point. If we're going to make a scandal, let's make it a good one."

"Oh, you maddening—!" she said, exasperated past the point of speech.

Bringing the horse nearer, he offered her his hand with a soft, beguiling smile. "Come away with me now. Don't hesitate. You know that I love you. This is our chance."

"Say yes!" someone in one of the nearby rows hollered. "Say yes to him!"

Others joined in.

"Don't be daft, girl! He loves you!" a big Cockney woman shouted from the pit.

"Go!" they all started shouting, cheering Robert on.

"I'm sure it's nobody's business!" Bel exclaimed.

He flashed her a dashing grin. "The ayes have it. Come, Bel. What good is anything if we're not together?"

Tears rushed into her eyes. His dark eyes shone with all the promise of the future he was offering. He waited faithfully, his hand outstretched, braving a very public rejection. God knew he deserved it, too, after all he had put her through.

She looked anxiously from the clamoring audience to her father. "Papa, what should I do?"

He gave her a teary-eyed smile. "Why, my dear, you should follow your heart, of course."

"What about Mick?"

"He only wants your happiness, as do I. He'll understand."

"Oh, Papa!" She hugged her father hard. He chuckled fondly as he released her.

Then the noise built to a crescendo; the whole audience cheered as Bel daringly climbed over the railing with a scandalous show of ankle that would have surely made the brazen Georgiana Hawkscliffe laugh. She took Robert's hand. He steadied her as she stepped down, gingerly lowering herself onto the horse behind him.

He drew her hands around his waist. "Put your arms around me," he whispered, "and never let me go."

"I love you!" At her joyous sob, she felt the rumble of his deep, tender laugh.

"Well, you'd better, bonny blue, because this time, our arrangement is permanent."

He turned and gave her a light, lingering kiss full of velvet promise for the night to come. Tears brimmed under her lashes as he ended the kiss and held her gaze for a moment, love glowing in his dark eyes. "I missed you," he whispered. Then he turned forward again, smiling more roguishly now.

"Hold on tight."

She clasped her hands around his lean middle.

With that, he pressed his heels into the horse's sides, and they galloped out of the theater and rode off into the stars.

Notice in The London Times Society Page
23rd September, 1814

After a private wedding ceremony in the chapel at Their Graces' ancestral pile in Cumberland last week, the Duke and Duchess of Hawkscliffe embarked to Vienna to take their honeymoon amid the festivities of the Great Congress.

Lady Jacinda Knight and her companion, Miss Carlisle, also joined Their Graces for the Continental holiday.

Adding to the family's happiness is the news that the decorated war hero Colonel Lord Damien Knight will be made a peer upon his arrival home from the Peninsula. We eagerly await the chance to express our thanks and congratulations to his lordship, who is expected to return before the month is out.

Elsewhere in Town, reports have reached us that the Duke of L— and the Marquess of W— were heard to exchange words in their longstanding rivalry for the favours of the notorious Harriette Wilson. . . .

HISTORICAL NOTE

> *I shall not say why and how I became, at the age of fifteen, the mistress of the Earl of Craven. Whether it was love, or the severity of my father, or the depravity of my own heart, or the winning arts of the noble Lord, which induced me to leave my paternal roof and place myself under his protection, does not now much signify: or if it does, I am not in the humour to gratify curiosity in this matter.*

So begins *The Lady and the Game*, the memoirs of Harriette Wilson. Her firsthand account of high life in the Regency demimonde was a primary source for this novel. The Cyprians' house in York Place actually belonged to Amy, the eldest of the famous courtesan sisters—Harriette had her own house in the New Road in Marylebone and later, in Trevor Square, Knightsbridge—but I condensed locations for the sake of unity. In real life Amy and Harriette, fierce rivals, could not have lived civilly under the same roof. In 1815, the year following my story, Harriette, aged thirty-five, moved to Paris as her fame in London began to wane. Amy turned respectable; Fanny died young; Julia Johnstone bore a total of twelve children. The youngest Wilson sister, Sophia, landed a viscount.

Marguerite Gardiner, who is also mentioned in the story, started out in life as a poor Irish girl of great beauty and ended up the Countess of Blessington, as well as a famed writer and confidante to Lord Byron. It is hoped the reader will forgive the author for taking the liberty of placing Lord and Lady Blessington's nuptials within the dates of this story; in actuality, they did not marry until 1818.

Politically the Tories' only foray into reform was in removing the death penalty for minor offenses and working toward a more humane penal code. Greater change would have to wait until after 1831, but when it came, it was driven in part by the vision and ferocious energy of Henry Brougham (later Lord Chancellor and First Baron of Brougham and Vaux). "Wickedshifts," as the diarist Creevy calls him, directed the attention of Parliament in 1816 to the whole question of charitable endowment and obtained a select committee to investigate the education of poor children; in 1820 Brougham became the defense lawyer in the trial of Queen Caroline. One wonders if his relationship with a free spirit like Harriette helped to shape his amazingly forward-thinking views on the rights of women.

The reactionary and repressive attitudes of the Tories, as exemplified by Sidmouth and Eldon, resulted in the government's failure to take any positive steps to deal with the problems of postwar England and led to public protests, one of which ended in the "Peterloo Massacre" of 1819. A savage attack on the Tory magnates still exists in Shelley's famous poem "The Mask of Anarchy." Wellington did not seem to suffer as badly in public opinion as the others did and later became prime minister.

As for Viscount Castlereagh and his ongoing battle with depression, after all his brilliant service, especially as foreign secretary, he took his life in 1822, slitting his throat with a penknife in his dressing room.

Finally, those familiar with the history of Lady Oxford and her "Harleian Miscellany" will no doubt recognize her as the model for my scandalous and beautiful Georgiana, duchess of Hawkscliffe and her variously sired brood. This grand dame of the ton was, of course, the inspiration for my new series about the Knight brothers, the first installment of which you have just read—and which I sincerely hope you will continue to enjoy.

—G.F.

P.S. The twins are next!

Lord of Fire
Gaelen Foley

After years of preparation, he has baited his trap well, luring the depraved members of Society into his devil's playground so he can earn their trust and uncover their secrets.

Yet no one in London suspects that Lord Lucien Knight is England's most cunning spy, an officer who has sacrificed his soul for his country. Now an unexpected intruder has invaded his fortress of sin, jeopardising his carefully laid plans - and igniting his deepest desires.

Beautiful, innocent Alice Montague finds herself at the mercy of scandalous Lord Lucien. But as he begins his slow seduction to corrupt her virtue, Alice glimpses a man tormented by his own choices, a man who promises her nothing but his undeniable passion. . .

Lord of Ice
Gaelen Foley

Damien Knight, the earl of Winterley, is proud, aloof, and tormented by memories of war.

Though living in seclusion, he is named guardian to a fellow officer's ward. Instead of the young homeless waif he was expecting, however, Miranda FitzHubert is a stunning, passionate beauty who invades his sanctuary and forces him back into society. Struggling to maintain honour and self-control, Damien now faces an ever greater threat: desire.

A bold, free spirit, Miranda has witnessed the darkest depths of Damien's soul - and has seen his desperate need for love. But before she can thaw his unyielding heart, she must endure a terrifying nightmare of her own . . .